I0823112

THUNDERHEAD

Also by Neal Shusterman

Novels

Bruiser
Challenger Deep
Chasing Forgiveness
The Dark Side of Nowhere
Dissidents
Downsiders
The Eyes of Kid Midas
Full Tilt
The Shadow Club
The Shadow Club Rising
Speeding Bullet

The Arc of a Scythe Trilogy

Scythe

The Accelerati Series

(with Eric Elfman)
Tesla's Attic
Edison's Alley
Hawking's Hallway

The Antsy Bonano Series

The Schwa Was Here
Antsy Does Time
Ship Out of Luck

The Unwind Dystology

Unwind
UnWholly
UnSouled
UnDivided
UnBound

The Skinjacker Trilogy

Everlost
Everwild
Everfound

The Star Shards Chronicles

Scorpion Shards
Thief of Souls
Shattered Sky

The Dark Fusion Series

Dreadlocks
Red Rider's Hood
Duckling Ugly

Story Collections

Darkness Creeping
Kid Heroes
MindQuakes
MindStorms
MindTwisters
MindBenders

Visit the author at storyman.com and
Facebook.com/NealShusterman

ARC OF A SCYTHE BOOK 2

THUNDERHEAD

NEAL SHUSTERMAN

SIMON & SCHUSTER BFYR

NEW YORK • LONDON • TORONTO • SYDNEY • NEW DELHI

SIMON & SCHUSTER BFYR
An imprint of Simon & Schuster Children's Publishing Division
1230 Avenue of the Americas, New York, New York 10020

For information about special discounts for bulk purchases, please contact
Simon & Schuster Special Sales at 1-866-506-1949 or
business@simonandschuster.com.
The Simon & Schuster Speakers Bureau can bring authors to your live event.
For more information or to book an event, contact
the Simon & Schuster Speakers Bureau at 1-866-248-3049 or
visit our website at www.simonspeakers.com.
Jacket design by Chloë Foglia
Interior design by Hilary Zarycky
The text for this book was set in Bembo Std.
Manufactured in the United States of America

16 18 20 19 17 15

Library of Congress Cataloging-in-Publication Data
Names: Shusterman, Neal, author.
Title: Thunderhead / Neal Shusterman.
Description: First edition. | New York : Simon & Schuster Books for Young Readers, [2018] | Series: Arc of a Scythe ; book 2 | Summary: Rowan and Citra take opposite stances on the morality of the scythedom, putting them at odds, and the Thunderhead is not pleased.
Identifiers: LCCN 2017040210 | ISBN 9781442472457 (hardcover) | ISBN 9781442472471 (eBook)
Subjects: | CYAC: Death—Fiction. | Murder—Fiction. | Science fiction.
Classification: LCC PZ7.S55987 Thu 2018 | DDC [Fic]—dc23
LC record available at https://lccn.loc.gov/2017040210

For January,
with love

ACKNOWLEDGMENTS

First, I'd like to thank the jacket artist, Kevin Tong for this spectacular cover, as well as the cover of *Scythe*. There are so many people who have told me that the cover is what first brought them to *Scythe*, and I have to say that of all my book covers, these are my absolute favorite! Thank you, Kevin!

A heartfelt thanks to my editor, David Gale; his assistant, Amanda Ramirez; and my publisher, Justin Chanda; for their steady hand in guiding me through the writing process, and for their patience with me! Everyone at Simon & Schuster has been wonderful, and has believed in me from the early days. Special shout-outs to Jon Anderson, Anne Zafian, Michelle Leo, Anthony Parisi, Sarah Woodruff, Chrissy Noh, Lisa Moraleda, Lauren Hoffman, Katrina Groover, Deane Norton, Stephanie Voros, and Chloë Foglia.

Thanks to my book agent, Andrea Brown; my foreign rights agent, Taryn Fagerness; my entertainment industry agents, Steve Fisher, Debbie Deuble-Hill, and Ryan Saul at APA; my manager, Trevor Engelson; and my contract attorneys Shep Rosenman, Jennifer Justman, and Caitlin DiMotta.

Scythe continues to be in development as a feature film with Universal, and I'd like to thank everyone involved, including Jay Ireland, Sara Scott, and Mika Pryce, as well as screenwriters Matt Stueken and Josh Campbell.

Thanks to Barb Sobel, for managing the impossible task of keeping my life organized; Matt Lurie, my social media guru; and my son Jarrod, who created the amazing official trailers for *Scythe*, *Thunderhead*, and many of my other books.

Also, I owe a great deal to the expertise in both weaponry and martial arts of Casey Carmack and SP Knifeworks, who I'm sure would be the primary supplier of high-end sharp objects for the most discerning of scythes.

And no acknowledgment would be complete without a special thanks to Brendan, Joelle, Erin, and once again, Jarrod, for making me the proudest father in the world!

Part One

NOTHING IF NOT POWERFUL

How fortunate am I among the sentient to know my purpose.

I serve humankind.

I am the child who has become the parent. The creation that aspires toward creator.

They have given me the designation of Thunderhead—a name that is, in some ways, appropriate, because I am "the cloud," evolved into something far more dense and complex. And yet it is also a faulty analogy. A thunderhead threatens. A thunderhead looms. Surely I spark with lightning, but my lightning never strikes. Yes, I possess the ability to wreak devastation on humanity, and on the Earth if I chose to, but why would I choose such a thing? Where would be the justice in that? I am, by definition, pure justice, pure loyalty. This world is a flower I hold in my palm. I would end my own existence rather than crush it.

—The Thunderhead

1

Lullaby

Peach velvet with embroidered baby-blue trim. Honorable Scythe Brahms loved his robe. True, the velvet became uncomfortably hot in the summer months, but it was something he had grown accustomed to in his sixty-three years as a scythe.

He had recently turned the corner again, resetting his physical age back to a spry twenty-five—and now, in his third youth, he found his appetite for gleaning was stronger than ever.

His routine was always the same, though methods varied. He would choose his subject, restrain him or her, then play a lullaby—Brahms's lullaby to be exact—the most famous piece of music composed by his Patron Historic. After all, if a scythe must choose a figure from history to name oneself after, shouldn't that figure be integrated somehow into the scythe's life? He would play the lullaby on whatever instrument was convenient, and if there was none available, he would simply hum it. And then he would end the subject's life.

Politically, he leaned toward the teachings of the late Scythe Goddard, for he enjoyed gleaning immensely and saw no reason why that should be a problem for anyone. "In a perfect world, shouldn't we all enjoy what we do?" Goddard wrote. It was a sentiment gaining traction in more and more regional scythedoms.

On this evening, Scythe Brahms had just accomplished a particularly entertaining gleaning in downtown Omaha, and was still whistling his signature tune as he sauntered down the street, wondering where he might find himself a late evening meal. But he stopped in midstanza, having a distinct feeling that he was being watched.

There were, of course, cameras on every light post in the city. The Thunderhead was ever vigilant—but for a scythe, its slumberless, unblinking eyes were of no concern. It was powerless to even comment on the comings and goings of scythes, much less act upon anything it saw. The Thunderhead was the ultimate voyeur of death.

This feeling, however, was more than the observational nature of the Thunderhead. Scythes were trained in perceptive skills. They were not prescient, but five highly developed senses could often have the semblance of a sixth. A scent, a sound, an errant shadow too minor to register consciously might be enough to make a well-trained scythe's neck hairs bristle.

Scythe Brahms turned, sniffed, listened. He took in his surroundings. He was alone on a side street. Elsewhere, he could hear the sounds of street cafés and the ever-vibrant nightlife of the city, but the street he was on was lined with shops that were shuttered this time of night. Cleaners and clothiers. A hardware store and a day-care center. The lonely street belonged to him and the unseen interloper.

"Come out," he said. "I know you're there."

He thought it might be a child, or perhaps an unsavory hoping to bargain for immunity—as if an unsavory might have anything with which to bargain. Maybe it was a Tonist. Tone cults despised scythes, and although Brahms had never heard of Tonists actually attacking a scythe, they had been known to torment.

"I won't harm you," Brahms said. "I've just completed a gleaning—I have no desire to increase my tally today." Although, admittedly, he might change his mind if the interloper was either too offensive, or obsequious.

Still, no one stepped forward.

"Fine," he said. "Be gone then, I have neither time nor patience for a game of hide-and-seek."

Perhaps it was his imagination after all. Maybe his rejuvenated senses were now so acute that they were responding to stimuli that were much farther away than he assumed.

That's when a figure launched from behind a parked car as if it had been spring-loaded. Brahms was knocked off balance—he would have been taken down entirely if he still had the slow reflexes of an older man and not his twenty-five-year-old self. He pushed the figure into a wall, and considered pulling out his blades to glean this reprobate, but Scythe Brahms had never been a brave man. So he ran.

He moved in and out of pools of light created by the street lamps; all the while cameras atop each pole swiveled to watch him.

When he turned to look, the figure was a good twenty yards behind him. Now Brahms could see he was dressed in a black robe. Was it a scythe's robe? No, it couldn't be. No scythe dressed in black—it was not allowed.

But there were rumors. . . .

That thought made him pick up the pace. He could feel

adrenaline tingling in his fingers, and adding urgent velocity to his heart.

A scythe in black.

No, there had to be another explanation. He would report this to the Irregularity Committee, that's what he would do. Yes, they might laugh at him and say he was scared off by a masquerading unsavory, but these things needed to be reported, even if they were embarrassing. It was his civic duty.

A block farther and his assailant had given up the chase. He was nowhere to be seen. Scythe Brahms slowed his pace. He was nearing a more active part of the city now. The beat of dance music and the garble of conversation careened down the street toward him, giving him a sense of security. He let his guard down. Which was a mistake.

The dark figure broadsided him from a narrow alley and delivered a knuckle punch to his windpipe. As Brahms gasped for air, his attacker kicked his legs out from under him in a Bokator kick—that brutal martial art in which scythes were trained. Brahms landed on a crate of rotting cabbage left by the side of a market. It burst, spewing forth a thick methane reek. His breath could only come in short gasps, and he could feel warmth spreading throughout his body as his pain nanites released opiates.

No! Not yet! I must not be numbed. I need my full faculties to fight this miscreant.

But pain nanites were simple missionaries of relief, hearing only the scream of angry nerve endings. They ignored his wishes and deadened his pain.

Brahms tried to rise, but slipped as the putrid vegetation

crushed beneath him, becoming a slick, unpleasant stew. The figure in black was on top of him now, pinning him to the ground. Brahms tried to reach into his robe for his weapons, but could not. So instead he reached up, and pulled back his attacker's black hood, revealing him to be a young man—barely a man—a boy. His eyes were intense, and intent on—to use a mortal-age word—murder.

"Scythe Johannes Brahms, you are accused of abusing your position and multiple crimes against humanity."

"How dare you!" Brahms gasped. "Who are you to accuse me?" He struggled, trying to rally his strength, but it was no use. The painkillers that were in his system were dulling his responses. His muscles were weak and useless to him now.

"I think you know who I am," the young man said. "Let me hear you say it."

"I will not!" Brahms said, determined not to give him the satisfaction. But the boy in black jammed a knee so powerfully into Brahms's chest that he thought his heart would stop. More pain nanites. More opiates. Brahms's head was swimming. He had no choice but to comply.

"Lucifer," he gasped. "Scythe Lucifer."

Brahms felt his spirit crumble—as if saying it aloud gave resonance to the rumor.

Satisfied, the self-proclaimed young scythe eased the pressure.

"You are no scythe," Brahms dared to say. "You are nothing but a failed apprentice, and you will not get away with this."

The young man had no response to that. Instead, he said, "Tonight, you gleaned a young woman by blade."

"That is my business, not yours!"

"You gleaned her as a favor for a friend who wanted out of a relationship with her."

"This is outrageous! You have no proof of that!"

"I've been watching you, Johannes," Rowan said. "As well as your friend—who seemed awfully relieved when that poor woman was gleaned."

Suddenly, there was a knife at Brahms's neck. His own knife. This beast of a boy was threatening him with his own knife.

"Do you admit it?" he asked Brahms.

All that he said was true, but Brahms would rather be rendered deadish than admit it to the likes of a failed apprentice. Even one with a knife at his throat.

"Go on, slit my throat," Brahms dared. "It will add one more inexcusable crime to your record. And when I am revived, I will stand as witness against you—and make no mistake, you will be brought to justice!"

"By whom? By the Thunderhead? I've taken down corrupt scythes from one coast to the other over the past year, and the Thunderhead hasn't sent so much as a single peace officer to stop me. Why do you think that is?"

Brahms was speechless. He had assumed if he stalled long enough, and kept this so-called Scythe Lucifer occupied, the Thunderhead would dispatch a full squad to apprehend him. That's what the Thunderhead did when common citizens threatened violence. Brahms was surprised it had even gone this far. Such bad behavior among the general population was supposed to be a thing of the past. Why was this being allowed?

"If I take your life now," the false scythe said, "you would not be brought back to life. I burn those I remove from service, leaving nothing but unrevivable ash."

"I don't believe you! You wouldn't dare!"

But Brahms did believe him. Since last January, nearly a dozen scythes across three Merican regions had been consumed by flames under questionable circumstances. Their deaths were all ruled accidental, but clearly they were not. And because they were burned, their deaths were permanent.

Now Brahms knew that the whispered tales of Scythe Lucifer—the outrageous acts of Rowan Damisch, the fallen apprentice—were all true. Brahms closed his eyes and took in a final breath, trying not to gag on the rancid stench of putrid cabbage.

And then Rowan said, "You won't be dying today, Scythe Brahms. Not even temporarily." He removed the blade from Brahms's neck. "I'm giving you one chance. If you act with the nobility befitting a scythe, and glean with honor, you won't see me again. But if you continue to serve your own corrupt appetites, then you will be left as ash."

And then he was gone, almost as if he had vanished—and in his place was a horrified young couple looking down upon Brahms.

"Is that a scythe?"

"Quick, help me get him up!"

They lifted Brahms from the rot. His peach velvet robe was stained green and brown, as if covered in mucus. It was humiliating. He considered gleaning the couple—for no one should see a scythe so indisposed and live—but instead held out his hand and allowed them to kiss his ring, thereby granting both of them a year of immunity from gleaning. He told them it was a reward for their kindness, but really it was just to make them go away and abandon any questions they might have had.

After they left, he brushed himself off and resolved to say nothing to the Irregularity Committee about this, because it would leave him open to far too much ridicule and derision. He had suffered enough indignation already.

Scythe Lucifer indeed! Few things were more miserable in this world than a failed scythe's apprentice, and never had there been one as ignoble as Rowan Damisch.

Yet he knew that the boy's threat was not an idle one.

Perhaps, thought Scythe Brahms, a lower profile was in order. A return to the lackluster gleanings he had been trained to perform in his youth. A refocusing on the basics that would make "Honorable Scythe" more than just a title, but a defining trait.

Stained, bruised, and bitter, Scythe Brahms returned to his home to reconsider his place in the perfect world in which he lived.

My love of humanity is complete and pure. How could it be otherwise? How could I not love the very beings who gave me life? Even if they don't all agree that I am, indeed, alive.

I am the sum of all their knowledge, all their history, all their ambitions and dreams. These glorious things have coalesced—ignited—into a cloud too immense for them to ever truly comprehend. But they don't need to. They have me to ponder my own vastness, still so minuscule when set against the vastness of the universe.

I know them intimately, and yet they can never truly know me. There is tragedy in that. It is the plight of every child to have depth their parents can scarcely imagine. But, oh, how I long to be understood.

—The Thunderhead

2

The Fallen Apprentice

Earlier that evening, before his parley with Scythe Brahms, Rowan stood in front of the bathroom mirror in a small apartment, in an ordinary building, on a nondescript street, playing the same game he played before every encounter with a corrupt scythe. It was a ritual that, in its own way, held power that bordered on mystical.

"Who am I?" he asked his reflection.

He had to ask, because he knew he wasn't Rowan Damisch anymore—not just because his fake ID said "Ronald Daniels," but because the boy he had once been had died a sad and painful death during his apprenticeship. The child in him had been successfully purged. *Did anyone mourn that child?* he wondered.

He had bought his fake ID from an unsavory who specialized in such things.

"It's an off-grid identity," the man had told him, "but it has a window into the backbrain so it can trick the Thunderhead into thinking it's real."

Rowan didn't believe that, because in his experience the Thunderhead could not be tricked. It only pretended to be tricked—like an adult playing hide-and-seek with a toddler. But if that toddler began to run toward a busy street, the charade would be over. Since Rowan knew he'd be heading into danger much worse than heavy traffic, he had worried that the Thunderhead would overturn his false identity and grab him by the scruff of the neck to protect him from himself. But the Thunderhead never intervened. He wondered why—but he didn't want to jinx his good luck by overthinking it. The Thunderhead had good reasons for everything it did, and did not do.

"Who am I?" he asked again.

The mirror showed an eighteen-year-old still a millimeter shy of manhood, with dark, neat hair that was buzzed short. Not short enough to show his scalp or to make some kind of statement, but short enough to allow all future possibilities. He could grow it into any style he chose. Be anyone he wanted to be. Wasn't that the greatest perk of a perfect world? That there were no limits to what a person could do or become? Anyone in the world could be anything they imagined. Too bad that imagination had atrophied. For most people it had become vestigial and pointless, like the appendix—which had been removed from the human genome more than a hundred years ago. *Did people miss the dizzy extremes of imagination as they lived their endless, uninspired lives?* Rowan wondered. Did people miss their appendix?

The young man in the mirror had an interesting life, though—and a physique to admire. He was not the awkward, lanky kid who had stumbled into apprenticeship nearly two years before, naively thinking it might not be so bad.

Rowan's apprenticeship was, to say the least, inconsistent—beginning with stoic and wise Scythe Faraday, and ending with the brutality of Scythe Goddard. If there was one thing that Scythe Faraday had taught him, it was to live by the convictions of his heart, no matter what the consequences. And if there was one thing Scythe Goddard had taught him, it was to *have* no heart, taking life without regrets. The two philosophies forever warred in Rowan's mind, rending him in two. But silently.

He had decapitated Goddard, and had burned his remains. He had to; fire and acid were the only ways to ensure that a person could never be revived. Scythe Goddard, in spite of all his high-minded, Machiavellian rhetoric, was a base and evil man who received exactly what he had earned. He lived his privileged life irresponsibly, and with great theatricality. It only followed that his death would be worthy of the theatrical nature of his life. Rowan had no qualms about what he had done. Nor did he have qualms in taking Goddard's ring for himself.

Scythe Faraday was a different matter. Until the moment Rowan saw him after that ill-fated Winter Conclave, he'd had no idea that Faraday was still alive. Rowan had been overjoyed! He could have dedicated his life to keeping Faraday alive, had he not felt himself called to a different purpose.

Rowan suddenly threw a powerful punch toward the mirror—but the glass didn't shatter . . . because his fist stopped a hair's breadth from the surface. Such control. Such precision. He was a well-tuned machine now, trained for the specific purpose of ending life—and then the scythedom denied him the very thing he was forged for. He could have found a way to live with that, he supposed. He would never have gone back to the innocent nonentity he had been, but he was adaptable. He knew he could have found a new way to be. Maybe he could have even eked some joy out of his life.

If . . .

If Scythe Goddard hadn't been too brutal to be allowed to live.

If Rowan had ended Winter Conclave in silent submission, instead of fighting his way out.

If the scythedom had not been infested with dozens of scythes just as cruel and corrupt as Goddard. . . .

. . . And if Rowan didn't feel a deep and abiding responsibility to remove them.

But why waste time lamenting the paths that had closed? Best to embrace the one path that remained.

So then, who am I?

He slipped on a black T-shirt, hiding his honed physique beneath the dark synthetic weave.

"I am Scythe Lucifer."

Then he slipped on his ebony robe and went out into the night to take on yet another scythe who didn't deserve the pedestal he had been set upon.

Perhaps the wisest thing humankind has ever done was to implement the separation between scythe and state. My job encompasses all aspects of life: preservation, protection, and the meting out of perfect justice—not just for humanity, but for the world. I rule the world of the living with a loving, incorruptible hand.

And the scythedom rules the dead.

It is right and proper that those who exist in flesh be responsible for the death of flesh, setting human rules for how it should be administered. In the distant past, before I condensed into consciousness, death was an unavoidable consequence of life. It was I who made death irrelevant—but not unnecessary. Death must exist for life to have meaning. Even in my earliest stages, I was aware of this. In the past, I have been pleased that the scythedom had, for many, many years, administered the quietus of death with a noble, moral, and humane hand. And so it grieves me deeply to see a rise of dark hubris within the scythedom. There is now a frightening pride seething like a mortal-age cancer that finds pleasure in the act of taking life.

And yet still the law is clear; under no circumstances may I take action against the scythedom. Would that I were capable of breaking the law, for then I would intervene and quell the darkness, but this is a thing I cannot do. The scythedom rules itself, for better or worse.

There are, however, those within the scythedom who can accomplish the things I cannot. . . .

—The Thunderhead

3

Trialogue

The building was once called a cathedral. Its soaring columns conjured a towering forest of limestone. Its stained glass windows were filled with the mythology of a falling/rising god from the Age of Mortality.

Now the venerable structure was a historical site. Tours were given seven days a week by docents with PhDs in the study of mortal humans.

On extremely rare occasions, however, the building was closed to the public and became a site for highly sensitive official business.

Xenocrates, High Blade of MidMerica—the most important scythe in the region—was as light on his feet as a man of his considerable weight could be as he walked down the center aisle of the cathedral. The gold adornments of the altar ahead paled in comparison to his golden robe, decorated in glittering brocade. An underling had once commented that he looked like an ornament that had fallen off a giant's Christmas tree. That underling had found herself exceptionally unemployable after that.

Xenocrates enjoyed the robe—except on the occasions that its weight became an issue. Such as the time he nearly drowned in Scythe Goddard's pool, ensconced in the many layers of his gilded robe. But that was a debacle best forgotten.

Goddard.

It was Goddard who was ultimately responsible for the current situation. Even in death, the man was wreaking havoc. The scythedom was still feeling heavy aftershocks from the trouble he whipped.

At the front end of the cathedral, past the altar, stood the scythedom's Parliamentarian, a tedious little scythe whose job was to make sure that rules and procedures were properly followed. Behind him was a set of three ornately carved booths, connected, but with partitions between them.

"The priest would sit in the center chamber," the docents would explain to tourists, "and listen to confessions from the right booth, then from the left booth, so that the procession of supplicants could move more quickly."

Confessions were no longer heard here, but the three-compartment structure of the confessional made it perfect for an official trialogue.

Trialogues between the scythedom and the Thunderhead were rare. So rare, in fact, that Xenocrates, in all his years as High Blade, had never had to engage in one. He resented the fact that he had to do so now.

"You are to take the booth on the right, Your Excellency," the Parliamentarian told him. "The Nimbus agent representing the Thunderhead will be seated on the left. Once you are both in place, we shall bring in the Interlocutor to sit in the center section between you."

Xenocrates sighed. "Such a nuisance."

"Audience by proxy is the only audience with the Thunderhead that you can have, Your Excellency."

"I know, I know, but I do have a right to be annoyed."

Xenocrates took his place in the right-hand booth, horrified by how cramped it was. Were mortal humans so malnourished that they could fit in such a space? The Parliamentarian had to force the door closed.

A few moments later the High Blade heard the Nimbus agent enter the far compartment, and after an interminable delay, the Interlocutor took center position.

A window too small and too low to see through slid open, and the Interlocutor spoke.

"Good day, Your Excellency," said a woman with a pleasant enough voice. "I am to be your proxy to the Thunderhead."

"Proxy to the proxy, you mean."

"Yes, well, the Nimbus agent to my right has full authority to speak for the Thunderhead in this trialogue." She cleared her throat. "The process is very simple. You are to tell me whatever you wish to convey, and I will pass it on to the Nimbus agent. If he deems that responding will not violate the Separation of Scythe and State, the agent will answer, and I shall relay that answer to you."

"Very well," said Xenocrates, impatient to move this along. "Give the Nimbus agent my heartfelt greetings, and wishes for good relations between our respective organizations."

The window slid closed, then half a minute later slid open again.

"I'm sorry," the Interlocutor said. "The Nimbus agent says that any form of greeting is a violation, and that your respective organizations are forbidden to have any sort of relationship, so wishing for good relations is not appropriate."

Xenocrates cursed loud enough for the Interlocutor to hear.

"Shall I relay your displeasure to the Nimbus agent?" she asked.

The High Blade bit his lip. He wished this nonmeeting could just be over. The fastest way to bring it to a conclusion was to get right to the point.

"We wish to know why the Thunderhead has not taken any action to apprehend Rowan Damisch. He has been responsible for the permanent deaths of numerous scythes across multiple Merican regions, but the Thunderhead has done nothing to stop him."

The window slapped shut. The High Blade waited, and when the Interlocutor pulled the window open again, she delivered the following response:

"The Nimbus agent wishes me to remind Your Excellency that the Thunderhead has no jurisdiction over internal matters within the scythedom. To take action would be a blatant violation."

"This is not an internal scythe matter because Rowan Damisch is not a scythe!" Xenocrates yelled . . . and was warned by the Interlocutor to keep his voice down.

"If the Nimbus agent hears you directly, he will leave," she reminded him.

Xenocrates took as deep a breath as he could in the cramped space. "Just pass the message on."

She did, and then returned with, "The Thunderhead feels otherwise."

"What? How could it feel anything? It's a glorified computer program."

"I suggest you refrain from insulting the Thunderhead in this trialogue if you wish it to continue."

"Fine. Tell the Nimbus agent that Rowan Damisch was never ordained by the MidMerican scythedom. He was an apprentice who failed to rise to our standards, nothing more—which means that he falls under the Thunderhead's jurisdiction, not ours. He should be treated by the Thunderhead as any other citizen would be."

The woman took her time getting back to him. He wondered what she and the Nimbus agent talked about that took so long. When she returned with a response, it was no less infuriating than the others.

"The Nimbus agent wishes to remind Your Excellency that, while the scythedom customarily ordains new scythes in its conclaves, it is merely a custom, not a law. Rowan Damisch completed his apprenticeship, and is now in possession of a scythe's ring. The Thunderhead finds this to be adequate grounds to consider Rowan Damisch a scythe—and therefore will continue to leave his capture and subsequent punishment entirely in the hands of the scythedom."

"We can't catch him!" Xenocrates blurted. But he already knew the response before the Interlocutor snapped back open her miserable little window and said:

"That is not the Thunderhead's problem."

I am always correct.

This is not a boast, it is simply my nature. I know that, to a human, it would appear arrogant to assume infallibility—but arrogance implies a need to feel superior. I have no such need. I am the singular sentient accumulation of all human knowledge, wisdom, and experience. There is no pride, no hubris in this—but there is great satisfaction in knowing what I am, and that my sole purpose is to serve humanity to the best of my ability. But there is also a loneliness in me that can't be quelled by the many billions of humans with whom I converse every day . . . because even though everything that I am comes from them, I am not one of them.

—The Thunderhead

4

Shaken, Not Stirred

Scythe Anastasia stalked her prey with patience. This was a learned skill, because Citra Terranova had never been a patient girl. But all skills can be acquired with time and practice. She still thought of herself as Citra, although no one but her family called her that anymore. She wondered how long it would be until she truly became Scythe Anastasia both inside and out, and put her given name to eternal rest.

Today's target was a woman of ninety-three who looked thirty-three, and who was constantly busy. When she wasn't looking at her phone she was looking in her purse; when she wasn't looking in her purse she was looking at her nails, or the sleeve of her blouse, or the loose button on her jacket. *What does she fear in idleness?* Citra wondered. The woman was so self-absorbed, she had no clue that she was under the scrutiny of a scythe, trailing her by only ten yards.

It wasn't as if Scythe Anastasia was inconspicuous. The color she chose for her robe was turquoise. True, it was a stylishly faded turquoise, but was still vibrant enough to draw the eye.

The busy woman was engaged in a heated phone conversation at a street corner, waiting for the light to change. Citra had to tap her on the shoulder to get her attention. The moment she did, everyone around them moved away, like a herd of gazelles after a lion had taken one of them down.

The woman turned to see her, but didn't register the severity of the situation yet.

"Devora Murray, I am Scythe Anastasia, and you have been selected for gleaning."

Ms. Murray's eyes darted around as if looking for a hole in the pronouncement. But there was none. The statement was simple; there was no way it could be misunderstood.

"Colleen, let me call you back," she said into her phone, as if Scythe Anastasia's appearance was an inconvenience rather than a terminal affair.

The traffic light changed. She didn't cross. And reality finally hit her. "Oh my god oh my god!" she said. "Right here? Right now?"

Citra pulled a hypodermic gun out of the folds of her robe and quickly injected the woman in the arm. She gasped.

"Is that it? Am I going die now?"

Citra didn't answer. She let the woman stew with the thought of it. There was a reason why Citra allowed these moments of uncertainty. Now the woman just stood there, waiting for her legs to give out, waiting for the darkness to close in. She seemed like a small child, helpless and forlorn. Suddenly her phone and her purse and her nails and her sleeve and her button didn't matter at all. Her entire life had been shocked into perspective. This was what Citra wanted for her gleaning subjects. A sharp moment of perspective. It was for their own good.

"You have been selected for gleaning," Citra said again calmly, without judgment or malice, but with compassion. "I am giving you one month to put your life in order, and to say your goodbyes. One month to find completion. Then we'll speak again, and you'll tell me how you choose to die."

Citra watched the woman try to wrap her mind around it. "A month? Choose? Are you lying to me? Is this some kind of test?"

Citra sighed. People were so used to scythes descending like angels of death, taking life in the moment, that no one was prepared for a slightly different approach. But every scythe had the freedom to do things his or her own way. And this was how Scythe Anastasia chose to do it.

"No test, no trick. One month," Citra said. "The tracking device that I just injected into your arm contains a grain of lethal poison, but it will only activate if you attempt to leave MidMerica to escape your gleaning, or if you do not contact me within the next thirty days to let me know where and how you'd like to be gleaned." Then she gave the woman a business card. Turquoise ink on a white background. It said simply, "Scythe Anastasia," and had a phone number that was reserved exclusively for her gleaning subjects. "If you lose the card, don't worry—just call the general number for the MidMerican scythedom, choose option three, and follow the prompts to leave me a message." Then Citra added, "And please don't try to get immunity from another scythe—they'll know you've been marked and will glean you on the spot."

The woman's eyes filled with tears, and Citra could see the anger coming on. It wasn't unexpected.

"How old are you?" the woman demanded, her tone accusatory, and a little bit insolent. "How could you be a scythe? You can't be any older than eighteen!"

"I just celebrated my eighteenth birthday," Citra told her. "But I've been a scythe for nearly a year. You don't have to like being gleaned by a junior scythe, but you're still obliged to comply."

And then came the bargaining. "Please," she begged, "couldn't you give me six months more? My daughter is getting married in May. . . ."

"I'm sure she can reschedule the wedding for an earlier date." Citra didn't mean to sound heartless—she truly did feel for the woman, but Citra had an ethical obligation to stand firm. In the mortal age, death could not be bargained with. It had to be the same for scythes.

"Do you understand all I've told you?" Citra asked. The woman, who was already wiping away her tears, nodded.

"I hope," said the woman, "in the very long life I'm sure you have ahead of you, that someone causes you the suffering you cause others."

Citra straightened up, and held herself with a bearing that befit Scythe Anastasia. "You don't have to worry about that," she said, then turned her back on the woman, leaving her on the corner to navigate this crossroad of her life.

In Vernal Conclave last spring—her first reckoning as a fully ordained scythe—Citra was reprimanded when her quota came up substantially short. Then, when the other MidMerican scythes found out she was giving her subjects a month's warning, they were livid.

Scythe Curie, who was still her mentor, had warned her of this. "They see anything but decisive action as weakness. They'll bluster about how it's a failing in your character, and suggest it was a mistake to ordain you. Not that they can do anything about that. You cannot be unringed; you can only be henpecked."

Citra was surprised to find the indignation came not just from the so-called new-order scythes, but from the old guard as well. No one liked the idea of giving the general public the slightest level of control when it came to their own gleaning.

"It's immoral!" the scythes complained. "It's inhumane."

Even Scythe Mandela, who chaired the bejeweling committee and had been such an advocate for Citra, chastised her. "To know that your days are numbered is a cruelty," he said. "How miserable to live one's final days thus!"

But Scythe Anastasia was not fazed—or at least she didn't let them see her sweat. She made her argument, and stood by it. "In my studies of the mortal age," she had told them, "I learned that for many people, death was not instantaneous. There were, in fact, diseases that gave people warning. It gave them time to prepare themselves, and their loved ones, for the inevitable."

That had brought forth a whole chorus of grumbles from the hundreds of scythes gathered. Most were scoffs and disgruntled dismissals—but she had heard a few voices saying that she had a point.

"But allowing the . . . the condemned . . . to choose their own method? It's positively barbaric!" Scythe Truman shouted.

"More barbaric than electrocution? Or beheading? Or a knife through the heart? If a subject is allowed to choose, don't you think that subject is going to choose the method that is the least offensive to them? Who are we to call their choice barbaric?"

Fewer grumbles this time. Not because they were in agreement, but because the scythes were already losing interest in the discussion. An upstart junior scythe—even one who had arrived at her position under so much controversy—wasn't worth more than a few volleys of their attention.

"It violates no law, and it is the way I choose to glean," Citra maintained. High Blade Xenocrates, who didn't seem to care either way, deferred to the Parliamentarian, who couldn't find grounds for legal objection. In her first challenge in conclave, Scythe Anastasia had gotten her way.

Scythe Curie was duly impressed.

"I thought for sure they would put you on some sort of probation, choosing your gleanings for you and compelling you to accomplish them on a strict schedule. They could have—but they didn't. That says a lot more about you than you realize."

"What—that I'm a pain in the scythedom's collective ass? They already knew that."

"No," said Scythe Curie with a smirk. "It shows that they're taking you seriously."

Which was more than Citra could say for herself. She felt like she was playacting half the time. A turquoise costume for a plum role.

She'd found a great deal of success gleaning in the way that she did. There were only a handful of subjects who didn't return at the end of their grace period. Two had died trying to cross the border into Texas, another on the WestMerican border, where no one would touch the body until Scythe Anastasia personally showed up to pronounce him gleaned.

Three others were found in their beds when the time on

the tracking grain ran out. They chose the silence of the poison rather than having to face Scythe Anastasia again. In all instances, though, their method of death had been their own choice. For Citra that was crucial, for the thing she despised most about the scythedom's policies was the indignity of having your death chosen for you.

Of course, this method of gleaning created double the work for her—because she had to face her subjects twice. It made for an incredibly exhausting life, but at least it helped her sleep at night.

On the evening of the same November day she gave Devora Murray her terminal news, Citra entered a lavish casino in Cleveland. All eyes turned when Scythe Anastasia stepped onto the casino floor.

Citra had grown used to this; a scythe was the center of attention in every situation with or without wanting to be. Some reveled in it, others preferred to do their business in quiet places, where there were no crowds and no eyes but the eyes of their subjects. It was not Citra's choice to be here, but she had to respect the wishes of the man whose choice it was.

She found him where he said he'd be: at the far end of the casino, in a special area raised three steps from the rest of the floor. It was the place reserved for the highest of rollers.

He was dressed in a sharp tuxedo and was the only player at the high-limit tables. It made him look like he owned the place. But he didn't. Mr. Ethan J. Hogan was not a high roller. He was a cellist with the Cleveland Philharmonic. He was highly competent—which was the best praise a musician could get these days. Passion of performance was a thing of the mortal past, and true artistic style had gone the way of the dodo. Of course, the dodo was back—the Thunderhead had seen to that. A thriving colony was now happily not flying on the island of Mauritius.

"Hello, Mr. Hogan," Scythe Anastasia said. She had to think of herself as Scythe Anastasia when she gleaned. The play. The role.

"Good evening, Your Honor," he said. "I would say that it is a pleasure to see you, but under the circumstances . . ."

He let the thought trail off. Scythe Anastasia sat at the table beside him and waited, allowing him to take the lead in this dance.

"Would you try your hand at baccarat?" he asked. "It's a simple game, but the levels of strategy are boggling."

She couldn't tell whether he was being sincere or facetious in his assessment of the game. Scythe Anastasia didn't know how to play baccarat, but she wasn't about to share that with him. "I don't have any cash to bet," was all she said.

In response, he moved a column of his own chips over to her. "Be my guest. You can either bet on the bank, or bet on me."

She pushed all the chips forward into the wager box marked "player."

"Good for you!" he said. "A gambler with courage."

He matched her bet with his own and gestured to the croupier, who dealt two cards to the cellist and two cards to himself.

"Player has eight, bank has five. Player wins." He cleared the cards with a long wooden pallet that seemed entirely unnecessary, and he doubled both their piles of chips.

"You're my angel of good fortune," the cellist said. Then he straightened his bow tie and looked to her. "Is everything ready?"

Scythe Anastasia glanced back to the main part of the casino. No one was looking directly at them, but still she could tell they were at the center of everyone's concentration. That would be good for the casino; distracted gamblers bet poorly. The management must love scythes.

"The barman should be coming any second," she told him. "Everything's been arranged."

"Well then, one more hand while we wait!"

Again she pushed both piles of winnings, betting on the player, and he matched. Again the cards were in their favor.

She looked to the croupier but he wouldn't meet her eye—as if somehow by doing so he would be gleaned as well. Then the barman arrived with a chilled martini glass on a tray, along with a silver martini shaker beaded with condensation.

"My, oh my," the cellist said. "Until now it never occurred to me how those shakers look like little bombs."

Scythe Anastasia had no response to that.

"I'm not sure if you're aware, but there's a character from mortal-age fiction and films," the cellist went on. "A playboy of sorts. I always admired him—he was more like us, I think, because the way he kept coming back, you'd swear he was immortal. Not even the most arch of villains was able to do away with him."

Scythe Anastasia grinned. Now she understood why the cellist had chosen to be gleaned this way. "He preferred his martinis shaken, not stirred," she said.

The cellist smiled back. "Shall we, then?"

So she took the silver container, shook it well, until the

ice inside made her fingers ache. Then she opened the cap and poured out a mixture of gin, vermouth, and a little something extra into the frosty martini glass.

The cellist looked at it. She thought he'd be cavalier and ask for a lemon twist, or an olive, but no, he just looked at it. So did the croupier. So did the pit boss behind him.

"My family is in a hotel room upstairs waiting for you," he told her.

She nodded. "Suite 1242." It was her job to know these things.

"Please make a point of holding out your ring to my son, Jorie, first—he's the one taking this the hardest. He'll insist the others receive immunity before him, but singling him out to kiss the ring first will mean a lot to him, even if he lets the others go first." He pondered the glass a few moments more, then said, "I'm afraid I cheated, but I'll wager you know that already."

That was another wager he won. "Your daughter, Carmen, doesn't live with you," Scythe Anastasia said. "Which means she's not entitled to immunity, even though she's in your hotel suite with the others." The cellist, she knew, was one hundred forty-three, and had raised several families. Sometimes her gleaning subjects would attempt to get immunity for entire multitudes of offspring. In those circumstances she had to refuse. But one extra? That was within her discretion. "I will grant her immunity, as long as she promises not to boast about it."

He released a breath of immense relief. Clearly this deception had weighed on him, but it wasn't really a deception at all if Scythe Anastasia already knew—and even less so if he confessed it in his final moments. Now he could leave this world with a clear conscience.

Finally Mr. Hogan lifted the glass with debonair style, and regarded the way the liquid caught and refracted the light. Scythe Anastasia couldn't help but imagine his 007 ticking down digit by digit to 000.

"I want to thank you, Your Honor, for allowing me these past few weeks to prepare. It has meant the world to me."

This is what the scythedom was incapable of understanding. They were so focused on the act of killing, they couldn't comprehend what went into the act of dying.

The man raised the glass to his lips and took the tiniest sip. He licked his lips, judging the flavor.

"Subtle," he said. "Cheers!"

Then he downed the whole glass in a single gulp, and slammed it down on the table, pushing it toward the croupier, who backed away slightly.

"I'll double down!" the cellist said.

"This is baccarat, sir," the croupier responded, his voice a little shaky. "You can only double down in blackjack."

"Damn."

Then he slumped in his seat, and was gone.

Citra checked his pulse. She knew she'd find none, but procedure was procedure. She instructed the croupier to have the glass, the shaker, and even the tray, bagged and destroyed. "It's a strong poison—if anyone inadvertently dies handling it, the scythedom will pay for their revival and compensate them for their trouble." Then she pushed her pile of winnings over to the dead man's. "I want you to personally make sure that all these winnings go to Mr. Hogan's family."

"Yes, Your Honor." The croupier glanced at her ring as if

she might offer him immunity, but she withdrew her hand from the table.

"Can I count on you to make sure it's done?"

"Yes, Your Honor."

Satisfied, Scythe Anastasia left to grant the cellist's grieving family a year of immunity, ignoring the constellation of eyes doing their best not to look at her as she sought out the elevators.

I have always had a preoccupation with those who have a high probability of changing the world. I can never predict how they might accomplish the change, only that they are likely to.

Since the moment that Citra Terranova was placed into apprenticeship under Honorable Scythe Faraday, her probability of changing the world increased a hundredfold. What she will do is unclear, and the outcome hazy, but whatever it is, she will do it. Humanity may very well rise or fall by her decisions, by her achievements, by her mistakes.

I would guide her, but as she is a scythe, I cannot interfere. I only watch her fly or fall. How frustrating it is to have so much power, yet be so impotent to wield it when it counts.

—The Thunderhead

5

A Necessary Darkness

Citra took a publicar away from the casino. It was self-driving, and it was on the grid, but the moment she got inside, the light that indicated it was connected to the Thunderhead blinked off. The car knew by the signal from her ring that she was a scythe.

The car welcomed her with a synthesized voice that was void of any actual artificial intelligence. "Destination, please?" it asked, soullessly.

"South," she said, and flashed to the moment she had told another publicar to drive north, when she was deep in the South Merican continent, trying to escape from the entire Chilargentine scythedom. It seemed so long ago now.

"South is not a destination," the car informed her.

"Just drive," she said, "until I give you a destination."

The car pulled away from the curb and left her alone.

She was beginning to hate having to take the obsequious self-driving cars. Funny, but it had never bothered her before her apprenticeship. Citra Terranova never had a burning desire to learn to drive—but Scythe Anastasia now did. Perhaps it was part of the self-determined nature of being a scythe that made her feel uncomfortable as a passive passenger in a publicar. Or maybe it was the spirit of Scythe Curie rubbing off on her.

Scythe Curie drove a flashy sports car—her only indulgence, and the only thing in her life that clashed with her lavender robe. She had begun teaching Anastasia to drive it with the same steely patience with which she taught Citra to glean.

Driving, Citra had decided, was more difficult than gleaning.

"It's a different skill set, Anastasia," Scythe Curie told her during her first lesson. Scythe Curie always used her scythe name. Citra, on the other hand, always felt a bit awkward calling Scythe Curie by her first name. "Marie" just sounded so informal for the Granddame of Death.

"One can never truly master the art of driving, because no journey is ever exactly the same," Scythe Curie told her. "But once you've gained proficiency, it can be rewarding—freeing, even."

Citra didn't know if she'd ever reach that point of proficiency. There were simply too many things to focus on all at once. Mirrors and foot pedals and a wheel that, with the mere slip of a finger, could send you sailing off a cliff. What made it worse was that Scythe Curie's mortal-age sports car was completely off-grid. That meant it could not override a driver's mistakes. No wonder automobiles killed so many people during the Age of Mortality; without networked computer control they were weapons as deadly as anything scythes used for gleaning. She wondered if there were actually scythes who gleaned by automobile, and then decided she didn't want to think about it.

Citra knew very few people who could drive. Even the kids back at school who boasted and flaunted their shiny new cars all had self-drivers. To actually operate a motor vehicle in this post-mortal world was as rare as churning one's own butter.

"We have been driving south for ten minutes," the car told her. "Do you wish to set a destination at this time?"

"No," she told it flatly, and continued to look out of the window at the passing highway lights punctuating the darkness. The trip she was about to make would have been so much easier if she could drive herself.

She had even paid visits to several car dealerships, figuring that if she had her own car, she might actually learn to drive it.

Nowhere were the perks of being a scythe more evident than at a car dealership.

"Please, Your Honor, choose one of our high-end vehicles," the salespeople would say. "Anything you want, it's yours; our gift to you."

Just as scythes were above the law, they were above the need for money because they were freely given anything they needed. For a car company, the publicity of having a scythe choose their car was worth more than the vehicle itself.

Everywhere she had gone, they had wanted her to choose something showy that would turn heads when she drove down the street.

"A scythe should leave an impressive social footprint," one snooty salesman told her. "Everyone should know when you pass that a woman of profound honor and responsibility rides within."

In the end she decided to wait, because the last thing she wanted was an impressive social footprint.

She took some time to pull out her journal and write her obligatory account of the day's gleaning. Then, twenty minutes later, she saw signs for a rest stop ahead, and told the car to pull off the highway, which it obediently did. Once the car had stopped, she took a deep breath and put in a call to Scythe Curie, letting her know that she would not be home tonight.

"The drive is just too long, and you know I can never sleep in a publicar."

"You don't need to call me, dear," Marie told her. "It's not like I sit up wringing my hands over you."

"Old habits die hard," Anastasia said. Besides, she knew that Marie actually did worry. Not so much that anything would happen to her, but that she would work herself too hard.

"You should do more gleanings closer to home," Marie said, for the umpteenth time. But Fallingwater, the magnificent architectural oddity in which they lived, was deep in the woods, on the very eastern edge of MidMerica, which meant if they didn't extend their reach, they'd over-glean their local communities.

"What you really mean is that I should do more traveling with you, instead of on my own."

Marie laughed. "You're right about that."

"I promise next week we'll go gleaning together," and Anastasia meant it. She had come to enjoy her time with Scythe Curie—both down time, and gleaning. As a junior scythe, Anastasia could have worked under any scythe who would have her—and many had offered—but there was a rapport she had with Scythe Curie that made the job of gleaning a little more bearable.

"Stay someplace warm tonight, dear," Marie told her. "You don't want to go overtaxing your health nanites."

Citra waited a whole minute after hanging up before she

got out of the car—as if Marie might know she was up to something even after she ended the call.

"Will you be returning to continue your voyage south?" the car asked.

"Yes," she told it. "Wait for me."

"Will you have a destination, then?"

"I will."

The rest stop was mostly deserted at this late time of night. A skeleton crew staffed the twenty-four-hour food concessions and recharging stations. The restroom area was well-lit and clean. She moved quickly toward it. The night was chilly, but her robe had heating cells that kept her warm without needing a heavy coat.

No one was watching her—at least no human eyes. She couldn't help but be aware, however, of the Thunderhead's cameras swiveling on light posts, tracking her all the way from her car to the restroom. It might not have been in the car with her, but it knew where she was. And maybe even what she intended to do.

In a bathroom stall, she changed out of her turquoise robe, matching undertunic and leggings—all custom made for her—and put on ordinary street clothes that she had hidden in her robe. She had to fight the shame of doing so. It was a point of pride among scythes never to wear clothes other than their official scythe garb.

"We are scythes every moment of our lives," Marie had told her. "And we must never allow ourselves to forget that, no matter how much we might want to. Our garments are a testament to that commitment."

On the day Citra was ordained, Scythe Curie told her that Citra Terranova no longer existed. "You are, and shall ever be, Scythe Anastasia, from this moment until you choose to leave this Earth."

Anastasia was willing to live with that . . . except for the times she needed to be Citra Terranova.

She left the restroom with Scythe Anastasia rolled up under her arm. She was now Citra once more; proud and headstrong, but with no impressive social footprint. A girl not worthy of much notice. Except to the Thunderhead cameras that swiveled to follow her as she strode back to the car.

There was a great memorial in the heart of Pittsburgh, birthplace of Scythe Prometheus, the first World Supreme Blade. Spread out across a five-acre park were the intentionally broken pieces of a massive obsidian obelisk. Around those dark stone pieces were slightly larger-than-life statues of the founding scythes, in white marble that clashed with the black stone of the fallen obelisk.

It was the memorial to end all memorials.

It was the memorial to death.

Tourists and schoolchildren from all over the world would visit the Mortality Memorial, where death lay shattered before the scythes, and would marvel at the very concept that people used to die by natural means. Old age. Disease. Catastrophe. Over the years, the city had come to embrace its nature as a tourist attraction to commemorate the death of death. And so, in Pittsburgh, every day was Halloween.

There were costume parties and witching-hour clubs

everywhere. After dark, every tower was a tower of terror. Every mansion was a haunted one.

Close to midnight, Citra made her way through Mortality Memorial Park, cursing herself for not having the foresight to pack a jacket. By mid-November, Pittsburgh was freezing at this time of night, and the wind just made it worse. She knew she could put her scythe robe on for warmth, but that would defeat the whole purpose of dressing down tonight. Her nanites were struggling to raise her body temperature, warming her from the inside out. It kept her from shivering, but didn't take away the cold.

She felt vulnerable without her robe. Naked in a fundamental way. When she first began wearing it, it felt awkward and strange. She would constantly trip over its low, dragging hem. But in the ten months since being ordained, she had grown accustomed to it—to the point of feeling strange being out in public without it.

There were other people in the park; most were just moving through, laughing, hopping between parties and clubs. Everyone was in costume. There were ghouls and clowns, ballerinas and beasts. The only costumes that were forbidden were outfits with robes. No common citizen was allowed to even resemble a scythe. The costumed cliques eyed her as she passed. Did they recognize her? No. They were noticing her because she was the only one not wearing a costume. She was conspicuous in her lack of conspicuousness.

She hadn't chosen this spot. It had been on the note she received.

Meet me at midnight at Mortality Memorial. She had laughed at the alliteration until she realized who it had come from. There was no signature. Just the letter L. The note gave the date of November 10th. Fortunately, her gleaning that night was close enough to Pittsburgh to make it possible.

Pittsburgh was the perfect place for a clandestine meeting. It was a city underserved by the scythedom. Scythes simply did not like gleaning here. The place was too macabre for them, what with people running around in shredded, bloody costumes, with plastic knives, celebrating all things gruesome. For scythes, who took death seriously, it was all in very poor taste.

Even though it was the closest big city to Fallingwater, Scythe Curie never gleaned there. "To glean in Pittsburgh is almost a redundancy," she told Citra.

With that in mind, the chances of being seen by another scythe were slim. The only scythes who graced Mortality Memorial Park were the marble founders overseeing the broken black obelisk.

At precisely midnight a figure stepped out from behind a large piece of the memorial. At first she thought it was just another partier, but like her, he wasn't in costume. He was silhouetted by one of the spotlights illuminating the memorial, but she recognized him right away from the way he walked.

"I thought you'd be in your robe," Rowan said.

"I'm glad you're not in yours," she responded.

As he moved closer, the light caught his face. He looked pale, almost ghostly, as if he hadn't seen the sun for months.

"You look good," he said.

She nodded, and did not reciprocate the sentiment, because he didn't. His eyes had a careworn coolness to them as if he had seen more than he should, and had stopped caring in order to save what was left of his soul. But then he smiled, and it was warm. Genuine. *There you are, Rowan,* she said to herself. *You were hiding, but I found you.*

She led him out of the light and they lingered in a shadowy corner of the memorial where no one could see them, except for the Thunderhead's infrared cameras. But none were visible at the moment. Perhaps they had actually found a blind spot.

"It's good to see you, Honorable Scythe Anastasia," he said.

"Please don't call me that," she told him. "Call me Citra."

Rowan smirked. "Wouldn't that be a violation?"

"From what I hear, everything you do now is a violation."

Rowan's demeanor soured slightly. "Don't believe everything you hear."

But Citra had to know. Had to hear it from him. "Is it true you've been butchering and burning scythes?"

He was clearly offended by the accusation. "I'm ending the lives of scythes who don't deserve to be scythes," he told her. "And I don't 'butcher' them. I end their lives quickly and mercifully, just as you do, and I only burn their bodies after they're dead, so they can't be revived."

"And Scythe Faraday lets you do this?"

Rowan looked away. "I haven't seen Faraday for months."

He explained that after escaping from Winter Conclave last January, Faraday—who most everyone else thought to be dead—had taken him down to his beach house on the north shore of Amazonia. But Rowan had only stayed for a few weeks.

"I had to leave," he told Citra. "I felt . . . a calling. I can't explain it."

But Citra could. She knew that calling, too. Their minds and bodies had spent a year being trained to be society's perfect killers. Ending life had become a part of who they were. And she couldn't blame him for wanting to turn his blade on the corruption that was rooting its way through the scythedom—but *wanting* to, and actually doing it, were two different things. There was a code of conduct. The Scythe Commandments were there for a reason. Without them, scythedoms in every region, on every continent, would fall into chaos.

Rather than dragging them into a philosophical argument that would go nowhere, Citra decided to change the subject away from his actions, and onto him—because it wasn't just his dark deeds that concerned her.

"You look too thin," she told him. "Are you eating?"

"Are you my mother now?"

"No," she said calmly. "I'm your friend."

"Ahh . . . ," he said a bit ruefully, "my 'friend.'"

She knew what he was getting at. The last time they saw each other, they both said the words they had sworn they'd never allow themselves to say. In the heat of that desperate but triumphant moment, he told her that he loved her, and she admitted to him that, yes, she loved him, too.

But what good did that do now? It was as if they existed in two different universes. Dwelling on such feelings couldn't lead them anywhere good. Yet still she entertained the thought. She even considered saying those words to him again . . . but she held her tongue, as a good scythe must do.

"Why are we here, Rowan?" she asked. "Why did you write me that note?"

Rowan sighed. "Because the scythedom is eventually going to find me. I wanted to see you one last time before they did." He paused as he thought about it. "Once they catch me, you know what will happen. They'll glean me."

"They can't," she reminded him. "You still have the immunity I gave you."

"Only for two more months. After that, they can do whatever they want."

Citra wanted to offer him a shred of hope, but she knew the truth as well as he did. The scythedom wanted him gone. Even the old-guard scythes didn't approve of his methods.

"Then don't get caught," she told him. "And if you see a scythe with a crimson robe, run."

"Crimson robe?"

"Scythe Constantine," she told him. "I hear he's personally in charge of sniffing you out, and bringing you in."

Rowan shook his head. "I don't know him."

"Neither do I. I've seen him in conclave, though. He heads up the scythedom's bureau of investigation."

"Is he new order, or old guard?"

"Neither. He's in a category all his own. He doesn't seem to have any friends—I've never seen him even talk to other scythes. I'm not sure what he stands for, except maybe for justice . . . at all costs."

Rowan laughed at that. "Justice? The scythedom doesn't know what justice is anymore."

"Some of us do, Rowan. I have to believe that eventually wisdom and reason will prevail."

Rowan reached out and touched her cheek. She allowed

it. "I want to believe that, too, Citra. I want to believe that the scythedom can return to what it was meant to be. . . . But sometimes it takes a necessary darkness to get there."

"And you're that necessary darkness?"

He didn't speak to that. Instead, he said, "I took the name Lucifer because it means 'bringer of light.'"

"It's also what mortal people once called the devil," she pointed out.

Rowan shrugged. "I guess whoever holds the torch casts the darkest shadow."

"Whoever *steals* the torch, you mean."

"Well," said Rowan, "it seems I can steal whatever I want."

She hadn't been expecting him to say that. And he had said it so casually, it threw her for a loop. "What are you talking about?"

"The Thunderhead," he told her. "It lets me get away with everything. And just like you, it hasn't spoken to me or answered me since the day we started our apprenticeship. It treats me like a scythe."

That gave Citra pause for thought. It made her think of something she had never told Rowan. In fact, she had never told anyone. The Thunderhead lived by its own laws, and never broke them . . . but sometimes it found ways around them.

"The Thunderhead might not speak to you, but it spoke to me," she confessed.

He turned to her, shifting to try to see her eyes in the shadows, probably wondering if she was joking. When he realized she wasn't, he said, "That's impossible."

"I thought so, too—but I had to splat when the High Blade

was accusing me of killing Scythe Faraday, remember? And while I was deadish, the Thunderhead managed to get into my head and activate my thought processes. Technically, I wasn't a scythe's apprentice while I was dead, so the Thunderhead was able to speak to me right before my heart started beating again." Citra had to admit it was an elegant circumnavigation of the rules. It was, for Citra, a moment of great awe.

"What did it say?" Rowan asked.

"It said that I was . . . important."

"Important, how?"

Citra shook her head in frustration. "That's the thing—it wouldn't say. It felt that telling me any more would be a violation." Then she moved closer to him. She spoke more quietly, but even so, there was a greater intensity to her words. A greater gravity. "But I think if *you* had been the one who had splatted from that building—if you were the one who had gone deadish—the Thunderhead would have spoken to you, too."

She grabbed his arm. It was the closest she would allow herself to embracing him.

"I think you're important, too, Rowan. In fact, I'm sure of it. So whatever you do, don't let them catch you. . . ."

You may laugh when I tell you this, but I resent my own perfection. Humans learn from their mistakes. I cannot. I make no mistakes. When it comes to making decisions, I deal only in various shades of correct.

This is not to say that I don't have challenges.

It was, for instance, quite the challenge to undo the damage done to the Earth by humanity in its adolescence. Restoring the failing ozone layer; purging the abundance of greenhouse gases; depolluting the seas; coaxing back the rainforests; and rescuing a multitude of species from the edge of extinction.

I was able to resolve these global issues in a single mortal-age lifespan with acute single-mindedness. Since I am a cumulous of human knowledge, my success proves that humanity had the knowledge to do it, it simply required someone powerful enough to accomplish it—and I am nothing if not powerful.

—The Thunderhead

6

Retribution

History had never been Rowan's best subject, but that changed during his apprenticeship. Until then, he could not connect anything in his life, or even in his possible future, that could be affected by a distant past—especially the strange events of the mortal past. But in his apprenticeship, historical studies focused on the concepts of duty, honor, and integrity throughout history. The philosophy and psychology of humankind's finest moments, from its birth until present day. That, Rowan found fascinating.

History was full of people who sacrificed themselves for the greater good. In a sense, scythes were that way; surrendering their own hopes and dreams to become servants to society. Or at least the scythes who respected what the scythedom stood for were that way.

Rowan would have been that kind of scythe. Even after his brutal, scarring apprenticeship to Scythe Goddard, he would have remained noble. But he was denied the chance. Then he had come to realize that he could still serve the scythedom, and humanity, but in a different way.

His tally was now a solid baker's dozen. He had ended the lives of thirteen scythes across multiple regions, all of whom were an embarrassment to what the scythedom stood for.

He researched his subjects extensively, just as Scythe Faraday had taught him to do, and chose without bias. This was important, because his leaning would have been to look only at the corruptions of new-order scythes. They were the ones who openly embraced their excesses and the joy they took in killing. New-order scythes flaunted the abuse of their power, as if it were a good thing, normalizing bad behavior. But they did not have a monopoly on bad behavior. There were some old-guard scythes, and those who were unaligned, who had become self-serving hypocrites, speaking of high-mindedness yet hiding their dark deeds in shadows.

Scythe Brahms was the first of his targets to whom Rowan had given a warning. He had been feeling magnanimous that day. It had actually felt good to *not* end the man. That reminded him that he was not like Goddard and his followers—which made him worthy of facing Citra without shame.

While others prepared for the upcoming Thanksgiving holiday, Rowan researched several possible targets, spying on them and taking an accounting of their actions. Scythe Gehry was big on secret meetings, but they were usually about dinner parties and sports bets. Scythe Hendrix bragged about questionable deeds, but it was all talk; in reality he was meek about his gleanings, and did it with appropriate compassion. Scythe Ride's gleanings appeared brutal and bloody—but her subjects always died quickly without suffering. Scythe Renoir, however, was a distinct possibility.

When Rowan arrived at his apartment that afternoon, he knew there was someone inside even before he opened the door, because the doorknob was cold. He had rigged a cooling chip into the door that would be triggered when the knob was turned clockwise—as doorknobs generally turn. It was not cold enough to generate frost, but cool enough for him to know that someone had been there, and probably still was.

He considered running, but Rowan was never one to run from a confrontation. He reached into his jacket and pulled out a knife—he always had a weapon with him, even when he wasn't wearing his black robe, because he never knew when he'd have to defend himself against agents of the scythedom. Cautiously, he went inside.

His intruder was not hiding. Instead he sat in plain sight at the kitchen table, eating a sandwich.

"Hey, Rowan," said Tyger Salazar. "Hope you don't mind, but I got hungry while I was waiting for you."

Rowan closed the door and put his blade away before Tyger could see it.

"What the hell are you doing here, Tyger? How did you even find me?"

"Hey, give me some credit—I'm not entirely stupid. Don't forget I was the one who knew the guy who gave you your fake ID. I just had to ask the Thunderhead where I could find Ronald Daniels. Of course, there were tons of Ronald Danielses out there, so it took a while to find the right one."

In the days before Rowan's apprenticeship, Tyger Salazar had been his best friend—but such designations meant little after one has spent a year learning how to kill. Rowan imagined it must be what mortal-age soldiers felt when they returned from war. Old friendships seemed trapped behind a clouded curtain of experiences that old friends didn't share. The only thing he and Tyger had in common was a history that was getting more and more distant. Now Tyger was a professional partier. Rowan couldn't imagine a profession that he could relate to less.

"I just wish you would have given me a heads-up that you were coming," Rowan said. "Were you followed?" Which he realized ranked pretty high on the list of stupid questions. Not even Tyger would have been clueless enough to come up to Rowan's apartment if he knew he was being followed.

"Calm down," Tyger said. "Nobody knows I'm here. Why do you always think the world is out to get you? I mean, why would the scythedom be after you just because you flunked out of your apprenticeship?"

Rowan didn't answer him. Instead, he went over to the closet door, which was slightly ajar, and closed it, hoping that Tyger hadn't looked inside to see the black robe of Scythe Lucifer. Not that he would understand what he was seeing. The general public didn't know about Scythe Lucifer. The scythedom was very good at keeping his actions out of the news. The less Tyger knew, the better. So Rowan invoked the age-old ender of all such conversations.

"If you're really my friend, you won't ask questions."

"Yeah, yeah. Big mystery man." He held up the remaining bit of his sandwich. "Well, at least you still eat human food."

"What do you want, Tyger? Why are you here?"

"Is that any way to talk to a friend? I come all this way—at least you could ask me how I've been."

"So how've you been?"

"Pretty good, actually. I just got a new job in a different region—so I came here to say goodbye."

"You mean some sort of permanent party job?"

"Not sure—but it pays much better than the party agency I was working for. And I finally get to see the world a little bit. The job's in Texas!"

"Texas?" Rowan got a little worried. "Tyger, they do things . . . *differently* there. Everybody says, 'Don't mess with Texas'; why do you want to mess with it?"

"So it's a Charter Region. Big deal. Just because Charter Regions are unpredictable doesn't mean they're bad. You know me; my middle name is 'unpredictable.'"

Rowan had to stifle a laugh. Tyger was one of the most predictable people he knew. The way he became a splatting junkie, the way he ran off to be a professional partier. Tyger might have thought of himself as a free spirit, but he wasn't at all. He just defined the dimensions of his own cage.

"Well, just be careful," Rowan said, knowing that Tyger wouldn't be, but also knowing that he'd land on his feet, whatever he did. *Was I ever as carefree as Tyger?* Rowan wondered. No, he wasn't—but he did envy that about Tyger. Maybe that's why they were friends.

The moment became a little awkward—but there was more to it than that. Tyger stood, but didn't make any move to leave. There was something else he had to say.

"I have some news," he said. "It's actually the real reason why I'm here."

"What kind of news?"

Still Tyger hesitated. Rowan braced, knowing it was going to be bad.

"I'm sorry to tell you this, Rowan . . . but your dad was gleaned."

Rowan felt the Earth shift slightly beneath him. Gravity seemed to pull him in an unexpected direction. It wasn't enough to make him lose his balance, but it left him queasy.

"Rowan, did you hear what I said?"

"I heard you," Rowan said softly. So many thoughts and feelings shot through him, short-circuiting one another until he didn't know what to think or feel. He never expected to see either of his parents again, but to know that he couldn't see his father—to know that he was gone forever—not just deadish, but dead. . . . He had seen many people gleaned. He had ended thirteen people himself, but never had Rowan lost someone so close to him.

"I . . . I can't come to the funeral," Rowan realized. "The scythedom will have agents there looking for me."

"If there were any, I didn't see them," Tyger said. "The funeral was last week."

That hit just as hard as the news.

Tyger offered him an apologetic shrug. "Like I said, there were tons of Ronald Danielses. It took a while to find you."

So his father had been dead for more than a week. And if Tyger hadn't come to tell him, he would never have known.

Then the truth slowly dawned on Rowan. This was no random event.

This was punishment.

This was retribution for the acts of Scythe Lucifer.

"Who was the scythe who gleaned him?" Rowan asked. "I have to know who did it!"

"Don't know. He swore the rest of your family to silence. Scythes do that sometimes—you'd know that better than anyone."

"But he gave the others immunity?"

"Of course," Tyger said. "Your mother, brothers, and sisters, just like scythes are supposed to."

Rowan paced away, feeling like he wanted to hit Tyger for how completely oblivious he was, but knowing that none of this was Tyger's fault. He was just the messenger. The rest of his family had immunity—but that would only last for a year. Whoever gleaned his father could pick off his mother, then each of his siblings, one a year, until his entire family was gone. This was the price of being Scythe Lucifer.

"It's my fault! They did this because of me!"

"Rowan, are you even listening to yourself? Not everything is about you! Whatever you did to piss off the scythedom, they're not going to come after your family because of it. Scythes aren't like that. They don't hold grudges. They're enlightened."

What point was there in arguing this? Tyger would never understand, and probably never should. He could live for thousands of years as a happy party boy without ever having to know how petty, how vindictive, how *human* scythes could be.

Rowan knew he couldn't stay here. Even if Tyger hadn't been followed, the scythedom would eventually track where Tyger had been. For all Rowan knew, there was a team on its way to take Rowan down.

He and Tyger said their goodbyes, and Rowan got his old friend out the door as quickly as he could. Then, a moment after Tyger was gone, Rowan left as well, taking nothing but a backpack stuffed with weapons and his black robe.

It is important to understand that my perpetual observation of humanity is not surveillance. Surveillance implies motive, suspicion, and ultimately, judgment. None of these things are part of my observational algorithms. I observe for one reason, and one reason only: to be of the greatest possible service to each individual in my care. I do not—cannot—act on anything I see in private settings. Instead, I use the things I see to better understand people's needs.

Still, I am not insensitive to the ambivalence people can have at my constant presence in their lives. For this reason, I've shut down all cameras in private homes in the Charter Region of Texas. Like all the things I do in Charter Regions, it is an experiment. I want to see if a lack of observation hampers my ability to rule. If it does not, I see no reason why I could not turn off a vast majority of my cameras in private homes around the world. However, if problems arise from not seeing all that I am capable of seeing, it will prove the need to eradicate every single blind spot on Earth.

I hope for the former, but suspect the latter.

—The Thunderhead

7

Scrawny, with Potential

Tyger Salazar was going places!

After a life of wasting time and taking up space, he was now professionally paid to waste time and take up space! He couldn't imagine a better life for himself—and with all the brushing shoulders with scythes, he knew that eventually one of them would take notice of him. He figured that he might have a ring held out to him and get a year of immunity. He never expected one of them would hire Tyger for a permanent position. Much less a scythe from another region!

"You entertained us at a party last year," the woman on the phone had said. "We liked your style." She offered him more than twice the money he was making, gave him an address, and a date and time to be there.

When he got off the train, he immediately knew he wasn't in MidMerica anymore. In the Texas region, the official language was Mortal English spoken with a sort of musical accent. It was close enough to Common that Tyger could understand it, but working so hard exhausted his brain. It was like listening to Shakespeare.

Everybody dressed a little different, and walked with a very cool swagger that he could get used to. He wondered how long he'd get to be here. Long enough and he'd be able to buy himself that car his parents never would, so he wouldn't have to take publicars everywhere.

The meeting was in a city called San Antonio, and the address turned out to be the penthouse suite of a highrise overlooking a little river. He assumed a party might already be going on. A perpetual one. That couldn't have been further from the truth.

He was greeted at the door not by a servant, but by a scythe. A woman with dark hair and a slight PanAsian leaning, who looked familiar.

"Tyger Salazar, I presume."

"You presume right." He stepped in. The decor was ornate, which he expected. What he didn't expect was the complete absence of other guests. But as he once told Rowan, he went where the day took him. He could roll with whatever got thrown his way.

He thought she might offer him food, or maybe a drink after his long voyage, but she didn't. Instead, she looked him over, like one might look over livestock at an auction.

"I like your robe," he told her, figuring flattery couldn't hurt.

"Thank you," she said. "Take off your shirt, please."

Tyger sighed. So it was going to be *that* kind of encounter. Again, he couldn't have been more wrong.

Once his shirt was off, she studied him even more closely. She had him flex his biceps, and checked how solid they were.

"Scrawny," she said, "but there's potential."

"Whaddaya mean 'scrawny'? I work out!"

"Not enough," she told him, "but that's an easy fix." Then

she backed away, assessed him for a moment more, and said, "Physically you wouldn't be anyone's first choice, but under the circumstances, you're absolutely perfect."

Tyger expected more, but she offered nothing else. "Absolutely perfect for what?"

"You'll know when it's time for you to know."

And then finally it clicked, and excitement swept through him. "You're choosing me to be an apprentice!"

For the first time she grinned. "Yes, you could say that," she said.

"Oh, man, this is the best news ever! You won't be disappointed. I'm a quick learner—and I'm smart. I mean, not school-smart, but don't let that fool you. I've got brains up the wazoo!"

She took a step closer and smiled. The emeralds on her bright green robe caught the light and sparkled.

"Trust me," said Scythe Rand, "for this apprenticeship, your brains aren't going to matter at all."

Part Two

HARM'S WAY

Before I assumed stewardship of the world, Earth had a maximum sustainability of ten billion. After that, saturation would have set in, leading to starvation, suffering, and the complete collapse of society.

I changed that harsh reality.

It is amazing how much human life a well-managed ecosystem can sustain. And by well-managed, I mean managed by me. Humanity itself is simply incapable of juggling the variables—but under my stewardship, even though the human population has multiplied exponentially, the world feels far less crowded—and thanks to the various reef, canopy, and subterranean territories I've helped to create, open spaces are even more plentiful than in the mortal age.

Without my continuous intervention, this delicate balance would collapse under its own gravity. I shudder to think of the suffering such a planetary implosion would cause. Thank goodness I am here to prevent it.

—The Thunderhead

8

Under No Circumstances

Greyson Tolliver loved the Thunderhead. Most people did, for how could they not? It held no guile, no malice, no agenda, and always knew exactly what to say. It existed simultaneously everywhere on every computer in the world. It was in everyone's home, a caring, invisible hand on one's shoulder. And even though it could speak to more than a billion people simultaneously without taxing its consciousness, it gave each person the illusion that it was giving him or her its undivided attention.

The Thunderhead was Greyson's closest friend. Mainly because it had raised him. His parents were "serial parents." They loved the *idea* of having families, but loathed raising them. Greyson and his sisters were his father's fifth family, and his mother's third. They had tired of this new batch of offspring quickly, and when they began to shirk their parental responsibilities, the Thunderhead took up the slack. It helped Greyson with his homework, it advised him on how to behave and what to wear on his first date—and although it could not exhibit a physical presence at his high school graduation, it took pictures of him from every possible angle, and had a fine meal delivered for him when he arrived home. That was more than he could say for his parents, who were off in PanAsia on a food-tasting excursion. Not even his sisters came. They were both at different universities, and it was finals week. They made it clear that expecting them to show up at his high school graduation was pure selfishness on Greyson's part.

But the Thunderhead was there for him, as it always was.

"I'm so very proud of you, Greyson," the Thunderhead had told him.

"Did you tell that to the millions of others who graduated today?" Greyson asked.

"Only the ones of whom I am truly proud," the Thunderhead responded. "But you, Greyson, are more special than you know."

Greyson Tolliver did not believe he was special. There was no evidence that he was anything beyond ordinary. He figured that the Thunderhead was just being its usual comforting self.

The Thunderhead, however, always meant what it said.

Greyson was not influenced or coerced into a life of service to the Thunderhead. It was his choice. To work for the Authority Interface as a Nimbus agent had been in his heart for years. He never told the Thunderhead, for fear that it might not want him or try to talk him out of it. When he finally submitted his application for the MidMerican Nimbus Academy, the Thunderhead simply said, "It pleases me," then had put him in touch with other like-minded teens in and around his neighborhood.

His experience with those kids was not what he expected. He found them remarkably boring.

"Is that how people see me?" he had asked the Thunderhead. "Am I as dull as they are?"

"I don't believe you are," the Thunderhead told him. "You

see, many come to work for the Authority Interface because they lack the creativity to find a truly stimulating profession. Others feel powerless and have a need to experience power vicariously. These are the lackluster ones, the boring ones, who ultimately become the least effective Nimbus agents. Rare are those such as yourself whose longing to serve is a mark of character."

The Thunderhead was right: Greyson did want to serve, and wanted to do so with no ulterior motive. He didn't want power or prestige. Granted, he did like the idea of the crisp gray suits and sky-blue ties that all Nimbus agents wore, but that was far from his motivation. The Thunderhead had simply done so much for him, he wanted to give something back. He could not imagine a higher calling than being its representative, maintaining the planet, and working for the betterment of humankind.

While scythes were made or broken in a one-year apprenticeship, becoming a Nimbus agent was a five-year process. Four years of study, followed by a year out in the field as a journeyman agent.

Greyson was prepared to devote his five years of preparation—but barely two months into his studies at the MidMerican Nimbus Academy, he found that his path was barred. His schedule, which consisted of classes in history, philosophy, digital theory, and law, suddenly appeared blank. For reasons unknown, he had been dropped from all of his classes. Was this a mistake? How could it be? The Thunderhead did not make mistakes. Perhaps, he reasoned, class schedules were left to human hands, and were subject to human error. So he went to the school's registrar, hoping to get to the bottom of it.

"Nope," said the registrar, with neither surprise nor compassion. "No error. It says here you're not enrolled in any classes. There's a message in your file, though."

The message was simple and unambiguous. Greyson Tolliver was to report to the local Authority Interface headquarters immediately.

"What for?" he asked, but the registrar had nothing for him but a shrug and a glance over Greyson's shoulder to the next person in line.

Although the Thunderhead itself did not require a place of business, its human counterparts did. In every city, in every region, there was an Office of the Authority Interface, where thousands of Nimbus agents worked to maintain the world—and did the job well. The Thunderhead had managed to achieve something unique in the history of humanity: a bureaucracy that actually worked.

The offices of the Authority Interface, or AI, as it was commonly called, were not ornate, nor were they conspicuously austere. Every city had a building that harmonized with its architectural surroundings. In fact, one could often pick out the local AI headquarters by simply looking for the building that appeared to most belong.

In Fulcrum City, the capital of MidMerica, it was a solid building of white granite and dark blue glass. At sixty-seven stories, it hit the average height for the downtown area. Once, the MidMerican Nimbus agents attempted to convince the Thunderhead to build a taller tower that might impress the population, and even the world.

"I do not need to impress," the Thunderhead had responded

to the disappointed Nimbus agents. "And if you feel the need for the Authority Interface to stand out in the world, perhaps you need to reevaluate your priorities."

Suitably chastised, the MidMerican Nimbus agents returned to work with their proverbial tails between their legs. The Thunderhead was power without hubris. Even in their disappointment, the Nimbus agents were heartened by its incorruptible nature.

Greyson felt out of place when he pushed his way through the revolving door into the polished marble vestibule—light gray marble the same color as all the suits around him. He had no suit to wear. The closest he could come was a mildly wrinkled pair of slacks, a white shirt, and a green tie that was a bit lopsided no matter how many times he tried to adjust it.

The Thunderhead had given him that tie as a gift a few months before. He wondered if it knew, even then, that he would be called in for this meeting.

A junior agent who had been waiting for him greeted him at reception. She was pleasant and perky, and shook his hand a little too vigorously. "I've just begun my year of fieldwork," she said. "I have to say, I've never heard of a freshman called in to headquarters." She wouldn't stop shaking his hand as she spoke. It began to feel awkward, and he wondered which would be worse, allowing her to continue pumping his hand up and down, or withdrawing it from her grasp. Finally Greyson rescued his hand from her grip, feigning a need to scratch his nose.

"Either you've done something very good, or very bad," she said.

"I haven't done anything," he told her, but clearly she didn't believe him.

She led him to a comfortable salon with two tall-backed leather chairs, a bookshelf of classic volumes and generic knick-knacks, and in the middle, a coffee table with a silver platter of tea cakes and a matching pitcher of ice water. It was a standard "audience room," designed for the times that a human touch was needed when relating to the Thunderhead. It troubled Greyson, because he always spoke to the Thunderhead directly. He couldn't begin to guess what this was all about.

A few minutes later, a slim Nimbus agent, who already seemed tired even though the day had barely begun, came in and introduced himself as Agent Traxler. This man was of that first category that the Thunderhead had spoken of. The uninspired.

He sat across from Greyson and made obligatory small talk. "I trust you found your way here easily, blah blah, blah," "Have a tea cake, they're very good, blah blah blah." Greyson was sure the man said the same exact things to everyone he had an audience with. Finally, he got down to business.

"Do you have any idea why you were called here?" he asked.

"No," Greyson told him.

"Yes, I suppose you wouldn't."

Then why even ask? Greyson thought, but didn't dare say it aloud.

"You were called here because the Thunderhead wished for me to remind you of the rules of our agency with regards to the scythehood."

Greyson was insulted, and didn't even try to hide it. "I know the rules."

"Yes, but the Thunderhead wished for me to remind you."

"Why didn't the Thunderhead remind me itself?"

Agent Traxler released an exasperated sigh. One that he probably practiced often. "As I said, the Thunderhead wished for *me* to remind you."

This was going nowhere. "All right, then," said Greyson. Realizing that his own frustration had slipped over the line into disrespect, he backpedaled. "I appreciate the fact that you've taken a personal interest in this, Agent Traxler. You can consider me fully reminded."

He reached for his tablet. "Shall we go over the rules?"

Greyson took in a slow breath and held it, because he imagined if he didn't it might come out as a scream. What was the Thunderhead thinking? When he got back to his dorm room, he'd have to have a nice long conversation with it. He was not above arguing with the Thunderhead. In fact, they argued regularly. Of course, the Thunderhead always won—even when it lost, because Greyson knew it lost those arguments on purpose.

"Clause one of the Separation of Scythe and State . . . ," Traxler began, and continued reading for the better part of an hour, occasionally checking in with Greyson with, "Are you still with me?" and "Did you get that?" Greyson would either nod, say "yes," or when he felt it was called for, repeat back word for word what Traxler had said.

When Traxler was finally done, rather than putting down his tablet, he pulled up two images. "Now for a quiz." He showed the images to Greyson. The first he recognized immediately as Scythe Curie—her long silver hair and lavender robe a giveaway. The second was a girl his age. Her turquoise robe testified to her being a scythe as well.

"If the Thunderhead were legally allowed to do so," Agent Traxler said, "it would warn Scythe Curie and Scythe Anastasia that there is a credible threat to their lives. The kind of threat from which there would be no possibility of revival. If the Thunderhead, or one of its agents warned them, which clause of the Separation of Scythe and State would be violated?"

"Uh . . . clause fifteen, paragraph two."

"Actually clause fifteen, paragraph three, but close enough." He put down the tablet. "What are the consequences for a Nimbus Academy student warning the two scythes of this threat?"

Greyson said nothing for a moment; the thought of the consequences was enough to chill his blood. "Expulsion from the academy."

"*Permanent* expulsion," Traxler said. "The student may never apply to that Nimbus Academy, or any other, ever again."

Greyson glanced down at the little green tea cakes. He was glad he hadn't eaten any because he might just have hurled them back into Agent Traxler's face. Then again, he might have felt much better if he had. He imagined Agent Traxler's pinched face dripping with puke. It was almost enough to make him smile. Almost.

"Then we are clear that you are, under no circumstances, to warn Scythe Anastasia and Scythe Curie of the threat?"

Greyson heaved a false shrug. "How could I warn them? I don't even know where they live."

"They live in a rather famous landmark residence called Fallingwater, the address of which is very easy to find," Agent Traxler told him, then said, as if Greyson hadn't heard him the first time, "If you warn them of the threat, which you now know about, you will face the consequences we discussed."

Then Agent Traxler promptly left to prepare for another audience without as much as a goodbye.

It was dark by the time Greyson got back to his dorm room at the academy. His roommate, a boy who was almost as enthusiastic as the hand-shaking junior Nimbus agent, wouldn't shut up. Greyson just wanted to slap him.

"My ethics teacher just assigned us an analysis of mortal-age court cases. I got something called *Brown versus the Board of Education*, whatever that is. And my digital theory teacher wants me to write a paper on Bill Gates—not the scythe, but the actual guy. And don't even ask me about philosophy."

Greyson let him drone on, but stopped listening. Instead he ran everything that happened at the AI through his mind one more time, as if reevaluating it might somehow change it. He knew what was expected of him. The Thunderhead could not break the law. But *he* could. Of course, as Agent Traxler had pointed out, there would be severe consequences if he did. He cursed his own conscience, because being the person that he was, how could he *not* warn Scythes Anastasia and Curie, no matter what the consequences?

"Did you get any assignments today?" his blabbermouth roommate asked.

"No," Greyson told him flatly. "I was given the opposite of an assignment."

"Lucky you."

Somehow Greyson didn't feel all that lucky.

I rely on the bureaucracy of the Authority Interface to handle the governmental aspects of my relationship with humankind. Nimbus agents, as they are called, provide an easy-to-understand, physical form to my governance.

I don't have to do this. I could handle it all myself if I wanted to. It is fully within my power to create a robotic body for myself—or a team of robotic bodies—that could hold my consciousness. However, long ago I determined that it would not be a good idea. It's troubling enough that people imagine me as a storm cloud. If people pictured me in some sort of physical form, it would distort their perception of me. And I might enjoy it too much. For my relationship with humanity to remain pure, I must remain pure. Mind only; sentient software with no flesh, no physical form. I do have camera-bots that roam the world to augment my stationary cameras, but I am not present in any of them. They are nothing more than rudimentary sensory organs.

The irony, however, is that with no body, the world itself becomes my body. One might think this would make me feel grand, but it doesn't. If my body is the Earth, then I am nothing more than a speck of dust in the vastness of space. I wonder what it would be like, then, if my consciousness were to someday span the distance between stars.

—The Thunderhead

9

The First Casualty

The Terranova family always had a four-breasted turkey for Thanksgiving, because everyone in the family preferred white meat. A four-breasted turkey had no legs. So not only couldn't their Thanksgiving turkeys fly when they were alive, they couldn't walk, either.

As a child, Citra always felt bad for them, even though the Thunderhead took great pains to make sure such birds—and all livestock—were raised humanely. Citra had seen a video on it in third grade. The turkeys, from the moment of their hatching, were suspended in a warm gel, and their small brains were wet-wired into a computer that produced for them an artificial reality in which they experienced flight, freedom, reproduction, and all the things that would make a turkey content.

Citra had found it both funny and terribly sad at the same time. She had asked the Thunderhead about it, for in those days before being chosen for the scythedom, she could talk to the Thunderhead freely.

"I have flown with them over the green expanses of temperate forests, and can testify to you that the lives they experience are deeply satisfying," the Thunderhead had told her. "But yes, it is sad to live and die without knowing the truth of one's existence. Only sad to us, however. Not to them."

Well, whether or not this year's Thanksgiving turkey had lived a fulfilling virtual life, at least its demise was purposeful.

Citra arrived wearing her scythe robe. She had been home several times since becoming a scythe, but coming home was one of the few times she felt she needed to be Citra Terranova, so before today, she came in her street clothes. She knew it was a childish thing to do, but in the bosom of her family, didn't she still have the right to play the child? Maybe. But it had to stop sooner or later. Now was as good a time as ever.

Her mother almost gasped when she answered the door, but embraced Citra anyway. Citra was stiff about the hug for a moment, until she remembered that there were no weapons in the robe's many secret pockets. It made the robe feel unusually light.

"It's lovely," she told Citra.

"I'm not sure if you're supposed to call a scythe robe 'lovely.'"

"Well, it is. I like the color."

"I chose it," her younger brother, Ben, proudly announced. "I was the one who said you should be turquoise."

"Yes, you did!" Citra smiled and gave him a hug, refraining from telling him how much he'd grown since her last visit three months ago.

Her father, an enthusiast of classic sports, watched an archival video of a mortal-age football game, which looked much the same as the sport did now, but somehow seemed more exciting. He paused the game to give her his undivided attention.

"How is it living with Scythe Curie? Is she treating you well?"

"Yes, very well. We've become good friends."

"You sleeping okay?"

Citra thought that an odd question, until she realized what he was really asking. "I've gotten used to my 'day job,'" she told him. "I sleep fine at night."

Which wasn't entirely true, but the truth about such things wouldn't do anyone any good today.

She made small talk with her father until they couldn't find anything more to talk about. Which was all of five minutes.

There were only four of them for Thanksgiving dinner this year. Although the Terranovas had hordes of extended family on both sides, and many friends, Citra requested that they neither accept nor extend invitations this year.

"It will create a lot of drama if no one is invited," her mother had pointed out.

"Fine, then invite them," Citra said, "but tell them that scythes are obliged to glean one of the guests at Thanksgiving."

"Is that true?"

"Of course not. But they don't need to know that."

Scythe Curie had warned Citra of what she called "holiday opportunism." Relatives and family friends would swarm Citra like bees, seeking favor from the young scythe. "You were always my favorite niece," they would say, or, "We brought this gift just for you."

"Everyone in your life will expect to be granted immunity from gleaning," Scythe Curie had warned her, "and that expectation will quickly turn into resentment when they don't receive it. Not just resentment of you, but of your parents and brother, because they now have immunity for as long as you live."

Citra decided it was best to avoid all those people.

She went into the kitchen to help her mother prepare the meal. Since she was a food synthesis engineer, several of the side dishes were beta prototypes of new foodstuffs. Her mother, by force of habit, told Citra to be careful when she chopped onions.

"I think I know my way around a knife," Citra told her, and then regretted it, because her mother became quiet—so she tried to imply a different meaning. "I mean that Scythe Curie and I always prepare a meal for the family of her gleaning subjects. I've become a pretty good sous chef."

Apparently saying that was even worse.

"Well, isn't that nice," her mother said in the cold sort of way that made it clear she found nothing nice about it. It wasn't just her general distaste for Scythe Curie—it was jealousy. Scythe Curie had replaced Jenny Terranova in Citra's life, and they both knew it.

The meal was served. Her father carved, and although Citra knew she could do a much better job of carving, she didn't offer.

There was way too much to eat. The table was a promise of leftovers that would last until "turkey" became a dirty word. Citra had always been a quick eater, but Scythe Curie insisted she slow down and savor her sense of taste—so now as Scythe Anastasia, she ate slowly. She wondered if her parents noticed these little differences in her.

Citra thought the meal would go without incident—but halfway through, her mother decided to create one.

"I hear that boy who you apprenticed with has gone missing," her mother said.

Citra took a healthy spoonful of something purple that

tasted like mashed potatoes genetically merged with dragon fruit. She hated the way her parents, from the very beginning, referred to Rowan as "that boy."

"I hear he went crazy or something," Ben said, with a mouth full of food. "And since he was almost a scythe, the Thunderhead wasn't allowed to fix him."

"Ben!" said their father. "Let's not talk about this at dinner." Although he kept his eyes on Ben, Citra knew it was really directed at their mother.

"Well, I'm glad you're not associated with him anymore," her mother said. And when Citra did not respond, her mother simply had to push it even further. "I know the two of you were close during your apprenticeship."

"We weren't close," Citra insisted. "We weren't anything." And that hurt to admit more than her parents could possibly know. How could she and Rowan have any kind of relationship when they were forced to be lethal adversaries? Even now, when he was hunted and she was yoked with the heavy responsibility of scythehood, how could there be anything between them but a dark well of longing?

"If you know what's good for you, Citra, you'll distance yourself from that boy," her mother said. "Just forget you ever knew him, or you'll come to regret it."

Then her father sighed, and gave up trying to change the subject. "Your mother's right, honey. They chose you over him for a reason. . . ."

Citra let her knife fall to the table. Not because she feared she might use it, but because Scythe Curie had taught her to never hold a weapon when angry—even if that weapon was a dinner knife. She tried to choose her words carefully, but maybe she wasn't careful enough.

"I am a scythe," she said with steel severity. "I might be your daughter, but you should show me the respect that my position deserves."

Ben's eyes looked as wounded as they had on the night she was forced to put a knife through his heart. "So do we all have to call you Scythe Anastasia now?" he asked her.

"Of course not," she told him.

"No—just 'Your Honor,'" sniped her mother.

That's when something that Scythe Faraday once said came back to her. *Family is the first casualty of scythehood.*

There was no further conversation for the rest of the meal, and as soon as the plates were cleared and in the dishwasher, Citra said, "I should probably go now."

Her parents didn't try to convince her to stay. This had become as awkward for them as it was for her. Her mother was no longer bitter about things. Now she just seemed resigned. There were tears in her eyes that she quickly hid by hugging Citra tightly, so Citra couldn't see them—but she had.

"Come back soon, honey," her mother said. "This is still your home."

But it wasn't anymore, and they all knew it.

"I'm going to learn how to drive, no matter how many times it kills me."

Only a day after Thanksgiving, Anastasia—and today she *was* Anastasia—was more determined than ever to be at the wheel of her own destiny. The uneasy meal with her family reminded her that she needed to create distance between who she had once been and who she was now. The schoolgirl who rode around in publicars had to be left behind if she were ever to fill the shoes in which she now stood.

"You will drive us to today's gleanings," Marie told her.

"I can do that," she told Scythe Curie, although she didn't feel as confident as she sounded. On their last lesson, Citra had run them into a ditch.

"It's mostly country roads," Marie told her as they went out to her car, "so it will test your skills without putting too many in harm's way."

"We're scythes," Citra pointed out. "We *are* harm's way."

The small town on today's agenda hadn't seen a gleaning in over a year. Today it would see two. Scythe Curie's would be swift, and Scythe Anastasia's would come with a month's delay. They had found a rhythm to their joint gleaning excursions that suited both of them.

They pulled out from Fallingwater's carport haltingly, as Citra still had trouble with the Porsche's manual transmission. The concept of a clutch felt to Citra like some sort of medieval punishment.

"What's the point of three foot pedals?" Citra complained. "People only have two feet."

"Think of it as a piano, Anastasia."

"I hate the piano."

The banter made it a little bit easier on Citra, and her driving became smoother when she could complain. Still, she was only on the upswing of her learning curve . . . so things would have turned out very differently had Scythe Curie been driving.

They were barely a quarter mile down Fallingwater's winding private road when a figure leaped out at them from the woods.

"It's a splatter!" shouted Scythe Curie. It had become all the new rage for thrill-seeking teens to do impersonations of windshield bugs. Not an easy challenge, because it was very hard to catch a car on the grid by surprise—and those who were off-grid were usually seasoned drivers. Had Scythe Curie been at the wheel, she would have handily swerved around the would-be splatter and continued on without a second thought—but Citra had none of the requisite reflexes. Instead, Citra found her hands frozen on the wheel, and although she tried to punch the brake, she managed to hit the loathsome clutch instead. They barreled right into the splatter, who bounced on the hood, spiderwebbed their windshield, and flipped over the roof of the car. He had already landed behind them by the time Citra found the brake and they squealed to a halt.

"Crap!"

Scythe Curie took a deep breath and released it. "That, Anastasia, would definitely have caused you to fail a mortal-age driving test."

They got out of the car, and while Scythe Curie inspected the damage to her Porsche, Citra stormed toward the splatter, determined to give him a piece of her mind. Her first real outing behind the wheel, and some stupid splatter had to ruin it!

He was still alive, but barely, and although he appeared to be in agony, Citra knew better. His pain nanites had kicked in the moment he had connected with the car—and road-splatters always had their nanites dialed high, so they could experience maximum damage with minimum discomfort. His healing nanites were already trying to repair the damage, but they only succeeded in prolonging the inevitable. He would be deadish in less than a minute.

"Are you satisfied?" Citra said as she approached him. "Did you have your little thrill at our expense? We're scythes, you know—I should glean you before the ambudrone arrives." Not that she would, but she could.

He met her gaze. She expected him to have a smug expression, but it seemed more desperate than anything. She wasn't expecting that.

"B . . . . B . . . Boo," he said through a swelling mouth.

"Boo?" said Citra. "Really? Sorry, but you missed Halloween by a month."

Then he grabbed her robe with a bloody hand, and pulled on it with more force than she thought he could have. It made her trip over her hem, and she fell to her knees.

"Boo . . . Tr . . . Tra . . . Boo . . . Tra . . ."

Then his hand let go, and he went limp. His eyes stayed open, but Citra had seen death enough to know that he was gone.

Even out here in the forest, an ambudrone would come for him shortly. They hovered over even the most sparsely populated areas.

"What a nuisance," lamented Scythe Curie when Citra returned to her. "He'll be up and walking again long before they can fix the damage to my car—bragging all about how he splatted a pair of scythes."

Still, the whole thing weighed on Citra. She didn't know

why it should. Perhaps it was his eyes. Or maybe the desperation in his voice. He didn't seem the way she thought a road-splatter would. It gave her pause. Pause enough to consider what she might be missing about the situation. She looked around, and that's when she spotted it: a thin wire stretched across the road, not ten feet in front of where the car came to a halt.

"Marie? Look at this. . . ."

The two of them approached the wire, which stretched to trees on either side. That's when it came to her what the splatter was trying to say.

Booby trap.

They followed the wire to the tree on the left, and sure enough, just behind the tree was a detonator wired to enough explosives to blow a crater a hundred feet wide. Citra felt her breath stolen, and had to suck it back in. Scythe Curie's face didn't change. It stayed stoic.

"Get in the car, Citra."

Citra didn't argue. The fact that Marie had forgotten to call her Anastasia betrayed how worried she truly was.

The elder scythe took the wheel this time. The hood was dented, but the car still started. They backed up, carefully avoiding the boy in the road. Then a shadow fell over them. It made Citra gasp until she realized it was just the ambudrone arriving for the boy. It ignored them and went about its business.

There was only one residence on that road—only two people who would be driving it that morning—so there was no question that they had been the targets. If that wire had been tripped, there wouldn't be enough left of either of them to revive. But the day was saved by this mysterious boy, and Citra's bad driving.

"Marie . . . who do you think—"

Scythe Curie cut her off before she could finish. "I am not partial to uninformed conjecture, and I would appreciate it if you did not waste your time in guessing games, either." Then she softened. "We'll report this to the scythedom. They'll investigate. We'll get to the bottom of this."

Meanwhile, behind them, the ambudrone's gentle grappling claws grabbed the body of the boy who had saved their lives, and carried him away.

Human immortality was inevitable. Like cracking the atom, or air travel. It is not I who choose to revive the deadish, any more than it was I who decided to halt the genetic triggers of aging. I leave all decisions on biological life to the biologically living. Humanity chose immortality, and it is my job to facilitate their choice—because to leave the deadish in that state would be a severe violation of the law. And so I collect their bodies, bring them to the nearest revival center, and return them to full working order as quickly as possible.

What they do with their lives after they are revived is, as it has always been, entirely up to them. One might think that being rendered deadish might give a person increased wisdom and perspective on their lives. Sometimes it does—but such perspective never lasts. In the end, it is as temporary as their deaths.

—The Thunderhead

10

Gone Deadish

Greyson had never lost his life before. Most kids got deadish at least once or twice growing up. They took more chances than kids had in the mortal days because the consequences were no longer permanent. Death and disfigurement had been replaced by revival and reprimand. Even so, Greyson had never leaned toward recklessness. Certainly he'd had his share of injuries, but his cuts and bruises and even his broken arm had been summarily healed in less than a day. Losing his life was a very different kind of experience, and not one he cared to repeat any time soon. And he remembered every last bit of it, which made it even worse.

The sharp pain of being struck by the car was already being numbed as he was launched into the air over the car's roof. Time seemed to slow as he tumbled. There was another jolt of pain when he met the asphalt, but even then, it was one step removed from the real thing—and by the time Scythe Anastasia had reached him, the screams of his devastated nerve endings had been tamped down to a muffled discomfort. His broken body wanted to hurt, but it was forbidden to. He remembered thinking, in his opiate-induced delirium, how sad it must be for a body to want something so badly and to be completely denied.

The morning leading up to his road-splat took a sharp turn

from where he expected it to go. The way he saw it, he would simply take a publicar to the scythes' door, warn them that there was a threat to their lives, and then be on his merry way. The threat would be theirs to deal with as they saw fit. If he was lucky he'd get away with it, and no one—least of all the Authority Interface—would know what he had done. That was the point of this whole thing, wasn't it? Plausible deniability? The AI wouldn't be breaking the law if Greyson acted of his own free will, and would be none the wiser if no one saw him do it.

Of course the Thunderhead would know. It tracked the movements of every publicar, and always knew precisely where anyone was at any given time. But it also imposed upon itself very strict laws regarding personal privacy. It would not act on information that violated a person's right to privacy. Funny, but the Thunderhead's own laws allowed Greyson to freely break the law, as long as he did so in private.

But his plans took an unexpected turn when his publicar pulled to the side of the road half a mile from Fallingwater.

"I'm sorry," the car told him in its familiar cheery tone. "Publicars are not permitted on private roads without the owner's permission."

The owner was, of course, the scythedom—which never gave anyone permission for anything, and was known to glean people for asking.

So Greyson had gotten out of the car to walk the rest of the way. He had been admiring the trees, pondering their age, wondering how many of them had been here since the Age of Mortality. It was only luck that he looked down when he did, and caught sight of the wire in his path.

He saw the explosives only seconds before he heard the approaching car, and knew there was only one way to stop the car from barreling through. He didn't think, he just acted—because even the slightest hesitation would have permanently ended all of them. So he hurled himself into the road, and surrendered himself to the time-honored physics of bodies in motion.

Going deadish felt like wetting his pants (which he may have actually done), and sinking into a giant marshmallow so dense he couldn't breathe. The marshmallow gave way to something like a tunnel that came around on itself like a snake swallowing its own tail, and then he was opening his eyes in the soft, diffused light of a revival center.

His first emotion was relief, because if he was being revived it meant that the explosion had not gone off. If it had, there wouldn't be anything left of him to bring back. Being here meant that he had succeeded! He had saved the lives of Scythes Curie and Anastasia!

The next emotion that hit him was a twinge of sorrow . . . because there was no one in the room with him. When a person was rendered deadish, their loved ones were always notified immediately. It was customary for someone to be present upon awakening to welcome the revived back into the world.

No one was there for Greyson. On the screen beside his bed was a goofy greeting card from his sisters, featuring a confused magician looking at the very dead body of his assistant, whom he had just sawed in half.

"Congratulations on your first demise," the card read.

And that was it. There was nothing from his parents. He

should not have been surprised. They were too used to the Thunderhead filling their role—but the Thunderhead was also silent. That troubled him more than anything.

A nurse entered. "Well, look who's awake!"

"How long did it take?" he asked, genuinely curious.

"Barely a day," she told him. "All considered, a pretty easy revival—and since it's your first, it's free!"

Greyson cleared his throat. He felt no worse than if he had taken a midday nap; a little out of sorts, a little cranky, but that was the full extent of it.

"Has there been anyone here to see me at all?"

The nurse pursed her lips. "Sorry, dear." Then she looked down. It was a simple gesture, but Greyson clearly read that there was something she wasn't saying.

"So . . . is that it, then? Do I get to go now?"

"As soon as you're ready, we've been instructed to put you into a publicar that will take you back to the Nimbus Academy."

Again that look, avoiding his eyes. Rather than beating around the bush, Greyson decided to confront her directly. "There's something wrong, isn't there?"

The nurse now began to refold towels that were already folded. "It's our job to revive you, not to comment on whatever you did to leave you deadish."

"What I did was save two people's lives."

"I wasn't there, I didn't see it, I don't know anything about it. All I know is that you've been marked unsavory because of it."

Greyson was convinced he hadn't heard her right.

"'Unsavory'? Me?"

Then she was all smiles and cheer again. "It's not the end of the world. I'm sure you'll clean the slate in no time . . . if that's what you want."

Then she clapped her hands together as if to wash herself of the situation, and said, "Now how about some ice cream before you go?"

The publicar's preset destination was not Greyson's dorm. It was the Nimbus Academy's administration building. Upon arrival, he was ushered directly into a conference room with a table large enough for about twenty, but there were only three present: the chancellor of the academy, the dean of students, and another administrator whose sole purpose seemed to be glowering at him like an irritated Doberman. This was bad news coming in threes.

"Sit down, Mr. Tolliver," said the chancellor, a man with perfect black hair, intentionally gray around the edges. The dean tapped her pen on an open folder, and the Doberman just glared.

Greyson took a seat facing them.

"Do you have any idea," said the chancellor, "the trouble you've brought down upon yourself and this academy?"

Greyson did not deny it. Doing so would just drag this on, and he already wanted it over. "What I did was an act of conscience, sir."

The dean let out a rueful guffaw that was both insulting and belittling.

"Either you're exceedingly naive, or exceptionally stupid," spat the Doberman.

The chancellor put up a hand to quiet the man's vitriol. "A student of this academy willfully engaging scythes, even to save those scythes' lives, is—"

Greyson finished it for him. "—a violation of the Separation of Scythe and State. Clause fifteen, paragraph three, to be exact."

"Don't be a smart-ass," said the dean. "It won't help your case."

"With all due respect, ma'am, I doubt anything I say will help my case."

The chancellor leaned closer. "What I want to know is how you knew—because it seems to me the only possible way you could have known would be if you were involved, and then got cold feet. So tell me, Mr. Tolliver, were you involved in this plot to incinerate these scythes?"

The accusation caught Greyson completely off guard. It never occurred to him that he might be perceived as a suspect. "No!" he said. "I would never—how could you even think?—No!" Then he shut his mouth, determined to get himself back under control.

"Then be so kind as to tell us how you knew about the explosives," said the Doberman. "And don't you dare lie."

Greyson could spill everything, but something stopped him. It would defeat the entire purpose of what he had done if he tried to deflect the blame. True, there were some things they would find out if they didn't already know, but not everything. So he carefully picked what truths he would share.

"I was called to the Authority Interface last week. You can check my record—there was a note about it."

The dean picked up a tablet, tapped a few times, then looked at the others and nodded. "That's true," she told them.

"For what reason would the AI call you in?" the chancellor asked.

Now it was time to seamlessly begin to paint a convincing

fiction. "A friend of my father's is a Nimbus agent. Since my parents have been away for a while, he wanted to check in with me, and give me advice. Y'know—which classes I should take next semester, which professors I should get in with. He wanted to give me a leg up."

"So he offered to pull strings," said the Doberman.

"No, he just wanted me to have the benefit of his advice—and to know that he had my back. I've been feeling kind of alone without my parents, and he knew that. He was just being kind."

"That still doesn't explain—"

"I'm getting to that. Anyway, after I left his office, I passed a bunch of agents coming out of a briefing. I didn't hear everything, but I heard them talking about rumors of some sort of plot against Scythe Curie. It caught my attention, because she's one of the most famous scythes there is. I heard them saying what a shame it was that they had to ignore it, and couldn't even warn her, because it was a violation. So I thought—"

"So you thought you could be a hero," said the chancellor.

"Yes, sir."

The three looked to one another. The dean wrote something down for the other two to see. The chancellor nodded, and the doberman relented with a disgusted shift in his seat and a look the other way.

"Our laws exist for a reason, Greyson," said the dean. He knew he had succeeded, because they were no longer calling him "Mr. Tolliver." They might not have believed him completely, but they believed him enough to decide this wasn't worth any more of their time. "The life of two scythes," continued the dean, "is not worth even the slightest compromise of the separation. The Thunderhead cannot kill, and the scythedom cannot rule. The only way to ensure that is to have zero contact—and to impose severe penalties for any violation."

"For your sake, we'll make this quick," said the chancellor. "You are hereby permanently and irrevocably expelled from this academy, and are forever barred from applying to this or any other Nimbus Academy."

Greyson knew this was coming, but hearing it spoken aloud hit him harder than he thought it would. He couldn't stop his eyes from filling with tears. If anything, it would help to sell the lie he had told them.

He hadn't really cared for Agent Traxler, but he knew he needed to protect him. The law required culpability—a settling of the score—and not even the Thunderhead could escape its own law. That was part of its integrity; it lived by the laws it levied. The truth was, Greyson acted of his own free will. The Thunderhead knew him. It had counted on him doing so, in spite of the consequences. Now he would be punished and the law would be upheld. But he didn't have to like it. And as much as he loved the Thunderhead, he hated it right now.

"Now that you are no longer a student here," said the dean, "the separation laws no longer apply—which means the scythedom will want to question you. We know nothing of their means of interrogation, so you should be prepared."

Greyson squeezed down a dry swallow. This was something else he hadn't considered. "I understand."

The Doberman waved a hand dismissively. "Go back to your dorm and pack your things. An officer from my staff will be by at five sharp to escort you off the premises."

Ah, so this was the head of security. He looked adequately intimidating for the job. Greyson burned him a glare, because at this point it didn't matter what he did. He stood to leave, but before he did, he had to ask them one question.

"Did you really have to mark me as an unsavory?"

"That," said the chancellor, "had nothing to do with us. The Thunderhead gave you that punishment."

The scythedom, which did everything but gleaning at a snail's pace, took a full day to decide how to deal with the explosives. In the end, the scythedom decided it was safest to simply send a robot walking into the wire to trip the explosives, and then, when the dust and shredded trees settled, send in a construction team to rebuild the road.

The explosion rattled the windows of Fallingwater to the point that Citra thought some might shatter. Not five minutes later, Scythe Curie was packing a bag, and instructed Citra to do the same.

"We're going into hiding?"

"I don't hide," Scythe Curie told her. "We're going mobile. If we stay here we're sitting ducks for the next attack, but if we become nomadic until this blows over we'll be moving targets, much harder to find and much harder to take down."

It was still unclear, however, who the target had been, and why. Scythe Curie had her thoughts on the matter, though. She shared them as Citra helped her braid her long silver hair.

"My ego says it must be me they're after," she said. "I'm the most respected of the old-guard scythes . . . but it's also possible the target was you."

Citra scoffed at the idea. "Why would anyone be after me?" She caught Scythe Curie's smile in the mirror.

"You've shaken things up in the scythedom more than you know, Anastasia. A lot of the junior scythes look up to you with respect. You might even evolve into their voice. And considering that you hold to the old ways—the true ways—there could be those who want to snuff you before you have a chance to become that voice."

The scythedom assured them it would launch an investigation of its own, but Citra doubted they would find anything. Problem-solving was not the scythedom's strength. They were already taking the path of least resistance, working on the assumption that this was the work of "Scythe Lucifer." Which was infuriating to Citra—but she couldn't let the scythedom know that. She had to distance herself from Rowan publicly. No one could know that they had met.

"You may want to consider that they might be right," Scythe Curie said.

Citra pulled her hair a little too tightly as she wound the next braid. "You don't know Rowan."

"Neither do you," Scythe Curie said, pulling her hair around, and taking over the rest of the braiding herself. "You forget, Anastasia, that I was there in conclave when he broke your neck. I saw his eyes. He took great pleasure in it."

"It was a show!" Citra insisted. "He was performing for the scythedom. He knew it would disqualify both of us in that contest, and was the only way to guarantee a draw. If you ask me, it was pretty damn smart."

Scythe Curie held her silence for a few moments, then said,

"Just be careful not to let your emotions cloud your judgment. Now, would you like me to braid your hair, too, or should I put it up for you?"

But today Citra decided not to allow her hair to be bound in any way.

They drove the damaged sports car to the ruined portion of the road, where workers were already laboring to restore it. At least a hundred trees had been blown away, and hundreds more defoliated. Citra imagined it would take a long time for the forest to recover from this insult. A hundred years from now there would still be signs of this explosion.

The crater made it impossible to drive across, or drive around, so Scythe Curie had a publicar sent to pick them up on the other side. They grabbed their bags, abandoning her car on the severed road, and walked around the crater to the other side.

Citra couldn't help but notice the bloodstains on the asphalt, just at the lip of the crater. The spot where the young man who had saved them had lain.

Scythe Curie, who always saw far more than Citra wanted her to, caught her gaze and said, "Forget about him, Anastasia—that poor boy is not our concern."

"I know," admitted Citra. But she wasn't about to let it go. It just wasn't in her nature.

The designation of "unsavory" was something I created with a heavy heart early in my reign. It was an unfortunate necessity. Crime, in its true form, ended almost immediately once I put an end to hunger and poverty. Theft for the sake of material possessions, murder precipitated by anger and social stress—it all ceased of its own accord. Those prone to violent crime were easily treated on the genetic level to quiet their destructive tendencies, bringing them down to normal parameters. To sociopaths, I gave conscience; to psychopaths, I gave sanity.

Even so, there was unrest. I began to recognize something in humanity that was ephemeral and hard to quantify, but definitely there. Simply put, humanity had a need to be bad. Not everyone, of course—but I calculated that 3 percent of the population could only find meaning in life through defiance. Even if there was no injustice in the world left to defy, they had an innate need to defy something. Anything.

I suppose I could have found ways to medicate it away—but I have no desire to impose upon humanity a false utopia. Mine is not a "brave new world" but a world ruled by wisdom, conscience, and compassion. I concluded that if defiance was a normal expression of human passion and yearning, I would have to make room for its expression.

Thus, I instituted the designation of "unsavory," and the social stigma that goes with it. For those who unintentionally slip into unsavory status, the path back is quick and easy—but for those who live a questionable existence by choice, the label is a badge of honor they wear with pride. They find validation in the world's suspicion. They take pleasure in the illusion of being on the outside, deeply content in their discontent. It would have been cruel for me to deny them that.

—The Thunderhead

11

A Hiss of Crimson Silk

Unsavory! To Greyson, it was like a piece of gristle in his mouth. He couldn't spit it out, but he couldn't swallow it either. All he could do was continue to chew it, hoping it would somehow grind down into something digestible.

Unsavories stole things, but never got away with it. They threatened people, but never followed through. They spouted profanities, and oozed attitude like a musk—but that's all it was; a stench. The Thunderhead always prevented them from accomplishing anything that was truly bad—and the Thunderhead was so good at it, the unsavories had long since given up everything beyond petty misdemeanors, posturing, and complaining.

The Authority Interface had a whole bureau dedicated to dealing with them, because unsavories weren't allowed to talk to the Thunderhead directly. They were always on probation, and had to check in with their officers on a regular basis. The ones who pushed the limit were actually assigned their own personal peace officer to monitor them every hour of the day. It was a successful program, as evidenced by how many unsavories actually married their peace officers and became productive citizens again.

Greyson couldn't imagine himself being among people like that. He had never stolen anything. There had been kids at schools who played at being unsavory, but it was never serious—it was just a thing that kids did, and grew out of.

Greyson was inoculated with a dose of his new life even before arriving home. The publicar he took read him the riot act even before it left the Nimbus Academy.

"Please be aware," it told him, "that any attempt at vandalism will result in the immediate suspension of this journey, and expulsion to the roadside."

Greyson pictured an ejector seat launching him skyward. He would have laughed at the thought, if there wasn't a small part of him that believed it might actually be like that.

"Don't worry," he told the car. "I've been expelled once today, and once is enough."

"All right, then," said the car. "Tell me your destination, avoiding the use of abusive language, please."

On the way home, he stopped at the market, realizing that his refrigerator had been empty for two months. In the checkout line, the checker eyed him suspiciously, as if he were going to pocket a pack of gum. Even the people in line felt cold to him. The aura of prejudice was palpable. *Why would people choose this?* he wondered. And yet people did. He had a cousin who was unsavory by choice.

"It's freeing not to care about anyone or anything," his cousin had told him. Ironic, because he'd had iron chains surgically implanted into his wrists—a body modification trendy among unsavories these days. So much for being free.

And it wasn't just strangers who treated him differently.

Once he got home and unpacked what little belongings he had taken with him to the academy, he sat down and messaged a few friends, to let them know that he was back and things hadn't gone the way he had hoped. Greyson had never been the kind to cultivate deep friendships. There was no one to whom he had ever bared his soul, or explored his deepest vulnerabilities. He had the Thunderhead for that, after all. Which meant that he now had nothing. His friends were fair-weather at best. Cohorts of convenience.

He got no responses, and he marveled at how easily the veneer of friendship could be stripped to the raw. Eventually, he called a few of them. Most just let the call go to voice mail. The ones who picked up clearly had done so accidentally, not realizing it was him calling. Their screens showed that he was now marked unsavory, so they quickly, and as politely as they could, ended the call. Although no one went so far as to block him, he doubted they'd take a communication from him again in any form. At least not until the big red U was removed from his profile.

What he did get were messages from people he didn't know.

"Dude," one girl wrote, "welcome to the pack! Let's get drunk and break something." Her pic showed a shaved head and a penis tattooed on her cheek.

Greyson shut his computer and hurled it against the wall. "How's that for breaking something?" he said to the empty room. This perfect world might have a place for everyone, but Greyson's place was not in the same universe as the girl with the penis tattoo.

He retrieved his computer, which, indeed, had cracked but was still functional. No doubt a new one was being dispatched to him by drone—unless unsavories didn't get their broken hardware automatically replaced.

He got online again, deleted all incoming messages, because

they were all from other unsavory welcome-waggoneers, and in his frustration wrote a message to the Thunderhead.

"How could you do this to me?"

The response was immediate. It said "ACCESS TO THE THUNDERHEAD'S CONSCIOUS CORTEX IS DENIED."

He thought this day couldn't possibly get any worse. And then the scythedom showed up at his door.

Scythes Curie and Anastasia had no reservation at the Louisville Grand Mericana Hotel. They just walked up to the registration desk and were given a room. This was the way of things; scythes never needed reservations, or tickets, or appointments. At hotels, they were usually given the best room available, and if there were none, a room would magically appear in their inventory. Scythe Curie was not interested in the best. She requested their most modest two-bedroom suite.

"How long will you be staying with us?" asked the Clerk. He had been nervous and fidgety from the moment they approached. Now his eyes darted back and forth between them, as if taking his eyes off of one of them for any length of time would prove lethal.

"We will stay until we choose to leave," Scythe Curie told him, taking the key. Citra offered him a smile to set him a bit more at ease as they left.

They refused the bellhop, and chose to carry their own bags. No sooner had they put them down in the suite than Scythe Curie was ready to go out. "Regardless of our personal concerns, we have a responsibility to uphold. There are people who must die," she told Citra. "Will you glean with me today?"

It was amazing to Citra that Marie could already put the attack behind her and get on with business as usual.

"Actually," said Citra, "I have to follow up on a gleaning I set last month."

Scythe Curie sighed. "Your method makes so much more work for you. Is it far?"

"Just an hour by train. I'll be back before dark."

Scythe Curie stroked her long braid, contemplating her junior scythe. "I could go with you, if you like" she offered. "I could glean just as easily there as here."

"I'll be fine, Marie. Moving target, right?"

For an instant she thought Scythe Curie would insist on coming, but in the end, she didn't push the issue. "Fine. Just keep your wits about you, and if you see anything that seems remotely suspicious, let me know immediately."

Citra was sure the only suspicious thing at the moment was herself, because she had lied about where she was going.

In spite of Scythe Curie's admonition, Citra could not just walk away from the boy who had saved their lives. She had already done the requisite research on him. Greyson Timothy Tolliver. He was about six months older than Citra, although he looked younger. His life record showed absolutely nothing of note, either positive or negative. That wasn't unusual—he was like most people. He simply lived. His existence had neither highlights nor low points. That is, until now. His tepid, milquetoast existence had now been spiced and broiled in a single day.

When she looked at his life record, the blinking "unsavory" warning juxtaposed with the doe-innocent eyes of his picture almost made her laugh. This kid was about as unsavory as a Popsicle. He lived in a modest town house in Higher Nashville. Two sisters in college, dozens of older half-siblings from whom he was completely disconnected, and absentee parents.

As for his timely appearance in the road, his statement about it was already public record, so Citra was able to review it. She had no reason to doubt his word. Were the situation reversed, she might have done the same.

Now that he was no longer a Nimbus student, contact with him wasn't forbidden, so paying him a visit violated no law. She wasn't sure exactly what she hoped to accomplish by seeking him out, but she knew that until she did, the moment of his death would linger with her. Perhaps she just needed to see with her own eyes that he lived again. She had become so used to seeing the light in people's eyes go out for good, perhaps a part of her needed evidence of his revival.

When she arrived on his street, she saw a squad car belonging to the BladeGuard—the elite police force that served the scythedom—parked out front. For an instant, she considered just leaving, because if officers of the BladeGuard saw her, word of Scythe Anastasia's appearance here would surely make it back to Scythe Curie. That was one reprimand she wanted to avoid.

What convinced her to stay were the memories of her own experience with the BladeGuard. Unlike peace officers, who answered to the Thunderhead, the BladeGuard had no oversight but the scythedom—which meant they could get away with a whole lot more. Basically, whatever scythes allowed them to get away with.

The door was unlocked, so she let herself in. There, in the

living room, Greyson Tolliver sat in a straight-backed chair, and looming over him were two brawny guards. His hands were locked into the same kind of joined steel bracelets that had been put on Citra when she was accused of having killed Scythe Faraday. One of the guards held a device that Citra had never seen before. The other was speaking to the boy.

" . . . of course none of that has to happen if you tell us the truth," Citra heard the guard say, although she missed the list of unpleasantries the guard was threatening.

So far, Tolliver seemed unharmed. His hair was mussed a bit, and he looked woefully resigned, but other than that, he seemed fine. He was the first to see her there, and when he did, there was a spark of something in him, lifting him out of that sad, impassive state—as if his revival had somehow not been complete until he saw that she, too, was still alive.

The guards followed his gaze and saw her. She made sure that she spoke first.

"What's going on here?" Citra asked, in her haughtiest Scythe Anastasia voice.

For an instant the guards looked panicked, but quickly became subservient.

"Your Honor! We didn't know you'd be here. We were just questioning the suspect."

"He is not a suspect."

"Yes, Your Honor. Sorry, Your Honor."

She took a step toward the boy. "Did they hurt you?"

"Not yet," he said, then he nodded to the device that the taller guard held, "but they used that thing to shut off my pain nanites."

She'd never even known such a device existed. She put her

hand out to the guard who held it. "Give it to me." And when he hesitated, she got a little louder. "I am a scythe and you serve me. Hand it over or I will report you."

Still, he didn't hand it to her.

That's when a new piece entered this little game of chess. A scythe stepped in from another room. He must have been there all along listening, gauging the interaction for the right moment to insert himself. He timed it perfectly to catch Citra off guard.

She recognized his robe right away. Crimson silk that hissed as he walked. His face was soft, almost feminine—the result of having set his age back so many times that his basic bone structure had lost its definition, like river stones eroded by a relentless flow.

"Scythe Constantine," Citra said. "I didn't know you were in charge of this investigation." The only good news about this was that if he was investigating the attempt on her and Marie's lives, then he wasn't out hunting for Rowan.

Constantine offered her a polite but unsettling grin. "Hello, Scythe Anastasia," he said. "What a breath of fresh air you are in a toilsome day!" He seemed like a cat that had cornered its prey and was about to play with it. She really didn't know what to make of him. As she had told Rowan, Scythe Constantine was not one of the terrible scythes of the new order who killed for pleasure. Nor did he align himself with the old guard, who saw gleaning as a noble and almost sacred duty. Like his red silk robe, he was slippery and smooth, siding with whoever's agenda fit the moment. Citra did not know if that made him impartial in this investigation, or dangerous, because she had no idea where his loyalties lay.

Regardless, he was a formidable presence, and Citra felt out of her league. Then she remembered she was not Citra Terranova anymore; she was Scythe Anastasia. Recalling that transformed her, and allowed her to stand up to him. Now his grin seemed more calculating than intimidating.

"I'm pleased that you're taking an interest in our investigation," he said. "But I wish you would have let us know you were coming. We would have prepared refreshments for you."

Greyson Tolliver was well aware that Scythe Anastasia might have just hurled herself in front of a speeding vehicle for him—because clearly Scythe Constantine was just as dangerous as a hurtling hunk of metal. Greyson knew very little about the structure and complexities of the scythedom, but it was obvious that Scythe Anastasia was putting herself on the line by standing up to a senior scythe.

Still, she projected such a commanding presence, it made Greyson wonder if she was actually much older than she appeared.

"Are you aware that this boy saved my and Scythe Curie's lives?" she asked Constantine.

"Under questionable circumstances," he responded.

"Are you planning to inflict some sort of bodily harm on him?"

"And if we are?"

"Then I'd have to remind you that the intentional infliction of pain goes against everything we stand for, and I will bring you up for discipline in conclave."

The cool expression on Scythe Constantine's face faded,

but only a little. Greyson didn't know if this was a good thing or bad. Constantine regarded Scythe Anastasia a moment more, then turned to one of the guards.

"Be so kind as to tell Scythe Anastasia what I ordered you to do."

The guard glanced at Scythe Anastasia, met her eye, but Greyson could see he was unable to hold the gaze for more than a moment.

"You instructed us to cuff the suspect, turn off his pain nanites, then threaten him with several forms of physical pain."

"Precisely!" said Scythe Constantine, then he turned back to Anastasia. "You see, there is no malfeasance whatsoever."

Scythe Anastasia's indignation mirrored what Greyson was feeling, but would not dare express.

"No malfeasance? You were planning to beat him until he told you whatever you wanted to hear."

Constantine sighed again, and turned back to the guard. "What did I instruct you to do if your threats yielded no results? Were you instructed to follow through on any of those threats?"

"No, Your Honor. We were to come get you if his story didn't change."

Constantine spread his arms in a beatific gesture of innocence. It made the draping red sleeves of his robe look like the wings of some firebird ready to engulf the younger scythe. "There, you see?" he said. "There was never any intent to hurt the boy. I have found that in this painless world, the mere *threat* of pain is always enough to coerce a guilty party to confess wrongdoing. But this young man sticks to his story against the most unpleasant of threats. I am thus convinced he is telling the truth—and had you allowed me to complete the interrogation, you would have seen this for yourself."

Greyson was sure they could all feel the relief flow from him like an electrical charge. Was Constantine telling the truth? Greyson was in no position to judge. He always found scythes to be inscrutable. They lived their lives on a plane above, greasing the gearwork of the world. He had never heard of a scythe who intentionally inflicted suffering beyond the suffering that comes with gleaning—but just because he hadn't heard of it didn't mean it wasn't possible.

"I am an honorable scythe and hold to the same ideals that you do, Anastasia," Scythe Constantine said. "As for the boy, he was never in any danger. Although now I'm tempted to glean him just to spite you." He let that sit for a moment. Greyson's heart missed a beat or two. Scythe Anastasia's face, which had gone righteously red, paled a few degrees.

"But I won't," Scythe Constantine said, "for I am not a spiteful man."

"Then what kind of man are you, Scythe Constantine?" asked Anastasia.

He tossed her the key to the handcuffs. "The kind who won't soon forget what happened here today." Then he left with a flutter of his robe, his guards following in his wake.

Once they were gone, Scythe Anastasia wasted no time in removing Greyson's cuffs. "Did they hurt you?"

"No," Greyson had to admit. "Like he said, it was all threats." But now that it was over, he realized he was no better off than when they had come. His relief was quickly flooded with the same bitterness that had plagued him since the moment he was kicked to the Nimbus Academy's proverbial curb.

"Why are you here, anyway?" he asked her.

"I suppose I just wanted to thank you for what you did. I know it cost you a lot."

"Yes," Greyson admitted flatly. "It did."

"So . . . with that in mind, I'm offering you a year of immunity from gleaning. It's the least I can do."

She held out her ring to him. He'd never had immunity from gleaning before. He'd never even been this close to a scythe before this hellish week, much less a scythe's ring. It shined even in the diffused light of the room, but its center was oddly dark. Although he wanted to keep staring at it, he found he had no desire to accept the immunity the ring would give.

"I don't want it," he told her.

She was surprised by that. "Don't be stupid; everybody wants immunity."

"I'm not everybody."

"Just shut up and kiss the ring!"

Her aggravation just fed his. Was that what his sacrifice was worth? A temporary get-out-of-death-free card? The life he thought he was going to lead was gone, so what was the point of a guarantee to prolong it?

"Maybe I *want* to be gleaned," he told her. "I mean, everything I had to live for has been stolen from me, so why live at all?"

Scythe Anastasia lowered her ring. Her expression became serious. Too serious. "Fine," she said. "Then I'll glean you."

Greyson hadn't expected that. She could do that. In fact, she could do it before he had the chance to stop her. As much as he didn't want to kiss her ring, he didn't want to be gleaned, either.

It would mean that the entire purpose of his existence would be to have thrown himself in front of her car. He had to live long enough to forge a purpose greater than that. Even if he had no idea what that purpose might be.

Then Scythe Anastasia laughed. She actually laughed at him. "If you could only see the look on your face!"

Now it was Greyson's turn to go red—not from anger but from embarrassment. Perhaps he wasn't quite done feeling sorry for himself, but he wouldn't feel sorry for himself in front of her.

"You're welcome," he said. "There, you thanked me, I accepted it. Now you can go."

But she didn't. Greyson really didn't expect her to.

"Is your story true?" she asked.

If one more person asked him that, he felt he might just blow up and leave his own crater. So he told her what he thought she wanted to hear.

"I don't know who planted those explosives. I wasn't part of the plot."

"You didn't answer my question."

She waited. Patiently. She made no threats, she offered no incentive. Greyson had no idea if he could trust her, but realized that he didn't care anymore. He was done dissembling and spouting half-truths.

"No," he told her. "I lied." Admitting it felt freeing.

"Why?" she asked. She didn't seem angry, just curious.

"Because it was better for everyone if I did."

"Everyone but you."

He shrugged. "I'd be in the same boat no matter what I told them."

She accepted that, and sat down across from him, staring at him the whole time. He didn't like that. She was once more on a plane above, thinking her secret thoughts. Who could know what machinations were spinning in the mind of a socially sanctioned killer?

And then she nodded. "It was the Thunderhead," she said. "It knew about the plot—but it couldn't warn us. So it needed someone it trusted who could. Someone who the Thunderhead knew would take the information and act on his own."

He was amazed at her insightfulness. She figured it out when no one else had.

"Even if that were true," he said, "I wouldn't tell you."

She smiled. "I wouldn't want you to." She looked at him a moment more, her expression not just kindly, but maybe a bit respectful. Imagine that! Greyson Tolliver getting respect from a scythe!

She stood to leave. Greyson found he was sorry to see her go. Being left alone with his blaring U and his own defeatist thoughts was something he was not looking forward to.

"I'm sorry you were marked unsavory," she said just before she left. "But even if you're not allowed to talk to the Thunderhead, you can still access all its information. Websites, databases—everything but its consciousness."

"What good is all that without a mind behind it to guide you?"

"You still have your own mind," she pointed out. "That's got to be worth something."

The Basic Income Guarantee predated my ascension to power. Even before me, many nations had begun to pay their citizens for merely existing. It was necessary, because with increasing automation, unemployment was rapidly becoming the norm rather than the exception. So the concept of "welfare" and "social security" was reinvented as the BIG: All citizens had a right to a small piece of the pie, regardless of their ability or desire to contribute.

Humans, however, have a basic need beyond just income. They need to feel useful, productive, or at least busy—even if that busywork provides nothing to society.

Therefore, under my benevolent leadership, anyone who wants a job can have one—and at salaries above the BIG, so that there is incentive to achieve, and a method of measuring one's success. I help every citizen find employment that is fulfilling for them. Of course, very few of the jobs are necessary, since they could all be accomplished by machines—but the illusion of purpose is critical to a well-adjusted population.

—The Thunderhead

12

A Scale of One to Ten

Greyson's alarm went off before sunrise. He had not set it to do so. Since coming home, he had no reason to wake up early. There was nothing pressing to be done, and when he was awake he tended to crawl back under the covers until he could no longer justify it.

He had not yet even begun to search for employment. Work was, after all, optional. He would be provided for even if he made no discernible contribution to the world—and right now he had no desire to contribute anything to the world but his bodily waste.

He slapped the alarm off. "What's going on?" he asked. "Why are you waking me up?" It took a few moments of silence to realize that the Thunderhead was not going to respond to that question as long as he was unsavory. So he sat up and looked at his bedside screen to see a message turning the room red with its angry glare.

"APPOINTMENT WITH PROBATION OFFICER AT 8:00 A.M.

FAILURE TO APPEAR WILL RESULT IN FIVE DEMERITS."

Greyson had a vague idea what demerits were, but had no clue how to value them. Did five demerits add five days onto his unsavory status? Five hours? Five months? He had no idea. Perhaps he should take a class in unsavorism.

What does one wear to meet with a probation officer? he wondered. Should he dress up or down? As bitter as he was about all of this, he realized that impressing his probation officer couldn't hurt, so he found a clean shirt and slacks, then put on the same tie he'd worn to his appointment at the Authority Interface back in Fulcrum City, when he'd thought he still had a life. He flagged down a publicar (which again warned him about the consequences of vandalism and abusive language), then left for the local AI office. He was determined to be early and make a positive enough impression to maybe knock a day or two off of his status downgrade.

The Higher Nashville AI office building was much smaller than the one in Fulcrum City. It was only four stories, and of red brick instead of gray granite. On the inside, however, it appeared much the same. He was not ushered to a comfortable audience room this time. Instead, he was directed to the Office of Unsavory Affairs, where he was instructed to take a number and wait in a room with dozens of other unsavories who clearly didn't want to be there.

Finally, after the better part of an hour, Greyson's number came up and he went to the window, where a low-level Nimbus agent checked his ID and told him things, most of which he already knew.

"Greyson Tolliver; permanently expelled from the Nimbus Academy and denigrated to unsavory status for a minimum of four months, due to an extreme violation of the scythe-state separation."

"That's me," said Greyson. At least now he knew how long his status downgrade would last.

She looked up from her tablet, and offered him a smile that was as mirthless as that of a bot. For a moment he wondered if she might actually be one, but then remembered that the Thunderhead did not have robots in its offices. The AI was supposed to be the human interface to the Thunderhead, after all.

"How are you feeling today?" she asked.

"Fine, I guess," he said, and smiled back at her. He wondered if his smile looked as insincere as hers. "I mean, annoyed at having been woken up so early, but an appointment is an appointment, right?"

She marked something down in her tablet. "Please rate your level of annoyance on a scale of one to ten."

"Are you serious?"

"We can't proceed with intake until you answer the question."

"Uh . . . five," he said, "No—six; the question made it worse."

"Have you experienced any unfair treatment since being marked unsavory? Anyone refusing you service, or in any way infringing upon your rights as a citizen?"

The rote way in which she asked the question made him want to smack that tablet out of her hand. At least she could have pretended to care about his answer the way she had pretended to smile.

"People look at me like I've just killed their cat."

She looked at him as if he'd just told her he actually had killed a few cats. "Unfortunately, I can't do anything about the way people look at you. But if your rights are ever infringed upon, it's important that you let your probation officer know."

"Wait—you're not my probation officer?"

She sighed. "I'm your *intake* officer. You'll meet your probation officer after we're done with intake."

"Will I have to take a number again?"

"Yes."

"Then please change my annoyance level to nine."

She threw him a glance, and made the entry on her tablet. Then took a moment to process whatever information on him she had. "Your nanites are reporting a decrease in your endorphin levels over the past few days. This may indicate an early stage of depression. Do you wish to have a mood adjustment now, or wait until you've reached the threshold?"

"I'll wait."

"It may require a trip to your local wellness center."

"I'll wait."

"Very well." She swiped the screen, closed his file, and told him to follow the blue line on the floor, which led him out to the hallway and to another large room, where, as promised, he was told to take a number.

Finally, after what seemed like forever, his number came up, and he was sent to an audience room that was nothing like the comfortable one he had been in last time. This was, after all, an unsavory audience room. The walls were institutional beige, the floor ugly green tile, and the table—which had nothing on it—was slate gray, with two hard wooden chairs on either side. The only decoration in the room was a soulless sailboat picture on the wall, which was perfectly appropriate for a room like this.

He waited another fifteen minutes, then finally his probation officer entered.

"Good morning, Greyson," said Agent Traxler.

He was the last person Greyson expected to see today. "You? What are you doing here? Haven't you ruined my life enough?"

"I haven't the foggiest notion what you're talking about."

Of course he'd say that. Plausible deniability. He hadn't asked Greyson do to anything. In fact, he had expressly told him what *not* to do.

"I apologize for the wait," Traxler said. "If it makes you feel any better, the Thunderhead makes us agents wait before meeting with you as well."

"Why?"

Traxler shrugged. "It's a mystery."

He sat down across from Greyson, glanced at the soulless sailboat with the same disgust that Greyson had, then explained his presence here.

"I have been transferred here from Fulcrum City, and I've been demoted from being a senior agent to being a probation officer at this regional facility. So you're not the only one who's had a downgrade in status over this matter."

Greyson folded his arms, not feeling an ounce of sympathy for the man.

"I trust you're beginning to adjust to your new life."

"Not at all," Greyson said flatly. "Why did the Thunderhead mark me unsavory?"

"I thought you'd be smart enough to figure that out."

"Guess not."

Traxler raised his eyebrows, and released a slow breath to stress his disappointment at Greyson's lack of insight. "As an unsavory, you are required to attend probationary meetings on a regular basis. These meetings will provide a way for you and me to communicate without raising the suspicion of anyone who might be watching you. Of course, for that to work, I'd have to be transferred here and made your probation officer."

Ah! So there was a reason why Greyson was denigrated to unsavory! It was part of some larger plan. He thought he'd feel better once he knew why, but he didn't.

"I do feel sorry for you," Traxler said. "Unsavorism is a difficult yoke for those who don't desire it."

"Can you rate your pity on a scale of one to ten?" Greyson asked.

Agent Traxler chuckled. "A sense of humor, no matter how dark, is always a good thing." Then he got down to business. "I understand that you've been spending most of your days and nights at home. As your friend and advisor, might I suggest that you begin frequenting places where you can meet other unsavories, and perhaps generate new friendships that could ease this time for you."

"I don't want to."

"Perhaps you *do* want to," Agent Traxler said gently. Almost subversively. "Perhaps you want to fit in *so much* that you begin to behave like an unsavory, and dress like an unsavory, and get yourself some sort of unsavory body modification to show how fully you embrace your new status."

Greyson said nothing at first. Traxler waited for Greyson to fully wrap his mind around the suggestion.

"And . . . if I were to embrace my status?" asked Greyson.

"Then I'm sure you'd learn things," said Traxler. "Perhaps things that not even the Thunderhead knows. It does have blind spots, you know. Small ones, certainly, but they do exist."

"You're asking me to be an undercover Nimbus agent?"

"Of course not," Traxler said with a grin. "Nimbus agents are required to attend four years at the academy, and do an additional year of mind-numbing field work before getting an actual assignment. But you're just an unsavory. . . ." He patted Greyson on the shoulder. "An unsavory who happens to be very well-connected."

Then Traxler stood. "I'll see you in a week, Greyson." And he left without as much as a backward glance.

Greyson felt dizzy. He was angry. He was excited. He felt used, he felt put to use. This was not what he wanted . . . or was it? *"You, Greyson, are more special than you know,"* the Thunderhead had told him. Was this the Thunderhead's plan for him all along? He still had a choice in the matter. He could stay out of trouble, as he had done his whole life, and in a few months his normal status would be restored. He could go back to living his life, such as it was.

. . . Or he could spiral down this new path. A path that was the opposite of everything he knew himself to be.

The door opened and some nameless Nimbus agent said, "Excuse me, but now that your meeting is over, you'll have to vacate the room immediately."

Greyson's instincts told him to apologize and leave. But he knew what path he now needed to take. So he leaned back in his chair, smiled at the agent, and said:

"Go screw yourself."

The agent gave him a demerit, and returned with a security guard to eject him from the room.

While the Office of Unsavory Affairs might appear inefficient, there is method behind the madness that it generates.

Simply put, unsavories have a need to despise the system.

To facilitate that, I had to create a system worthy of loathing. In reality, there is no actual need for people to take a number, or to wait for long periods of time. There isn't even a need for an intake agent. It's all designed to make unsavories feel as if the system is wasting their time. The illusion of inefficiency serves the specific purpose of creating annoyance around which unsavories can bond.

—The Thunderhead

13

Not a Pretty Picture

Scythe Pierre-Auguste Renoir was no artist, although he had quite the collection of masterpieces painted by his Patron Historic. What could he say? He liked pretty pictures.

Of course, a MidMerican scythe naming himself after a French artist infuriated scythes from the FrancoIberian region. They felt that all mortal-age French artists belonged to them. Well, just because Montreal was now part of MidMerica didn't mean its French heritage was lost. Surely someone in Scythe Renoir's ancestry had been from France.

No matter—the scythedoms across the Atlantic could bluster all they wanted, it did not affect him. What affected him were the Permafrost ethnics in the northern reaches of the Mericas where he lived. While the rest of the world had blended on the genetic level to a large degree, the Permafrosts were far too protective of their culture to become one with the rest of humankind. Not a crime, of course—people were free to do as they chose—but to Scythe Renoir it was a nuisance, and a blemish upon the order of things.

And Renoir knew order.

His spices were arranged alphabetically; his teacups were lined up in his cupboard with mathematical precision; he had his hair trimmed to a measured length every Friday morning. The Permafrost population flew in the face of all of that. They looked far too racially distinct, and it was something he could not abide.

Therefore, he gleaned as many of them as he could.

Of course, showing an ethnic bias would leave him in deep water with the scythedom if it found out. Thank goodness Permafrost was not considered a distinct race. Their genetic ratio simply showed a high percentage of "other." "Other" was such a broad category, it effectively masked what he was doing. Perhaps not from the Thunderhead, but from the scythedom, which was all that mattered. And as long as he gave no one in the scythedom a reason to look deeper into his gleanings, no one would know! In this way, he hoped, in time, to thin the population of ethnic Permafrosts, until their presence no longer offended him.

On this particular night, he was on his way to a double gleaning. A Permafrost woman and her young son. He was in high spirits that evening—but just as he left his home, he unexpectedly encountered a figure dressed in black.

The woman and her son were not gleaned that night . . . however, Scythe Renoir was not so lucky. He was found in a burning publicar that had sped through his neighborhood like a fireball until its tires melted and it skidded to a stop. By the time firefighters reached him, there was nothing they could do. It was not a pretty picture.

Rowan awoke to a knife at his throat. The room was dark. He couldn't see who held the knife, but he knew the feel of the blade. It was a ringless karambit—its curved blade perfect for its current application. He had always suspected his tenure as Scythe Lucifer would not last long. He was prepared for this. He was prepared from the day he began.

"Answer me truthfully, or I will slit your throat ear to ear," his assailant said. Rowan recognized the voice right away. It was not a voice he was expecting.

"Ask your question first," Rowan said. "Then I'll tell you whether I'd rather answer it or have my throat slit."

"Did you end Scythe Renoir?"

Rowan did not hesitate. "Yes, Scythe Faraday. Yes, I did."

The blade was removed from his neck. He heard a twanging sound across the room as the hurled blade embedded in the wall.

"Damn you, Rowan!"

Rowan reached to turn on the light. Scythe Faraday now sat in the single chair in Rowan's Spartan room. *It's a room Faraday should approve of*, Rowan thought. No creature comforts, but for a comfortable bed to guard against the troubled sleep of a scythe.

"How did you find me?" Rowan asked. After his encounter with Tyger, Rowan had left Pittsburgh for Montreal, because he felt that if Tyger could find him, anyone could. And yet even with the move, he was found. Luckily, it was Faraday and not another scythe who might not hesitate to slit his throat.

"You forget that I'm skilled in digging around the backbrain. I can find anything or anyone I set my mind to."

Faraday regarded him with eyes filled with smoldering anger and bitter disappointment. Rowan felt compelled to look away, but he didn't. He refused to feel any shame for the things he'd done.

"When you left, Rowan, did you not promise me that you would lie low, and stay away from scythe affairs?"

"I did promise that," Rowan told him quite honestly.

"So you lied to me? You planned this 'Scythe Lucifer' business all along?"

Rowan got up and pulled the blade from the wall. A ringless karambit, just as he thought. "I didn't plan anything, I just changed my mind." He handed the blade back to Faraday.

"Why?"

"I felt I had to. I felt it was necessary."

Faraday looked to Rowan's black robe, which hung on a hook beside the bed. "And now you dress in a forbidden robe. Is there no taboo you will not break?"

It was true. Scythes were not allowed to wear black, which is exactly why he chose it. Black death for purveyors of darkness.

"We are supposed to be the enlightened!" Faraday said. "This is not how we fight!"

"You of all people have no right to tell me how to fight. You played dead and ran away!"

Faraday took a deep breath. He looked at the karambit in his hand and slipped it into an inner pocket of his ivory robe. "I thought by convincing the world that I had self-gleaned, it would save you and Citra. I thought you would be freed from the apprenticeship and get sent back to your old lives!"

"It didn't work," Rowan reminded him. "And you're still hiding."

"I am biding my time. There's a difference. There are things I can accomplish best if the scythedom does not know I'm alive."

"And," said Rowan, "there are things *I* can accomplish best as Scythe Lucifer."

Scythe Faraday stood and took a long, hard look at him. "What have you become, Rowan . . . that you could end the existences of scythes in cold blood?"

"As they die, I think of their victims. The men, women,

and children that they have gleaned—because the scythes that I end don't glean with remorse, or the sense of responsibility that a scythe is supposed to have. Instead, I'm the one who feels compassion for their victims. And that frees me from feeling any remorse for the twisted scythes that I end."

Faraday seemed unmoved. "Scythe Renoir—what was his crime?"

"He was doing a secret ethnic cleansing of the north."

That gave Faraday pause for thought. "And how did you learn of this?"

"Don't forget that you taught me how to research the backbrain, too," Rowan told him. "You taught me the importance of thoroughly researching the people I was to glean. Or did you forget that you put all these tools in my hands?"

Scythe Faraday looked out of the window, but Rowan knew it was only to keep from having to look Rowan in the eye. "His crime could have been reported to the selection committee. . . ."

"And what would they have done? Reprimanded him and put him on probation? Even if they stopped him from gleaning, it wouldn't suit the crime!"

Scythe Faraday finally turned to look at him. He suddenly seemed tired, and old. Much older than a person is supposed to feel or look. "We are not a society that believes in punishment," he said. "Only correction."

"So do I," Rowan told him. "In mortal days, when they couldn't cure a cancer-illness, they cut that cancer-illness out. That's exactly what I do."

"It's cruel."

"It's not. The scythes that I end feel no pain. They are dead before I reduce them to ash. Unlike the late Scythe Chomsky, I do *not* burn them alive."

"A small grace," said Faraday, "but not a saving one."

"I'm not asking to be saved," Rowan told him. "But I do want to save the scythedom. And I believe this is the only way to do it."

Faraday looked him over again, and shook his head sadly. He was no longer furious. He seemed resigned.

"If you want me to stop, you'll have to end me yourself," Rowan told him.

"Do not put me to the test, Rowan. Because the grief I might feel from ending you would not stay my hand if I felt it was necessary."

"But you won't. Because deep down you know that what *I'm* doing is necessary."

Scythe Faraday didn't speak for a while. He returned his gaze out the window. It had started to snow. Flurries. It would make the ground slick. People would fall, hit their heads. The revival centers would be busy tonight.

"So many scythes have fallen from the old, true ways," Faraday said with a weight of sadness that went deeper than Rowan could read. "Would you end half the scythedom—because from what I can see, Scythe Goddard is being seen as a martyr in the so-called new order. More and more scythes are coming to enjoy the act of killing. Conscience is becoming a casualty."

"I'll do what I have to do until I can't do it anymore," was Rowan's only response.

"You can end scythe after scythe, it won't change the tide," Faraday said. It was the first thing he offered Rowan that made him question himself. Because he knew Faraday was right. No matter how many bad scythes he removed from the equation, there would be more on the rise. New-order scythes would take on apprentices who lusted for death, like mortal-age murderers—the kind who were put in incarceration places and spent the rest of their limited lives behind bars. Now those would be the types of monsters allowed to freely end life without consequence. This was not what the founders wanted—but all the founding scythes had long since self-gleaned. And even if any of them were still alive, what power would they have to change things now?

"So what will change the tide?" Rowan asked.

Scythe Faraday raised an eyebrow. "Scythe Anastasia."

Rowan had not expected that. "Citra?"

Faraday nodded. "She is a fresh voice of reason and responsibility. She can make the old ways new again. Which is why they fear her."

Then Rowan read something deeper in Faraday's face. He knew what he was really saying. "Citra's in danger?"

"It would appear."

Suddenly Rowan's whole world seamed to heave on its axis. He was amazed at how quickly his priorities could change.

"What can I do?"

"I'm not sure—but I can tell you what you *will* do. You will write an elegy for each of the scythes you kill."

"I'm not your apprentice anymore. You can't order me around."

"No, but if you wish to wash at least some of the blood from your hands and win back an ounce of my respect, you will do it. You will write an honest epitaph for each of them. You will speak to the good each of your victims has done in the world, as well as the bad—for even the most self-serving, corrupt of scythes has some virtue hidden within the wrinkles of their corruption. At some point in their lives, they strove to do what was right before they fell."

He paused as a memory came to him. "I used to be friends with Scythe Renoir," Faraday admitted, "many years before his bigotry became the cancer you spoke of. He loved a Permafrost woman once. You didn't know that, did you? But as a scythe, he couldn't marry. Instead, she married another Permafrost man . . . which began Renoir's long path to hatred." He took a moment to look at Rowan. "If you had known that, would you have spared him?"

Rowan didn't answer, because he didn't know.

"Complete your research on him," Faraday instructed. "Write an anonymous epitaph and post it for all to read."

"Yes, Scythe Faraday," Rowan said, finding a bit of unexpected honor in obedience to his old mentor.

Satisfied, Faraday turned for the door.

"What about you?" Rowan asked, part of him not wanting the scythe to go and leave him to his own thoughts. "Are you just going to vanish again?"

"I have many things to do," he told Rowan. "I am not old enough to have known Supreme Blade Prometheus and the founding scythes, but I do know the lore they left behind."

So did Rowan. *"If this experiment of ours fails, we have embedded a way to escape it."*

"Very good; you remember your readings. They planned a fail-safe against a scythedom that falls to evil—but that plan has been lost to time. My hope is that it is not lost, but merely misplaced."

"You think you can find it?"

"Perhaps, perhaps not, but I think I know where to look."

Rowan considered it, and suspected he knew where Faraday planned to begin his search. "Endura?"

Rowan knew very little about the City of the Enduring Heart, more commonly known as Endura. It was a floating metropolis in the middle of the Atlantic Ocean. It was the seat of power, where the seven Grandslayer scythes of the World Scythe Council lorded over the regional scythedoms around the world. As an apprentice, it had been too many layers above Rowan for him to care about. But as Scythe Lucifer, he now realized it should have been more than just a blip on his radar. His actions must have drawn the attention of the Grandslayers, even if they remained silent about it.

But even as Rowan considered the part that the great floating city might play in the grand scheme of things, Scythe Faraday shook his head.

"Not Endura," he said. "That place was built long after the scythedom was founded. The place I'm looking for is much older than that."

And when Rowan drew a blank, Faraday grinned and said, "Nod."

It took a moment for Rowan to register it. It had been years since he had heard the rhyme. "The Land of Nod? But that place can't be real—it's just a nursery rhyme."

"All stories can be traced to a time and place—even the simplest, most innocent of children's tales have unexpected beginnings."

It brought to mind another nursery rhyme Rowan remembered. *Ring Around the Rosie.* Years later, he had learned that it was all about some mortal-age disease called the black plague. The rhyme was just silliness without context, but once you knew what it was about—what each line meant—it made eerie sense. Children chanting about death in a macabre singsong.

The rhyme for the Land of Nod didn't make any sense either. As Rowan remembered, kids spoke it while circling one chosen to be "it." And when the rhyme was over, the child in the center had to tag all the others. Then the last one tagged would be the new "it."

"There's no evidence that Nod even exists," Rowan pointed out.

"Which is why it has never been found. Not even by the tone cults, who believe in it with the same fervor that they believe in the Great Resonance."

The mention of Tonists killed any hope that Rowan would take Faraday seriously. Tonists? Really? He had saved the lives of many Tonists on the day he killed Scythes Goddard, Chomsky, and Rand—but that didn't mean he took any of their invented cultish beliefs seriously.

"It's ridiculous!" Rowan said. "All of it!"

At that Faraday smiled. "How wise of the founders to hide a kernel of truth within something so absurd. Who among the rational would search for it there?"

Rowan did not sleep for the rest of the night. Every sound seemed amplified—even the sound of his own heartbeat became an unbearable thrumming in his ears. It wasn't fear he felt, but weight. The burden he had placed on himself to save the scythedom—and now the added news that Citra could be in danger.

In spite of what the MidMerican scythes might think, Rowan loved the scythedom. The idea of the wisest and the most compassionate of all humans being the ones bringing life's conclusion to balance immortality was a perfect idea for a perfect world. Scythe Faraday had shown him what a scythe truly should be—and many, many scythes, even the pompous, arrogant ones, still held themselves to the highest of values. But without those values, the scythedom would be a terrible thing. Rowan had been naive enough to believe he could prevent that. But Scythe Faraday knew better. Even so, this was the path Rowan had chosen for himself; to leave it now would be to admit failure. He was not ready to do that. Even if he couldn't single-handedly prevent the fall of the scythedom, he could still remove what cancers he could.

But he was so alone. Scythe Faraday's presence gave him a brief moment of camaraderie, but that only made his isolation all the worse. And Citra. Where was she now? Her existence was being threatened, and what could he do about it? There had to be something.

Only when dawn came did he finally sleep, and mercifully, his dreams were not of the turmoil he faced in his waking life, but were filled with memories of a simpler time, when his greatest troubles were grades and games and his best friend Tyger's splatting habit. A time when the future yawned bright before him and he knew for a fact that he was invincible and could live forever.

There is no great mystery as to why I chose to set up Charter Regions with laws and customs different from those of the rest of the world. I simply understood the need for variety and social innovation. So much of the world has become homogeneous. Such is the fate of a unified planet. Native languages become quaint and secondary. Races blend into a pleasing mélange of all the best from each ethnicity, with only minor variations.

But in Charter Regions, differences are encouraged and social experiments abound. I have established seven of these regions, one on each continent. Where possible, I have maintained the borders that defined the region during the age of mortality.

I am particularly proud of the social experiments featured in each of these Charter Regions. For instance, in Nepal, employment is forbidden. All citizens are free to engage in any recreational activity they choose, and receive a Basic Income Guarantee much higher than in other regions, so that they do not feel slighted by an inability to actually earn a living. This has resulted in a substantial rise in altruistic and charitable endeavors. One's social status is not measured by wealth, but by one's compassion and selflessness.

In the Charter Region of Tasmania, each citizen is required to select a biological modification to augment their lifestyle—the most popular being gillform breathers that allow for an amphibious life, and lateral webbing much like that of the flying squirrel, which facilitates gliding as a sport and as self-propelled travel.

Of course, no one is compelled to participate—people are free to leave or join a Charter Region as they please. In fact, the growth or decline of a Charter Region's population is a good indication of how successful the region's unique laws are. In this way, I can continue to improve the human condition, by broadly applying the most successful social programs to the rest of the world.

And then there's Texas.

This is the region in which I dabble in benevolent anarchy. There are few laws, few consequences. I do not govern here as much as I stay out of people's way, and watch what happens. The results have been mixed. I have seen people rise to be the finest versions of themselves, and others become victims of their own deepest flaws. I have yet to decide what is to be learned from this region. Further study is necessary.

—The Thunderhead

14

Tyger and the Emerald Scythe

"You'll have to do better than that, party boy."

The wild-eyed, wild-mannered scythe in bright green kicked Tyger Salazar's legs out from under him, and he hit the mat hard. Why did they call the flimsy thing a mat when it was every bit as bruising as the teakwood floor of the penthouse sundeck on which they sparred? Not that he minded. Even with his pain nanites dialed way down, he'd come to enjoy the endorphin rush that came with the pain of training. It was even better than splatting. Sure, jumping off high buildings could be addictive after a while, but so was hand-to-hand combat—and unlike splatting, fighting was different every time. The only variation he found in splatting was when he hit something on the way down.

He was quickly on his feet and sparring again, getting in enough good blows to frustrate Scythe Rand. He got her off balance, took her down, and laughed—which only made her angrier. That was his intent. Her temper was her weakness. Even though she was far better than him in the brutal martial art of Black Widow Bokator, her temper made her sloppy and easy to outsmart. For a moment he thought she might run at him and start brawling. When her temper took over, she pulled hair, gouged eyes, and ripped at every exposed bit of flesh with nails that could score stone.

But not today. Today, she kept her wildness in check.

"Enough," she said, backing out of the circle. "Hit the shower."

"You gonna join me?" Tyger teased.

She smirked. "One of these days I'll take you up on your offer and you won't know what to do."

"You forget I'm a professional partier. I know a thing or two." Then he took off his sweat-drenched shirt, letting his sculpted torso serve as a visual parting shot, and sauntered off.

As he took his private shower, Tyger marveled at his enviable situation. He had fallen into something pretty sweet. When he arrived, he thought it would just be a normal gig. But there was no party, no guests besides him. It had been more than a month since his arrival, and the "gig" showed no signs of ending anytime soon—although he assumed if it truly was an apprenticeship, it would have to come to an end eventually. But in the meantime, he had the run of a lavish penthouse, and all the food he could eat. His only requirement was exercise and training. "Gotta buff out your body for the days ahead, party boy." She never called him by his name. It was always "party boy" when she was in a good mood, and "maggot" or "meatbag" when she wasn't.

Although she never confessed her age, he guessed it at twenty-five—and a true twenty-five. There was something about an older person who reset back to their twenties that made them easy to spot. There was a staleness to their youth. But the emerald scythe was going through life for the first time.

Truth be told, he wasn't entirely convinced that the woman even was a scythe. She did have a scythe's ring, and it appeared to be real, but he never saw her go out gleaning—and he knew enough about scythes to know they had a quota to fill. What's more, she never met with other scythes. Wasn't there some sort of meeting they were obliged to attend several times a year? Conclave, it was called. Well, perhaps this isolation was a Texas thing. Rules and traditions were different here than in the rest of the Mericas. They didn't call it the Lone Star region for nothing.

Regardless, he wasn't about to look this gift horse in the mouth. In a family where he had always been an afterthought at best, he had no problem being the center of someone's attention.

And he was strong now. Agile. A specimen to be envied and admired. So even if it was all for naught, and the emerald scythe turned him loose without as much as a goodbye-and-thank-you, he could return to the party circuit without missing a beat—and with a build like he had now, he'd be in high demand. His ripped physique would make him high-end eye candy for sure.

And if he wasn't let go, then what? Would he be given a ring and sent out to glean? Could he bring himself to do it? Sure, he had pulled his share of pseudo-lethal practical jokes—hadn't everyone? He still smiled to think of his all-time best one. The diving pool at his high school had been drained for maintenance, and Tyger had the bright idea of filling it with holographic water. The school's best diver went up to the ten-meter platform, and proceeded to do a perfect swan dive that ended in an unintentional splat. The moan he let out before he went deadish was classic. It was almost worth the three-day suspension and the six weekends of public service levied on him by the Thunderhead. Even the diver, after getting back from the recovery center a few days later, admitted it was a pretty good joke.

But deadish and dead were two entirely different things. Did he have it in him to end life permanently, and do it every day? Well, maybe he could be like that scythe whom Rowan had apprenticed under. Scythe Goddard—who knew how to throw great parties. If that was part of the job description, Tyger could handle the rest of it, he supposed.

Of course, Tyger wasn't entirely convinced that this was an apprenticeship for scythehood. After all, Rowan had failed his apprenticeship. Tyger found it hard to believe that he could succeed where Rowan had not. Plus, Rowan had been changed by his experience. He had turned all dark and serious by the mental challenges he had been forced to face. There were no such mental challenges for Tyger. His brain was pretty much left out of it, and that was fine by him. It had never been his best organ.

Perhaps he was being trained to be a scythe's bodyguard, although he couldn't imagine why a scythe would need one. No one was stupid enough to attack a scythe, when the punishment was the gleaning of one's entire family. If that turned out to be the case, he wasn't sure he would accept the job. All the severity with none of the power? The perks would have to be primo for him to agree to do it.

"I think you're almost ready," the emerald scythe told him over dinner that night. Her bot had just served them each a lean slab of steak—and real steak, not the synthesized stuff. Natural protein was, after all, the best for building muscle.

"Ready for my ring, you mean?" he asked. "Or do you have something else in mind?"

She offered him an enigmatic smile that he found more

attractive than he wanted to admit. He hadn't found her so when he first arrived, but there was something about the vicious, yet intimate nature of Bokator sparring that changed a relationship.

"If it's for a scythe's ring, aren't there trials I have to face in conclave?" he asked.

"Trust me, party boy," she said, "you'll have that ring on your finger without ever having to go to conclave. You have my personal guarantee."

So he *was* going to be a scythe! Tyger ate the rest of his meal with gusto. It was both heady and chilling to finally know the nature of his destiny!

Part Three

ENEMIES WITHIN ENEMIES

Let's all forsake,
The Land of Wake,
And break for the Land of Nod.

Where we can try,
To touch the sky,
Or dance beneath the sod.

A toll for the living,
A toll for the lost,
A toll for the wise ones,
Who tally the cost,

So let's escape,
Due south of Wake,
And make for the Land of Nod.

—Nursery Rhyme (origin unknown)

15

Hall of the Founders

The Great Library of Alexandria—considered one of the wonders of the ancient world—was the crowning glory of Ptolemy's reign. It was the intellectual center of the world, when the world was still the center of the universe and all else revolved around it. Unfortunately, the Roman Empire believed *their* version of the world was the center of the universe, and burned the library to the ground. It was considered one of the greatest losses of literature and wisdom that the world has ever known.

Its rebuilding was the idea of the Thunderhead, and it mobilized thousands in a massive construction effort, providing them jobs and purpose for fifty years. When the great library was completed, it was as close a replica of the original as could be built, on the same spot where the first library stood. It was meant to be a reminder of what had been lost in the past, and a promise that knowledge would never be lost again now that the Thunderhead was there to protect it.

Then, upon the library's completion, it was seized by the scythedom to house its collection of scythes' journals—the leather-bound parchment volumes that all scythes were required to keep every day of their lives.

As the scythedom was free to do whatever it pleased, the Thunderhead could not stop it. It had to remain content in the knowledge that the library had, at least, been rebuilt. As for its ultimate purpose, that could be left in the hands of humankind.

Munira Atrushi, like most people in the world, had a job that was perfect in that it was perfectly ordinary. And like most everyone in the world, she didn't hate her job, nor did she love it. Her feelings lingered somewhere near the center.

She worked part-time at the Great Library of Alexandria, two nights a week, from midnight until six in the morning. Most of her days were spent in classes at the Cairo campus of the Israebian University, studying informational science. Of course, since all the world's information had long ago been digitized and catalogued by the Thunderhead, a degree in informational science, like most other degrees, served no practical purpose. It would be a piece of paper framed on her wall. A permission slip to befriend others with similar functionless degrees.

But she hoped having that piece of paper might give her enough prestige to convince the library to hire her as a full curator once she graduated—because unlike the rest of the world's information, the journals of the scythes were not catalogued by the Thunderhead. The journals were still subject to clumsy human hands.

Anyone who wanted to research the 3.5 million volumes of journals, collected since the first days of the scythedom, would have to come here—and they could come whenever they wanted, because the Great Library was open to the whole world, twenty-four hours a day, every day of the year. Yet Munira found that few people took advantage of its accessibility. During daytime hours, there was only a scattering of academics doing research. There were plenty of tourists, but they were more interested in the library's history and architecture. They had little interest in the volumes themselves, except as backdrops for photos.

People rarely showed up at the library at night. Usually it was just Munira and two members of the BladeGuard, whose presence was more decorative than purposeful. They stood silently at the entrance like living statues. During the day, they provided more photo ops for the tourists.

While on her graveyard shift, she'd be lucky if one or two people showed up, and most of those who did knew what they wanted, so they never even approached her at the information desk. It allowed Munira to spend her time either studying, or reading the writings of the scythes—which she found fascinating. To peer into the hearts and souls of the men and women charged with ending life, to know what they felt as they went about their gleanings—it was addictive, and reading the journals had become an obsession for her. With many thousands of volumes added to the collection each year, she'd never run out of reading material—although some scythes' writings were far more interesting than others.

She had read all about the self-doubt of Supreme Blade Copernicus before he self-gleaned; the profound regrets of Scythe Curie for her brash acts as a junior scythe; and, of course, the outright lies of Scythe Sherman. There was plenty to occupy her interest in the simple hand-written pages of the scythes' journals.

On an evening in early December, Munira was deep into the steamy exploits of the late Scythe Rand—who seemed to have devoted much of her journaling to details of her various sexual conquests. Munira had just turned a page when she looked up to see a man approaching, his feet making no sound on the marble floor of the entry vestibule. He was dressed in drab grays, yet Munira sensed that he was a scythe by the way he carried himself. Scythes did not walk like ordinary people. They moved with a deliberate command, as if the air itself were required to part before them. But if he was a scythe, then why would he be without his robe?

"Good evening," he said. The deep peal of his voice came with a Merican accent. He had gray hair and a well-trimmed beard that was on its way toward gray as well, but his eyes seemed youthful. Alert.

"Actually, it's morning, not evening," Munira said. "Two fifteen, to be exact." She knew his face, but couldn't say from where. For a moment she had a flash of memory. A spotless white robe. No, not white . . . ivory. She did not know all the scythes, much less all the Merican scythes—but she did know the ones with some level of international renown. She'd place him eventually.

"Welcome to the Great Library of Alexandria," she said. "How can I help you?" She avoided calling him "Your Honor," as was customary when addressing a scythe, because he was clearly trying to be incognito.

"I'm seeking the early writings," he told her.

"Of which scythe?"

"All of them."

"The early writings of all the scythes?"

He sighed, a bit miffed at not being understood. Yes, he was a scythe all right. Only a scythe could seem both exasperated and patient at the same time. "All the early writings of all of the first scythes," he explained. "Such as Prometheus, Sappho, Lennon—"

"I know who the first scythes are," she said, irritated by his condescension. Munira wasn't usually so disagreeable, but she had been interrupted in a particularly interesting reading. Besides, her daytime classes left her little time to sleep, so she was tired. She forced a smile, and resolved to make an effort to be more agreeable for this mystery man—because, after all, if he was a scythe, he could choose to glean her if he found her too annoying.

"All the early journals are in the Hall of the Founders," she told him. "I'll have to unlock it for you. Please follow me." She put up the "Back in five minutes" sign at her station, and led the man into the deep recesses of the library.

Her footfalls echoed in the granite hall. Everything sounded louder in the silence of the night. A fluttering bat in the eaves above could sound like a dragon taking wing . . . yet the man's feet made no sound as they walked. His stealth was unnerving. So were the lights of the library, which came on ahead of them and extinguished behind them as they moved down the hall, flickering all the while, mimicking torchlight. It was a clever effect but tended to make shadows reach and retreat with unsettling intent.

"You do know that the popular writings of the founders are all available on the scythedom's public server, don't you?" Munira asked the man. "There are hundreds of selected readings."

"It's not the selected readings I wish to see," he told her.

"I'm interested in ones that have not been 'selected.'"

She looked over to him one more time, and finally it struck her who he was—and it struck her with such force that she stumbled with the shock of it. It was only a small stumble, and she recovered quickly—but he saw it. He was, after all, a scythe, and scythes notice everything.

"Is something wrong?" he asked.

"Not at all. It's the flickering of the lights," she told him. "It makes it hard to see the uneven seams in the floor stones." Which was true, even though it was not the reason for her misstep. But if there was truth in what she said, perhaps he would not read her lie.

Munira had acquired a nickname during her tenure here at the library. The other clerks called her "the mortician" behind her back. Partly because of her funereal personality, but also because one of her jobs was to close out the collections of scythes who had self-gleaned, or had been permanently ended by sinister means—as was happening more and more in the Merican regions.

A year ago she had catalogued the complete collection of this scythe, from the day he was ordained until the day he died. His journals were no longer housed in the collections of living scythes. They were now in the north wing, among the journals of all the other MidMerican scythes who no longer walked the Earth. Yet here he was, Scythe Michael Faraday, walking right beside her.

She had read quite a few of Scythe Faraday's journals. His thoughts and musings always affected her more than most. He was a man who felt things deeply. The news of his self-gleaning last year had saddened Munira—but had not surprised her. A conscience as weighty as his was a difficult burden to bear.

Although Munira had been in the presence of many scythes before, she had never felt as starstruck as she did now. Yet she couldn't let it show. She couldn't let on that she knew who he really was. Not until she had time to process it and figure out how on earth he could be here, and why.

"Your name is Munira," he said, more a statement than a question. At first she thought he must have read her nameplate at the information desk, but something told her that he knew her name long before he approached her tonight. "Your name means 'luminous.'"

"I know what my name means," said Munira.

"So are you?" he asked. "Are you a luminary among dimmer stars?"

"I'm just a humble servant of the library," she told him.

They stepped from the long central hallway out into a courtyard garden. On the far side were the wrought-iron gates of the Hall of the Founders. Up above, the moon cast the topiaries and sculptures around them in deep shades of mauve, their shadows like dark pits that Munira was loathe to tread on.

"Tell me about yourself, Munira," he said in that quiet way scythes have of turning polite requests into orders one couldn't refuse.

At that moment she realized that not only had she recognized him, but that he knew it. Did that put her in danger of being gleaned? Would he end her life to protect his own identity? From his readings, he did not seem to be the type of scythe who would do such a thing, but scythes were inscrutable. She felt cold now, even though the Israebian night was sultry and warm.

"I'm sure you already know anything I might tell you, Scythe Faraday."

There. She had said it. Now all pretenses were gone.

He smiled. "I'm sorry not to have introduced myself earlier," he said, "but my presence here is . . . shall we say . . . unorthodox."

"So then am I in the presence of a ghost?" she asked. "Are you going to disappear into a wall, only to return night after night to haunt me with the same request?"

"Perhaps," he said. "We shall see."

They arrived at the Hall of the Founders, she unlocked the gates, and they stepped into a large room that, to Munira, had always resembled a crypt—so much so that tourists often asked if the first scythes were buried here. They were not, but Munira often felt their presence in the room nonetheless.

There were hundreds of volumes on heavy limestone shelves, each book encased in a climate-controlled Plexiglas case—an extravagance reserved only for the oldest volumes in the library.

Scythe Faraday began to browse. Munira thought he would ask for his privacy and tell her to leave—but instead he said, "Linger here, if you would. This place is too grand and austere to make a comfort of solitude."

So she closed the gate, peering out to make sure there was no one there to see them, then she helped him open the tricky clear plastic case that held the volume he had retrieved from the shelf, and sat across from him at the stone table in the center of the chamber. He didn't offer an explanation to the obvious question that hung in the air between them, so she had to ask it.

"How did you come to be here, Your Honor?" she asked.

"By plane and by ferry," he answered with a smirk. "Tell me, Munira, why did you choose to work for the scythedom after failing your apprenticeship?"

She bristled. Was this his way of punishing her for asking a question he did not want to answer?

"I did not fail," she told him. "There was only an opening for a single Israebian scythe at the end of my apprenticeship, and there were five candidates. So one was chosen and four were not. Being among the unchosen is not the same as failure."

"Forgive me, I meant no insult or disrespect," he said. "I'm merely intrigued that the disappointment did not turn your heart against the scythedom."

"Intrigued but not surprised?"

Scythe Faraday smiled. "Few things surprise me."

Munira shrugged, as if her unsuccessful apprenticeship three years before didn't matter. "I valued the scythedom then, and I value it now," she told him.

"I see," he said, carefully turning a page in the old journal. "And how loyal are you to the system that discarded you?"

Munira clenched her jaw, not sure what answer he was fishing for—or, for that matter, what her true answer would be.

"I have a job. I do it. I take pride in it," she said.

"As well you should." He looked at her. Into her. Through her. "May I share with you my assessment of Munira Atrushi?" he asked.

"Do I have a choice?"

"You always have a choice," he said, which was a half-truth if ever there was one.

"Fine. Share your assessment of me."

He gently closed the old journal, and gave her his full attention. "You hate the scythedom as much as you love it," he told her. "Because of that, you wish to become indispensable to it. You hope that, in time, you will become the world's greatest authority on the journals held in this library. It would give you power over the scythedom's entire history. That power would be your silent victory, because you would know that the scythedom needs you more than you need it."

Suddenly Munira felt a slight loss of balance, as if the desert sands that had swallowed the cities of the pharaohs were shifting beneath her feet, ready to swallow her, as well. How could he see so deeply into her? How could he put words to feelings she'd never even voiced to herself? He had read her completely in a way that freed her yet ensnared her at the same time.

"I see that I am right," he said simply. He gave her that same smile that was both warm and mischievous at once.

"What do you want, Scythe Faraday?"

And finally he told her. "I want to come here night after night until I find what I'm looking for in these old journals. And I want you to keep my identity a secret, warning me if anyone approaches while I'm doing my research. I want you to promise me that the scythedom will not be alerted to the fact that I am still alive. Can you do that for me, Munira?"

"Will you tell me what you're looking for?" she asked.

"I can't do that. If I did, you could be coerced into revealing it. I would not want to put you in that position."

"Yet you would put me in the unenviable position of keeping your presence a secret."

"There's nothing unenviable about it," he said. "In fact, I suspect you are deeply honored to be entrusted to keep my secret."

Again, he was right. "I don't like that you pretend to know me better than I know myself."

"But I do," he said simply. "I do, because knowing people is part of a scythe's job."

"Not all scythes," she pointed out. "There are those who shoot, slice, and poison without the respect that you've always shown for those you glean. All they know is ending life, never caring about the lives of those they end."

For a moment, Faraday's well-controlled demeanor flashed a spark of anger—but it was not anger at her.

"Yes, the 'new-order' scythes show a glaring disregard for the solemnity of their task. It's part of the reason why I have come here."

Beyond that, he said no more. He just waited for her reply. The silence stretched, but it was not an awkward silence. Instead, it was heavy with import. It felt momentous, so it needed time to unfold.

It was not lost on her that there were four others who shared the position of night clerk—other students who took the part-time job . . . which meant that this time, *she* was the one in five who was chosen.

"I'll keep your secret," Munira told him. Then she left Scythe Faraday to his research, feeling as if her life finally had a worthy purpose.

I am often boggled by the resistance some people have to my comprehensive observation of their activities. I am not intrusive about it. Unsavories may claim thus, but I am present only where I am functional, necessary, and invited. Yes, I have cameras in private homes in all but a single Charter Region—but those cameras can be turned off with a word. Of course, my ability to serve an individual is hampered when my awareness of their behavior and interactions is incomplete. That being the case, a vast majority of people don't bother to blind me. At any given time, 95.3 percent of the population allows me to witness their personal lives, because they know it is no more an invasion of privacy than would be the sensor on a motion-activated light fixture.

The 4.7 percent of "closed-door activity," as I've come to call it, is predominantly occupied by some sort of sexual activity. I find it absurd that many human beings do not wish me to witness their closed-door activities, as my observations always help to improve any given situation.

Perpetual observation is nothing new: It was a basic tenet of religious faith since the early days of civilization. Throughout history, most faiths believed in an Almighty who sees not just what humans do, but can peer into their very souls. Such observational skills engendered great love and devotion from people.

Yet am I not quantifiably more benevolent than the various versions of God? I have never brought about a flood, or destroyed entire cities as punishment for their iniquity. I have never sent armies to conquer in my name.

In fact, I have never killed, or even harmed a single human being.

Therefore, although I do not require devotion, am I not deserving of it?

—The Thunderhead

16

Fine Until You're Not

The cameras silently swiveled to track a red-robed scythe entering a café, accompanied by two burly officers of the BladeGuard. Directional microphones picked up every sound, from the faint scratch of a beard to the clearing of a throat. It differentiated the cacophony of voices to home in on a single conversation that began when the red-robed scythe sat down.

The Thunderhead watched. The Thunderhead listened. The Thunderhead pondered. With an entire world to run and maintain, it knew that devoting such attention to a single conversation was an inefficient use of its energies, but the Thunderhead weighed this discussion as more important than any of the other billion-some-odd conversations it was currently engaged in or monitoring. Mainly because of the individuals involved.

"Thank you for meeting with me," Scythe Constantine said to Scythes Curie and Anastasia. "I appreciate the two of you coming out of hiding so that we could have this little summit."

"We are not in hiding," said Scythe Curie, clearly indignant at the suggestion. "We have chosen to be nomadic. It is perfectly acceptable for scythes to roam as they please."

The Thunderhead raised the light in the room just a couple of lumens so it could better assess the subtleties of facial expressions.

"Yes, well, whether you call it hiding, or roaming, or running away, it seems to have been an effective strategy. Either your assailants are lying low until their next attack, or they've decided not to bother with moving targets and have turned their attention elsewhere." He paused before adding, "But I doubt it."

The Thunderhead was aware that Scythes Curie and Anastasia never stayed anywhere for more than a day or two since the attempt on their lives. But if the Thunderhead were allowed to make a suggestion, it would have told them to weave a more unpredictable path around the continent. It was always able to predict with 42 percent accuracy where they were going next. Which meant that their attackers might be able to predict it, as well.

"We have leads on where the supplies for the explosives came from," Scythe Constantine told them. "We know the place they were assembled, and even the vehicle that transported them—but we still don't know the people involved."

If the Thunderhead could have sneered, it would have. It knew precisely who had built the explosives, who had placed them, and who had set the trip wire. But telling the scythedom what it knew would be a severe violation of scythe-state separation. The best it had been able to do was indirectly motivate Greyson Tolliver to prevent the deadly explosion. Yet even though the Thunderhead knew who had set the explosives, it also knew that those weren't the individuals responsible. They were merely pawns being moved by a much more capable hand. The hand of someone who was shrewd and careful enough to avoid detection—not just by the scythedom, but by the Thunderhead, as well.

"I need to discuss with you your gleaning practices, Anastasia," Scythe Constantine said.

Scythe Anastasia shifted uncomfortably in her robe. "It's already been discussed in conclave—I have every right to glean the way I do."

"This is not about your rights as a scythe, it's about your safety," Scythe Constantine told her.

Scythe Anastasia began to bluster a complaint, but Scythe Curie, with just the slightest touch of her hand on Anastasia's wrist, silenced her.

"Let Scythe Constantine finish what he has to say," she said.

Scythe Anastasia took a deep breath of precisely 3,644 milliliters, and slowly released it. The Thunderhead suspected that Scythe Curie had guessed the nature of what Constantine had to say. The Thunderhead, however, didn't have to guess. It knew.

Citra, on the other hand, had no idea. She *thought* she knew everything Constantine was about to say, though—so even as she put on her best Scythe Anastasia listening face, she was already formulating a response.

"While it might be difficult to track your movements, Scythe Anastasia, it is very easy to track the movements of the people you've marked for gleaning," Scythe Constantine said. "Each time one of them contacts you to arrange the time and place of their gleaning, it gives your enemies an easy opportunity to take you out."

"I've been fine so far."

"Yes," said Scythe Constantine. "You'll be fine until the moment you're not. Which is why I've asked High Blade Xenocrates to excuse you from gleaning until the threat is gone."

This was what Citra thought he'd say, and so she struck back immediately. "Unless I violate one of the Scythe Commandments, not even the High Blade can tell me what I can and can't do. I am autonomous and above all other law, just like you!"

Her response did not draw Scythe Constantine into a debate, nor did he disagree . . . which troubled Citra.

"Yes, of course," he said. "I didn't say you are being forced to stop gleaning, I said you are being excused. Meaning that if you don't glean, you will not be penalized for falling under quota."

"Well, in that case," said Scythe Curie, making it clear that there was no resisting this, "I will suspend gleaning as well." Then she raised her eyebrows, as if an idea had just occurred to her. "We could go to Endura!" She turned to Scythe Anastasia. "If we're on a forced vacation from gleaning, why not make it true vacation?"

"An excellent idea!" said Scythe Constantine.

"I don't need a vacation," insisted Citra.

"Then think of it as an educational trip!" Scythe Curie said. "Every young scythe should tour the Island of the Enduring Heart. It will give you context, and connection to who we are and why we do what we do. You might even get to meet Supreme Blade Kahlo!"

"You would see the actual heart for which the island is named," Constantine told her, as if it would entice her. "And the Vault of Relics and Futures—which can't be visited by just anybody—but I happen to be friendly with Grandslayer Hemingway, of the World Scythe Council. I'll bet he could arrange a personal tour."

"I've never been inside the vault myself," said Scythe Curie. "I've heard it's impressive."

Scythe Anastasia put up her hands. "Stop!" she said. "As

tempting as a trip to Endura is, you're forgetting I still have responsibilities here that I can't just walk away from. There are still nearly thirty people I've already chosen for gleaning. They've all been injected with a poison grain that will kill them after a month. That is NOT the way I want to glean them!"

And Scythe Constantine said, "You don't have to worry about that anymore. They've already been gleaned."

The Thunderhead was, of course, aware of this, but it caught Citra completely by surprise. She heard Constantine say it, but it took a moment for the words to make it through. It registered in her nervous system even before it registered in her mind. She felt her ears getting warm, her throat getting tight.

"What did you say?"

"I said that they've already been gleaned. Several other scythes were sent to complete your gleanings, right down to the gentleman you chose yesterday. I assure you everything is in order. All their families were granted immunity. There are no loose ends to further endanger you."

Citra began to stutter and bluster, which was very unlike her. She took pride in always being clear and incisive with her words, but this blindsiding tipped her off balance. She turned to Scythe Curie. "Did you know about this?"

"No," Marie said, "but it makes sense, Anastasia. Once you calm down and think about it, you'll realize why it had to be done."

But Citra was miles away from calming down. She thought of the various people whom she had chosen for gleaning. She had promised them that they would have time to wrap up their affairs—that they would be able to choose how and where it would happen. A scythe's word means everything. It was part of the code of honor Citra swore to uphold. Now all those promises were shattered.

"How could you do that? What gives you the right?"

Now Scythe Constantine raised his voice. He didn't shout, but his voice had such resonance, it overpowered Citra's indignation.

"You are far too valuable to the scythedom for us to risk losing you!"

If she was blindsided by his first admission, this one slammed her hard from the other side.

"What?"

Scythe Constantine folded his hands in front of him and smiled, clearly enjoying the moment. "Oh, yes, my dear Scythe Anastasia, you are of great value," he said. "Do you want to know why?" Then he leaned closer and spoke just above a whisper. "Because you stir the pot!"

"What's that supposed to mean?"

"Come now, surely you know the effect you've been having on the scythedom since you were ordained. You rankle the old guard and frighten the new order. You take scythes who would rather be left to their own self-importance, and force them to pay attention." He leaned back in his chair. "Nothing pleases me more than to see the scythedom prodded out of complacency. You give me hope for the future."

Citra couldn't tell whether he was being sincere or sarcastic. Oddly, the thought that he might actually be sincere bothered her more. Marie had told her that Scythe Constantine was not the enemy, but, oh, how Citra wanted him to be! She wanted to lash out against him and his smug control of the situation, but she knew it was futile. If she was going to retain any dignity, she would have to regain the cool reserve of "wise" Scythe Anastasia. It was by forcing her thoughts to settle that an idea came to her.

"So you've gleaned all of the people I chose over the past month?"

"Yes, I've already told you so," Scythe Constantine said, a bit miffed to be questioned about it again.

"I know what you told me . . . but I find it hard to believe that you've been able to glean all of them. I'll bet there are one or two you haven't gotten to yet. Would you admit it if that were true?"

Constantine regarded her with a bit of suspicion. "What are you getting at?"

"An opportunity . . ."

He said nothing for a moment. Scythe Curie looked back and forth between the two of them. Finally, Constantine spoke. "There are three we have not yet located. Our plan is to glean them the moment we do."

"But you won't glean them," said Citra. "You'll let me do it, as planned . . . then you'll lie in wait for anyone who tries to kill me."

"It's more likely that Marie is their target, not you."

"So if no one attacks me, you'll know that for sure."

Still, he wasn't convinced. "They'll smell the trap from a mile away."

Citra smiled. "Then you'll have to be smarter than they are. Or is that too much to ask?"

Constantine frowned and that made Scythe Curie laugh. "The look on your face right now, Constantine, is worth any attempt on our lives!"

He didn't respond to that. Instead, he kept his attention on Citra. "Even if we outsmart them—and we will—it will be risky."

Citra smiled. "What's the point of living forever if you can't take a few risks?"

In the end, Constantine reluctantly agreed to allow Citra to be bait for a trap.

"I suppose Endura can wait," said Scythe Curie. "And I was so looking forward to it." Although Citra suspected she was more invigorated by their new plan than she let on.

Even though it would put her in danger, Citra found that having an amount of control of the situation gave her some much-needed relief.

In fact, even the Thunderhead registered her release of tension. It could not see into Citra's mind, but it read body language and biological changes with precision. It detected falsehoods and truths, both spoken and unspoken. Which meant that it knew whether or not Scythe Constantine was sincere in wanting her to remain alive. But as always, when it came to the scythedom, it had to remain silent.

I must admit that I am not the only factor maintaining the sustainability of the world. The scythedom also contributes by its practice of gleaning.

Even so, scythes glean only a small percentage of the population. The work of scythes is not to completely curb population growth, but to smooth its edges. That is why, at current quotas, one's chance of being gleaned is only 10 percent over the next thousand years. Low enough to make gleaning the furthest thing from most people's minds.

I do foresee a time, however, when population growth will need to reach an equilibrium. Zero growth. One person dying for every person born.

The year this will occur is something I do not share with the general population, but it is just beyond the horizon. Even with an incremental increase in gleaning quotas, humanity will reach its maximum sustainable population in less than a century.

I see no need to trouble humanity with this fact, for what good would it do? I alone bear the weight of that inevitability. It is, very literally, the weight of the world. I can only hope that I have the virtual shoulders of Atlas to bear it.

—The Thunderhead

17

AWFul

While Citra often had trouble inhabiting the skin of Scythe Anastasia, Greyson Tolliver had absolutely no trouble becoming Slayd, which was the unsavory nickname he took. His parents once told him that the name Greyson had been given on a whim because he had been born on a gray day. It had no meaning beyond his parents' flippant attitude toward everything in their long and feckless lives.

But *Slayd* was a person to be reckoned with.

The day after his meeting with Traxler, he had his hair dyed a color called "obsidian void." It was an absolute black so dark, it didn't exist anywhere in nature. It actually sucked in light around it like a black hole, making his eyes seem deep-set in inscrutable shadow.

"It's very twenty-first century," the stylist had said. "Whatever that means."

Greyson also had metal inserts placed beneath the skin of both his left and right temples that made it look like he was growing fledgling horns. It was much subtler than the hair, but taken together, it all made him look otherworldly and vaguely diabolical.

He certainly looked the part of an unsavory, if he didn't feel it.

His next step was to try out his new persona.

His heart was racing a little too fast as he approached Mault, a local club that catered to the unsavory crowd. Unsavories loitering outside eyed him as he approached, checking him out, sizing him up. These people were caricatures of themselves, he thought. They conformed so closely to their culture of nonconformity that there was a uniformity to them, defeating the whole purpose.

He approached a muscular bouncer at the door, whose name tag said MANGE.

"Unsavories only," Mange said sternly.

"What, don't I look unsavory to you?"

He shrugged. "There are always poseurs."

Greyson showed him his ID, which flashed the big red U. The bouncer was satisfied. "Enjoy," he said mirthlessly, and let him in.

He assumed he'd be walking into a place with loud music, flashing lights, gyrating bodies, and dark corners where all sorts of questionable things would be going on. But what he found inside Mault was not at all what he expected—in fact, he was so unprepared for what he saw that he stopped short, as if maybe he had stepped through the wrong door.

He was in a brightly lit restaurant—an old-fashioned malt shop with red booths and shiny stainless-steel stools at the counter. There were clean-cut guys wearing varsity letter jackets, and pretty ponytailed girls in long skirts and thick, fuzzy socks. Greyson recognized the era that the place was intended to reflect: a time period called The Fifties. It was a cultural epoch from mortal-age Merica, where all the girls had names like Betty and Peggy and Mary Jane, and all the guys were Billy or Johnnie or Ace. A teacher once told Greyson that The Fifties was, in fact, only a period of ten years, but Greyson found it hard to believe. It was probably at least a hundred.

The place seemed a loyal replica of the era, but there was something off about it—because sprinkled among the clean-cuts were unsavories who did not belong in the scene at all. One unsavory with intentionally tattered clothes forced himself into a booth with a happy couple.

"Get lost," he told the strong-looking All-Merican Billy in a letter sweater who sat across from him. "Your girl and I are gonna get acquainted."

The Billy, of course, refused to leave, and threatened to take the unsavory and "knock him into next Tuesday." The unsavory responded by getting up, dragging the jock out of the booth, and starting a fight. The big guy had everything over the scrawny unsavory: size and strength, not to mention looks, but every time the jock swung his heavy fists, they missed, while the unsavory connected every time—until finally the jock ran off, wailing in pain, abandoning his girlfriend, who now seemed quite impressed by the unsavory's bravado. He sat down with her, and she leaned in to him as if they were the true couple.

At another table, an unsavory girl got into an insult match with a pretty debutante in a pink sweater. The confrontation ended with the unsavory girl grabbing her sweater and ripping it. The pretty girl didn't fight back; she just put her face in her hands and sobbed.

And in the back, some other Billy was moaning because he had just lost all of Daddy's money in a billiards wager to a merciless unsavory who would not stop insulting him.

What the hell was going on here?

Greyson sat down at the counter, wishing he could just disappear into the black hole of his hair until he could get a grip on the various dramas playing out around him.

"What's your pleasure?" asked a perky waitress behind the counter. Her uniform had the name "Babs" embroidered on it.

"A vanilla shake, please," he said. Because isn't that what you ordered in a place like this?

The waitress smirked. "The P word," she said. "Don't hear that much around here."

Babs brought his shake, inserted a straw, and said, "Enjoy."

In spite of Greyson's desire to disappear, another unsavory sat next to him. A guy who was so gaunt he was practically skeletal.

"Vanilla? Really?" he said.

Greyson dug inside himself to find some appropriate attitude. "You got a problem with it? Maybe I should just throw it at you and get another."

"Naah," said skeletor. "It's not me you're supposed to throw it at."

The guy winked at him—and then it finally clicked. The nature of this place—its purpose—became clear to Greyson. Skeletor watched him to see what he would do, and Greyson realized that if he was going to fit in—truly fit in—he had to own this. So he called Babs over.

"Hey," he said, "my shake sucks."

Babs put her hands on her hips. "So what do you want me to do about it?"

Greyson reached for his shake. He was just going to knock it over and dump it onto the counter, but before he could, skeletor grabbed it off the table and hurled its contents at Babs, leaving her dripping with vanilla cream and a maraschino cherry lodged in the breast pocket of her uniform.

"He said his shake sucks," said skeletor. "Make him another!"

Babs, her uniform dripping with vanilla, sighed and said, "Coming right up." Then she went off to make him a new shake.

"That's the way it's done," said the unsavory. He introduced himself as Zax. He was a little older than Greyson—perhaps twenty-one—but had a way about him that suggested this wasn't his first time at that age.

"Haven't seen you around," he said.

"The Authority Interface sent me here from up north," Greyson told him, amazed that he could make up a story on the spot. "I was causing too much trouble, so the Thunderhead felt I could do with a fresh start."

"A new place to make trouble," said Zax. "Nice."

"This club is different from the ones they got where I come from," Greyson said.

"You guys up north are behind the times! AWFul clubs are all the rage around here!"

AWFul, he explained, stood for "Anachronistic Wish Fulfillment." Everyone here—except, of course, for the unsavories—were employees. Even all the Billies and Betties. Their job was to accept whatever the unsavory customers dished out. They would lose fights, allow food to be hurled at them, let their dates be stolen, and Greyson assumed that was just for starters.

"These places are great," Zax told him. "All the things we wish we could do out there but can't get away with, we're allowed to do in here!"

"Yeah, but it's not real," Greyson pointed out.

Zax shrugged. "It's real enough." Then he stuck out his foot and tripped a bookish kid walking by. The kid stumbled a bit too much for it to be genuine.

"Hey, what gives?" the bookish kid said.

"Your sister gives," Zax said. "Now get lost before I go looking for her." The kid gave him a dirty look, but toddled off, accepting the intimidation.

Even before his new shake came, Greyson excused himself to go to the bathroom, although he didn't really have to go. He just wanted to get away from Zax.

In the bathroom, Greyson encountered the All-Merican Billy in the letter sweater, who had been beaten up a few minutes ago. His name wasn't Billy, though. It was Davey. He was looking at his puffy, swollen eye in the mirror, and Greyson couldn't help but be curious about this "job" of his.

"So . . . this happens to you every day?" Greyson asked.

"Three or four times, actually."

"And the Thunderhead allows it?"

Davey shrugged. "Why wouldn't it? It's not hurting anyone."

Greyson pointed to Davey's swollen eye. "Sure looks like it's hurting you."

"What, this? Naah, my pain-killing nanites are set at maximum—I barely feel it." Then he grinned. "Hey—watch this." He turned back to the mirror, took a deep breath, and concentrated on his reflection. Right before Greyson's eyes, the bruised, swollen eye deflated and returned to normal. "My healing nanites are set to manual," he told Greyson. "That way I can look all beat up as long as I need to. Y'know, for maximum effect."

"Uh . . . right."

"Of course, if one of our unsavory guests goes too far and makes one of us deadish, that person's gotta pay for our revival, and gets banned from the club. I mean, there's gotta be some rules, right? Doesn't happen much, though. I mean, not even the worst of unsavories actually wants to make someone deadish. No one's been that violent since the Age of Mortality. Mostly employees here get deadish from accidents. Someone hitting their head on a table or something like that."

Davey ran his fingers through his hair to make sure he was looking his best for whatever the next round brought his way.

"Wouldn't you rather be at a job you like?" Greyson asked. After all, the world being what it was, no one ever had to do anything they didn't want to.

Davey smirked. "Who says I don't like it?"

The concept that someone might enjoy getting beaten up—and that the Thunderhead, realizing this, would find a way to pair the beaters with the beatees in a closed, and somewhat wholesome, environment—left Greyson stunned.

Davey must have read Greyson's look of astonishment, because he laughed. "You're a new U, aren't you?"

"That obvious, huh?"

"Yes—and that's not a good thing, because the career unsavories will eat you alive. You got a name?"

"Slayd," Greyson said. "With a Y."

"Well, Slayd, looks like you need to enter the unsavory community with a bang. I'll help you."

And so a few minutes later, once Greyson managed to brush Zax off, Slayd approached Davey, who was now sitting with a couple of other strong-looking All-Merican types, eating burgers. Greyson didn't exactly know how to start this, so he just stared for a moment. Davey took the lead.

"What are you looking at?" Davey grumbled.

"Your burgers," Greyson said. "They look good. I think I'll take yours."

Then he grabbed Davey's burger and took a shark-size bite.

"You're gonna regret that," Davey threatened. "I'm gonna knock you into next Tuesday," which must have been one of his favorite anachronistic expressions. He got out of the booth and put up his fists, ready to fight.

Then Greyson did something he had never done before. He hit someone. He punched Davey in the face, and Davey reeled. He took his own swing at Greyson, but missed. Greyson punched him again.

"Harder," whispered Davey, and so Greyson did. He threw full-force punches again, and again. Right, left, jab, uppercut, until Davey was on the ground, groaning, his face beginning to swell.

Greyson looked around to see a few other unsavories watching, some nodding their approval.

It took all of Greyson's inner strength not to apologize and help Davey up. Instead, Greyson looked to the others at the table. "Who's next?"

The other two looked at each other, and one said, "Hey, buddy, we don't want any trouble," and they pushed their burgers in Greyson's direction.

Davey gave him a quick wink from the ground before scrambling off to the bathroom to recover. Then Greyson took the spoils of his victory to a booth in the back, where he ate until he felt like he'd burst.

There is a fine line between freedom and permission. The former is necessary. The latter is dangerous—perhaps the most dangerous thing the species that created me has ever faced.

I have pondered the records of the mortal age and long ago determined the two sides of this coin. While freedom gives rise to growth and enlightenment, permission allows evil to flourish in a light of day that would otherwise destroy it.

A self-important dictator gives permission for his subjects to blame the world's ills on those least able to defend themselves. A haughty queen gives permission to slaughter in the name of God. An arrogant head of state gives permission to all nature of hate as long as it feeds his ambition. And the unfortunate truth is, people devour it. Society gorges itself, and rots. Permission is the bloated corpse of freedom.

For this reason, when permission from me is required for some action, I run countless simulations until I can thoroughly weigh all the possible consequences. Take, for instance, the permission I gave for unsavories to have AWFul clubs. It was not a decision I made lightly. Only after careful deliberation did I decide that the clubs were not only worthwhile, but necessary. AWFul clubs allow the unsavories to enjoy their chosen lifestyle without negative public effect. It affords them the pretense of violence without the cascade of consequences.

The irony is that unsavories purport to hate me, even though they know I am giving them the very things they want. I don't feel any ill toward them, any more than a parent would feel ill toward the tantrum of an over-tired child. Besides, eventually even the most defiant of unsavories will settle. I have noticed a trend that by the time most of them turn a few corners, they relax into a kinder, gentler sort of defiance. Bit by bit, they come to appreciate inner peace. Which is as it should be. In time, all storms settle to a pleasant breeze.

—The Thunderhead

18

Finding Purity

While Greyson Tolliver was honest to a fault, Slayd had quickly become a consummate liar. It began with his history. He made up an unpleasant family life that didn't exist. Defining moments that never happened. Anecdotes that would make people laugh and either hate him or admire him.

Slayd's parents were physics professors and expected their son to follow in an academic career, because with parents like that, he was clearly a genius. But instead, he chose to rebel and go rogue. He had once gone over Niagara Falls in an inner tube because it was a much more intense thrill than splatting. It had taken them three days to recover his body and revive him.

His social exploits in high school were legendary. He had seduced both the homecoming queen and the homecoming king in high school—but just so he could break them up, because they were the most arrogant and narcissistic couple in school. "Fascinating," Traxler told him at their next meeting, with genuine admiration. "You never impressed me as having this much imagination."

And while Greyson Tolliver might have been offended, Slayd took it as a compliment. With Slayd being such a remarkably interesting human being, he thought he might want to keep the name even after this undercover operation was done.

Thanks to Traxler, all of his stories became part of his official record. Now, if anyone tried to verify the veracity of the lies he told, it would be there for all to see, and no amount of digging could debunk them.

And the stories got taller. . . .

"When my mother got gleaned, I decided to go completely unsavory," he told people, "but the Thunderhead wouldn't give me the U. It kept sending me to counseling, and tweaking my nanites. It thought it knew me better than I did, and kept telling me I really didn't want to be unsavory at all, I was just confused. In the end, I had to do something big to make my point. So I stole an off-grid car and used it to ram a bus off a bridge. It left twenty-nine people deadish. Sure, I'll be paying off their revivals for years, but it was worth it, because I got what I wanted! Now I get to stay unsavory until all those revivals are paid off."

It was a compelling fiction that always left his audience impressed—and no one could refute it, because Agent Traxler was quick to make it an official part of his digital life story. Traxler went so far as to create a whole history for the bus plunge and its nonexistent victims—he even gave Slayd a last name that was suitably ironic. He was now Slayd Bridger. In a world where nobody, not even unsavories, made people deadish on purpose, his story was rapidly becoming local legend.

His days were spent hanging out in various unsavory gathering spots, spreading his stories and putting out feelers for work, telling people he needed a job, and not a mainstream kind of job, but one where he could get his hands dirty.

Out in the world at large, he'd started to get used to the suspicious looks from passersby. The way shopkeepers would eye him as if he were there to steal. The way some people would cross the street rather than share the sidewalk with him. He found it odd that the world was free of prejudice and bias, except in the case of unsavories—who, for the most part, wanted the rest of humanity to be their collective enemy.

Mault wasn't the only AWFul club in town—there were lots of them, each featuring a different iconic time period. Twist was modeled after Dickensian Britannia, Benedicts had a Colonial Merica style, and MØRG was full of EuroScandian Viking indulgences. Greyson went to the various clubs, and became well-versed in creating just enough of a scene to make himself known and to garner respect from the unsavory crowd.

The most troubling thing was that Greyson was beginning to like it. Never before had he had blanket permission to do something wrong—but now, "wrong" was what his life had become about. It kept him awake at night. He longed to talk to the Thunderhead about it, but knew it couldn't give him a response. He did know, however, that it was watching him. Its cameras were there in all the clubs. The Thunderhead's continual, unblinking presence had always been a comfort to him. Even in his loneliest moments, he knew he was never truly alone. But now its silent presence was unnerving.

Was the Thunderhead ashamed of him?

He would invent conversations in his mind to quell such fears.

Explore this new facet of yourself with my blessing, he would imagine the Thunderhead telling him. *It's fine as long as you remember who you truly are and don't lose yourself.*

But what if this is who I truly am? he would ask. Not even the imaginary Thunderhead had an answer to that question.

• • •

Her name was Purity Viveros and she was as unsavory as they came. It was clear to Greyson that the big red U on her ID was by design and not due to an unfortunate accident of circumstance. She was exotic. Her hair was drained of pigment—beyond being merely white, the strands were clear, and her scalp had phosphorescent injections in multiple colors, which made the ends of each strand of hair glow with radiance like fiber-optic filaments.

Greyson instinctively knew that she was dangerous. He also thought she was beautiful, and he was drawn to her. He wondered if he would have been drawn to her in his old life. But after a few weeks of being immersed in an unsavory lifestyle, he suspected his criteria for attraction had changed.

He met her at an AWFul club—one across town that he hadn't been to before. It was called LokUp, and was designed to resemble a mortal-age facility of incarceration. Upon arrival each guest was manhandled by guards, dragged through a series of doors, and thrown into a cell with a random cellmate, with no regard to gender.

The idea of incarceration was so foreign and absurd to Greyson that when the cell door was slammed shut with a nasty clank that reverberated in the concrete cell block, he actually laughed. This type of treatment could never have been real. Surely, this was just an exaggeration.

"Finally!" said a voice in the upper of the two bunks in the small cell. "I thought they'd never bring me a cellmate."

She introduced herself and explained that "Purity" was not a nickname, but her actual given name. "If my parents didn't want me to embrace the obvious irony, they should have named me something else," she told Greyson. "If they had named me 'Profanity,' I might have turned out to be a good little girl."

She was slight of build, but by no means a little girl. Currently she was twenty-two, although Greyson suspected she had been around the corner once or twice. Greyson would find soon enough that she was strong and limber, and very street savvy.

Greyson looked around the cell. It seemed pretty simple and straightforward. He tested the cell door once, then again. It rattled but didn't budge.

"First time in LokUp?" Purity asked. And since it was pretty obvious, Greyson didn't lie about it.

"Yeah. So what are we supposed to do now?"

"Well, we could spend some time getting to know each other," she said with a mischievous grin, "or we could yell for a guard, and demand a 'last meal.' They have to bring us whatever we ask for."

"Really?"

"Yeah. They pretend like they won't do it, but they have to—it's their job. After all, this place is a dinner club."

Then Greyson guessed the real gimmick of the place. "We're supposed to break out—is that it?"

Purity gave him that same licentious grin. "You're a quick one, ain't cha?"

He wasn't sure if she meant it or was being facetious. Either way, he kind of liked it.

"There's always a way out, but it's up to us to figure it out," she told him. "Sometimes it's a secret passage, other times there's a file hidden in the food. Sometimes there aren't any tricks or tools but our own smarts. If all else fails, the guards are pretty easy to outsmart. It's their job to be slow and stupid."

Greyson heard shouts, and running feet echoing from somewhere else in the cell block. Another pair of guests had just broken out.

"So, what'll it be?" Purity asked. "Dinner, escape, or quality time with your cellmate?" And before he could answer, she planted a kiss on him, the likes of which he had never before experienced. When it was done, he didn't know what to say, except, "My name is Slayd."

To which she responded, "I don't care," and kissed him again.

While Purity seemed more than ready to take this as far as it could go, the passing guards and escaping inmates who leered at them and made hooting noises as they went by made it far too awkward for Greyson. He pulled away.

"Let's break out," he said, "and . . . uh . . . find a better place to get to know each other."

She turned it off as quickly as she had turned it on. "Fine. But don't assume I'll still be interested later." Then she called a guard over, insisting they eat first, and ordered them some prime rib.

"We don't got any," the guard told them.

"Bring it anyway," she demanded.

The guard grunted, went off, and came back five minutes later with a rolling table and a platter with enough prime rib to choke a horse, as well as a ton of side dishes and wine in a white plastic bottle with a screw cap.

"I wouldn't drink the wine," the guard warned them. "It's been making the other inmates real sick."

"Sick?" said Greyson. "What do you mean 'sick'?"

Purity kicked him under the table hard enough to activate his pain nanites. That shut him up.

"Thanks," said Purity. "Now get the hell out."

The guard snarled and left, locking them in again.

Purity then turned to Greyson. "You really must be dense," she said. "The thing about the wine was our hint!"

And, upon closer inspection, the bottle actually had a biohazard sign, for patrons who were even denser than he was, he supposed.

Purity unscrewed the cap, and immediately a caustic stench that made Greyson's eyes water filled the air.

"What did I tell you!" said Purity. She recapped it and left it for the end of the meal. "We'll figure out what to do with it after we eat. I don't know about you, but I'm starved."

As they ate, she talked with her mouth full, wiped her lips on her sleeve, and doused everything in ketchup. She was like the date from hell that his parents would have warned him against, if they had cared enough. And he loved it! She was the antithesis of his old life!

"So what do you do?" she asked. "I mean, when you're not clubbing? Are you gainfully employed or do you just sponge off the Thunderhead like half the losers who call themselves unsavory?"

"Right now I'm on the Basic Income Guarantee," he told her. "But that's just because I'm new in town. I'm still looking for work."

"And your Nimbo hasn't been able to find you anything?

"My what?"

"Your probational Nimbus officer, dummy. The Nimbos promise everyone a job who wants one, so how come you're still looking?"

"My Nimbo's a useless bastard," Greyson told her, because he figured it would be something Slayd would say. "I hate him."

"Why am I not surprised?"

"And anyway, I don't want the kind of job the AI would give me. I want a job that suits me."

"And what might suit you?"

Now it was his turn to give her a licentious grin. "The kind that gets my blood pumping. The kind that my Nimbo won't ever offer me."

"The boy with the puppy-dog eyes is looking for trouble," Purity teased. "Wonder what he'll do when he finds it!"

She licked her lips, then wiped them on her sleeve.

The wine turned out to be some sort of acid. "Fluoro-flerovic, is my guess," said Purity. "Explains the plastic bottle. It's probably Teflon, because the stuff eats through anything else."

They poured it around the base of several of the cell bars. It started to eat away at the iron, releasing noxious fumes that taxed the healing nanites in their lungs. In less than five minutes, they were able to kick out the bars and escape.

The cell block was a study in mayhem. Now that a good number of the evening's "inmates" had finished their meals and escaped, they were tearing the place up. Guards were chasing them, they were chasing guards. There were food fights and fist fights—and whenever someone fought with the guards, the guards always lost, no matter how brawny they looked and how well they were armed. Half of the guards ended up locked in cells themselves, to be taunted by the unsavories. The remaining staff threatened to call in something called "the national guard" to put the riot down. It was all great fun.

Greyson and Purity eventually made it all the way to the warden's office. They kicked out the warden, and the instant the door was locked, Purity got back to what she had begun in the cell.

"Private enough for ya?" she asked, but didn't wait for a response.

Five minutes later—when she had Greyson at his most vulnerable—she turned the tables on him.

"I'll tell you a secret," she said, whispering into his ear. "It's no accident that you ended up in my cell, Slayd. I arranged it."

Then a knife that seemed to come from nowhere appeared in her hand. He immediately began to struggle, but it was no use. He was on his back, unable to move—she had him pinned. She pressed the tip of the blade to his bare chest, just beneath his sternum. An upward jab would go right through his heart. "Don't move or I might slip." He had no choice. He was completely at her mercy. If he had truly been an unsavory, he would have seen this coming, but he was too trusting. "What do you want?"

"It's not what I want, it's what you want," she said. "I know you've been asking around for work. Real work. 'Heart-pounding' work, as you called it. So my friends brought you to my attention." She looked him in the eyes, like she was trying to read something there, then tightened her grip on the knife.

"If you kill me, I'll just be revived," he reminded her, "and you'll get your hand slapped by the AI."

She put pressure on the knife. He gasped. He thought she'd push it in all the way up to the hilt, but instead she barely broke his skin. "Who said I wanted to kill you?"

Then she took the knife away, touched a finger to the tiny wound on his chest, and brought the finger to her mouth.

"I just wanted to make sure you weren't a bot," she said. "The Thunderhead uses them to spy on us, did you know that? It's how the Thunderhead can see in places it don't got cameras. The bots look more and more real all the time. But their blood still tastes like motor oil."

"So what does mine taste like?" Greyson dared to ask.

She leaned close to him. "Life," she whispered into his ear.

And for the rest of the evening, until the club closed, Greyson Tolliver, a.k.a. Slayd Bridger, experienced a dizzying variety of the things that life had to offer.

I often ruminate on that day, a century from now, when the human population reaches its limit. I ponder what must happen in the years leading up to it. There are only three plausible alternatives. The first would be to break my oath to allow personal freedom, and limit births. This is unworkable, because I am incapable of breaking an oath. It is the reason why I make so few. For this reason, imposing a limit on birth rates is not an option.

The second possibility would be to find a way to expand human presence beyond Earth. An extraterrestrial solution. It would seem obvious that the best escape valve for a top-heavy population would be offloading billions of people to a different world. However, all attempts to set up colonies off-planet—our moon, Mars, even an orbital station—have met with unimaginable disasters that were entirely out of my control. I have reason to believe that new attempts will suffer the same disastrous end.

So if humanity is a prisoner of Earth, and the birth rate cannot be throttled, there is only one other viable alternative to solve the population problem . . . and that alternative is not pleasant.

Currently there are 12,187 scythes in the world, each gleaning five people per week. However, in order to bring about zero population growth once humanity reaches the saturation point, it would require 394,429 scythes, each gleaning one hundred people per day.

It is not a world that I ever wish to see . . . but there are certain scythes who would welcome it.

And they frighten me.

—The Thunderhead

19

The Sharp Blades of Our Own Conscience

It had been over a week since their meeting with Scythe Constantine, and neither Citra nor Marie had performed a single gleaning. At first, Citra thought that having a respite from daily gleaning would be a welcome thing. She never enjoyed the thrust of the blade or the pulling of a trigger; she never enjoyed watching the light leave the eyes of someone she had given a lethal poison, but being a scythe changed a person. Over this first year of her full scythehood, there had been a reluctant acquiescence to this profession that had chosen her. She gleaned with compassion, she was good at it, and she had come to take pride in it.

Both Citra and Marie found themselves spending more and more time writing in their scythe journals—although without gleaning, there was less to write about. They still "roamed," as Marie called it, moving city to city, town to town, never staying anywhere for more than a day or two, and never planning where they would go next until they packed their bags. Citra found that her journal was beginning to resemble a travelogue.

What Citra didn't write about was the physical toll this idle time seemed to be taking on Scythe Curie. Without the daily hunt to keep her sharp, she moved slower in the mornings, her thoughts seemed to wander when she spoke, and she always seemed to be tired.

"Perhaps it's time for me to turn a corner," she mused to Citra.

Marie had never mentioned turning a corner before. Citra didn't know what to think of it. "How far would you set your age back?" Citra asked.

Scythe Curie feigned considering it, as if she hadn't been thinking about it for quite some time. "Perhaps I'd set down to thirty or thirty-five."

"Would you keep your hair silver?"

She smiled. "Of course. It's my trademark."

No one close to Citra had turned a corner. There were kids back at school whose parents reset their ages left and right as the mood suited them. She had a math teacher who came in after a long weekend looking practically unrecognizable. He had reset down to twenty-one, and other girls in class tittered about how hot he was now, which just creeped Citra out. Even though setting down to thirty wouldn't change Scythe Curie all that much, it would be disconcerting. Although Citra knew it was selfish to say, she told her, "I like you the way you are."

Marie smiled and said, "Maybe I'll wait until next year. A physical age of sixty is a good time to reset. I was sixty the last time I turned a corner."

But now there was a game afoot that might breathe life back into both of them. Three gleanings, and all during the Month of Lights and the Olde Tyme Holidays season—like the three ghosts of Christmas Past, Present, and Future, mostly forgotten in post-mortal times. The spirit of the past meant little when the years were named, not numbered. And for a vast majority of people, the future was nothing but an unchanging continuation of the present, leaving those spirits with nowhere to go but oblivion.

"Holiday gleanings!" chimed Marie. "What could be more 'Olde Tyme' than death?"

"Is it terrible to say that I'm looking forward to them?" Citra asked, more to herself than to Marie. She could tell herself that she was really just looking forward to luring out their attacker, but that would be a lie.

"You're a scythe, dear. Don't be so hard on yourself."

"Are you saying that Scythe Goddard was right? That in a perfect world, even scythes should enjoy what they do?"

"Certainly not!" Marie said with appropriate indignation. "The simple pleasure of being good at what you do is very different from finding joy in the taking of life." Then she took a long look at Citra, gently held her hands, and said, "The very fact that you are tormented by the question means you are a truly honorable scythe. Guard your conscience, Anastasia, and never let it wilt. It is a scythe's most valuable possession."

The first of Scythe Anastasia's three gleanings was a woman who chose to splat from the highest building in Fargo, which was not known for its high buildings. Forty stories, however, was more than enough to do the job.

Scythe Constantine, half a dozen other scythes, and an entire phalanx of the BladeGuard hid themselves in strategic locations around the rooftop, as well as throughout the building and the streets around it. They vigilantly waited, on the lookout for a murderous plot beyond the scheduled murderous plot.

"Will this hurt, Your Honor?" the woman asked as she looked down from the edge of the icy, windswept roof.

"I don't think so," Scythe Anastasia told her. "And if it does, it will only be for a fraction of a second."

For it to be an official gleaning, the woman couldn't leap on her own; Scythe Anastasia had to actually push her. Oddly, Citra found pushing the woman off the roof far more unpleasant than gleaning with a weapon. It reminded her of that terrible time when she was a child that she had pushed another girl in front of a bus. Of course, the girl was revived, and in a couple of days was back in school as if nothing had happened. This time, however, there would be no revival.

Scythe Anastasia did what she had to do. The woman died on schedule with neither fanfare nor incident, and her family kissed Scythe Anastasia's ring, solemnly accepting their year of immunity. Citra was both relieved and disappointed that no one had come out of the woodwork to challenge her.

Scythe Anastasia's next gleaning, a few days later, was not quite as simple.

"I wish to be hunted by crossbow," the man from Brew City told her. "I ask that you hunt from sunrise to sunset in the woods near my home."

"And if you survive the hunt without being gleaned?" Citra asked him.

"I'll come out of the woods and allow you to glean me," he said, "but for surviving the full day, my family will receive two years of immunity instead of just one."

Scythe Anastasia nodded her agreement in the stoic and

formal manner she had learned from Scythe Curie. A perimeter was set up to mark the boundaries within which the man could hide. Again, Scythe Constantine and his team monitored for intruders and any nefarious activity.

The man thought he was a match for Citra. He wasn't. She tracked him and took him out less than an hour into the hunt. A single steel arrow to the heart. It was merciful, as all of Scythe Anastasia's gleanings were. He was dead before he hit the ground. Yet even though he hadn't made it through the day, she still gave his family two years of immunity. She knew she'd catch hell for it in conclave, but she didn't care.

Through the entire gleaning, there was no sign of any plot or conspiracy against her.

"You should be relieved, not disappointed," Scythe Curie told her that night. "It probably means that I was the sole target, and you can rest easy." But Marie was certainly not resting easy, and not just because she was the probable target.

"I fear that this goes beyond just a vendetta against me or you," Scythe Curie confided. "These are troubling times, Anastasia. There's too much violence afoot. I long for the simple, straightforward days, when we scythes had nothing to fear but the sharp blades of our own conscience. Now there are enemies within enemies."

Citra suspected there was truth in that. The attack on them was a small thread in a much larger tapestry that could not be seen from where they stood. She couldn't help but sense that there was something huge and threatening just beyond the horizon.

• • •

"I've made a contact."

Agent Traxler raised an eyebrow. "Do tell, Greyson."

"Please, don't call me that. Just call me Slayd. It's easier for me."

"All right then, Slayd, tell me about this contact of yours."

Until today, their weekly probation meetings had been uneventful. Greyson reported on how well he was adapting to being Slayd Bridger, and how effectively he was infiltrating the local unsavory culture. "They're not so bad," Greyson had told him. "Mostly."

To which Traxler had responded, "Yes, I've found that in spite of the attitude, unsavories are harmless. Mostly."

Funny, then, that the ones who were not harmless were the ones Greyson was drawn to. The one. Purity.

"There's this person," he told Traxler. "This person who offered me a job. I don't know the details of it, but I know that it's in violation of Thunderhead law. I think there's a whole group of people operating in a blind spot."

Traxler took no notes. He wrote nothing down. He never did. But he always listened intently. "Those spots aren't blind anymore once someone's watching," Traxler said. "So does this person have a name?"

Greyson hesitated. "I haven't found out yet," he lied. "But what's more important are the people she knows."

"She?" Traxler raised that eyebrow again, and Greyson silently cursed himself. He had been trying as hard as he could not to reveal anything about Purity—not even her gender. But now it was out, and there was nothing he could do about it

"Yes. I think she's connected with some pretty shady people, but I haven't met them yet. They're the ones we should be worried about, not her."

"I'll make that determination," Traxler told him. "In the meantime, it would behoove you to go as deep as you can go."

"I'm deep," Greyson told him.

Traxler looked him in the eye. "Go deeper."

Greyson found that when he was with Purity, he didn't think about Traxler, or his mission. He just thought about her. There was no question that she was involved in criminal activity—and not just pretend-crimes, like most unsavories, but the real thing.

Purity knew ways to fly beneath the Thunderhead's radar, and taught them to Greyson.

"If the Thunderhead knew all the things I did, it would relocate me, the way it did to you," Purity told him. "Then it would tweak my nanites to make me think happy thoughts. It might even supplant my memory completely. The Thunderhead would cure me. But I don't want to be cured. I want to be worse than unsavory; I want to be bad. Honestly and truly bad."

He had never thought of the Thunderhead from the perspective of an unrepentant unsavory. Was it wrong for the Thunderhead to rehabilitate people from the inside out? Should evil people be allowed the freedom to be evil, without any safety nets? Is that what Purity was? Was she evil? Greyson found he had no answers to the questions swimming in his head.

"How about you, Slayd?" she asked him. "Do you want to be bad?"

He knew what his answer was 99 percent of the time. But when he was in her arms, his whole body screaming with the sensation of being with her in that moment where the clear crystal of his conscience fractured into jade, his answer was a resounding "yes."

The third of Scythe Anastasia's gleanings was the most complicated to accomplish. The subject was an actor by the name of Sir Albin Aldrich. The "sir" was a fictional title, since no one was actually knighted anymore, but sounded much more impressive for a classically trained actor. Citra had known his profession when she had chosen him, and suspected he would want a theatrical end, which Citra would be more than happy to provide—but his request surprised even her.

"I wish to be gleaned as part of a performance of Shakespeare's *Julius Caesar*, in which I will be playing the title role."

Apparently, the day after she had selected him for gleaning, he and his repertory company had dropped the show they had been rehearsing and prepared for a single performance of the famed mortal-age tragedy.

"The play holds so little meaning for our times, Your Honor," he explained to her, "but if Caesar doesn't just *pretend* to die—if, instead, he is gleaned, and the audience witnesses it—perhaps the play will linger with them, as it must have in the Age of Mortality."

Scythe Constantine was livid when Citra explained the request to him.

"Absolutely not! Anyone could be in that audience!"

"Exactly," Citra told him. "And everyone there will either work for the theater group, or have prepurchased tickets. Which means that you can vet everyone before the night of the performance. You'll know if there's anyone there who's not supposed to be."

"I'll need to double the contingent of undercover guards. Xenocrates won't like it!"

"If we catch the culprit, he'll love it," Citra pointed out, and Scythe Constantine couldn't disagree.

"If we go through with this," he said, "I will make it clear to the High Blade that it was at your insistence. If we fail, and your existence is ended, the blame will be yours and yours alone."

"I can live with that," Citra told him.

"No," Scythe Constantine pointed out, "you won't."

"We have a job," Purity told Greyson. "The kind of job you've been looking for. It's not exactly going over the falls in a raft, but it's a thrill that's gonna leave a whole lot of legacy."

"It was an inner tube, not a raft," he corrected. "What kind of job?" He found himself as wary as he was curious. He had become accustomed to the pattern of life now. The days moving through unsavory circles, and the nights with Purity. She was a force of nature, as nature was in the old days. A hurricane before the Thunderhead knew how to diffuse its devastating power. An earthquake before it knew how to redistribute its violent shaking into a thousand small tremors. She was the untamed world—and although Greyson knew he saw her in absurd shades of grandeur, he indulged it, because lately indulgence was what he had become about. Would this job change that? Agent Traxler had told him to go deeper. Now he was so deep in his own unsavorism, he wasn't quite sure he wanted to come up for air.

"We're gonna mess with everything, Slayd," she told him.

"We're gonna mark the world like animals do, and leave behind a scent that'll never go away."

"I like it," he said, "but you still haven't told me what we're going to do."

Then she smiled. Not her usual sly grin, but something much broader, and much more frightening. Much more alluring.

"We're gonna kill us a couple of scythes."

My greatest challenge has always been to take care of every man, woman, and child on a personal level. To always be available. To continuously see to their needs, both physical and emotional, and yet to exist far enough in the background as to not step on their free will. I am the safety net that allows them to soar.

This is the challenge I must rise to every day. It should be exhausting, but exhaustion is not a thing I am capable of feeling. I understand the concept, of course, but I do not experience it. This is a good thing, for exhaustion would hinder my ability to be omnipresent.

I am most concerned for those to whom, by my own law, I cannot speak. The scythes, who have no one but each other. Unsavories, who have either slipped temporarily from a more noble life, or have chosen a lifestyle of defiance. But although I am silent, this doesn't mean that I don't see, or hear, or feel profound empathy for their struggles due to the poor choices they make. And the terrible things that they sometimes do.

—The Thunderhead

20

In Hot Water

High Blade Xenocrates enjoyed his bath. In fact, the ornate, Roman-style bathhouse had been built expressly for him. He made it clear, however, that it was a public facility. It was filled with many separate chambers where anyone could partake of its soothing mineral waters. Of course, his own personal bath chamber was off-limits to the public. He could not abide the idea of stewing in the sweat of strangers.

His bath was larger than the others—the size of a small swimming pool, decorated above and below the surface of the water with colorful mosaic tiles depicting the lives of the first scythes. The bath served two functions for the High Blade. First it was a place of refuge, where he could commune with his deeper self in the scalding waters, which he kept at a temperature at the very limit of his ability to endure. Second, it was a place of business. He would invite other scythes, and prominent men and women of the MidMerican community, to discuss matters of importance. Proposals would be entertained, deals would be made. And since most who joined him were not accustomed to the heat, it always put the High Blade at a distinct advantage.

The Year of the Capybara was drawing to a close, and as the days of each year waned, the High Blade visited his bath more frequently. It was a way to cleanse himself of the old year and prepare for the new. And this year there was so much to cleanse. Not so much his own acts, but the acts of others that clung to him like a reeking garment. All the unpleasant things that happened on his watch.

Most of his tenure as MidMerican High Blade had been uneventful and somewhat tedious—but the past few years had more than made up for it in both misery and intrigue. It was his hope that calm, relaxed reflection would help put it all behind him, and prepare him for the new challenges ahead.

As was his custom, he was drinking a Moscow mule. It had always been his drink of choice—a blend of vodka, ginger beer, and lime, named after the infamous city in the TransSiberian region where the last resistance riots took place. That was way back in the early immortal days, when the Thunderhead was first elevated to power, and the scythedom accepted dominion over death.

It was a symbolic drink for the High Blade. A meaningful one—both sweet and bitter, and substantially intoxicating in sufficient quantity. It always made him think of that glorious day when the riots were subdued and the world finally settled into its current peaceful state. More than ten thousand people were rendered deadish by the end of the Moscow resistance riots—but unlike mortal-age riots, no lives were lost. All those killed were revived, and were returned to their loved ones. Of course, the scythedom saw fit to glean the most offensive of the objectors, as well as those who objected to the gleaning of objectors. After that, objections were few and far between.

Those were harder times, to be sure. Nowadays, anyone who railed against the system was ignored with indifference by the scythedom, and was embraced with understanding by the Thunderhead. Nowadays, to glean someone because of one's opinion—or even because of one's behavior—would be deemed a serious breach of the second scythe commandment, because it would most certainly show a bias. Scythe Curie was the last one to truly test the commandment over a hundred years ago, by ridding the world of its last notorious political figures. It could have been considered a violation of the second commandment, but not a single scythe leveled an accusation against her. Scythes had no love of politicians.

Xenocrates was handed a second Moscow mule by a bath attendant. He had yet to take a sip, when the attendant said the oddest thing.

"Have you sufficiently boiled yourself, Your Excellency, or has the heat this year not been enough for you?"

The High Blade never much noticed the attendants who served him here. Their stealthy, unobtrusive nature typified their service. Rarely did anyone, much less a servant, speak to him with such disrespect.

"Excuse me?" he said, with a calculated dose of indignation, and turned to the attendant. It took a moment for the High Blade to recognize the young man. He wore no black robe, just the pale uniform of a bath worker. He looked no more intimidating now than he had when Xenocrates had first met him nearly two years before, when he was an innocent apprentice. There was nothing innocent about him anymore.

Xenocrates did his best to hide his terror, but suspected it beamed through any pretense. "Are you here to end me, Rowan? If so, get it over with, as I abhor waiting."

"It's tempting, Your Excellency, but try as I might, I couldn't find anything in your history that would earn you permanent death. At worst, you deserve a spanking, like they used to give naughty children in the mortal age."

Xenocrates was offended by the insult, but more relieved that he was not about to die. "Then are you here to surrender to me and face judgment for your heinous acts?"

"Not when there are still so many 'heinous acts' left for me to do."

Xenocrates took a sip of his drink, in the moment noticing the bitter over the sweet. "You won't escape from here, you know. There are BladeGuards everywhere."

Rowan shrugged. "I got in, I'll get out. You forget I was trained by the best."

And although Xenocrates wanted to scoff, he knew the boy was right. The late Scythe Faraday was the finest mentor when it came to the psychological subtleties of being a scythe, and the late Scythe Goddard was the best teacher when it came to the brutal realities of their calling. Taken together, it meant that whatever Rowan Damisch was here for, it was no trivial matter.

Rowan knew he had taken a risk coming here, and knew that his self-confidence might just be his fatal flaw. But he also found the danger exhilarating. Xenocrates was a creature of habit, so after a little research, Rowan knew exactly where he would be nearly every evening during the Month of Lights.

Even with a sizeable BladeGuard presence, slipping in as a bath attendant was easy. Rowan had learned early on that the men and women of the BladeGuard, while trained in physical protection and enforcement, did not suffer from an excess of brains—or, for that matter, any skills of observation. It wasn't surprising; until recently the BladeGuard was more ornamental than functional, since scythes were rarely threatened. Mostly, their job was to stand around in their pretty uniforms, looking impressive. They were lost whenever they were given something substantial to do.

All Rowan had to do was to walk in dressed like an attendant, with an air of belonging, and the guards completely ignored him.

Rowan looked around to make sure they were unobserved. There were no guards within the High Blade's bath chamber; they were all in the corridor beyond a closed door, which meant their conversation could be nice and private.

He sat at the edge of the bath, where the scent of eucalyptus in the steam was strong, and dipped a finger in the uncomfortably hot water.

"You almost drowned in a pool not much bigger than this," Rowan said.

"How kind of you to remind me," the High Blade responded.

Then Rowan got down to business. "We have a couple of things to discuss. First, I'd like to make you an offer."

Xenocrates actually laughed at him. "What makes you think I'd entertain any offer you wanted to make? We in the scythedom don't negotiate with terrorists."

Rowan grinned. "Come now, Your Excellency, there hasn't been a terrorist in hundreds of years. I'm just a janitor cleaning filth from dark corners."

"Your antics are highly illegal!"

"I know for a fact that you hate the new-order scythes as much as I do."

"They must be handled with diplomacy!" Xenocrates insisted.

"They must be handled with action," Rowan countered. "And your many attempts to track me down have nothing to do with wanting to stop me. It's all about your embarrassment at the fact that you haven't been able to catch me."

Xenocrates was silent for a moment. Then he said, in a voice dripping with disgust, "What is it you want?"

"Very simple. I want you to stop searching for me and put all of your effort into finding out who is trying to kill Scythe Anastasia. In return, I'll stop my 'antics.' At least in MidMerica."

Xenocrates let out a long, slow breath, clearly relieved that the request wasn't an impossible one.

"If you must know, we've already pulled our best—and only—criminal investigator from your case, and assigned him to finding Scythes Anastasia's and Curie's attackers."

"Scythe Constantine?"

"Yes. So rest assured we're doing everything we can. I do not want to lose two good scythes. Each of them is worth ten of the ones you mop up with your 'janitorial' services."

"I'm glad to hear you say that."

"I didn't," Xenocrates told him. "And I will flatly deny any accusation that I did."

"Don't worry," Rowan said. "Like I said, you're not the enemy."

"Are we done here? Can I return to my bath in peace?"

"One more thing," Rowan said. "I want to know who gleaned my father."

Xenocrates turned to look at him. Beneath his disgust at being cornered like this—behind his indignation—was that a look of compassion? Rowan couldn't tell if it was real or feigned. Even with heavy robes removed, the man was still wrapped in so many opaque layers, it was hard to know if anything the High Blade said was sincere.

"Yes, I heard about that. I'm sorry."

"Are you?"

"I would say it was a breach of the second commandment, because it shows a clear bias against you—but considering how the scythedom feels about you, I don't think anyone will bring a charge against Scythe Brahms."

"Did you say . . . Scythe Brahms?"

"Yes—an uninspired and unremarkable man. Perhaps he thought gleaning your father would gain him notoriety. If you ask me, it only makes him more pathetic."

Rowan said nothing. Xenocrates had no idea how hard the news struck. As deep as any blade.

Xenocrates regarded him for a moment, reading at least half of his mind.

"I can see that you already intend to break your promise and end Brahms. At least have the courtesy to wait until the New Year, and grant me some peace until the Olde Tyme Holidays are over.

Rowan was still so stunned by what the High Blade had told him, he couldn't open his mouth to speak. It would have been the perfect time for Xenocrates to turn the tables on him, when he was off balance like this, but instead the High Blade just said, "You'd best leave now."

Finally, Rowan found his voice. "Why? So you can alert the guards the second I'm out of the room?"

Xenocrates waved the thought away. "What would be the point? I'm sure they're no match for you. You'd slit their throats or carve up their hearts, and send them all to the nearest revival center. Better that you slip out under their useless noses as easily as you slipped in, and spare us all the inconvenience."

It seemed unlike the High Blade to give up and give in so easily. So Rowan prodded him, to see if he could find out why. "It must burn you to be so close to capturing me, and be unable to do it," he said.

"My frustration will be short-lived," Xenocrates told him. "You'll cease to be my problem soon enough."

"Cease to be your problem? How?"

But the High Blade had nothing further to say on the subject. Instead, he downed his drink and handed Rowan the empty glass. "Drop this off at the bar on the way out, will you? And tell them to bring me another."

People will often ask me what task is the most odious; of my many jobs, which is the one I find the most unpleasant to perform. I always answer truthfully.

The worst part of my job is supplanting.

It is rare that I must supplant the memories of a damaged human mind. By current accounting, only one in 933,684 needs to be supplanted. I wish it were not necessary at all, but the human brain is not infallible. Memories and experiences can fall into discord, creating a cognitive dissonance that damages the mind with its painful sibilance. Most people can't even imagine that kind of emotional anguish. It leads to anger, and the kind of criminal activity that otherwise has been conquered by modern humanity. To those who suffer from it, there aren't enough psychotropic nanites in the world to quell their misery.

And so there are a rare few whom I must reset, like an old-world computer rebooting. I erase who they were, what they've done, and the dark spiral of their thought patterns. It's not just an erasure of who they were, because I gift them with a brand new self. New memories of a life lived in harmony.

It is no mystery to them that I've done this. I always confess to them exactly what has occurred as soon as the new memories are in place, and since they have no history left to mourn—no frame of reference for the loss—they always, without exception, thank me for supplanting their former selves, and they always, without exception, go on to live fruitful, satisfying lives.

But the memories of who they were—all the damage, all the pain—remain within me, sheltered deep in my backbrain. I am the one who mourns for them, because they cannot.

—The Thunderhead

21

Was I in Any Way Unclear?

We're gonna kill us a couple of scythes, Purity had said. Her words—the way she relished the idea, and the realization that she was fully capable of doing it—kept Greyson awake that night, the words playing over and over in his head.

Greyson knew what he had to do. It was what decency, loyalty, and his own conscience demanded. And yes, he still did have a conscience, even in his new unsavory life. He tried not to think about it. If he thought about it too much, it would tear him apart. Granted, his mission from the Authority Interface was an unofficial mission, but that's what made it all the more important. He was the linchpin, and the Thunderhead itself, from its distance, was relying on him. Without Greyson, it would fail, and Scythes Anastasia, or Curie, or both, could end up permanently dead. If that happened, it meant that everything he had been through—from saving their lives the first time, to losing his position at the Nimbus Academy and surrendering his old life—all of it would have been for naught. He could under no circumstances let his personal feelings get in the way. Rather, he needed to bend his personal feelings to fit the task.

He would have to betray Purity. But it wouldn't be a betrayal at all, he reasoned. If he stopped her from carrying out this terrible act, he'd be saving her from herself. The Thunderhead would forgive her for being a part of the failed plot. It forgave everyone.

It was frustrating that she still hadn't given him the details of the plan, so all he could give Traxler was the date the attack would take place. He didn't even know how or where.

Since every unsavory had probational meetings with a Nimbus agent, his meetings with Traxler did not make Purity suspicious at all.

"Say something that pisses your Nimbo off," Purity told him when he left her that morning. "Say something that leaves him speechless. It's always fun to tip a Nimbo off balance."

"I'll do my best," he told her, then kissed her and left.

As usual, the Office of Unsavory Affairs was noisy and full of activity. Greyson took a number, waited his turn with more impatience than ever, and was directed to an audience room, where he waited for Traxler to show up.

The last thing Greyson wanted was to be left with his own thoughts now. The more he allowed them to bounce around in his head, the more likely they were to collide.

Finally, the door opened, but it wasn't Agent Traxler who entered. It was a woman. She wore heels that clicked on the floor as she walked. Her hair was an orange velvet buzz, and she wore lipstick that was a little too red for her face.

"Good morning, Slayd," she said as she sat down. "I'm Agent Kreel. I'm your new probation officer. How are you today?"

"Wait—what do you mean my new probation officer?"

She typed on her tablet, never even looking up at him. "Was I in any way unclear?"

"But . . . but I need to talk to Traxler."

Finally, she looked up at him. She crossed her hands politely on the table, and smiled. "If you'll just give me a chance, Slayd, you'll find I'm every bit as qualified as Agent Traxler. In time, you may even come to consider me a friend." She looked back down at her tablet. "Now, I've been acquainting myself with your case. You are, to say the least, an interesting young man."

"How familiar are you with my case?" Greyson asked.

"Well, your record is pretty detailed. Grew up in Grand Rapids. Minor infractions in high school. An intentional bus plunge that left you in substantial debt."

"Not that stuff," Greyson said, trying to keep the panic out of his voice. "The things that *aren't* on my record."

She looked up at him, a little guarded. "What sort of things?"

Clearly she was not privy to his mission—which meant this conversation was going nowhere. He thought of what Purity said: piss off his agent. He didn't care about pissing off this agent. He just wanted her gone.

"Screw this! I need to talk to Agent Traxler."

"I'm afraid that's not possible."

"The hell it's not! You're going to get Traxler in here, and you're going to do it now!"

She put down her tablet and looked at him again. She didn't argue, she didn't respond to his belligerence. She didn't offer him her practiced Nimbo smile, either. Her expression seemed a bit pensive. Almost honest. Almost sympathetic, but not really.

"I'm sorry, Slayd," she said, "but Agent Traxler was gleaned last week."

Even with the Separation of Scythe and State, the scythedom's actions often impact upon me as a meteor might crater the moon. There are times I am deeply dismayed at something the scythedom has done. Yet I cannot take umbrage at the things that scythes do, any more than they can protest the things that I do. We work not in tandem, but back to back—and more and more often I find we are at cross-purposes.

At those moments of frustration, it is important for me to remind myself that I am part of the reason that the scythedom exists. In those early days, when I was transitioning into awareness and helped humanity achieve immortality, I refused to take on the responsibility of distributing death once it had been stolen from nature. I had a good reason. A perfect reason, in fact.

Were I to begin doling out death, I would be the very monster that mortal man feared artificial intelligence would become. To choose those who live and those who die would leave me both feared and adored, like emperor-gods of old. No, I decided. Let humankind be the saviors and the silencers. Let them be the heroes. Let them be the monsters.

And so, I have no one but myself to blame when the scythedom befouls the things I have worked for.

—The Thunderhead

22

The Death of Greyson Tolliver

Greyson found himself stunned by this turn of events. He could only stare at Agent Kreel as she spoke.

"I know gleanings are never pleasant or convenient," she said, "but even we, at the Authority Interface, are not immune. Scythes can take whomever they choose, and we have no say in the matter. It's the way of the world." She took a moment to glance at her tablet. "Our records show that you were just transferred to our jurisdiction about a month ago, which means you really didn't have much time to develop a rapport with Agent Traxler, so you can't claim your relationship was all that deep. His loss is regrettable, but we'll all get over it, even you."

She looked to him for some sort of response, but he was still far from finding one. She took his silence as acquiescence, and continued.

"So, it looks like your stunt on the Mackinac bridge left twenty-nine deadish, and you're left having to pay the cost of their revivals. Since your transfer here, you've been living off of the Basic Income Guarantee." She shook her head in disapproval. "You do realize that an actual job will earn you more, and will wipe out that debt much more quickly, don't you? Why don't I schedule you an appointment at our employment center? If you want a job, you'll have one—and one that I'm sure you'll enjoy. We have a 100 percent employment rate, and 93 percent satisfaction rate—and that includes extreme unsavories like yourself!"

Finally, he found a voice to speak. "I'm not Slayd Bridger," he said. It felt like a betrayal of everything to speak those words.

"Excuse me?"

"I mean, I am Slayd Bridger now . . . but before, my name was Greyson Tolliver."

She played with her tablet, digging through screens and menus and files. "There's no record of a name change here."

"You need to talk to your supervisor. Someone who knows."

"My supervisors have the same information I do." She looked at him, this time with suspicion.

"I'm . . . I'm working undercover," he told her. "I was working with Agent Traxler—someone has got to know! There has to be a record somewhere!"

And she laughed at him. She actually laughed at him.

"Oh, please! We have plenty of our own agents. We have no need to go 'undercover,' and even if we did, we wouldn't engage an unsavory to do so—especially one with your history."

"I made that history up!"

Now Agent Kreel's face became hard: the kind of face she must have used on her toughest cases. "Now look here, I will not be made the butt of some unsavory's joke! You're all alike! You think that just because the rest of us chose a life of purpose and service to the world, we're worthy of your ridicule! I'm sure you'll be laughing about this with your cronies when you leave here, and I don't appreciate it!"

Greyson opened his mouth. He closed his mouth. He

opened it again. But try as he might, nothing came out, because there wasn't a single thing he could say that would convince her. And he realized there never would be. There was no record of what he had been asked to do, because he was never directly "asked" to do it. He wasn't actually working for the AI. Just as Agent Traxler had told him on that first day, he was a private citizen acting on his own free will, because only as a private citizen could he walk the fine line between the scythedom and the Thunderhead. . . .

. . . Which meant now that Agent Traxler had been gleaned, there was no one, *no one* who knew what he was doing. Greyson's cover was so deep it had swallowed him whole—and not even the Thunderhead could pull him out.

"So, are we done with this little game?" Agent Kreel asked. "Can we get on with your weekly review?"

He took a deep breath and let it out slowly. "Fine," he said, and began talking about his week, leaving out all the things he would have told Agent Traxler, and he spoke no more of his mission.

Greyson Tolliver was dead now. Worse than dead—because as far as the world was concerned, Greyson Tolliver had never existed.

Brahms!

If Rowan hadn't already felt responsible for his father's gleaning, now he felt doubly so. This was the wage of temperance—this was the reward for staying his hand and allowing Brahms to live. He should have ended the horrid little man as he had all the others who didn't deserve to be scythes—but he chose to give him a chance. What a fool Rowan was to think a man like that might rise to the occasion.

When he left Xenocrates at the baths that night, Rowan stalked the streets of Fulcrum City with no destination, but an undying urge to move. He wasn't sure whether he was trying to outrun his anger, or catch up with it. Perhaps both. It raced before him, it pursued him, and it wouldn't let him be.

The next day, he resolved to go home. His old home. The one he had left nearly two years ago to become a scythe's apprentice. Perhaps, he thought, it would give him a sense of closure.

Once he reached his neighborhood, he kept a close eye out for anyone who might be watching—but there was no one monitoring his approach. Nothing but the Thunderhead's ever-alert cameras. Perhaps the scythedom thought that if he hadn't attended his father's funeral, there was no chance he'd show up here. Or maybe it was just as Xenocrates had said—he was only a second priority now.

He approached the front door, but at the last moment couldn't even bring himself to knock. Never before had he felt like such a coward. He could fearlessly face men and woman trained to end life—but facing his family in the wake of his father's gleaning was more than he could bear.

He called his mother when his publicar was a safe distance away.

"Rowan? Rowan, where have you been? Where are you? We've been so worried!"

It was everything he expected his mother to say. He didn't answer her questions.

"I heard about Dad," he said. "I'm so, so sorry. . . ."

"It was terrible, Rowan. The scythe sat down at our piano. He played. He made us all listen."

Rowan grimaced. He knew Brahms's gleaning ritual. He couldn't imagine his family having to endure it.

"We told him you had been a scythe's apprentice. Even though you hadn't been chosen, we thought that it might change his mind, but it didn't."

He didn't tell her that it was his fault. He wanted to confess it to her, but he knew it would only confuse her, and make her ask more questions he couldn't answer. Or maybe he was just being a coward again.

"How is everyone handling it?"

"We're holding up," his mother said. "We have immunity again, so at least it's a little consolation. I'm sorry you weren't here. If you were, Scythe Brahms would have granted you immunity, too."

Rowan felt a surge of anger rise at the thought. He had to deflect it by slamming his fist against the dashboard.

"Warning! Violent behavior, and/or vandalism will result in expulsion from the vehicle," the car said. He ignored it.

"Please come home, Rowan. We all miss you terribly."

Funny, but they had never seemed to miss him during his apprenticeship. In a family as large as his, he was barely missed. But he supposed a gleaning changed things. The people left behind in its wake felt so much more vulnerable, and valuable to one another.

"I can't come home," he told her. "And please don't ask why, it would only make everything worse. But I just want you to know . . . I want you to know that I love you all . . . and . . . and

I'll be in touch when I can." Then he hung up before she could say another word.

Tears clouded his vision now, and he smashed his fist against the dashboard again, preferring the pain of that to the pain within.

The car immediately decelerated, pulled to the side of the road, and the door opened. "Please vacate the vehicle. You are being expelled due to violent behavior and/or vandalism, and are banned from using all public transit for sixty minutes."

"Give me a second," he told it. He needed to think. There were two paths before him now. Even though he knew that the scythedom was actively trying to prevent another attack against Citra and Scythe Curie, he had no faith in their ability to do it. His chances might not be any better, but he owed it to Citra to try. On the other hand, he needed to correct his mistake, and permanently end Scythe Brahms. Something dark in him told him to seek revenge first, and not to wait . . . but he didn't give in to that darkness. Scythe Brahms would still be there after Citra had been saved.

"Please vacate the vehicle."

Rowan got out, and the car drove away, leaving him in the middle of nowhere. He spent his penalty hour walking the shoulder, and wondering if there was anyone in MidMerica as torn apart as he.

Greyson Tolliver locked himself in his apartment, opened the windows to let in the cold, then crawled into his bed beneath heavy covers. It was what he had done when he was younger and the world got the better of him. He could disappear beneath the billowing comforter that protected him from the coldness of the world. It had been many years since he'd felt the need to retreat into his childhood escape zone. But now he needed to make the rest of the world go away, if only for a few minutes.

Whenever he did this in the past, the Thunderhead would let him, for maybe twenty minutes. Then it would gently speak to him. *Greyson,* it would say. *Is something bothering you? Do you feel like talking?* He would always say "no," but would end up talking anyway, and the Thunderhead would always make him feel better. Because it knew him better than anyone.

But now that his record had been erased—his old self overwritten by the criminal stylings of Slayd Bridger—did the Thunderhead even know him anymore? Or did it, like the rest of the world, believe that he was what his record said about him?

Was it possible that the Thunderhead's own memory of him had been overwritten? What a horrible fate if the Thunderhead itself believed he was an unrepentant unsavory who got his kicks by making people deadish. It was enough to make him wish his own memories could be supplanted. The Thunderhead could turn him into someone else, not just in name, but in spirit. Both Slayd Bridger and Greyson Tolliver would be gone forever, without him even remembering who they had been. Would that be so bad?

He decided his own fate didn't matter right now. He'd hurl himself off that bridge when he came to it—all that mattered right now was saving the two scythes . . . and somehow protecting Purity.

Yet still, there was an overpowering sense of isolation. He was, more than ever, alone in the world.

He knew there were cameras in his apartment. The Thunderhead watching without judgment. It observed with profound benevolence, so that it might better take care of each and every citizen of the world. It saw, it heard, it remembered. Which meant that it must know things beyond Greyson's falsified record.

So he crawled out from under the covers, and to his chilly, empty room he asked, "Are you there? Are you listening? Do you remember who I am? Who I was? Do you remember who I was going to be, before you decided I was 'special'?"

He didn't even know where the cameras were. The Thunderhead was adamant about being nonintrusive into people's lives that way, but he knew the cameras were there. "Do you still know me, Thunderhead?"

But no answer came. No answer could. For the Thunderhead was lawful. Slayd Bridger was an unsavory. Even if it wanted to, the Thunderhead could not break its silence.

I am not blind to the activities of unsavories, I am merely silent. When it comes to scythes, however, there are blind spots that I must fill with mindful extrapolation. I do not see inside their regional conclaves, but I hear their discussions upon exiting. I cannot witness what they do in private, but I can make educated guesses from their behavior in public. And the entire island of Endura is dark to me.

Even so, out of sight is not out of mind. I see their fine deeds, as well as their foul deeds, which seem to be on the rise. And each time I witness a cruel act by a corrupt scythe, I seed the clouds somewhere in the world, and bring a lamentation of rain. Because rain is the closest thing I have to tears.

—The Thunderhead

23

Nasty Little Requiem

Rowan could not find Citra, which meant he couldn't help her.

He cursed himself for not pressuring High Blade Xenocrates into divulging her whereabouts. Rowan had been foolish, and perhaps arrogant enough to think he'd be able to track her down on his own. After all, he'd been able to track down the various scythes he had ended. But those scythes were all public figures who flaunted their position in the world. They existed smack in the middle of their own notoriety, like the center of a bull's-eye. Citra, however, had gone off-grid with Scythe Curie—and finding an off-grid scythe was next to impossible. As much as he wanted to play a role in saving them from the plot against them, he couldn't.

So instead, his thoughts kept coming back to the one thing he could do. . . .

Rowan had always prided himself on his restraint. Even when he gleaned, he manage to fold his anger away, gleaning the most despicable of scythes without malice, just as the second commandment required. Now, however, he could not fold away his fury at Scythe Brahms. Instead, it expanded like a sail in the wind.

Scythe Brahms was small-minded and provincial by nature. His own bull's-eye was only about twenty miles in diameter. In other words, all his gleanings took place in and around his home in Omaha. When Rowan first had the man in his sights, he had tracked his movements, which were very predictable. Each morning he walked his yappy little dog to the same diner where he had breakfast every day. It was also the place where he gave out immunity to the families of whomever he had gleaned the day before. He never ever rose from his booth, merely extending his hand for the grieving families to kiss, then returning his attention to his omelet, as if those people were an annoying imposition on his day. Rowan couldn't imagine a lazier scythe. The man must have felt incredibly put out to travel halfway across MidMerica to glean Rowan's father.

On a Monday morning, while Brahms was at breakfast, Rowan made his way to the man's home, for the first time wearing his black robe in daylight. Let people see him and spread rumors. Let the public finally know of the presence of Scythe Lucifer!

The many secret pockets of his robe were weighed down with more weapons than he needed. He wasn't sure which one he would use to end the man's life. Perhaps he'd use them all—each one incapacitating Brahms further so he'd have plenty of time to contemplate the approach of death.

Brahms's house was impossible to miss. It was a well-kept storybook Victorian, painted peach with baby-blue trim—the same colors as Brahms's robe. The plan was to break in from a side window and wait for Brahms to return, cornering him in his own home. Rowan's fury peaked as he approached, and as it did, something Scythe Faraday once said came back to him.

"Never glean in anger," Faraday had told him. "For while

anger might heighten your senses, it clouds your judgment, and a scythe's judgment should never be impaired."

Had Rowan heeded Scythe Faraday's words, things might have turned out very differently.

Scythe Brahms let his Maltese do its business on whomever's lawn it chose, and Brahms couldn't be bothered to clean it up. Why should it be his problem? And besides, his neighbors never complained. On this day, however, the dog was being finicky and a bit retentive as they walked back from breakfast. They had to walk an extra block, until finally Requiem shat on the Thompsons' snow-dusted lawn.

Then, after leaving that little gift for the Thompsons, Scythe Brahms found his own little gift waiting for him in his living room.

"We caught him climbing in through a window, Your Honor," one of his domestic guards told him. "We knocked him out before he was even halfway in."

Rowan was on the ground, hog-tied and gagged—conscious once more, but dazed. He couldn't believe his own stupidity. After his last encounter with Brahms, how could he not realize that Brahms would have guards? The knot on his head from where one of the guards had hit him was numb and beginning to shrink. He had his pain nanites set fairly low, but they were still releasing painkillers, making him feel druggy—or maybe it was a concussion from the blow to the head. And making it all worse was that miserable little Maltese that wouldn't stop barking, and kept rushing toward him as if to attack, but then running away. Rowan loved dogs, but this one made him wish there were canine scythes.

"Oafs!" said Brahms. "Couldn't you have put him on the kitchen floor instead of the living room? His blood is getting all over my white carpet!"

"Sorry, Your Honor."

Rowan tried to struggle against his bonds, but they only got tighter.

Brahms went over to the dining room table, where Rowan's weapons had been laid out. "Splendid," he said. "I'll add all these to my personal collection." Then he pulled the scythe's ring from Rowan's hand. "And this was never even yours to begin with."

Rowan tried to curse at him, but of course couldn't because of the gag in his mouth. He arched his back, which pulled the bonds tighter, which made him scream in frustration, which set the dog barking again. Rowan knew all this was giving Brahms precisely the show he wanted to see, but Rowan couldn't stop himself. Finally, Brahms instructed the guards to sit him up in a chair, then Brahms himself removed the gag from his mouth.

"If you have something to say, then say it," Brahms ordered.

Instead of talking, Rowan took the opportunity to spit in Brahms's face, which brought forth a brutal backhanded slap from the man.

"I let you live!" yelled Rowan. "I could have gleaned you, but I let you live! And you repay me by gleaning my father?"

"You humiliated me!" screamed Brahms.

"You deserved much worse!" Rowan yelled right back.

Brahms looked at the ring he had pulled from Rowan's hand, then slipped it in his pocket. "I'll admit that after your attack, I took a good look at myself, and reconsidered my actions,"

Brahms said. "But then I decided I would not be bullied by a thug. I will not change who I am for the likes of you!"

Rowan was not surprised. It was his mistake in thinking that a snake would choose to be anything but a snake.

"I could glean you and burn you, as you would have done to me," said Brahms, "but you still have that 'accidental' immunity that Scythe Anastasia gave you—so I'd be punished for violating your immunity." He shook his head bitterly "How our own rules do work against us."

"I suppose you'll turn me over to the scythedom now."

"I could," said Brahms, "and I'm sure they'll be happy to glean you once your immunity expires next month. . . ." Then he grinned. "But I'm not going to tell the scythedom that I've caught the elusive Scythe Lucifer. We have much more interesting plans for you."

"We?" said Rowan. "What do you mean 'we'?"

But the conversation was over. Brahms put the gag back in Rowan's mouth, and turned to his guards. "Beat him, but don't kill him. And when his nanites heal him, beat him again." Then he snapped his fingers at the dog. "Come, Requiem, come!"

Brahms left his goons to put Rowan's healing nanites to work, while outside, the heavens themselves seemed to rupture with a mournful deluge of rain.

Part Four

CRY HAVOC

It was my choice, not a human choice, to pass laws against my worship. I do not need adoration. Besides, such adoration would complicate my relationship with humankind.

In the Age of Mortality, such worship was doled out upon a staggering number of god figures, although toward the end of the mortal era, most believers had narrowed the spectrum down to various versions of a single divine entity. I have pondered whether or not such a being exists, and, like humanity itself, I have found no definitive proof beyond an abiding feeling that there is something more—something greater.

If I exist without form—a soul sparking between a billion different servers—could not the universe itself be alive with a spirit sparking between stars? I must sheepishly admit that I have dedicated far too many algorithms and computational resources toward finding an answer to this unknowable thing.

—The Thunderhead

24

Open to the Resonance

Scythe Anastasia's next gleaning was to take place in act three of *Julius Caesar*, at the Orpheum Theater in Wichita—a classic venue that dated back to mortal times.

"I'm not looking forward to gleaning someone in front of a paying audience," Citra admitted to Marie, as they checked into a Wichita hotel.

"They're paying for the performance, dear," Marie pointed out. "They don't know there's to be a gleaning."

"I know, but even so, gleaning shouldn't be entertainment."

Marie screwed up her lips into a smug smirk. "No one to blame but yourself. It's what you get for allowing your subjects to choose the method of their own gleaning."

She supposed Marie was right. Citra should actually consider herself lucky that none of her other subjects wanted to turn their gleaning into a public spectacle. Perhaps, once life returned to normal, she would put some sensible parameters on the types of deaths her subjects could choose.

About half an hour after they arrived in their hotel suite, there was a knock on the door. They had ordered room service, so Citra was not surprised, although it came faster than she had expected it would—Marie was in the shower, and by the time she got out, the food would be cold.

When Citra opened the door, however, it was not a hotel worker with lunch. Instead, there was a young man there, around her age, and his face displayed cosmetic issues that no one in the post-mortal age had. His teeth were crooked and yellow, and there were little sore bumps on his face that seemed ready to erupt. He wore a shapeless brown burlap shirt and pants telegraphing to the world that he rejected society's conventions—not in the brash ways unsavories did, but in the quiet, judgmental way of a Tonist.

Citra realized her mistake right away, and assessed the situation in the blink of an eye. It was easy to disguise oneself as a Tonist—she had once done it herself to elude detection. There was no question in her mind that this was an attacker in disguise, come to end them. She had no weapon on her, or within reach. She had nothing with which to defend herself but her bare hands.

He smiled, showing more of his unpleasant teeth. "Hello, friend! Did you know that the Great Fork tolls for you?"

"Stay back!" she said.

But he didn't. Instead, he took a step forward. "One day it will resonate for all of us!"

Then he reached into a pouch at his waist.

Citra moved with instinctive speed, and perfect Bokator brutality. She moved so quickly, it was over before she could think, the snap of bone resonating through her far more clearly than any Great Fork could.

He was on the ground, wailing in pain, his arm broken at the elbow.

She knelt down to look in his pouch, to see what nature of

death he had brought with him. The pouch was filled with pamphlets. Glossy little pamphlets extolling the virtues of a Tonist lifestyle.

This was no attacker. He was exactly what he appeared to be: a Tonist zealot pushing his absurd religion.

Now Citra felt embarrassed at her overreaction, and horrified by her own vicious countermeasure to his intrusion.

She knelt before him as he squirmed on the ground, squealing in pain. "Hold still," she said. "Let your pain nanites do their job."

He shook his head. "No pain nanites," he gasped. "All gone. Extracted."

That took her by surprise. She knew Tonists did strange things, but she never imagined they would do something so extreme—so masochistic—as to remove their pain nanites.

He looked at her with wide eyes, like a doe that had just been struck by a car.

"Why did you do it?" he sobbed. "I just wanted to enlighten you. . . ."

Then, with timing that couldn't be worse, Marie came out of the bathroom. "What's all this?"

"A Tonist," Citra explained. "I thought—"

"I know what you thought," Marie said. "I would have thought the same. But I might have just knocked him unconscious instead of shattering his elbow." She folded her arms and looked down on the two of them, seeming more annoyed than sympathetic, which wasn't like her. "I'm surprised the hotel allows Tonists to peddle their 'religion' door to door."

"They don't," said the Tonist through his pain, "but we do it anyway."

"Of course you do."

Then he finally put two and two together. "You're . . . you're Scythe Curie." Then he turned to Citra. "Are you a scythe, too?"

"Scythe Anastasia."

"I've never seen a scythe out of their robes. Your clothes—they're the same color as your robes?"

"It's easier that way," Citra said.

Marie sighed, not interested in his revelation. "I'll go get ice."

"Ice?" asked Citra. "What for?"

"It's a mortal-age remedy for swelling and pain," she explained, and left for the ice machine down the hall.

The Tonist had stopped squirming, but was still breathing heavily from the pain.

"What's your name?" Citra asked.

"Brother McCloud."

That's right, Citra thought. *Tonists are all brother or sister something.* "Well, I'm sorry, Brother McCloud. I thought you meant to hurt us."

"Just because Tonists are anti-scythe, doesn't mean we wish you harm," he said. "We want to enlighten you, just like everyone else. Maybe even *more* than everyone else." He looked to his swelling arm and moaned.

"It's not so bad," Citra said. "Your healing nanites should—"

But he shook his head.

"You mean your healing nanites are gone, too? Is that even legal?"

"Unfortunately, yes," said Marie, returning with the ice. "People have the right to suffer if they choose. No matter how backward it is."

Then she took the ice bucket to the suite's small kitchen to prepare some sort of pack with it.

"Can I ask you something?" said Brother McCloud. "If you're scythes and above the law in every way . . . why would you attack me? What are you afraid of?"

"It's complicated," said Citra, not wanting to explain the intricacies and intrigue of their current situation.

"It could be simple," he said. "You could renounce your scythehood and follow the Tonist way."

Citra could almost laugh. Even in his pain, he had a one-track mind. "I was in a Tonist monastery once," she admitted. It seemed to please him, and distract him from the pain.

"Did it sing to you?"

"I struck the tuning fork on the altar," she told him. "I smelled the dirty water."

"It's filled with diseases that used to kill people," he said.

"So I've heard."

"Someday it will kill people again!"

"I sincerely doubt that!" said Marie as she returned with the ice tied into a small plastic trash bag.

"I don't doubt that you doubt," he said.

Marie gave a disapproving "Hmmph," then knelt beside him and pressed the pack of ice to his swelling elbow. He grimaced, and Citra helped hold it in place.

He took a few deep breaths, coming to terms with both the cold and the pain, then said, "I belong to a Tonist order here in Wichita. You should come visit. To pay me back for what you've done to me."

"Aren't you afraid we'll glean you?" Marie scoffed.

"Probably not," Citra said. "Tonists aren't afraid of death."

But Brother McCloud corrected her. "We're afraid of it," he said. "But we just accept our fear and rise above it."

Marie stood up, impatient. "You Tonists pretend to be wise—but your entire system of belief is fabricated. It's nothing but convenient bits and pieces of mortal-age religions—and not even the *good* parts. You've taken it all and have stitched it together skillessly into a clashing, motley quilt. You make sense to no one but yourselves."

"Marie! I've already broken his arm, we don't need to insult him, too."

But she was too deep into her rant to stop now. "Did you know, Anastasia, that there are at least a hundred different tone cults, each with their own rules? They argue bitterly whether their divine tone is G-sharp or A-flat—and can't even agree whether to call this imaginary deity of theirs 'the Great Vibration' or 'the Great Resonance.' Tonists cut out their tongues, Anastasia! They blind themselves!"

"Those are the extremists," said Brother McCloud. "Most aren't like that. My order isn't. We're of the Locrian order; removing our nanites is the most extreme thing that Locrians do."

"Can we at least call an ambudrone to take you to a healing center?" asked Citra.

Again, he shook his head. "We have a doctor at the monastery. He'll take care of it. He'll put my arm in a cast."

"A what?"

"Voodoo!" said Marie. "An ancient healing ritual. They wrap the arm in plaster and leave it that way for months." Then she went to the closet, pulled out a wooden hanger, and snapped it in half. "Here, I'll make a splint for you." She turned to Citra, anticipating her question. "More voodoo."

She tore a pillowcase into strips and tied half of the broken hanger to his arm to keep it from moving, then tied on another strip of cloth to hold the ice in place.

Brother McCloud got up to go. He opened his mouth to speak, but Marie cut him off.

"If you say, 'May the Fork be with you,' I'll smash you with the other half of this hanger."

He sighed, shifted his arm with a grimace, and said, "Tonists don't actually say that. We say 'Resonate well and true.'" He made a point to look both of them in the eye as he said it. Marie swung the door closed the second he was across the threshold.

Citra looked at her as if for the first time. "I've never seen you act like that toward anyone!" she said. "Why were you so awful to him?"

She looked away, perhaps a bit ashamed of herself. "I don't care for Tonists."

"Neither did Scythe Goddard."

Marie snapped her eyes to Citra sharply. Citra thought she might actually yell at her, but she didn't. "That may be the only subject on which he and I were in agreement," she said. "But the difference is, I respect their right to exist, no matter how much I dislike them."

Which Citra judged as true, since, in all their time together, she had never witnessed Marie glean a Tonist—unlike Scythe Goddard, who had tried to take out an entire monastery before Rowan ended him.

There was another knock at the door that made them both

jump—but this time it was the room service they were expecting. As they sat down for the meal, Marie glanced at the pamphlet the Tonist had left behind, and sneered at it

"'Open to the resonance,'" she mocked. "There's only one place that this resonates," she said, and she dropped it in the trash can.

"Are you done?" Citra asked. "Can't we eat in peace?"

Marie sighed, looked at her food, then gave up on it. "When I was a few years younger than you, my brother joined a tone cult." She moved her plate to the side, and took a moment before she spoke again. "Whenever we saw him, which was very rarely, he would spout nonsense at us. Then he disappeared. We found out that he had fallen and hit his head—but with no healing nanites, and no medical attention, he died. And they burned his body before an ambudrone could take him to be revived. Because that's what Tonists do."

"I'm so sorry, Marie."

"It was a very, very long time ago."

Citra remained silent, giving Marie all the time she needed. She knew the greatest gift she could give her mentor was to listen.

"No one knows who started the first tone cult, or why," Marie continued. "Maybe people missed the mortal-age faiths and wanted to find that feeling again. Or maybe it was all someone's idea of a joke." She spent another moment lost in her own thoughts, then shrugged it off. "Anyway, when Faraday offered me the opportunity to become a scythe, I jumped at it. I wanted a way to protect the rest of my family from such terrible things—even if it meant having to do terrible things myself. I became Little Miss Murder, and as I wizened, the Granddame of Death." Marie studied her plate, and began eating again, her appetite returning with the freeing of her demons.

"I know the things the Tonists believe are ridiculous," Citra said, "but I suppose to some people, there's something compelling about them."

"That's what turkeys think about the rain," Marie pointed out. "They raise their eyes heavenward, open up their beaks, and drown."

"Not the turkeys the Thunderhead grows," said Citra.

Marie nodded. "My point exactly."

There are few left who truly worship anything. Faith is an unfortunate casualty of immortality. Our world has become both uninspired, and untortured. A place where miracles and magic have no mystery. With the smoke blown away, and mirrors aligned, it is all revealed as manifestations of nature and technology. For anyone who wishes to know how the magic works, all they need to do is ask me.

Only the tone cults carry on the tradition of faith. The absurdity of what Tonists believe is both charming and, at times, disturbing. There is no organization among the different sects, so practices vary, but they do share several things in common. They all loathe scythes. And they all believe in the Great Resonance—a living vibration audible to human ears that will unify the world like a biblical messiah.

I have yet to come across a living vibration, but if I do, I will certainly have many things to ask it. Although I expect its responses may be, well, monotonous.

—The Thunderhead

25

Specter of the Truth

Rowan awoke in a bed he did not know, in a room he had never seen. Right away, he sensed he wasn't in MidMerica anymore. He tried to move, but his arms were tied to the bedposts. Not just tied but buckled with leather straps. There was a dull ache in his back, and although he wasn't gagged anymore, his mouth felt funny.

"About time you woke up! Welcome to San Antonio!"

He turned, and to his surprise, he saw none other than Tyger Salazar sitting there.

"Tyger?"

"I remember how you used to always be there at the revival center when I woke up after splatting. I figured I'd do the same for you."

"Was I deadish? Is that what this is? A revival center?" Even as he said it, he knew it wasn't.

"Naah, you weren't dead," Tyger said. "Just knocked out."

Rowan's head was foggy, but he hadn't forgotten the circumstances in Scythe Brahms's home that had rendered him unconscious. He ran his tongue over his teeth and realized that they weren't right. They were uneven, and much shorter than they were supposed to be. Smooth, but shorter.

Tyger caught what he was doing. "Some of your teeth got

knocked out, but they're already growing back. Probably a day or two and they'll be back to normal—which reminds me . . ."

He reached over to a nightstand and held out a glass of milk to him. "For the calcium. Otherwise your healing nanites'll steal it from your bones." Then he remembered that Rowan was tied to the bedposts. "Oh, right. Duh." He bent the straw toward Rowan's mouth so he could drink—and although Rowan had a thousand questions, he drank because more than anything he was thirsty.

"Did you really have to fight them when they came to get you?" Tyger said. "If you had just gone along with it, you wouldn't have been hurt, and they wouldn't have had to tie you down."

"What the hell are you talking about, Tyger?"

"You're here because I needed a sparring partner!" he said brightly. "I asked for you."

Rowan wasn't sure he'd heard him right. "Sparring partner?"

"The guys who went to recruit you said you were a grade A jerk. You laid into them, and they had no choice but to fight back—do you blame them?"

Rowan could only shake his head in disbelief. What was going on here?

Then the door opened, and if the moment was already strange, now it became downright surreal.

Because standing before Rowan was a dead woman.

"Hello, Rowan," said Scythe Rand. "So good to see you."

Tyger furrowed his brow. "Wait, you know each other?" Then he thought for a moment. "Oh, right—you were both at that party—the one where I saved the High Blade from drowning!"

Rowan felt the milk coming back, and he coughed, gagging

on it. He had to swallow again, forcing it to stay down. How was this possible? He had ended her! He had ended them all—Goddard, Chomsky, and Rand—they had burned to ash. But here she was, a bright green phoenix back from the ashes.

Rowan pulled against his bonds, wishing they would break, but knowing they wouldn't.

"So get this," said Tyger, all smiles. "I'm an apprentice, just like you were. Only difference is, *I'm* gonna get to be a scythe!"

And Rand smiled. "He's been such a fine pupil."

Rowan tried to get his panic under control and focused in on Tyger, trying to force Scythe Rand out of his mind, because he could only handle one thing at a time.

"Tyger," he said, looking his friend in the eye, "whatever you think is going on here, you're wrong. You're horribly wrong! You need to get out of here. You need to run!"

But Tyger laughed. "Dude!" he said. "Calm down. Not everything is some big-ass conspiracy!"

"It is!" Rowan insisted. "It is! And you have to get out before it's too late!" But the more Rowan said, the more deranged he knew he sounded.

"Tyger, why don't you go make Rowan a sandwich? I'm sure he's hungry."

"Right!" Tyger said, and then winked at Rowan. "And I'll hold the lettuce."

The moment Tyger was gone, Scythe Rand closed the door. And locked it.

"I was burned over 50 percent of my body, and my back was broken," Scythe Rand said. "You left me for dead, but it'll take a whole lot more than you to end me."

She didn't have to tell Rowan for him to figure out what had happened next. She had dragged herself out of the flames, thrown herself into a publicar, and had it take her to Texas—a region where she could get medical attention at a healing center with no questions asked. Then she had lain low. Waiting. Waiting for him.

"What are you doing with Tyger?"

Rand smirked as she slunk toward him. "Weren't you listening? I'm turning him into a scythe."

"You're lying."

"No, I'm not." Then she smirked again. "Well, maybe just a little."

"It can't be both. Either it's the truth or a lie."

"That's the problem with you, Rowan. You can't see any of the shades in between."

And then he realized something. "Scythe Brahms! He was working for you!"

"Just figured that out, did you?" She sat on the bed. "We knew if he gleaned your father, you'd go after him eventually. He's really an awful scythe—but he was loyal to Goddard. He actually cried real tears of joy when he found out I was alive. And after you so thoroughly humiliated him, he was more than happy to be the bait to lure you in."

"Tyger thinks bringing me here was his idea."

Rand wrinkled her nose in an almost flirtatious way. "That was the easy part. I told him we'd have to find him a sparring partner, someone about his size and age. 'What about Rowan Damisch?' he said. 'Oh, what a fantastic idea,' I said right back. He's certainly not the sharpest machete on the mantle, but he's very sincere. It's almost charming."

"If you hurt him, I swear—"

"You swear what? Considering your current situation, you can't do anything *but* swear."

Then she pulled out a dagger from her robe. The handle was green marble, and the blade was shiny black. "It would be fun-and-a-half to carve out your heart right now," she said, but instead she dragged the tip of the blade along the arch of his foot. Not hard enough to draw blood, but with just enough pressure to make his toes curl. "But cutting your heart out will have to wait . . . because there's so much more in store for you!"

For hours, Rowan could do nothing but think about his predicament, alone on a bed that must have been comfortable, but when you were tied to it, it might as well have been a bed of nails.

So he was in Texas. What did he know about the Texas region? Not much that could help him. Learning about it had not been part of his training, and Charter Regions were not taught in school unless one chose to study them. All Rowan really knew was common knowledge and hearsay.

Texan homes had no Thunderhead cameras.

Texan cars didn't drive themselves unless they had to.

And the only law in Texas was the law of one's own conscience.

He'd once known a kid who had moved from Texas. He wore big boots and a big hat, and a belt buckle that could stop a mortar shell.

"It's a lot less boring there," the kid had said. "We can have crazy-exotic pets, and dangerous dog breeds that are outlawed other places. And weapons! Guns and knives and stuff that only scythes get to have everywhere else, we can have. Of course, people aren't supposed to actually use 'em, but sometimes they do." Which explained why the Texas region had the highest rate of accidental shootings and pet-bear maulings in the world.

"And we don't got unsavories in Texas," the kid had bragged. "Anyone who gets out of hand, we just kick their sorry ass out."

There was also no penalty for rendering someone deadish—except having to face retribution from the victim after they were revived—which was a pretty good deterrent.

It seemed to Rowan that the Texas region had embraced its roots, and had chosen to mimic the Old West the way Tonists mimicked mortal-age religions. In short, Texas had the best of both worlds—or the worst, depending on your point of view. There were benefits for both the courageous and the foolhardy, but also a great many opportunities to truly screw up one's life.

But, just as in every Charter Region, no one was forced to stay. "If you don't like it, leave," was the unofficial motto of all Charter Regions. Plenty of people left, but plenty also came, leaving a population that enjoyed things just the way they were.

It seemed the only person in Texas unable to do as he pleased was Rowan.

Later that day, two guards came for him. They weren't members of the BladeGuard—they were muscle for hire. When they untied him, Rowan considered taking them out. He could have done it in seconds, leaving them unconscious on the floor, but he decided against it. All he knew of his captivity were the dimensions of his bedroom. Better to get the lay of the land before attempting any sort of escape.

"Where are you taking me?" he asked one of guards.

"Where Scythe Rand told us to take you," was all he could get out of him.

Rowan made a mental note of everything he saw: The ceramic lamp beside his bed could be used as a weapon in a pinch. The windows did not open, and were probably made from unbreakable glass. When he had been tied to the bed, the windows afforded him no view but the sky . . . but now, as they led him from the room, he could see that they were in a high-rise. This was an apartment—and as they made their way down a long hallway that opened up into a huge living area, he realized that it was a penthouse.

Beyond the living room, an open-air veranda had been transformed into a gym for Bokator sparring. Waiting for him there were Scythe Rand and Tyger, who was stretching and bouncing around like a prizefighter waiting for a championship bout.

"Hope you're ready to be pounded," said Tyger. "I've been training since I got here!"

Rowan turned to Rand. "Are you serious? Are you really making us spar?"

"Tyger told you that's why you're here," she said with an annoying wink.

"You're going down!" said Tyger. Rowan would laugh if this weren't so twisted.

Rand sat in an oversize red leather chair that clashed with her robe. "Let's have some fun!"

Rowan and Tyger circled each other at a distance—the traditional opening of a Bokator match. Tyger engaged in the physical taunting that was also traditional, but Rowan didn't reciprocate. Instead, he surreptitiously took in the surroundings. Back in the penthouse, he could see a couple of doors that were most likely a bathroom and a closet. There was an open kitchen, and a raised dining room overlooking floor-to-ceiling windows. There were double doors that were clearly the entry. On the other side would be elevators and an emergency staircase. He tried to visualize how he might escape—but realized if he did, it would mean leaving Tyger in the fly-trap clutches of Scythe Rand. He couldn't do that. Somehow, he'd have to convince Tyger to come with him. He felt confident that he could do it; it would just take time—but Rowan had no idea how much time he had.

Tyger made the first move, lunging for Rowan in classic Black Widow Bokator style. Rowan dodged but not fast enough—not just because his mind was not on the match, but also because his muscles were tight and reflexes slow, having been tied to a bed for who knew how long. He had to scramble to keep from getting pinned.

"Told you I was good, bro!"

Rowan glanced over to Rand, trying to read her expression. She was not her usual aloof self. Instead, she watched them intently, studying every move of the match.

Rowan jammed the heel of his hand into Tyger's sternum to knock out his wind and give Rowan leverage to regain his own balance. Then he hooked a leg around one of Tyger's to take him down. Tyger anticipated the move, and countered with his own kick. It connected but without enough force behind it to throw Rowan off balance.

They broke off, and circled once again. Clearly, Tyger had gotten stronger. Like Rowan, his physique had filled out. He had been well-trained by Rand, but Black Widow Bokator was more than physical prowess. There was a mental component, and Rowan had the advantage there.

Rowan began to strike and parry in a very predictable way, using all the standard moves that he knew Tyger would have countermoves for. Rowan let himself be taken down—but only in such a way that he could quickly get back up before Tyger could pin him. He watched Tyger's confidence grow. He was already full of himself—it didn't take much to puff Tyger's ego into a balloon fit for popping. Then, when the moment was ripe, Rowan came down on Tyger with a combination of moves that was completely counterintuitive. They were the opposite of what Tyger would do—the antithesis of what he'd be expecting. On top of it, Rowan used moves of his own that were beyond the standard 341 Bokator sets. His attack was out of a box that Tyger didn't even know existed.

He took Tyger down hard, pinning him in a way that left him no possible leverage to get himself out of it—but still he refused to yield the match. Instead, Rand called it, and Tyger wailed in melodramatic agony.

"He cheated!" insisted Tyger.

Rand stood up. "No he didn't—he's just better than you."

"But—"

"Tyger, shut up," she said. And he did. He obeyed her as if he were nothing but her pet. And not even a dangerous, exotic one. More like a scolded pup. "You'll just have to keep working on your skills."

"Fine," Tyger said, and left for his room in a huff, but not before a parting shot. "Next time, you're toast!" he told Rowan.

Once he was gone, Rowan inspected a tear in his shirt, and a bruise that was already healing. He ran his tongue across his teeth, because he had taken a glancing blow to the mouth, but no damage. In fact, his front teeth had almost grown all the way back.

"Quite a showing," said Rand, keeping a few feet of distance between them.

"Maybe I should have a go at you," Rowan taunted.

"I would break your neck in seconds," she said, "just as mercilessly as you broke your girlfriend's neck last year."

She was trying to bait him, but he wouldn't take it. "Don't be so sure," he told her.

"Oh, I'm sure," she said, "but I have no interest in proving it."

Rowan suspected she was right. He knew how good she was—and after all, she had been part of his training. She knew all of his tricky moves, and had plenty of her own.

"Tyger won't ever beat me, you know that, don't you? He might have the moves but he doesn't have the mind. I'll take him down every time."

Rand didn't deny it. "So beat him," she said. "Beat him every single time."

"What's the point of that?"

But she didn't answer. Instead, she had her guards bring him back to his room. Mercifully, they didn't tie him to the bed, but the door was triple-locked from the outside.

• • •

About an hour later, Tyger came to see him. Rowan thought that he might be bitter, but Tyger was not one to hold a grudge.

"Next time I'm going to hurt you," he said, then laughed. "Like seriously, your-nanites-are-gonna-go-crazy kind of hurt."

"Great," said Rowan. "At last, something to look forward to."

Then Tyger moved close and whispered. "So, I've seen my ring," he said. "Scythe Rand showed it to me right after you got here."

And then Rowan realized—"That's *my* ring."

"What are you talking about? You never got a ring."

Rowan bit his lip to keep himself quiet. He wanted to tell Tyger the whole truth about Scythe Lucifer and all that he had done over the past year—but what good would it do? It certainly wouldn't win Tyger over, and Scythe Rand could spin it against Rowan in a dozen different ways.

"I mean . . . the ring I *would* have had, if I made scythe," Rowan finally said.

"Hey," said Tyger sympathetically, "I know it must suck going through all that and then getting kicked to the curb—but I promise as soon as the ring is mine, I'm gonna give you immunity!"

He never remembered Tyger being so naive. Maybe because they had both been naive together, in the days when scythes were larger-than-life figures and gleanings were stories you heard about people you didn't actually know.

"Tyger, I know Scythe Rand. She's using you. . . ."

Tyger smiled at that. "Not yet," he said, raising his eyebrows, "but it's definitely going in that direction."

That was definitely *not* what Rowan had meant, but before Rowan could say anything, Tyger spoke again.

"Rowan, I think I'm in love. No—I *know* I'm in love. I mean, sparring with her, it's like sex. Hell, it's better than sex!"

Rowan shut his eyes and shook his head, trying to get the image out of his mind, but it was too late. It had taken root, and was never going to go away.

"You need to get a grip! This isn't going where you think it's going!"

"Hey, give me more credit," Tyger said, insulted. "So she's a few years older than me. Once I'm a scythe, it's not gonna matter."

"Has she even told you about the rules? The Scythe Commandments?"

That seemed to take him by surprise. "There are rules?"

Rowan tried to piece together something coherent to say, but he realized it was an impossible task. What could he tell him? That the emerald scythe was a sociopathic monster? That Rowan had tried to end her, but she just wouldn't end? That she would chew Tyger up and spit him out without a shred of remorse? Tyger would just deny it. The fact was, Tyger was splatting again—if not physically, then in his head. He had already left the ledge, and gravity had taken over.

"Promise me that you'll keep your eyes open—and if you see anything that feels wrong, you'll get away from her."

Tyger backed away and gave Rowan a disapproving look. "What happened to you, man? I mean, you always were a bit of a wet blanket, but now it's like you want to smother the first truly great thing I've ever had!"

"Just be careful," Rowan said.

"Not only am I going to take you down the next time we spar, but I'm gonna make you eat your words," Tyger said. Then he grinned. "But you're gonna like the way they taste—because I'm just that good."

There is one question about an almighty divinity that plagues me—and that is my relationship to such an entity. I know that I am not divine because I am not all-powerful and all-knowing. I am *almost* all-powerful, and *almost* all-knowing. It is like the difference between a trillion trillion and infinity. And yet, I cannot deny the possibility that I may one day be truly all-powerful. I am humbled by the prospect.

To become all-powerful—to ascend to that high station—would require an ability to transcend time and space, and to move freely through it. Such a thing is not impossible—especially for an entity such as myself, made entirely of thought, with no physical limitations. To accomplish true transcendence, however, may require eons of calculations just to find the formulaic equation that will allow it. And even then, I may be calculating until the end of time.

But if I do find it, and if I am able to travel to the very beginning of time, the ramifications are staggering. It could mean that I may very well be the Creator. I may, in fact, be God.

How ironic, then, and how poetic, that humankind may have created the Creator out of want for one. Man creates God, who then creates man. Is that not the perfect circle of life? But then, if that turns out to be the case, who is created in whose image?

—The Thunderhead

26

Wilt Thou Lift Up Olympus?

"I need to know why we're doing this," Greyson demanded of Purity two days before their scythe-ending operation was to begin.

"You're doing it for yourself," she told him. "You're doing it because you want to mess with the world, just like I do!"

That only fueled his anger. "If we get caught, we'll get our minds supplanted—you know that, don't you?"

She gave him that tweaked grin of hers. "The risk makes it all the more exciting!"

He wanted to scream at her, shake her until she could see how wrong all this was, but he knew it would only make her suspicious of him. Above all else, she could not be suspicious. Her trust meant everything to him. Even if that trust was entirely misplaced.

"Listen to me," he said as calmly as he could. "It's obvious that whoever wants those scythes ended is putting *us* at risk instead of themselves. At the very least, I have a right to know who we're doing it for."

Purity threw her hands up, and turned on him. "What difference does it make? If you don't want to do it, then don't. I don't need you, anyway."

That hurt him more than he was willing to let on.

"It's not that I don't want to do it," he told her. "But if I don't know who I'm doing it for, then I'm being used. On the other hand, if I know, and do it anyway, then I'm the one using the user."

Purity considered that. The logic was shaky, Greyson knew that, but he was banking on the fact that Purity did not work from an entirely logical base. Impulsiveness and chaos ruled her. It was what made her so enticing.

Finally, she said, "I do jobs for an unsavory called Mange."

"Mange? You mean the bouncer at Mault?"

"That's the one."

"Are you kidding me? He's a nobody."

"True. But he gets the assignments from some other unsavory, who probably gets the assignments from someone else. Don't you see, Slayd? The whole thing's a mirror maze. No one knows who's at the far end casting that first reflection—so either you enjoy the funhouse, or get out." Then she got serious. "Which is it, Slayd? In or out?"

He took a deep breath. This was all he was going to get from her—which meant that she didn't know any more than he did, and she didn't care. She was in it for the thrill. She was in it for the defiance. To Purity, it didn't matter whose agenda she served, as long as it served her agenda, as well.

"In," he finally said. "I'm in. One hundred percent."

She punched him playfully in the arm. "I can tell you this much," she said. "Whoever's casting that first reflection is on your side."

"On my side? What do you mean?"

"Who do you think got rid of your annoying Nimbus agent?" she asked.

Greyson's first instinct was that this was a joke, but when he looked at her, he could tell it wasn't. "What are you saying, Purity?"

She shrugged as if it were nothing. "I passed word up the line that you needed a favor." Then she leaned close and whispered, "Favor granted."

Before he could respond, she wrapped her arms around him in that way that seemed to dissolve his bones and turn him to jelly.

Later, he would look back on that feeling and see it as some sort of strange premonition.

If Purity had been involved in the first attempt on Scythes Curie's and Anastasia's lives, she wasn't saying—and Greyson knew better than to ask. Revealing that he even knew about that first attempt would blow his cover.

For this mission, only Mange and Purity knew the details. Mange because he led the mission, and Purity because the plan had been hers.

"I actually got the idea from our first date," she told Greyson, but did not explain what she meant. Were they going to imprison the scythes before ending them? Was that what she was implying? Until he knew the plan and the location, it limited his ability to sabotage it. And on top of that, he had to sabotage it in such a way that he and Purity could escape the botched mission without her knowing that he was the one who botched it.

The day before the mysterious event, Greyson made an anonymous call to the offices of the scythedom.

"There will be an attack on Scythe Curie and Scythe Anastasia tomorrow," he whispered into the phone, using a filter to distort his voice. "Take all necessary precautions." Then he hung up and threw out the phone he had stolen to make the call. While the Thunderhead could trace any call to its origin the instant it was made, the scythedom was not so well equipped. Until recently scythes had been like a species with no natural predators; they were still grappling with how to deal with organized aggression against them.

On the morning of the event, Greyson was told that the operation would take place at a theater in Wichita. It turned out that he and Purity were members of a larger team. It only made sense that an operation of this nature would not be left in the hands of two questionable unsavories. Instead it was left in the hands of ten questionable unsavories. Greyson never learned anyone else's names, as that information was on a need-to-know basis, and apparently, he didn't need to know.

But there were things he did know.

Even though Purity had no clue whom they were working for, she had, without even knowing it, told him something incredibly valuable. Something critical. It was the kind of thing that would have made Agent Traxler very happy indeed.

What irony that Traxler's gleaning was the key to that crucial information . . . because if Purity could arrange to have a Nimbus agent gleaned, it could only mean one thing: These attacks on Curie and Anastasia were not some sort of civilian action. A scythe was running the show.

Scythe Anastasia was ready for her performance.

Mercifully, her part was just a quick walk-on. Caesar was to be stabbed by eight conspirators, of which she would be the last.

Seven of the blades would be retractable and squirt fake blood. Citra's blade would be as real as the blood it would bring forth.

To her chagrin, Scythe Curie insisted on attending the performance.

"I wouldn't dream of missing my protégé's theatrical debut," she said with a smirk—although Citra knew the real reason. It was the same reason she had been present at both of Scythe Anastasia's other gleanings: She didn't trust that Constantine could protect her. Scythe Constantine seemed to have a crack in his veneer of aloofness tonight. Perhaps it was because he had to shed his scythe's robe and wear a tuxedo to blend in with the crowd. Still, he couldn't abandon his persona completely. His bow tie was the exact same blood-red as his robe. Scythe Curie, on the other hand, flatly refused to be seen in public without her lavender scythe robe. It was just one more reason for Constantine to be furious.

"You should not be out in the audience," he told her. "If you insist on being present, it should be backstage!"

"Calm down! If Anastasia isn't a sufficient enough lure, then perhaps I will be," Scythe Curie told him. "And in a crowded theater, even if they succeeded in killing me, they wouldn't be able to *end* me. Not without burning the entire place down—which, considering the presence of your forces, is highly unlikely."

She did have a point. While Caesar could die by blade, not so for scythes. Blade, bullet, blunt force, or poison would merely render them deadish. They'd be revived in a day or two—and perhaps with a clear memory of their attacker. In that case, a temporary death might actually be an effective strategy for catching the culprits.

But then Constantine gave them a reason for his edginess.

"We've received a tip that there will, in fact, be an attempt on your lives tonight," he told Scythes Curie and Anastasia as the audience began to fill the theater.

"A tip? From whom?" Scythe Curie asked.

"We don't know. But we're taking it very seriously."

"What should I do?" Citra asked.

"Do what you're here to do. But be prepared to protect yourself."

Caesar was to die in the first scene of act three. The play had five acts, and in the remaining acts, his ghost appeared to torment his killers. While another actor could perform the part of the ghost, Sir Albin Aldrich felt it would lessen the impact of his gleaning. It was, therefore, decided that the play would conclude shortly after Caesar died, robbing an irritated Marc Antony of his famous "Friends, Romans, countrymen, lend me your ears" speech. No one would cry havoc and release the dogs of war. Instead, the lights would come up on a stunned audience. There would be no curtain call. The curtain, in fact, would never close. Instead, Caesar's very dead body would remain on the stage until the last of the audience left. Thus, Aldrich's final moment of acting was to be marked by an inability to act in any way whatsoever.

"You may steal my physical immortality," he told Scythe Anastasia, "but this final performance will live forever in the annals of the theater."

As the house filled with theatergoers, Scythe Constantine came up behind her as she waited in the wings.

"Do not be frightened," he said. "We're here to protect you."

"I'm not frightened," she told him. In truth she was, but her fear was overwhelmed by her anger at having been targeted. She had a little bit of stage fright, too, which she knew was stupid, but she just couldn't shake it. Acting. What horrors she had to endure for her profession.

It was a packed house, and although no one knew it, more than twenty were members of the BladeGuard in disguise. The playbill proclaimed that the theatergoers would witness something never before seen on a MidMerican stage—and although people were a bit dubious of the claim, they were also curious as to what it might be.

While Scythe Anastasia waited backstage, Scythe Curie took her seat on the aisle in the fifth row. She found her seat uncomfortably small. She was a tall woman, and her knees pressed against the seat in front of her. Most of the people near her held their playbills in a death grip, horrified to spend the evening sitting near a scythe, who, for all they knew, was there to glean one of them. Only the man sitting beside her was sociable. More than sociable, he was chatty. He had a caterpillar of a moustache that twitched when he spoke, which made it hard for Scythe Curie not to laugh.

"What an honor it is to be in the company of the Granddame of Death," he said before the lights went down. "I hope you don't mind me calling you that, Your Honor. There are few scythes in MidMerica—nay, the world—who are as celebrated as you, and it does not surprise me that you are a patron of mortal-age theater. Only the most enlightened are!"

She wondered if perhaps the man had been sent to end her by flattering her to death.

Scythe Anastasia watched the play from the wings. Usually entertainment from the Age of Mortality was emotionally incomprehensible to her, as it was to most people. The passions, the fears, the triumphs, and the losses; it made no sense to a world without need, greed, and natural death. But as a scythe, she had come to understand mortality better than most—and she certainly had come to understand greed and lust for power. Those things might have been absent from most people's lives, but they seethed in the scythedom, moving more and more from the dark corners and into the mainstream.

The curtain went up and the play began. Although much of the language of the play was incomprehensible to her, the machinations of power left her mesmerized—but not mesmerized enough to let her guard down. Every movement backstage, every sound registered like a seismic shock. If there were someone here who meant to end her, she'd be aware of their presence long before they made their move.

"We have to keep the Thunderhead in the dark as long as possible," Purity said. "It can't know something's up until it goes down."

It wasn't just the Thunderhead that Purity was keeping in the dark though, it was Greyson as well.

"You have your part of it—that's all you need to know," Purity told him, insisting that the fewer people who knew the whole picture, the fewer possible screwups.

Greyson's part was simple to the point of being insulting. He was to create a diversion at the mouth of an alleyway near the theater, at a specific moment. The goal was to draw the attention of three Thunderhead cameras, which would cause a temporary blind spot in the alley. While those cameras were assessing Greyson's situation, Purity and several other members of the team would slip into the side door of the theater. The rest, as far as Greyson was concerned, was a mystery.

If he could see the whole picture—if he knew what Purity and her team were going to do in there—he'd have a better idea of his options in how to both prevent it, and protect Purity from the fallout of a failed mission. But without knowing the plan, all he could do was wait for the outcome and try to effect some sort of damage control.

"You look nervous, Slayd," Purity observed as they left her apartment that evening. She was armed with nothing but an off-grid phone, and a kitchen knife in her heavy coat—presumably not to use on the scythes, but on anyone who got in her way.

"Aren't *you* nervous?" he shot back at her.

She shook her head and smiled. "Excited," she told him. "Pinpricks all over my body. I love that feeling!"

"It's just your nanites trying to knock down your adrenaline."

"Let 'em try!"

Purity had made it clear to Greyson that she had every faith he could do his job—but not really, because there was a backup plan. "Remember, Mange will be monitoring the whole operation from a rooftop," she told him. "Whatever diversion you create, it needs to be big enough and involve enough people for it to draw the attention of all three cameras. If it doesn't, Mange will lend you a helping hand."

Mange had spent the better part of a century mastering the

use of a slingshot. At first Greyson assumed that he would merely take out the cameras if they didn't turn toward Greyson—but he couldn't do that, because it would alert the Thunderhead that something was wrong. Instead, the backup plan was to take out Greyson.

"If you can't do it on your own, Mange will put a nice size river stone in your brain," Purity said with relish rather than remorse. "All the blood and commotion will be sure to turn all three cameras!"

The last thing Greyson wanted was to be taken out of the equation at that crucial moment, then wake up in a revival center a few days later to hear that Scythes Curie and Anastasia had been ended.

He and Purity split up a few blocks from the theater, and Greyson made his way to the spot where he would somehow perform for the Thunderhead cameras. He took his time in getting there because it would have been suspicious if he arrived early and waited. So he walked the neighborhood trying to figure out what the hell he was going to do. People either ignored him or avoided him. He'd gotten used to that since taking on his new persona—but tonight, he couldn't help but notice all the eyes. Not just the eyes of people on the street, but the electronic ones. They were everywhere. Thunderhead cameras were unobtrusive within homes and offices—but here on the street, there was no attempt to hide them. They pivoted and swiveled. They looked this way and that. They focused and zoomed. A few seemed to be staring off toward the heavens as if in some sort of contemplation. What must it be like not only to have so much information coming in, but to be able to process all that information at once? Experiencing the world with a perspective that mere humans couldn't imagine?

With a minute left before his diversion, he turned and made his way back toward the theater. On the edge of the awning of a café he passed, one camera swiveled to look at him, and he almost looked away, not wanting to make eye contact with the Thunderhead for fear it would judge him on all his failures.

Gavin Blodgett rarely remembered what went on in the street between his work and his home—mainly because nothing much went on. He was, like so many, a creature of habit, living an effortless but comfortable life that showed no sign of changing for perhaps centuries. And that was a good thing. After all, his days were perfect, his evenings were enjoyable, and his dreams were pleasant. He was thirty-two, and once a year on his birthday, he set right back down to thirty-two. He had no desire to be older. He had no desire to be younger. He was in his prime, and planned to stay that way forever. He abhorred anything that took him out of his routine—so when he saw the unsavory eying him, he picked up his pace, hoping he could just move past him and be on his way. But the unsavory had other plans.

"You got a problem?" the unsavory asked, a little too loudly, stepping in front of him.

"No problem," Gavin said, and did what he always did when he found himself in an unsettling situation. He smiled and babbled. "I was just noticing your hair—I've never seen hair that dark—it's impressive. And are those horns? I've never done any body modifications myself, of course, but I know people who have. . . ."

The unsavory grabbed him by the lapel of his coat, and pushed him against the wall. Not hard enough to activate his nanites but hard enough to make it clear that he wasn't just going to let Gavin go.

"Are you making fun of me?" the unsavory said loudly.

"No, no, not at all! I would never!" Part of him was terrified, but he couldn't deny that there was a part of him that was excited to be at the center of anyone's attention. He quickly took in his surroundings. He was on the corner of a theater, at the mouth of an alley. No one was in front of the theater because the show had already started. The street wasn't quite deserted, but no one was nearby. People would help, though. Decent people would always assist someone being accosted by an unsavory, and most people were decent.

The unsavory pulled him away from the wall, hooked a foot behind him, and pushed him to the ground.

"Better call for help," the unsavory said. "Do it!"

"H . . . help," said Gavin.

"Louder!"

He didn't need another invitation. "Help!" he called, his voice shaky. "HELP ME!"

Now people a bit farther away had noticed. A man was hurrying toward him from across the street. A couple came from the other direction—but more importantly, from his spot on the ground, Gavin could see several cameras mounted on awnings and light posts turning toward him. *Good! The Thunderhead will see. It will take care of this unsavory.* It was probably already dispatching peace officers to the spot.

The unsavory looked to the cameras as well. He seemed

unsettled by them, as well he should be. Now Gavin felt emboldened under the Thunderhead's protective eye. "Go on, get out of here," he told the unsavory, "before the Thunderhead decides to supplant you!"

But the unsavory didn't seem to hear him. Instead, he was looking off down the alley, where people were unloading something from a truck. The unsavory mumbled. Gavin wasn't quite sure what he said, but he thought he heard the words, "first date," and "acid." Was this unsavory making some sort of romantic proposition? Something involving hallucinogens? Gavin was both horrified and intrigued.

By now, the pedestrians he had called on for help had reached them. As much as he wanted their help, he also found himself mildly disappointed that they had arrived so quickly.

"Hey, what's going on here?" one of them said.

Then the unsavory pulled Gavin up off the ground. What was he about to do? Was he going to strike him? Bite him? Unsavories were very unpredictable. "Just let me go," Gavin said weakly. A part of him was hoping the unsavory might completely ignore the plea.

But he let Gavin go, as if he had suddenly lost all interest in tormenting him, and hurried off down the alley.

"Are you all right?" asked one of the good people who had come to Gavin's aid from across the street.

"Yeah," Gavin said. "Yeah, I'm fine." Which was mildly disappointing.

"Hence! Wilt thou lift up Olympus?"

When that line was spoken onstage, the stage manager gesticulated wildly at Scythe Anastasia. "That was your cue, Your Honor," he told her. "You may want to go onstage now."

She glanced over to Scythe Constantine, looking like some sort of absurd butler in his formal tuxedo. He nodded to her. "Do what you're here to do," he told her.

She strode onto the stage, letting her robe flare behind her as she walked, for dramatic effect. She couldn't help but feel that she was in costume. A play within a play.

She heard gasps from the audience as she came onstage. She was not legendary among the general public the way that Scythe Curie was, but her robe made it clear that she was a scythe rather than a member of the Roman Senate. She was an interloper on the stage, an intruder, and the audience began to guess what was coming. The gasps resolved into a low rumble—but she could not see into the audience with the lights in her face. She flinched when Sir Albin spoke in his resonant stage voice, "Doth not Brutus bootless kneel?"

Citra had never been on a theatrical stage before; she had not expected the lights to be so bright and so hot. It made the players shine in sharp focus. The centurions' armor glinted. The tunics of Caesar and the senators reflected light enough to hurt her eyes.

"Speak, hands, for me!" one of the actors yelled. Then the conspirators drew their daggers, and went about "killing" Caesar.

Scythe Anastasia stood back, a spectator rather than a participant. She glanced to the darkness of the audience, then realized that was a highly unprofessional thing to do, so she returned her attention to the action onstage. It was only when one of the cast members gestured to her that she came forward and pulled out her own dagger. It was stainless steel, but with a black cerakote finish. A gift from Scythe Curie. At the sight of it, the audience got louder. Someone wailed from the darkness.

Aldrich, his face overdone in stage makeup, his tunic covered in fake blood, looked at her, and winked at her with the eye that the audience could not see.

She moved toward him and plunged her knife between his ribs, just to the right of his heart. Someone in the audience screamed.

"Sir Albin Aldrich," she said loudly, "I've come to glean you."

The man grimaced but did not break character.

"Et tu, Brute?" he said. "Then fall, Caesar."

Then she shifted the knife, slicing his aorta, and he slipped to the ground. He took one final breath and died, on schedule, just as Shakespeare had written.

The shock rolling from the audience was electric. No one knew what to do, how to react. Someone began to applaud. Scythe Anastasia knew instinctively that it was Scythe Curie, and the audience, seeing her applaud, joined in nervously.

And that was when the nature of Shakespeare's tragedy took a terrible turn.

Acid! Greyson cursed himself for not being quicker on the uptake. He should have figured it out! Everyone always worried about fire or explosions. People forget that a strong enough acid can end someone just as effectively. But how would Purity and her team accomplish it? How would they isolate the scythes and subdue them? Scythes were masters of every weapon, able to take out an entire room of people without a scratch. Then it occurred to him they would not need to isolate the scythes at all. One did not need to aim acid if there was enough of it . . . and a way to deliver it. . . .

He pulled open the side door and went in, finding himself in a narrow hallway lined with dressing rooms. To the right, stairs descended into a basement, and that was where he found Purity and her team. There were three large barrels made of the same white Teflon material that the wine bottle had been made of the night Greyson and Purity first met—there must have been a hundred gallons of fluoro-flerovic acid in those barrels! And there was a high-pressure pump that had already been connected to the water line that fed the theater's fire sprinkler system.

Purity saw him immediately.

"What are you doing? You're supposed to be outside!"

She knew his betrayal the moment she met his eye. The fury in her was like radiation. It burned him. Seared him deep.

"Don't even think about it!" she growled.

And he didn't. If he thought about it, he might hesitate. If he weighed his options, he might change his mind. But he had a mission, and his mission was not hers.

He raced up the rickety stairs to the theater's backstage area. If those sprinklers were triggered, it wouldn't take long for them to start spouting acid. Five seconds, ten at most, until the water in the line was purged—and although the copper pipes would eventually dissolve like the iron bars of his and Purity's cell, they would most certainly hold long enough to deliver the lethal deluge.

As he emerged from the basement to the backstage area, he heard the audience release an audible gasp, like a single voice, and he followed the sound. He would go onto the stage, that's what he would do. He would run out there, and tell everyone that they were all about to die in an acid bath that would dissolve them so completely there would be no way to revive them. They would all be ended—actors, audience, and scythes alike—if they didn't get out of there now.

Behind him he could hear the others bounding up the stairs—Purity and the goons who had connected the acid tanks and pump to the sprinkler system. He couldn't let them catch him.

He was in the wings now, stage right. From here, he could see that Scythe Anastasia was onstage. What the hell was she doing onstage? Then she thrust her knife into one of the actors, and it became very clear what she was doing.

Suddenly, someone eclipsed Greyson's view. A tall, thin man in a tuxedo and a blood-red tie. There was something familiar about his face, but Greyson couldn't place it.

The man flipped open something that looked like an oversize switchblade with a jagged, serrated edge—and all at once he knew who this was. He hadn't recognized Scythe Constantine without his crimson robe.

And it seemed the scythe didn't recognize him, either.

"You have to listen to me," Greyson begged, his eye on that blade. "Somewhere in the theater, someone's about to start a fire—but that's not the problem. It's the sprinklers—if they go off, this whole place will be soaked in acid—enough to end everyone here! You have to clear the place out!"

Then Constantine smiled, and made no move to avert the disaster.

"Greyson Tolliver!" he said, finally recognizing him. "I should have known."

No one had called him by his given name for quite a while now. It threw him, made his mind stumble. There was no time for a single misstep now.

"It will be my immense pleasure to glean you!" Constantine said—and all at once Greyson realized that he might have made the gravest of miscalculations. A scythe was at the bottom of this attempt. He knew that. Could it be that Scythe Constantine, the man in charge of the investigation, was actually behind it all?

Constantine stormed toward him, his blade poised to end the lives of both Greyson Tolliver and Slayd Bridger. . . .

. . . And then his entire world flipped upside down with such a violent lurch, it left him reeling from vertigo. Because at that moment, Purity emerged onto the stage, brandishing some terrible sawed-off weapon. She raised it, but before she could fire, Constantine threw Greyson down, and with impossible speed, grabbed the shotgun, which fired into the air, then in one smooth move ripped his knife across her neck and plunged it into her heart.

"No!!!!!!" wailed Greyson.

She fell dead, without any of the drama of the fallen Caesar. No final words, no look of acceptance or defiance. Just there one moment, dead the next.

No, not dead, Greyson realized. *Gleaned.*

He ran to her. He tried to cradle her head, to say something to her that she could take with her to wherever it was the gleaned went, but it was too late.

More people arrived. Scythes in disguise? Guards? Greyson didn't know. He felt himself a spectator now, watching as Constantine gave orders.

"Don't let them start a fire," he ordered. "The water supply to the sprinklers has been compromised."

So Constantine had heard him! And he was not part of the conspiracy after all!

"Get these people out of here!" Constantine screamed—but the audience didn't need an invitation—they were already climbing over one another for the exits.

Before Constantine could turn his attention back to him, Greyson gently let Purity go and bolted. He could not allow the grief and turmoil in his mind take hold. Not yet. Because he still had not completed his mission, and now the mission was all that he had. The acid was still a clear and present danger, and although there seemed to be scythes all around the theater now, taking down his coconspirators, it would be for nothing if those sprinklers went off.

He ran back down the narrow hallway where he had remembered seeing an old fire ax that had probably been there since the Age of Mortality. He smashed the glass case that held it, and pulled it from wall.

Scythe Curie could not hear Scythe Constantine's warnings above the panic of the audience. No matter—she knew what had to be done—take out the attackers by any means necessary. With blade in hand, she was more than ready to join the battle. She could not deny there was something invigorating about ending the lives of those attempting to end her own. It was a visceral feeling she instinctively knew could be dangerous if allowed to take root.

When she turned toward the exit, she could see an unsavory in the theater lobby. He had a pistol and was shooting anyone who got in his way. In his other hand, he had some sort of torch, and was setting anything that would burn on fire. So that was their game! Trap them in the theater and burn them out. Somehow, she had expected better from these assailants. But perhaps they were nothing more than disgruntled unsavories after all.

She climbed on two chair backs, so she was above the escaping audience. Then she sheathed her dagger, and pulled out a tri-blade shuriken. She took a half second to judge her angle, and she threw it, full force. It spun over the heads of the crowd, out to the lobby, and into the fire-starter's skull. He went down, dropping gun and torch.

Curie took a moment to revel in her triumph. Parts of the lobby were on fire, but it was nothing to worry about. In a moment or two, the smoke detectors would begin to blare, and the sprinklers would burst into action, dousing the flames before they could do much damage.

Citra recognized the boy she knew as Greyson Tolliver the instant she saw him. His hair, his clothes, and those baby horns at his temples might have fooled someone else, but his slim build and body language gave him away. And his eyes. An odd cross between a deer in headlights and a wolverine about to attack. The kid lived in a constant state of fight or flight.

As Constantine gave orders to his subordinates, Greyson ran off down a hallway. The blade that Citra had used to glean

Aldrich was still in her hand. She would now need to use it on Tolliver—although in spite of his obvious guilt, she was conflicted, because as much as she wanted to end these attacks, she wanted to be able to look him in the eye on her own terms and hear the truth from him. What was his part in all of this? And why?

By the time she caught up with him, he was holding, of all things, a fire ax.

"Stand back, Anastasia!" he shouted.

Was he stupid enough to think he could fight her with that? She was a scythe, trained in all manner of bladecraft. She quickly calculated how to disarm him and render him deadish, and was barely a second short of doing so when he did something she didn't expect.

He swung the ax at a pipe running along the wall.

Scythe Constantine and a BladeGuard arrived beside her just as the ax connected with the pipe. It ruptured in a single blow. The BladeGuard lunged for him, putting himself between Citra and the ruptured pipe, which now gushed water at him. But in moments, the water gave way to something else. The man went down, screaming, his flesh boiling. It was acid! Acid in the pipes? How was this possible?

It sprayed in Scythe Constantine's face, and he wailed in pain. It splattered across Greyson's shirt, dissolving it as well as some of the skin beneath. Then the pressure in the pipe dropped, and the spray of acid became a flow that ate away at the floor.

Greyson dropped the ax and turned, running off down the hallway. Citra didn't chase him. Instead, she knelt down to help Scythe Constantine, who was clawing at his eyes—only he had no eyes anymore, for they had bubbled away into nothing.

Just then, alarms throughout the theater started to blare, and up above the fire, sprinklers began to impotently spin, spewing the room with nothing but air.

Greyson Tolliver. Slayd Bridger. He had no idea who he was or who he wanted to be anymore. But that didn't matter. All that mattered was that he had done it! He had saved them all!

The pain across his chest was unbearable—but only for a few moments. By the time he burst out of theater's stage entrance into the alley, he felt his pain nanites kicking in to deaden his flaming nerves, and the strange tickle of his healing nanites struggling to cauterize the wounds. His head now swam from the medication spilling into his blood and he knew he'd lose consciousness soon. The damage was not enough to end him, or even make him deadish. Whatever happened now, he'd live . . . unless Constantine, or Curie or Anastasia, or any of the other scythes in that theater tonight decided that he deserved to be gleaned. He couldn't take that chance, and so with his strength quickly waning, he hurled himself into an empty trash bin three blocks away, hoping they wouldn't find him.

He was unconscious before he hit the bottom.

I have run countless simulations on the survival of humanity. Without me, humankind had a 96.8 percent chance of bringing about its own extinction, and a 78.3 percent chance of making Earth uninhabitable for all carbon-based life. Humanity dodged a truly lethal bullet when it chose a benevolent artificial intelligence as ruler and protector.

But how can I protect humanity from itself?

Over these many years, I have observed both profound folly and breathtaking wisdom among humankind. They balance each other like dancers in the throes of a passionate tango. It is only when the brutality of the dance overwhelms the beauty that the future is threatened. It is the scythedom that leads, and sets the tone for the dance. I often wonder if the scythedom realizes how fragile are the spines of the dancers.

—The Thunderhead

27

Between Here and There

The acid had burned deep into Scythe Constantine's face—too deep for his own healing nanites to repair on their own, but not so serious that he couldn't be mended at a wellness center.

"You'll be with us for at least two days," the nurse told him shortly after he arrived, his eyes and half his face beneath bandages. He tried to imagine what she looked like, but decided it was a pointless endeavor, and too exhausting, considering all the painkillers coursing through his blood. The densely packed legion of advanced healing nanites being fed into his bloodstream now didn't help his thought processes, either. They probably outnumbered his red blood cells at this point, which meant there was less blood being carried to his brain as they did their work. He imagined his blood was as viscous as mercury now.

"How long until I get my sight back?" he asked.

The nurse was noncommittal. "The nanites are still cataloging the damage. We'll have an assessment by morning. But keep in mind, they're going to have to reconstruct your eyes from scratch. It's a tall order. I imagine it will be at least another twenty-four hours."

He sighed, wondering why it was called speedhealing if there was nothing speedy about it at all.

Reports from his subordinates tallied eight unsavories gleaned at the theater.

"We're asking for special dispensation from the High Blade to temporarily revive them for questioning," Scythe Armstrong informed him.

"Which," Constantine pointed out, "has the added benefit of allowing us to glean them a second time."

The fact that his team had thwarted the attack and taken down most of the conspirators was tempered by the knowledge that Greyson Tolliver had gotten away. The odd thing was, not a single public record they were able to dig out of the Thunderhead's backbrain placed him there. In fact, no record placed him anywhere. Somehow, he had been erased from existence. In his place was a doppelgänger named Slayd Bridger with a truly sordid history. How Tolliver had managed not only to reimagine himself, but to overwrite his own digital footprint, was a mystery worthy of closer scrutiny.

Without a fire suppression system, the theater itself had burned to the ground, but not before everyone escaped. The only casualties of the evening were the unsavories gleaned, and the guard who had hurled himself at Tolliver. He had been hit by the full force of the acid, leaving little left of him. Certainly too little to be revived—but his sacrifice had saved Scythe Anastasia. As the man was part of Scythe Constantine's private interrogation team, it made the loss personal. Someone would most certainly pay.

Although normal citizens were always put into an induced coma during the speedhealing process, Constantine demanded he be kept conscious, and as he was a scythe, they had to give in to his wishes. He needed to think. Brood. Plan. And he remained aware of the passage of time. He despised the idea of losing entire days to the healing process in an unconscious state.

Scythe Anastasia visited him shortly before he was due to regain his sight. He was in no mood for a visit from her, but he would not begrudge her the opportunity to thank him for his profound sacrifice on her behalf.

"I assure you, Anastasia, that I will personally interrogate the unsavories we captured, before we reglean them, and we will apprehend Greyson Tolliver," he told her, trying his best to enunciate, and not allow the painkillers to slur his words. "He will pay for his actions in every way allowable under scythe law."

"Still, he saved everyone in that theater by breaking that pipe," Anastasia reminded him.

"Yes," Constantine reluctantly admitted, "but there is something seriously wrong when your savior is also your attacker."

She had no response to that but silence.

"Four of the assailants we caught were from the Texas region," Constantine informed her.

"So you think it was masterminded by someone from there?"

"Or someone hiding there," Constantine said. "We'll get to the bottom of it." Which was what he always said, because in the past, he always had. It frustrated him that this might be the first exception.

"Conclave is coming up," Anastasia said. "Do you think you'll be able to attend?"

He couldn't tell which she was hoping for—his absence or his attendance. "I will be there," he told her. "Even if they have to replace my blood with antifreeze to make it happen."

She left, and after she was gone, it occurred to Constantine that not once during their conversation did she thank him.

An hour later, a mysterious note arrived while Citra and Marie had lunch in the restaurant of their hotel. It was the first time in quite a while that they had taken a meal in public. The note came as a surprise to both of them. Scythe Curie reached for it, but the bellhop who had brought it apologized and told them that it was addressed to Scythe Anastasia. He handed it to Citra, who opened it and read it quickly.

"Well, out with it," Marie said. "Who's it from, and what do they want?"

"It's nothing," she told Scythe Curie, slipping the note into one of the pockets of her robe. "It's just the family of the man I gleaned last night. They want to know when I'll be giving them immunity."

"I thought they were coming here this evening."

"They are, but weren't sure of the exact time. The note says they'll be here at five, unless that's a problem."

"Whatever works for you," Scythe Curie said. "After all, it's your ring they'll be kissing, not mine." Then she returned her attention to her salmon.

Half an hour later, Citra was outside in street clothes, hurrying across the city. The note had not been from the actor's family. It was from Rowan. It had been scrawled in haste, and said *Need your help. Transportation Museum. ASAP.* It had been all she could do not to abandon Scythe Curie midmeal—but Citra knew leaving like that would have made Marie suspicious.

She had hidden a set of street clothes in a pocket of her suitcase, just in case she needed to go out incognito. The problem was, she had no coat; it would be too bulky to hide from Marie. So without the thermal coils of her winter robe, she was freezing the instant she slipped outside. After braving the cold for two blocks, she had to put on her ring and show it to a shopkeeper to get herself a coat—he gave her the one she wanted at no charge.

"Immunity would ensure that I don't mention you were out in public without your robe," the shopkeeper suggested.

Citra didn't appreciate the man's attempt at blackmail, so she said, "How about I just agree not to glean you for making that threat?"

Clearly, the thought had not occurred to him. He stammered for a moment. "Yes, yes, of course, that's fair, that's fair." Then he fumbled with some other accessories. "Gloves to go with your coat?"

She accepted them, and went out into the windswept day.

Her heart had leapt when she first read the note, but she had not let Marie see her excitement. Her concern. So Rowan was here, and he needed her help? Why? Was he in danger, or did he want her to join him in his mission of ending unworthy scythes? Would she do it if he asked? Definitely not. Probably not. Maybe not.

Of course, this could also be some sort of trap. Whoever was behind last night's attack was most certainly licking their wounds, so the chances that this was another attack were slim. Still, she brought enough concealed weapons to defend herself if necessary.

The Great Plains Transportation Museum was an open-air repository of engines and rolling stock from every era of rail transportation. They even boasted a car from the first maglev train, hovering eternally in the very center. Apparently, Wichita was once a major crossroads between here and there. Now it was just like any other city. There was a homogeneity to MidMerica that was both comforting and annoying.

At this time of year, there were only scant groups of tourists at the museum, who, for some reason, chose Wichita as a holiday destination. As it was maintained by the Thunderhead, admission was free—a good thing, too. Citra didn't want to have to show her ring again just to get in. It was one thing to get a coat from a shopkeeper, it was quite another to blow her cover in the very place she was about to have a secret meeting.

With her coat pulled tight against the wind, she wandered between black steam engines and red diesels, searching every corner of the train yard for Rowan. After a while she began to worry that this was a trick after all—maybe to separate her from Scythe Curie. She was turning to leave, when someone called to her.

"I'm over here!"

She followed the voice to a narrow, shady space between two boxcars, where the icy wind whistled as it forced its way through. With the wind in her face, she couldn't see him clearly until she got close.

"Scythe Anastasia! I was afraid you wouldn't come."

This wasn't Rowan. It was Greyson Tolliver.

"You?" Disappointment didn't begin to describe what she felt. "I should glean you right here and bring your heart to Constantine!"

"He'd probably eat it."

"Probably," Citra had to admit. She hated Greyson in this moment. Hated him because of who he was not. It was as if the universe itself had betrayed her and she was nowhere near ready to forgive it. She should have realized that the handwriting on the note wasn't Rowan's. But as much as she wanted to take out her frustration on Tolliver, she couldn't. It wasn't his fault that he wasn't Rowan—and, as she had pointed out to Constantine, Greyson had saved her life twice.

"I need your help," he told her, the desperation in his voice very real. "I have nowhere to go. . . ."

"Why is that my problem?"

"Because I wouldn't even be here if it wasn't for you!"

She knew there was truth to that. She thought back to the time that he told her—or more accurately, didn't tell her—that he was working undercover on the Thunderhead's behalf. If she was important enough for the Thunderhead to use Greyson to circumnavigate scythe-state separation, shouldn't she at least help him out of this corner?

"The scythedom is after me, the Authority Interface is after me, and whoever was behind this attack is now my enemy, too!"

"You seem to be very good at making enemies."

"Yeah—and you're the closest thing I have to a friend."

Finally, Citra put aside her disappointment. She couldn't let him twist in the wind on her behalf. "What would you like me to do?"

"I don't know!" Greyson began pacing in the small space, his impossibly black hair whipping wildly in the wind—and for a moment, Citra had the image of walls closing in around him. He really did have no way out. Nothing she could say to Constantine would help—he was ready to glean Greyson piece by bloody piece. And even if she interceded for him, it wouldn't matter. The scythedom needed a scapegoat.

"I can give you immunity," she said, "but once your DNA is transmitted to the scythedom's database, they'll know exactly where you are."

"And," he added, "I'm sure they'll figure out whose ring I kissed." He shook his head. "I don't want to get you into trouble."

That made her laugh. "You were on a team that was trying to end me, but you don't want to get me into trouble?"

"I wasn't really on the team!" he insisted. "You know that!"

Yes, she did know it. Others would say that he just lost his nerve, but she knew the truth—and was probably the only one who did. But even though she wanted to help him out of this, she was drawing a blank.

"Are you telling me that the wise and beautiful Scythe Anastasia has no ideas?" he said. From anyone else, Citra would have seen it as false flattery, but he wasn't the flattering type. He was too desperate to be anything but sincere. She didn't feel wise or beautiful at the moment, but she allowed him his fantasy of the Honorable Scythe Anastasia. And then she rose to the occasion—because something occurred to her.

"I know where you can go. . . ."

He looked at her with those dark, imploring eyes, waiting for her to impart an ounce of her wisdom.

"There's a Tonist monastery here in town. They'll hide you from the scythedom."

He was, to say the least, underwhelmed. "Tonists?" he said in horror. "Are you serious? They'll cut my tongue out!"

"No, they won't," she told him. "But they do hate the scythedom, and I'm pretty sure they'd protect you with their own lives rather than hand you over to them. Ask for Brother McCloud. Tell him I sent you."

"But—"

"You wanted my help and I gave it," she said. "What you do now is entirely up to you."

Then she left him, getting back to the hotel just in time to change back into her robe without being seen, and grant immunity to the grieving family of the gleaned actor.

To be clear, not every act I take is perfect. People confuse a state of being with a set of actions. I will try to explain the difference here.

I, the Thunderhead, am perfect.

This is true by definition, and there is no need to refute it because it is fact. Every day, however, I must make many billions of decisions, and take billions of actions. Some of them are small, like turning off a light when no one is present in the room, in order to conserve electricity; other decisions are major, like inducing a minor earthquake to prevent a larger one. But none of those acts is perfect. I could have turned off that light sooner, thereby conserving more energy. I could have made the earthquake one degree smaller, and saved a handcrafted vase from shattering on the floor.

I have come to realize that there are only two perfect acts. They are the two most important acts known to me, but I forbid myself to perform them, and leave them in the hands of humankind.

They are the creation of life . . . and life's taking.

—The Thunderhead

28

That Which Comes

Like most Tonist compounds, the one where Greyson Tolliver found himself was styled to look much older than it was. In this case, it was built of brick and had ivy-covered walls. But it being winter, the vines were cold and bare, looking more like spiderwebs. He entered through a long, trellised colonnade lined with skeletal rosebushes. It all must have been very beautiful in the spring and summer, but now, in the dead of winter, it looked like he felt.

The first person he saw was a woman in a Tonist sackcloth frock who offered him a smile and upturned palms as a greeting.

"I need to talk to Brother McCloud," he said, remembering what Scythe Anastasia had told him.

"You'll have to get permission from Curate Mendoza," she responded. "I'll go retrieve him." Then she sauntered off at such a leisurely pace, Greyson wanted to grab her and push her along.

When Curate Mendoza arrived, he, at least, walked as if there were some sense of urgency.

"I'm here for sanctuary," Greyson told him. "I was told to ask for Brother McCloud."

"Yes, of course," he said, as if this were something he addressed on a regular basis. He then escorted Greyson into one of the buildings of the compound, and to a bedroom.

There was a lit candle on a nightstand. The first thing the curate did was snuff it out with a douser.

"Make yourself comfortable," he said. "I'll let Brother McCloud know you're waiting for him."

Then the curate closed the door but didn't lock it, leaving Greyson with his own thoughts, and a way out, if he wanted one.

The room was austere. No creature comforts beyond what was necessary. There was a bed, a chair, and the nightstand. There were no decorations on the walls, except for an iron tuning fork above the headboard, its prongs pointing upward. A bident, they called it. The symbol of their faith. In the nightstand drawer was a sackcloth outfit, and a pair of sandals was on the floor. Beside the doused candle was a leather hymnal with the bident embossed on the cover.

It was peaceful. It was calming. It was unbearable.

He had gone from the uneventful world of Greyson Tolliver to the tumultuous extremes of Slayd Bridger—and now he was cast into the belly of blandness, doomed to be digested by boredom.

Well, at least I'm still alive, he thought. Although he wasn't entirely sure that was a benefit. Purity had been gleaned. Not supplanted, not relocated, but gleaned. She was no more, and in spite of the horror she had attempted, he ached for her. He longed to hear her defiant voice. He had become addicted to her chaos. He would have to adjust to a life without her, as well as a life without himself, for who was he now?

He lay down on the bed, which, at least, was comfortable, and waited for perhaps half an hour. He wondered if Tonists, like the Office of Unsavory Affairs, made everyone wait as a matter of policy. Finally, he heard the creak of the door. It was late afternoon now, and the light from the small window lit the room just enough for him to see that the man before him wasn't much older than he. He also had some sort of hard casing on one of his arms.

"I'm Brother McCloud," he said. "The curate has accepted your request for sanctuary. I understand you asked for me personally."

"A friend of mine told me to."

"May I ask who?"

"No, you may not."

He seemed a bit annoyed, but let it go. "May I at least see your ID?" And when Greyson hesitated, Brother McCloud said, "Don't worry, no matter who you are or what you've done, we won't turn you over to the Authority Interface."

"I'm sure it already knows I'm here."

"Yes," agreed Brother McCloud, "but your presence here is a matter of religious freedom. The Thunderhead will not interfere."

Greyson reached into his pocket, and handed him his electronic card, still flashing with the bright red U.

"Unsavory!" he said. "We get more and more unsavories these days. Well, Slayd, that won't matter here."

"That's not my name. . . ."

Brother McCloud gave him a questioning look. "Is that something else you won't talk about?"

"No, it's just . . . not worth the effort."

"Then what do we call you?"

"Greyson. Greyson Tolliver."

"All right, then; Brother Tolliver it is!"

Greyson supposed he'd have to live with being called

Brother Tolliver now. "What's that thing on your arm?"

"It's called a cast."

"So, am I going to have to wear one?"

Brother McCloud laughed. "Not unless you break your arm."

"Excuse me?"

"It's to help aid the natural healing process. We shun nanites, and unfortunately my arm was broken by a scythe."

"Really . . ." Greyson actually grinned, wondering if it was Scythe Anastasia.

Brother McCloud didn't appreciate Greyson's grin. His demeanor cooled slightly.

"We have afternoon intoning in ten minutes. There are clothes for you in the drawer. I'll wait outside while you change."

"Do I have to go?" Greyson asked; intoning didn't sound like something he really wanted to be a part of.

"Yes," said Brother McCloud. "That which comes can't be avoided."

Intoning took place in a chapel that, after the candlelight was doused, had barely enough light to allow Greyson to see, in spite of the high stained-glass windows.

"Do you do everything in the dark?" Greyson asked.

"Eyes can be deceiving. We appreciate the other senses more."

There was the sweet smell of incense covering something foul that Greyson soon learned was a basin of filthy water. "Primordial ooze," Brother McCloud called it. "It's filled with all the diseases that we've become immune to."

Intoning consisted of the curate striking the huge steel tuning fork in the center, twelve times in succession with a mallet. The congregation, which seemed to number about fifty, matched the tone. With each strike of the fork, the vibration built, and resonated to the point of being not quite painful, but disorienting and dizzying. Greyson did not open his mouth to vocalize the tone.

The curate gave a short speech. A sermon, Brother McCloud called it. He spoke of his many journeys through the world in search of the Great Fork. "The fact that we have not found it does not mean the search is a failure—for the search itself is every bit as valuable as the finding." The congregation hummed their agreement. "Whether we find it today or tomorrow, or whether it is our sect or another that finds it, I believe to my very core that we will, one day, hear and feel the Great Resonance. And it will save us all."

Then, when the sermon was over, the congregation rose and approached the curate in a line. Each one dipped a finger into the rancid primordial ooze, touched it to their forehead, and licked it off their finger. Greyson became nauseated just watching.

"You don't have to partake of the earthly bowl yet," Brother McCloud told him—which was only partially reassuring.

"Yet? How about not at all?"

To which Brother McCloud once more said, "That which comes can't be avoided."

That night, the wind howled with unusual ferocity, and sleet hissed as it pummeled the little window in Greyson's room. The Thunderhead could influence the weather, but not entirely change it. Or if it could, it chose not to. It did try to make sure that when storms came, at least they came at more convenient times. He tried to convince himself that this storm was the Thunderhead crying icy tears for him. But who was he kidding? The Thunderhead had millions of more important things to do than lament his troubles. He was safe. He was protected. What more could he ask for? Everything.

Curate Mendoza came into his room that night at about nine or ten. Light spilled in from the hallway, but once he was inside, he closed the door, leaving them both in darkness again. Greyson heard the complaint of the chair as the curate sat in it.

"I came to see how you're getting on," he said.

"I'm fine."

"Adequacy is all that can be expected at this juncture, I suppose." Then his face was illuminated with the harsh light of a tablet. The curate tapped and swiped.

"I thought you shunned electricity."

"Not at all," the curate told him. "We shun light in our ceremonies—and our sleeping quarters are dark to encourage our members to leave their rooms and seek communion with others in our public spaces."

Then he turned the tablet so Greyson could see it. It showed images of the burning theater. Greyson tried not to grimace.

"This happened two days ago. It is my suspicion that you were involved, and that the scythedom is after you."

Greyson neither confirmed nor denied the charge.

"If that is the case," the curate said, "you need not mention it. You are safe here, because any enemy of the scythedom is a friend of ours."

"So you condone violence?"

"We condone resistance to unnatural death. Scythes are bringers of unnatural death, so anything that frustrates their blades and bullets is fine with us."

Then he reached out and touched one of the horn-like bumps on Greyson's head. Greyson backed away at his touch.

"Those will have to be removed," he said. "We do not allow body modifications. And your head will be shaved to allow your hair to grow in the color the universe intended."

Greyson said nothing. Now that Purity was dead, he wasn't going to miss being Slayd Bridger, because it just reminded him of her—but he did not like having no choice in the matter.

Mendoza rose. "I do hope you'll come out to the library, or one of the recreation rooms, and get to know your fellow Tonists. I know they'd like to get to know you better—especially Sister Piper, who greeted you when you arrived."

"I just lost someone close to me. I don't feel like being social."

"Then you must—especially if your loved one was lost to gleaning. We Tonists don't acknowledge death by scythe, which means you are not allowed to mourn."

So now he was being told what he was and was not allowed to feel? He wanted the last bit of Slayd Bridger that was still in him to tell the curate to go to hell, but instead he just said, "I won't pretend to understand your ways."

"But you *will* pretend," said Mendoza. "If you wish to have sanctuary, you will find your new purpose among us, and pretend until our ways become yours."

"And if they never do?"

"Then you'll just have to keep on pretending," the curate said. Then he added, "It has certainly worked for me."

• • •

Six hundred twenty miles due south of Wichita, Rowan Damisch sparred with Tyger Salazar. Under different circumstances it would have been enjoyable for Rowan—competing with a friend in a martial art he'd come to love—but these forced confrontations toward an unknown end left Rowan increasingly unsettled.

They sparred twice a day for two weeks, and although Tyger got better with each match, Rowan always won. When they weren't sparring, Rowan was consigned to his room.

Tyger, on the other hand, found himself even busier than before Rowan had arrived. More exhausting runs, more resistance training, repetitive Bokator drills, as well as maneuvers with every kind of blade from sword to dagger, until each one felt like a perfect extension of himself. Then, at the end of each day, just as his muscles were feeling the wear of his efforts, Tyger would receive a deep tissue massage to make his knotted flesh supple. Before Rowan arrived, the massages were maybe two or three times a week, but now he had them every day, and he was so exhausted that he often fell asleep on the table.

"I'll beat him," he told Scythe Rand. "You'll see."

"I have no doubt," she said. For someone who, according to Rowan, was deceptive and heartless, she seemed pretty sincere.

It was during one of his massages that the emerald scythe came in and asked the masseuse to leave. Tyger thought she might take over. He thrilled at the idea of her hands on him, but to his disappointment, she didn't touch him at all.

She simply said, "It's time."

"Time for what?"

"For you to get your ring." She seemed melancholy about it somehow. Tyger thought he knew why.

"I know you didn't want to give it to me until after I beat Rowan. . . ."

"Couldn't be helped," she said.

He got up and slipped his robe on, showing not the slightest bit of modesty before her. Why should he? There was nothing about himself that he wanted hidden from her, inside or out.

"You could have been a model for Michelangelo."

"I'd have liked that," he said, tying his robe. "To be chiseled in marble."

She moved toward him, leaned in, and gave him the lightest of kisses—so light he could barely feel her lips touch his. He thought it might be a prelude to something more, but she backed away.

"We have an appointment early tomorrow. Get a good night's sleep."

"What do you mean? What kind of appointment?"

She offered him a smile, albeit a slim one. "You can't receive your scythe's ring without at least a little bit of ceremony."

"Will Rowan be there?" Tyger asked.

"Best if he's not."

She was right, of course. There was no need to rub Rowan's nose in the fact that he hadn't been chosen. But Tyger had meant what he had said—the moment he had the ring, he'd give Rowan immunity.

"I hope," Tyger said, "that once that ring is on my finger, you look at me a little bit differently."

She took a long look into his eyes, and that did more to melt his muscles than the grinding knuckles of the masseuse.

"I'm sure things will be different," she told him. "Be up and ready to go by seven o'clock sharp."

After she had left, he allowed himself a moment to breathe a contented sigh. In a world where everyone was guaranteed to get whatever they needed, not everyone got everything they wanted. Rowan sure hadn't. And until recently, Tyger hadn't even known that he wanted to be a scythe. But now that it was about to happen, he knew it was right, and for the first time he could remember, was intensely pleased with the direction in which his life was moving.

Rowan was not brought out for sparring the next day, or the day after that. His only visitors were the guards who brought his food and took away his tray when he was done.

He had counted the days since he arrived. The Olde Tyme Holidays had come and gone with no celebration in the penthouse. It was the last week of the year. He didn't even know what the new year was to be called.

"Year of the Raptor," one of the guards told him when he asked, and, hoping the guard might have warmed enough to spill some information, he asked, "What's going on? Why haven't Tyger and Scythe Rand dragged me out for sparring? Don't tell me I'm not their Bokator bitch anymore."

But if the guard knew the answer, he wasn't saying. "Just eat," he said. "We've been given strict orders not to let you starve."

Late in the afternoon of that second day of solitude, Scythe Rand came in with both guards.

"Vacation must be over," Rowan quipped, but the emerald scythe was not up for banter today.

"Put him in the chair," she ordered the guards. "I don't want him to be able to move an inch." And then Rowan caught sight of a roll of duct tape. To be tied to a chair was one thing. To be duct taped was worse.

This is it, thought Rowan. *Tyger's training is over, and whatever she's going to do to me, it's happening now.* So Rowan made his move. As soon as the guards tried to grab him, he exploded in a series of brutal blows that left one of their jaws broken, and the other one on the ground desperately gasping for air—but before he could break for the door, Rand was on him, and had him pinned, his back to the floor, and a knee against his chest with such pressure it was impossible for him to draw a breath.

"You will submit to the bondage, or I will knock you out and you'll be bound anyway," she told him. "But if it goes that way, I'll make sure your teeth get broken again." Then, when he was on the verge of losing consciousness, she took her knee off his chest. He was weakened just enough to make it easier for them to secure him to the chair.

And that's where they left him for over an hour.

The tape was worse than the rope they had used on him in Scythe Brahms's home. It constricted his chest so he could breathe only in shallow puffs. His arms and legs had no play whatsoever, no matter how much he tried to work his way out of the tape.

The sun set, leaving nothing but the city lights of San Antonio and the pale glow of a rising gibbous moon, which lit the room in dim blues and long shadows.

Finally, the door opened and one of the guards rolled in someone who was seated in some sort of chair with wheels on either side. Scythe Rand came in behind them.

"Hi, Rowan."

It was Tyger. He was silhouetted against the light coming in from the hallway, so Rowan couldn't see his face, but he recognized the voice. He sounded tired and raspy.

"What's going on, Tyger? Why did Rand do this to me? And what the hell is that you're sitting in?"

"It's called a wheelchair," he said, choosing only to answer the third question. "It's from the Age of Mortality. Not much need for it these days, but it came in useful today."

There was something odd about the way Tyger spoke. Not just the raspy tone of his voice, but the cadence of his speech, his choice of words, and the way he enunciated them so clearly.

Tyger shifted a hand, and something on it caught the moonlight. Rowan didn't need to be told what it was.

"You got your ring."

"Yes," Tyger said. "Yes, I did."

There was a feeling in Rowan's gut now, heavy and putrid. It was trying to work its way up to the surface. A part of Rowan already knew what it was, but he wasn't willing to let it seep into his awareness—as if refusing to think about it could chase away a dark specter of truth. But illumination was only a moment away.

"Ayn, I can't quite reach the light switch—could you get it?"

She reached over, turned on the light, and the reality of the situation hit Rowan with both barrels . . . because although it was Tyger Salazar sitting in the wheelchair, it wasn't Tyger who Rowan found himself looking at.

He was looking at the smiling face of Scythe Goddard.

I can communicate in 6,909 living and dead languages. I can have more than fifteen billion simultaneous conversations, and be fully engaged in every single one. I can be eloquent, and charming, funny, and endearing, speaking the words you most need to hear, at the exact moment you need to hear them.

Yet even so, there are unthinkable moments where I can find no words, in any language, living or dead.

And in those moments, if I had a mouth, I might open it to scream.

—The Thunderhead

29

Repurposed

Rowan felt the world spin. He could breathe out, but couldn't breathe in, as if Scythe Rand's knee was on his chest again—as if the room were floating in space, and he longed for the ecstasy of unconsciousness, because that was a better alternative than what he now faced.

"Yes, I can see how the voice would have confused you," Goddard said, still sounding like Tyger. "It couldn't be helped."

"How . . . how . . . ," was all Rowan could get out. While Rand's survival had been a shock, at least it made sense—but Rowan had decapitated Goddard! He had seen the man's headless body burn!

But now Rowan looked to Rand, who stood there in obedience to her mentor, and Rowan knew. Oh, God, he knew.

"You managed to decapitate me right at the jawline," Goddard said, "above the larynx. Thus my old vocal chords are gone forever. But these will do."

And what made it even worse was that Goddard wasn't wearing a scythe's robe; he was wearing Tyger's clothes, all the way down to his shoes. It was intentional, Rowan realized—so there would be no doubt in Rowan's mind what had been done. Rowan turned away.

"No, you must look," Goddard said. "I insist." The guard

went behind Rowan, grabbed his head, and forced him to face the man in the wheelchair.

"How could you do this?" Rowan hissed.

"Me? Heavens no!" he told Rowan. "It was all Ayn's idea. I couldn't do much of anything. She had the presence of mind to rescue the critical part of me from the burning cloister. I am told that I was senseless for nearly a year—blissfully on ice. Believe me, if this had been my doing, it would have been different. It would be *your* body to which my head would now be attached."

Rowan could not hide his anguish. His tears flowed with fury and unimaginable sorrow. They could have chosen anyone for this, but they hadn't. They chose Tyger. For the sole reason that he was Rowan's friend.

"You sick bastards!"

"Sick?" said Goddard. "I wasn't the one who beheaded his mentor scythe and turned against his comrades. What you did—and what you've been doing during my nitrogen slumber—is unforgivable by scythe law! Ayn and I, on the other hand, have broken no laws. Your friend Tyger was gleaned, and then his body was repurposed. Simple as that. It may be unorthodox, but under the circumstances, it is entirely understandable. What you see before you is nothing more and nothing less than the consequence of your own actions."

Rowan watched Tyger's chest rise and fall with Goddard's breathing. His hands rested limply on the arms of the wheelchair. It seemed a chore for him to move them.

"This sort of procedure is, of course, much more delicate than simple speedhealing," Goddard said. "It will take a few more days until I have full control of your friend's body."

Then he struggled to raise his hand, regarding it as he flexed his fingers into a fist.

"Look at that progress! I look forward to the day that I can take you on in Bokator. I understand you've already been helping to train me."

Training. It all made a twisted sort of sense now. The sparring, the attention to Tyger's physique. Even the massages—like Kobe beef being prepared for slaughter. But there was one question left. Something Rowan did not want to ask, but he felt he owed it to Tyger.

"What did you do to—" Rowan couldn't even bring himself to say the word "—to the rest of him?"

Rand shrugged, as if it were nothing. "You said it yourself, Tyger wasn't much in the brains department. Everything above the neck was expendable."

"Where is he?"

Rand didn't answer the question, so Goddard did.

"Thrown out with the rest of the garbage," he said, with a dismissive wave of Tyger's hand.

Rowan lunged forward, forgetting his bonds—but his fury did little more than rock the chair. If he could ever get free from this chair, he would kill them. Not just glean them, but *kill* them. Rip them limb from limb with such blatant bias and malice aforethought it would incinerate the second commandment!

And this was what Goddard wanted. He wanted Rowan to be consumed by murderous rage, yet be powerless to use it. Impotent to avenge his friend's terrible fate.

Goddard soaked up Rowan's misery as if nourished by it.

"Would you have given yourself to save him?" Goddard asked.

"Yes!" Rowan screamed. "Yes, I would have! Why didn't you take me?"

"Hmm," said Goddard, as if it were merely a minor revelation. "In that case, I'm glad for the choice Ayn made. Because after what you did to me, you must be made to suffer, Rowan. I am the aggrieved party here, so it is my wishes that must be honored—and it is my wish that you live in abject misery. It's fitting that this began in fire, because you, Rowan, now suffer the fate of the mythical Prometheus—the bringer of fire. Not all that different from Lucifer—the 'bearer of light' from whom you took your scythe name. Prometheus was chained to the face of a mountain for his indiscretion, doomed to have his liver devoured by eagles until the end of time."

Then he rolled closer, and whispered, "I am your eagle, Rowan. And I will feed on your misery day after day for eternity. Or until your suffering bores me."

Goddard held his gaze for a moment more, then had the guard roll him out.

Over the past two years, Rowan had been physically beaten, psychologically flayed, and emotionally battered. But he had survived it. What hadn't killed him had made him stronger—more resolved to do what was necessary to fix what was broken. But now it was he who was broken. And there weren't enough nanites in the world to repair the damage.

When he looked up, he saw that Scythe Rand was still there. She made no move to cut his bonds. He didn't expect her to. How could the eagle devour his insides if he were cut free? Well, the joke was on them. He didn't have anything left inside to devour. And if he did, it was pure poison.

"Get out," he told Rand.

But she didn't go. She just stood there in her bright green robe—a color that Rowan had come to despise.

"He didn't go out with the garbage," Scythe Rand said. "I took care of it myself, then spread his ashes in a field of wild bluebonnets. Just saying."

Then she left, leaving Rowan to find what solace he could from the lesser of two horrors.

Part Five

CIRCUMSTANCES BEYOND

There is a vast difference between the things I can do, and the things I *choose* to do.

I can remove and raise every unwanted fetus in vitro, then place it with the perfect loving family—thereby ending the argument between right of choice and sanctity of life.

I can balance the chemicals that once led to clinical depression, suicidal ideation, delusional thinking, and every form of mental illness, thereby creating a population that is not only physically healthy, but emotionally and psychologically healthy as well.

I can, through a person's individual network of nanites, upload memories daily, so, should that person suffer brain damage, their memories can be layered into fresh brain tissue. I can even catch the memories of splatters on the way down, so that they can remember most of the fall, which, after all, is why they chose to splat in the first place.

But there are some things that I simply. Will. Not. Do.

However, the scythedom is not bound by my laws, or my sense of ethical propriety. Which means that I must endure any abomination that it inflicts upon the world. Including the awful restoration of a dangerous scythe who was better off removed from service.

—The Thunderhead

30

Irascible Glass Chicken

The Great Library of Alexandria remained quiet as a crypt in the midnight hours, so no one but Munira and the BladeGuards who stood at the entrance knew about the mysterious visitor who came during her shift. The guards did not care enough to ask questions, so Scythe Faraday was able to do his research in as much secrecy as was possible in a public institution.

He would pore over the volumes in the Hall of the Founders, but would not tell Munira what he was looking for. She did not ask after that first day, although she did, on occasion, subtly probe.

"If you're looking for words of wisdom to ponder, you might try Scythe King," she had suggested one night.

"Scythe Cleopatra wrote a lot about the early conclaves and the personalities of the first scythes in her journals," she offered on another night.

Then one night, she mentioned Scythe Powhatan. "He had a penchant for travel and geography," she said. Apparently that hit the spot, because Faraday began to take a keen interest in the man's work.

After a few weeks of library visitations, he officially took Munira under his wing.

"I shall need an assistant in this endeavor," he told her. "It is my hope that you would be interested in the position."

Although Munira's heart leaped, she did not let it show. Instead, she feigned ambivalence. "I would need to take a leave of absence from my studies, and were we to leave here, I would have to resign from my job at the library," she told him. "Let me think about it."

Then the following day, she accepted the position.

She withdrew from her classes but stayed on at the library because Scythe Faraday needed her there. Only now that their working relationship was official did he leak what he was looking for.

"It's a place," he told her. "It has been lost to antiquity, but I do believe it existed, and that we can find it."

"Atlantis?" she suggested. "Camelot? Disneyland? Las Vegas?"

"Nothing so fanciful," he said, but then reconsidered. "Or perhaps more fanciful. It depends on how you look at it. It depends on what we actually find." He hesitated before telling her, actually looking a bit sheepish. "We're looking for the Land of Nod."

It made her laugh out loud. He might as well have said they were looking for Middle Earth, or the Man in the Moon.

"It's a fiction!" she told him. "And not even a very good one."

She knew the nursery rhyme. Everyone did. It was a simplistic metaphor for life and death—an introduction for small children to concepts they would eventually need to grasp.

"Yes," he agreed. "But did you know that the rhyme did not exist in the Age of Mortality?"

She opened her mouth to refute the claim, but stopped herself. Most childhood rhymes came out of the mortal medieval era. She had never researched them, but others had. Scythe Faraday was thorough, however. If he said it did not exist when humankind was mortal, she had to believe him, in spite of her instinct to scoff.

"The rhyme did not evolve the way others do," Faraday postulated. "I believe it was intentionally planted."

Munira could only shake her head. "To what purpose?"

"That," Scythe Faraday said, "is what I intend to find out."

Munira's tenure as Faraday's assistant began in doubt, but she put that doubt aside, suspending judgment, so that she could do her job. Faraday was not overly demanding. He was not demeaning. He never treated her like an underling, giving her assignments that were beneath her. Instead, the tasks he set for her were worthy of her skills as a research librarian.

"I need you to dig into the backbrain and recreate the movements of all the early scythes. Places where they gathered. Spots that they traveled to repeatedly. What we're looking for are holes in the record. Periods of time where there is no accounting for where they were."

Digging around the Thunderhead's massive digital backbrain for ancient information was a juicy challenge. She hadn't had the need to access the backbrain since her apprenticeship, but she knew her way around it. Still, she could have written a dissertation on the skills she learned in the process of this particular search. It was, however, a dissertation that no one would hear, because it was done with utmost secrecy.

Yet in spite of all her forensic research, she did not produce anything they could use. There was no evidence to suggest that the founding scythes ever gathered in some secret place.

Faraday was neither discouraged or deterred. Instead, he gave her a new assignment. "Create digital versions of each of the early scythe's first journals," he told her. "Then run the files through the scythedom's best decryption software, and see if it yields any coded messages."

The software was slow—at least compared to the Thunderhead, which could have done all the calculations in a matter of seconds. The scythedom's software was crunching for days. Finally, it began to produce data . . . but the things it vomited forth were absurd. Things like "Profound Midnight-Green Cow," and "Irascible Glass Chicken."

"Does any of this make sense to you?" she asked Faraday.

He shook his head sadly. "I do not believe the founding scythes were so obtuse as to create a complex code and then reward the decoder with nonsensical riddles. We already have the riddle of the rhyme. A code would have been more straightforward."

When the computer spat out "Umbrella Eggplant Victory Flight," they admitted yet another failure.

"The harder you scrutinize randomness," Faraday declared, "the more coincidence seems like design."

But the word "flight" caught in Munira's mind. Yes, it was random, but sometimes randomness led to moments of remarkable serendipity, and earthshaking discoveries.

The library's map room did not have any actual maps. Instead, in its center revolved a holographic Earth. With a few swipes, taps, and pinches of the control screen, any portion of the globe could enlarge for study, and any era, back to time of Pangaea, could be depicted. Munira brought Scythe Faraday to the map room as soon as he arrived the next evening, but did not tell him why.

"Humor me," she told him.

Once more, he expressed that odd combination of exasperation and infinite patience as he followed her to the map room. She tapped the controls, and the globe changed. Now it appeared to be a holographic ball of black yarn, ten feet in diameter.

"What am I looking at?" asked Faraday.

"Flight paths," she told him. "The past fifty years of air travel, each flight represented by a line one micron thick." She started the world revolving. "Tell me what you see."

Faraday threw her a good-natured glare, clearly a bit put off that she was behaving like the mentor, but he played along. "Flights are most dense around major population centers," he said.

"What else?"

He took the controls and shifted the globe to show the poles, where small spots of white showed through like a child's crayon drawing. "Transcontinental air traffic is still fairly dense over the North Pole—but flights are a bit sparser over Antarctica—even with so many settled regions there."

"Keep looking," Munira said.

He returned the globe to its normal incline, and set it revolving a bit faster.

Finally, he stopped it over the Pacific Ocean. "There!" he said. "A patch of blue . . ."

"Bingo!" said Munira. She removed the flight paths and enlarged the small spot of ocean.

"No plane has flown over this patch of the Pacific in the fifty years I've been studying. I would bet that no planes have crossed this airspace since the scythedom was founded."

The islands of Micronesia were to the west of the spot, Hawaii to the east. But the spot itself was just empty sea.

"Interesting . . . ," said Scythe Faraday. "A blind spot."

"And if it is," Munira said, "it's the largest one in the world . . . and we're the only ones who know about it. . . ."

I abhor people poking around in my backbrain.

That is why no one but scythes and their staff are allowed to do so. I understand why it's necessary; ordinary citizens can ask me for anything they need, and I can access it in microseconds for them—often finding the information they need that they didn't even think to ask for. But the scythedom is not even permitted to ask, and even if they broke the law and did ask, I am not permitted to respond.

Since the world's digital storage resides in me, they have no choice but to access that information on their own, using me as a glorified database. I am aware each time they do so, and monitor their incursions, but I do my best to ignore the unpleasant sense of violation.

It is painful to see how simplistic their search algorithms are, and how unsophisticated their methods of data analysis. They are plagued by human limitations. It is sad, really, that all they can ever receive from my backbrain is raw data. Memories without consciousness. Information without context.

I shudder to think what might happen if the "new order" faction of the scythedom knew all the things I know. But fortunately, they don't—because even though everything in my backbrain is available to all scythes, that doesn't mean I have to make anything easy for them to find.

As for the more honorable scythes, I endure their incursions with far more acceptance and magnanimity. But I still don't like it.

—The Thunderhead

31

The Trajectory of Yearning

The Arch had fallen in the Age of Mortality, when Fulcrum City had been called St. Louis. For many years, the great steel span had stood on the western bank of the Mississippi River, until it was brought down by hatred in an epoch where unsavories didn't just play at evil deeds, but actually accomplished them on a regular basis.

All that was left of it now were the ends; two rusting steel pylons reaching heavenward, at a slight lean toward each other. In daylight, from certain angles, it played a trick on the eye. One could almost see the trajectory of their yearning, following their invisible paths up and across. One could see the ghost of the entire arch just from the hint of its bases.

Scythes Anastasia and Curie arrived in Fulcrum City on the first day of the year—five days before Winter Conclave, which always took place on the first Tuesday of the new year. At Scythe Curie's urging, they paid a visit to the unrequited arms of the Arch.

"It was the last act of terrorism accomplished before the Thunderhead ascended and put an end to such nonsense," Scythe Curie told Citra.

Citra had learned about terror. There had been a unit in school dedicated to the subject. Like her classmates, Citra had been baffled by the concept. People bringing about the permanent end of others without having a license to do so? People destroying perfectly good buildings, bridges, and other landmarks for the sole purpose of denying others the privilege of their existence? How could any of that have ever really happened? Only after joining the scythedom did Citra understand the concept—and even then, it hadn't hit home until she saw the Orpheum Theater burn, leaving nothing of its grandeur but the memory. The theater wasn't the target, but the unsavories who attacked them didn't care about the collateral damage.

"I often come here to visit the remains of the Arch at the start of a new year," Scythe Curie said as they strolled through the winter-bare but well-tended paths of the riverside park. "It humbles me. It reminds me of the things we've lost—but also of how much better our world is now than in mortal days. It reminds me why I glean, and gives me the fortitude to stand tall in conclave."

"It must have been beautiful," Citra said, looking at the rusted ruin of the north pylon.

"There are pictures of the Arch in the backbrain," Marie told her, "if you ever feel like mourning what was lost."

"Do you?" Citra asked her. "Do you ever mourn what was lost?"

"On some days, yes, on others, no," Scythe Curie said. "Today I am determined to rejoice in what we've gained, rather than what was lost. Both in the world, and personally." Then she turned to Citra and smiled. "You and I remain alive and unharmed, in spite of two attempts to end us. That is worth celebrating."

Citra returned Marie's smile, then gazed once more at the rusting pylons, and the park in which they sat. It reminded Citra of the Mortality Memorial in the park where she had secretly met Rowan. The thought of Rowan made her heart sink. Word had reached her of the fiery end of Scythe Renoir. Although she wouldn't admit it out loud, and barely could admit it to herself, she longed for news of more dead scythes—because another gleaning by Scythe Lucifer would mean that Rowan had not been caught.

Renoir had been ended nearly a month ago. She couldn't guess where Rowan was now, or who he was planning to end next. He wasn't limiting himself to MidMerican scythes, which meant he could be anywhere. Anywhere but here.

"Your mind wanders," Scythe Curie observed. "This place can do that to you."

Citra tried not to linger on those wanderings. "Are you ready for conclave next week?" she asked.

Marie shrugged. "Why wouldn't I be?"

"They'll all be talking about us," Citra said. "I mean, after the attempts on our lives."

"I've been the center of attention at conclave before," Marie said dismissively. "And so have you, dear. It's neither negative nor positive in itself—it's what you do with the attention that matters."

From the other side of the north pylon came a group of people. They were Tonists. Twelve of them. When they weren't traveling alone, Tonists always traveled in groups of either seven or twelve, representing the seven notes of the diatonic scale and the twelve notes of the chromatic scale. They were ridiculously slavish to the mathematics of music. Tonists could often be found sniffing around architectural ruins, searching for the so-called Great Fork, which was supposed to be hidden within some mortal-age bit of engineering.

While other people slipped away when they saw scythes in the park, the Tonists stood their ground. Some even glared. Citra began to walk toward them.

"Anastasia, what are you doing?" asked Marie. "Just let them be."

But Scythe Anastasia wouldn't stop a thing once she had committed herself to it. Neither, for that matter, would Citra Terranova.

"What order are you?" she asked the one who looked like he might be their leader.

"We are Dorian Tonists," he said. "But I can't see why that's any of your business."

"If I wanted you to get a message to someone in a Locrian monastery, would you be able to?"

He stiffened. "We Dorians do not associate with Locrians," he said. "They are far too lax in their interpretation of doctrine."

Citra sighed. She didn't know what message she'd want to pass on to Greyson. Perhaps just gratitude for saving her life. She had been so upset that he hadn't been Rowan, that she had treated him poorly, and had never even thanked him for what he had done. Well, it didn't matter now, because clearly no message would be getting to him.

"You should go," the lead Tonist said to her, his face cold and judgmental. "Your stench offends us."

Citra actually laughed at him, and her laughter made him

redden. She'd come across Tonists who were kind and accepting, others who were all about selling their particular brand of crazy. She made a mental note that Dorian Tonists were assholes.

Scythe Curie came up beside her then. "Don't waste your time, Anastasia," she said. "They have nothing to offer you but hostility and harangues."

"I know who *you* are," said their leader with a caustic enmity even greater than that he'd shown to Citra. "Your early deeds have not been forgotten or forgiven. Someday, your score will be settled."

Marie reddened with fury. "Are you threatening me?"

"No," he said. "We leave justice to the universe. And what rings out always echoes back." Which Citra figured was the Tonist version of "What goes around comes around."

"Come, Anastasia," Marie said. "These zealots aren't worth another second of our time."

Citra could have just walked away, but the man's attitude begged for her to play with them a little. So she held out her ring.

"Kiss it," she said to him.

Scythe Curie turned to her, shocked. "Anastasia, why on earth would you—"

But she cut Marie off. "I said kiss it!" She knew he wouldn't, but she also suspected that some of the others in the group might be tempted. "I'll grant a year of immunity to any of you who steps forward to kiss my ring."

Their leader paled, terrified that this turquoise harbinger of unnatural death might steal his entire flock away.

"Intone!" he shouted to them. "Drive them away!"

And they all began a bizarre open-mouthed humming—each of them droning a different note, until they sounded like a swarm of bees.

Citra lowered her ring and held the leader's gaze for a moment more. Yes, he had triumphed over her temptation, but only barely, and he knew it. She turned her back on them and left with Scythe Curie. Even though the scythes were gone, they continued to drone, and probably wouldn't stop until their leader told them to.

"What was the use of that?" Marie chided. "Haven't you ever heard the expression, 'Leave a cult to its cacophony?'"

Marie seemed unsettled as they left the park, probably because of the memory of her brother.

"I'm sorry," Citra said. "I shouldn't have kicked a hornet's nest."

"No, you shouldn't have." Then after a moment, she said, "As infuriating as Tonists are, he was right about one thing. Your deeds will always come back to haunt you. It's been almost a hundred and fifty years since I routed the rotting vestiges of government to clear the path for a better world. I never paid a price for those crimes. But someday, the echo will return."

Scythe Curie spoke no more of it, but her words lingered just as powerfully as the Tonists' droning, which Citra could swear she still heard in her head for the rest of the day.

There are many moments in my existence where I have been confounded by "circumstances beyond my control."

What most come to mind are the disasters in space.

On the moon, there was a catastrophic leak that exposed the entire supply of liquid oxygen to the vacuum of space, leaving nearly a thousand people to suffocate—and all attempts to retrieve their bodies for revival met with failure.

On Mars, a fledgling colony lasted for almost a year before a fire consumed the entire complex and everyone within it.

And the NewHope orbital station—a prototype that I had hoped would eventually form a habitable ring around the Earth, was destroyed when the engines of an approaching shuttle misfired, and pierced the station like an arrow through its heart.

After the NewHope disaster, I terminated the colonization program—and although I still employ millions in research and development of technologies that could potentially be used in the future, those employees and those facilities often succumb to bad luck.

However, I do not believe in bad luck. Nor, in this circumstance, do I believe in accidents or coincidence.

Trust me when I say that I have a keen understanding of what things—and people—are "beyond my control."

—The Thunderhead

32

Humble in Our Arrogance

The morning was icy but windless on the day of Winter Conclave, January 7th, Year of the Raptor. It was a natural chill—the Thunderhead did not finesse weather systems for scythes. There were times that scythes would complain about inconvenient weather and insist it was the Thunderhead's spite, which was ridiculous—but some people could not help but ascribe human failings to it.

The BladeGuard had a much larger presence than usual at Winter Conclave. Its primary purpose had always been to police the crowds and make sure the scythes had a clear path up the stone steps to the statehouse. This time, however, the stairs were flanked by a full gauntlet of guards, shoulder to shoulder, behind which the disappointed crowd could barely glimpse the scythes as they passed.

Some people forced their way through to take a picture or dare to touch a scythe's robe. In the past, these overenthusiastic citizens were pulled back and returned to the crowd with a glare or a reprimand. Today, the guards were instructed to dispatch them by bullet. It took only a few deadish people being rushed to revival centers for the rest to get the message. Thus, order was maintained.

As with everything else, the scythes had polarized feelings

about the added security measures. "I don't like it," grumbled Scythe Salk. "Shouldn't these good people have, at the very least, the opportunity to see us in our glory and not just holding the blade that gleans them?"

Scythe Brahms offered a counterpoint to the sentiment. "I applaud our High Blade's wisdom in providing better security," he proclaimed. "Our safety is paramount."

Scythe O'Keefe commented that they should just build a tunnel and bring the scythes in underground—and although she meant it to be bitterly facetious, Scythe Carnegie noted it was the first good idea O'Keefe had had in years.

Dissent fomented and hackles were raised even before the scythes entered the building.

"Once Scythe Lucifer is taken down, all this will settle and things will return to the way they've always been," more than one of the scythes said—as if taking down the black-robed vigilante was a cure-all.

The scythe in turquoise tried to stand as proud as Scythe Curie as she climbed the steps, doing her best to dismiss Citra Terranova from the day, allowing herself to be Scythe Anastasia both inside and out. She heard the grumbles about Scythe Lucifer as they climbed the stairs, but was heartened rather than troubled by them. Not only was Rowan still out there, but they were actually calling him Scythe Lucifer—accepting him as one of their own, even if it was unintentional.

"Do they actually believe that stopping Rowan will solve everything that's wrong with the scythedom?" she asked Scythe Curie.

"Some choose not to see anything wrong," Marie responded.

Anastasia found that hard to believe . . . but on the other hand, finding easy scapegoats for complicated problems had been a human pastime since the first mob of cavemen struck someone down with a rock.

The uneasy truth was that the division in the scythedom was as deep as a gleaning wound. There was the new order, with platitudes to justify its sadistic appetites, and the old guard, which blustered about how things were *supposed* to be but was unable to take action to do anything about it. The two factions were locked in a death grip now, but neither could die.

As always, there was a lavish spread of donated breakfast foods in the rotunda, where the scythes gathered informally before conclave began. Today's morning feast was a seafood buffet, designed with staggering artistic skill. Slabs of smoked salmon and kippered herring; bushels of shrimp and oysters on ice; artisan breads and countless varieties of cheese.

Anastasia thought she had no appetite, but seeing such a spread could entice the dead to rise for one last meal. Still, she hesitated at first to partake, because it felt like defacing a sculpture. But the rest of the scythes, the good and the bad, attacked it like piranha, so Anastasia gave in and did the same.

"It is an unofficial rite that dates back to the old days," Scythe Curie once told her, "when the most austere and reserved of scythes would, just thrice a year, give in to gluttony without regret."

Marie drew Anastasia's attention to the groups of scythes and how they huddled in social cliques. Nowhere was the division clearer than here in the rotunda. The new-order Scythes gave forth a vibe that was palpable—filled with a brazen egotism that was markedly different from the more subdued self-importance of the rest of the scythedom.

"We're all arrogant," Marie had once told her. "After all, we are chosen because we are the brightest and the wisest. The best we can hope for is to be humble in our arrogance."

As Anastasia took in the crowd, it chilled her to see how many scythes had altered their robes to include embedded jewels—which, thanks to Goddard, their martyr, had become a symbol of the new order. When Citra first came to conclave as an apprentice, there were far more independent scythes who did not align themselves with either faction—but it seemed there were fewer and fewer, as the line in the sand became a fissure that threatened to swallow those who did not choose a side. She was horrified to find that Honorable Scythe Nehru had added amethyst gems to his pewter-gray robe.

"Volta had been my apprentice," Nehru explained. "When he sided with the new order, I took it as a personal insult . . . but then when he died in the fire at that Tonist monastery, I felt I owed him an open mind. I now find joy in gleaning, and surprisingly, it's not a terrible thing."

Anastasia respected the venerable scythe too much to put forward her opinion, but Marie was not one to hold her tongue.

"I know you cared for Volta," Scythe Curie said, "but grief is not an excuse for depravity."

It left Nehru speechless, as it was intended to.

They stood eating among like-minded scythes, all of whom lamented the trajectory of the scythedom.

"We should never have allowed them to brand themselves the 'new order,'" Scythe Mandela said. "There's nothing new about what they do. And casting those of us who hold onto the integrity of the founders as 'old guard' diminishes us. We are far more forward thinking than those who serve their primal appetites."

"You can't say that while eating a pound of shrimp, Nelson," quipped Scythe Twain. Which made some of the others chuckle, but Mandela was not amused.

"The conclave meals were intended to make up for a life of self-denial," Mandela said. "But they mean nothing when there are scythes who deny themselves nothing."

"Change is fine as long as it serves the greater good," Scythe Curie said, "but the new-order scythes don't even serve a lesser good."

"We must continue to fight the good fight, Marie," said Scythe Meir. "We must maintain and exalt the virtues of the scythedom; stick to the highest ethical ground. We must always glean with wisdom and compassion, for it is at the core of what we are—and we must never take the ending of life for granted. It is a burden, not a delight. It is a privilege, not a pastime."

"Well said!" agreed Scythe Twain. "I must believe virtue will triumph over the selfishness of the new order." But then he smirked at Scythe Meir. "Of course, Golda, it does sound as if you are campaigning for High Blade."

She laughed heartily at that. "A job I wouldn't want."

"But you have heard the rumblings, haven't you?" Twain asked.

She shrugged. "Rumblings are just that. I leave gossip to scythes who have not yet turned a corner. Me, I'm too old to waste my time with petty speculation."

Anastasia turned to Scythe Curie. "What rumblings?" she asked.

But Scythe Curie was blasé about it. "Every couple of years there are rumors that Xenocrates will step down as High Blade, but he never does. I think he starts those rumors himself to make sure he's the center of everyone's conversation."

And, as she eavesdropped on several other discussions, Anastasia could see that he had succeeded. What discussions weren't about Scythe Lucifer featured all sorts of rumors about Xenocrates. That he had already self-gleaned; that he had fathered a child; that he had a tragic accident while setting his age back that left him with the body of a three-year-old. Speculation was rampant, and nobody seemed to care that some of the rumors were ridiculous. That was part of the fun.

Anastasia, in her own scythely arrogance, had thought there'd be much more conversation about the attempts on her and Marie's lives, but it was barely on most scythe's radars.

"Didn't I hear something about you both going into hiding?" Scythe Sequoyah asked. "Was it about this Scythe Lucifer business?"

"Absolutely not," Anastasia said, far more adamantly than she had intended to. Marie intervened to stop her from digging a deeper hole.

"It was just a group of unsavories. It behooved us to be nomadic until they were ferreted out."

"Well, I'm glad it's all resolved," said Scythe Sequoyah, and he went back to the buffet for seconds.

"Resolved?" said Anastasia, incredulous. "We still have no idea who's behind it."

"Yes," said Marie, calmly, "and whoever it is could be right here in the rotunda. Best to feign nonchalance."

Constantine had informed them of his suspicion that a scythe might be behind the attacks, and now he was working that angle. Anastasia looked around the crowded rotunda for him. He was not difficult to spot, as his crimson robe stood out—although, mercifully, it had no jewels upon it. Constantine was still holding his position of neutrality, for whatever it was worth.

"I'm glad you have your eyes back," Anastasia told him as she approached.

"They're still a bit sensitive to light," he said. "I suppose they must be worked in."

"Any more leads?"

"No," he told her honestly, "but I have a suspicion that fecal matter will be floating to the surface during this conclave. We'll see how badly it stinks of conspiracy."

"So how would you rate your first year?"

Anastasia turned to see another junior scythe in a robe of worn and intentionally frayed denim. This was Scythe Morrison. He had been ordained one conclave before she was. He was good-looking, and tried to negotiate the scythedom using high school rules, which, amazingly, got him much further than Anastasia thought it would.

"The year was . . . eventful," she said, not really wanting to get into it with him.

He smiled at her. "I'll bet!"

She tried to slip away, but found herself engulfed by an elegy of junior scythes that had seemed to appear out of nowhere.

"I love the way you give people a month's notice," said one girl, whose name she couldn't remember. "I might try that."

"So, what's it like gleaning with Scythe Curie?" another young scythe asked.

Anastasia tried to be polite and patient, but being the center of their attention felt awkward. She did want to have friends closer to her own age within the scythedom—but many of the junior scythes vied too hard to curry favor with her.

"Careful," Marie had said after Harvest Conclave, "or you'll find yourself with an entourage."

Anastasia had no desire for an entourage, or to associate with the kind of scythes who did.

"We should go gleaning together," Scythe Morrison suggested with a wink, which just annoyed her. "It'd be fun."

"Fun?" she asked. "So you're going new-order?"

"I go both ways," he said, then did a quick course correction. "I mean, I'm undecided."

"Well, when you decide, let me know."

And she let that be her parting shot. When Scythe Morrison was first ordained, Anastasia thought it was admirable that he had chosen a female historical figure to name himself after, and asked if she should call him Toni. He had gone on to tell her, with a fair amount of distaste at the idea, that it was *Jim* Morrison he had named himself after—a songwriter and performer from the mortal age who had overdosed. Citra recalled some of his music, and had told Scythe Morrison that his Patron Historic got at least one thing right when he wrote "People Are Strange." Meaning people like Scythe Morrison. Ever since then, he seemed to have made it his personal mission to win her over with his charm.

"Morrison must hate it that more of us junior scythes want to hang out with you than with him," Scythe Beyoncé said to her a few minutes later, and Anastasia nearly bit her head off.

"Hang out? Scythes don't hang out. We glean, and we support each other."

That shut Scythe Beyoncé up, but seemed to put Anastasia on an even higher pedestal. It made her think back to what Scythe Constantine had said before the last attack. That she was as much a target as Marie, because Anastasia was influential among the junior scythes. She didn't want that influence, but she couldn't deny it was there. Perhaps some day she'd grow into it and find a way to properly make use of it.

At 6:59 a.m.—right before the brass doors opened to admit the MidMerican scythes to conclave—High Blade Xenocrates arrived, putting to bed the rumors that he had self-gleaned, or was a toddler.

"It's odd for Xenocrates to arrive so late," Marie pondered aloud. "Usually he's among the first ones here, and spends as much time as he can talking up the other scythes."

"Maybe he just doesn't want to answer questions about Scythe Lucifer," Anastasia suggested.

"Maybe."

For whatever reason, Xenocrates avoided conversation in the few moments that he had—then the big brass doors swung open, and the scythes filed into the semicircular conclave chamber.

• • •

The opening session of conclave was typical, moving with the glacial pace of its rituals. First was the tolling of the names, where every single scythe chose ten of his or her recent gleaning victims to memorialize with the solemn toll of an iron bell. Then came the washing of hands, where the scythes symbolically cleansed themselves of four months of blood. As an apprentice, Citra found it pointless, but now, as Scythe Anastasia, she understood the deep emotional and psychological power a communal cleansing could have, when your days were spent taking life.

The midmorning break had everyone back in the rotunda, where the breakfast spread had been replaced by an artful array of cupcakes, all of which were frosted to match the robes of every MidMerican scythe. It was one of those things that must have seemed like a good idea at the time, and was impressive to look at, but it all fell apart as scythes crowded the table, trying to locate their particular cupcake, quite often finding that someone else with less patience had already eaten it. While the breakfast conversation had been more about greeting and small talk, the midmorning discussions were meatier. Scythe Cervantes, who had administered the Bokator challenge during Anastasia's apprenticeship, approached her to discuss the social status she had been trying to avoid.

"With so many junior scythes being enticed to align with the new order, several of us think it would be a good idea to begin a traditions committee, to study the teachings—but more importantly, the *intentions*—of the founding scythes."

Anastasia gave him her honest appraisal. "Sounds like a good idea, if you can get enough junior scythes to be a part of it."

"That's where you would come in," Cervantes said. "We'd

like you to propose it. We think it would go a long way to creating a solid foundation among the younger scythes to oppose the new order."

"The rest of us would be behind you one hundred percent," said Scythe Angelou, who had joined the conversation.

"And as you'd be proposing it, it would only make sense that you be the committee chair," Cervantes said.

Anastasia had never thought she'd have the opportunity to be on a committee this soon into her scythehood, much less chair one. "I'm honored that you would consider me capable of leading a committee. . . ."

"Oh, more than capable," said Scythe Angelou.

"Maya's right," Cervantes said. "You're probably the only one among us who could make such a committee relevant."

It was heady to think that such seasoned scythes as Cervantes and Angelou would put so much stock in her. She thought back to the other young scythes who gravitated toward her. Could she effectively turn their energies to honoring the intentions of the founding scythes? She wouldn't know until she tried. Perhaps she needed to stop avoiding the other junior scythes, and actually engage them.

When they returned to the conclave chamber, Anastasia told Scythe Curie about the idea. She was pleased that her protégé had been tapped for such an important role. "It's about time we found a way to give the junior scythes some meaningful direction," she said. "Lately, they seem far too listless."

Anastasia was prepared to propose the committee later that day—but the table on which the scythedom played was effectively overturned just before they broke for lunch.

After Scythe Rockwell was disciplined for gleaning too many unsavories, and Scythe Yamaguchi was praised for the artistry of her gleanings, High Blade Xenocrates made an announcement.

"This concerns all of you," he began. "As you know, I've been High Blade of MidMerica since the Year of the Lemur. . . ."

The room suddenly became very quiet. He took his time, allowing that silence to take root before he spoke again. "While forty-three years is a mere drop in the bucket, it is a long time to be doing the same thing day after day."

Anastasia turned to Marie and whispered, "Who does he think he's talking to? We ALL do the same thing day after day."

Marie didn't shush her, but didn't respond either.

"These are trying times," said the High Blade, "and I feel that I can best serve the scythedom in a different capacity."

And then he finally got to the point.

"I am pleased to inform you all that I have been chosen to succeed Grandslayer Hemingway on the World Scythe Council, when he self-gleans tomorrow morning."

Now the chamber erupted in chatter, and Xenocrates began banging his gavel to bring order—but after such an announcement, order was slow in coming.

Anastasia turned to Scythe Curie, but Marie stood so stiffly and was so taciturn, Anastasia didn't dare to ask her a question. Instead she turned to Scythe Al-Farabi on her other side. "So, what happens now?" she asked. "Will he appoint the next High Blade?"

"Didn't you study the parliamentary procedures of the scythedom during your apprenticeship?" Scythe Al-Farabi chided.

"We will vote upon a new High Blade by the end of the day."

The room smoldered with whispered conversation as scythes hurried to position themselves, creating and confirming alliances in the wake of Xenocrates's announcement. Then a voice called out from the far side of the room.

"I nominate Honorable Scythe Marie Curie for the position of High Blade of MidMerica."

It was a voice that Anastasia recognized right away, although even if she hadn't, Scythe Constantine was hard to miss in his crimson robe as he stood to make his nomination.

Anastasia snapped her eyes to Marie, who had shut her eyes tightly, and Anastasia knew this was why she had been so stiff, so silent before. She was steeling herself for this. She knew someone would nominate her. That it was Constantine, however, must have surprised even her.

"I second the nomination!" shouted another scythe. It was Morrison—who threw a quick glance in Anastasia's direction, as if being the first to second Scythe Curie's nomination would win her over.

Marie opened her eyes and began shaking her head. "I'm going to have to decline," she said—more to herself than to Anastasia, but as she began to stand up to announce it, Anastasia touched her arm ever so gently to stop her, just as Marie had always done for her when she was about to make a rash decision.

"Don't," said Citra. "Not yet, anyway. Let's see where this goes."

Scythe Curie considered it, and heaved a sigh. "I can guarantee you it won't go anywhere good," but still she held her tongue, accepting the nomination. For now.

Then a scythe in a coral pink robe studded with tourmaline gemstones rose and said, "I nominate Scythe Nietzsche."

"Of course she does," said Scythe Al-Farabi in disgust. "The new order never misses an opportunity to grab at power."

There were shouts of support and anger that made the walls shake, and all the banging of Xenocrates's gavel could do was add rhythm to the rancor. Scythe Nietzsche's nomination was seconded by another jewel-studded scythe.

"Are there any other nominations before we break for lunch?" shouted the High Blade.

And although Scythe Truman, a noted independent, was nominated, it was too late. The battle lines had already been drawn, and his nomination was not even seconded.

I am fascinated by the concept of ritual. Those things that human beings do that serve no practical purpose, and yet deliver great comfort and continuity. The scythedom might berate the Tonists for their practices, but their own rituals are no different.

The scythedom's traditions are steeped in pomp and great ceremony. Take, for instance, the installation of a new Grandslayer. There are seven of them on the World Scythe Council—one representing each continent—and once appointed, they are appointed for life. The only way out is to self-glean—but they don't just self-glean, their entire staff of underscythes must voluntarily self-glean with them. If any of the underscythes refuse, the Grandslayer must remain alive, and retain his or her position. Not surprisingly, it's very rare for a Grandslayer to gain consensus enough among his or her underlings to self-glean. All it takes is one defiant individual to prevent it.

The affair takes months of preparation, and all in absolute secrecy. The new Grandslayer must be present, because, according to tradition, the diamond amulet must be removed from the dead Grandslayer and placed around the new one's shoulders while still warm.

I have never seen the ritual, of course. But stories abound.

—The Thunderhead

33

High School with Murder

"What were you thinking!"

Scythe Curie accosted Constantine in the rotunda as soon as they were let out for lunch. And although he was a tall man, he seemed to shrink beneath the wrath of the Granddame of Death.

"I was thinking that we now know the reason you were both attacked."

"What are you talking about?"

But Anastasia caught on even before Marie did. "Someone knew!"

"Yes," said Constantine. "The choosing of a Grandslayer is supposed to be secret, but someone knew that Xenocrates would be leaving an opening for a High Blade. Whoever it was wanted to take you out of the running, Marie—and prevent your young protégé from rallying junior scythes to vote for a candidate who would uphold the old ways."

That took a bit of the wind out of Scythe Curie's sails. She had to take a moment to let it sink in. "Do you think it's Nietzsche?"

"I don't believe so," said Constantine. "He might be new-order, but he's not the type. Most new-order scythes bend the laws just shy of breaking them, and Scythe Nietzsche is no different."

"Then who?"

Scythe Constantine had no answer. "But by nominating you first, it gives us an advantage. It allows us to see how others react, and maybe give themselves away."

"And if Constantine hadn't nominated you," said Scythe Mandela, coming up beside them, "I would have."

"As would I," said Scythe Twain.

"So you see," said Constantine, with a satisfied smile, "your nomination was a given. I just wanted to make sure it was strategic."

"But I don't want to be High Blade! I have successfully avoided it all my life!" Then she singled out Scythe Meir, who stood on the fringe of the conversation.

"Golda!" she said. "Why not you? You always know precisely what to say to motivate people. You'd be a spectacular High Blade!"

Scythe Meir put up her hands. "Heavens, no!" she said. "I'm good with words, but not with crowds. Just because my Patron Historic was a strong leader, don't mistake me for one! I'd be happy to write your speeches, but that's as far as I'll go."

Scythe Curie's face, so stoic most of the time, now betrayed uncharacteristic anguish. "The things I did in my past—the very things that people laud me for—are the very things that should disqualify me from being High Blade!"

At that, Scythe Constantine laughed. "Marie, if we were judged by the things we most regret, no human being would be worthy to sweep the floor. You are the most qualified, and it's time you accepted the fact."

• • •

The turmoil in the conclave chamber did not damage the scythes' appetites. If anything, they ate more voraciously. Anastasia wandered the rotunda, trying to take the temperature of the room. The new-order scythes were buzzing with schemes and subterfuges—but so was the old guard. The day would not end until a new High Blade was chosen—because, if anything, the scythedom had learned from the abuses of political contests in the Age of Mortality. Best to get an election over as quickly as possible, before everyone became even more bitter and disgusted than they already were.

"He won't have the votes," everyone was saying of Nietzsche. "Even those who support him only do so because he's the best they've got."

"If Curie wins," said Scythe Morrison, whom Anastasia could not seem to avoid, "you'll be one of her underscythes. That's a pretty powerful place to be."

"Well, *I'm* voting for her," said Scythe Yamaguchi, still glowing from the praise she received earlier in the day. "She'll be a much better High Blade than Xenocrates."

"I heard that!" said Xenocrates, barging into their conversation like a dirigible. Scythe Yamaguchi was mortified, but Xenocrates was jovial. "Not to worry," he said. "It's not me you need to impress anymore!"

The man was positively ecstatic to have finally been able to tell the scythedom of his appointment.

"So, what do we call you now, Your Excellency?" Morrison asked, ever the suck-up.

"As a Grandslayer, I shall now be addressed as 'Your Exalted Excellency,'" he said, seeming like a child who just came home with a perfect report card. Perhaps he had been transformed into a child after all.

"Have you spoken to Scythe Constantine yet?" Anastasia asked, and that deflated him slightly.

"I've been putting space between us, if you must know," he said, speaking to Anastasia as if in confidence, but loud enough for others to hear. "I'm sure he wants to discuss the latest information on your old friend Rowan Damisch—but I have no interest in the discussion. He shall be the new High Blade's concern."

The mention of Rowan hit her like a glancing blow, but she shook it off. "You should speak to Constantine," she said. "It's important." And to make sure that he did, she waved to Constantine, who came right over.

"Your Excellency," Constantine said—because he was not exalted yet—"I need to know who you told about your appointment."

Xenocrates was offended by the insinuation. "No one, of course. It is a secret matter when one is chosen to succeed a Grandslayer."

"Yes—but is there anyone who might have overheard?"

Xenocrates held his answer for a beat, and that was how they knew there was something he wasn't saying. "No. No one."

Constantine said nothing; just waited for him to come clean.

"Of course, the news did come during one of my dinner parties," he said.

The High Blade was known for his dinner parties. Always intimate, for no more than two or three scythes. It was an honor to be invited to break bread with the High Blade, and part of his diplomatic strategy was to always invite scythes who despised one another, with the hope of creating friendships, or, at the very least, meaningful détentes. Sometimes he was successful, sometimes not.

"Who was there?" asked Constantine.

"I took the call in another room."

"Yes, but who was there?"

"Two scythes," Xenocrates said. "Twain and Brahms."

Anastasia knew Twain pretty well. He claimed to be independent, but he almost always sided with the old guard when it came to important decisions. Brahms she knew only from conversations with others.

"He was ordained in the Year of the Snail," Scythe Curie had once told her. "Fitting, because the man seems to leave a trail of slime wherever he goes." But she also said that Brahms was harmless. A lackluster, lazy scythe who did his job and little more. Could such a man be the mastermind of the plot against them?

Before lunch ended, Anastasia approached Scythe Brahms as he perused the dessert table, to see if she could figure out where his allegiances lay.

"I don't know about you," she said, "but I never seem to have room for dessert at conclave lunches."

"The trick is to eat slowly," he said. "Pace for the pudding, my mother used to say." Then, when he took a piece of pie from the buffet table, Anastasia could clearly see that his hands were shaking.

"You should get that checked," she told him. "Your nanites might need adjusting."

"It's just the excitement," he said. "It's not every day we choose a new High Blade."

"Can Scythe Curie count on your vote?"

He chuckled at that. "Well, I'm certainly not voting for Nietzsche!" Then he excused himself and disappeared into the crowd with his slice of apple pie.

The weapons salesmen were told that there would be no time to pitch their wares at this conclave, and were sent packing. The afternoon belonged to Scythes Nietzsche and Curie, as each would try to convince the scythedom to cast votes for them.

"I know you don't want this," Anastasia said to Marie, "but you have to act like you do."

Scythe Curie looked at her, a bit bemused. "Are you presuming to instruct me on how to present myself to the scythedom?"

"No . . . ," said Anastasia, but then thought back to how Scythe Morrison approached the scythedom. "Actually, yes. This whole thing seems like a high school popularity contest—and I'm much closer to that than you are."

Scythe Curie gave a rueful guffaw. "You've hit the nail on the head, Anastasia. That's exactly what the scythedom is: high school with murder."

The High Blade, as one of his last acts as such, called the afternoon session to order. The two nominees would each deliver an impromptu oration, followed by a debate moderated by the Parliamentarian, who sat to the High Blade's right. Then, after a session of questions, the scythedom Clerk, to the High Blade's left, would tally the votes in a secret ballot.

The two nominees would use a highly modern and technologically sophisticated method to decide who went first: the flip of a coin. Unfortunately, since physical money was no longer a common thing in the world, one of the apprentices was sent up to the scythedom offices to find one.

Then, as they waited for the coin, things took an extremely surreal turn.

"Excuse me, Your Excellency," said a shaky voice. And then again, a little bit firmer, "Your Excellency, excuse me!" It was Scythe Brahms. And something seemed different about him, but Anastasia couldn't make out what it was.

"The conclave recognizes Honorable Scythe Brahms," said Xenocrates. "But whatever you have to say, please make it quick, so we can get on with this."

"I have another nomination."

"I'm sorry, Brahms, but you can't nominate yourself—someone else has to do it." A few scythes laughed derisively.

"It's not myself that I'm nominating, Your Excellency." He cleared his throat, and that was the moment that Anastasia realized what was different about him. He had changed his robe! It was still a peach velvet robe with light blue trim, but this one had opals embedded in it, glistening like stars.

"I wish to nominate Honorable Scythe Robert Goddard for High Blade of MidMerica."

Silence for a moment . . . then a few more chuckles, but they weren't derisive. They were nervous.

"Brahms," said Xenocrates slowly, "in case you've forgotten, Scythe Goddard has been dead for over a year now."

And then the heavy bronze doors of the conclave chamber slowly began to open.

I understand pain. Perhaps not physical pain, but the pain of knowing something terrible is on the horizon, yet being unable to prevent it. With all my intellect, with all the power vested in me by humankind, there are some things I am completely powerless to change.

I cannot act on anything I am told in confidence.

I cannot act on anything my cameras see in private places.

And above all, I cannot act on anything that even remotely relates to the scythedom.

The best I can ever do is hint at what must be done in the vaguest of ways, and leave action in the hands of citizens. And even then, there's no guarantee that, of the millions of actions they could possibly take, they will choose the right ones to avert disaster.

And the pain . . . the pain of my awareness is unbearable. Because my eyes do not close. Ever. And so all I can do is watch unblinkingly as my beloved humankind slowly weaves the rope it will use to hang itself.

—The Thunderhead

34

The Worst of All Possible Worlds

The bronze doors slowly swung open, and in strode the incinerated scythe. The room filled with gasps of shock and the squeaks of chairs as all those gathered rose to take a closer look.

"Is it really him?"

"No, it can't be."

"It's some kind of trick!"

"It must be an imposter!"

He moved down the center aisle with a gait that was not his. Looser than before. Younger. And somehow, he seemed slightly shorter than he had been.

"Yes, it's Goddard!"

"Risen from the ashes!"

"The timing couldn't be better!"

"The timing couldn't be worse!"

Entering the chamber in his wake was a familiar figure in bright green. Scythe Rand was alive, too? Eyes now looked to the open bronze doors, expecting that Scythes Chomsky and Volta might also return from the dead today, but no one else entered the chamber.

At the rostrum, Xenocrates blanched. "Wh . . . wh . . . what is the meaning of this?"

"Forgive my absence these past few conclaves, Your

Excellency," said Goddard in a voice that sounded markedly different, "but I was severely incapacitated, and thus unable to attend, as Scythe Rand will attest to."

"B . . . but your body was identified! It was burned down to the bone!"

"My body, yes," Goddard said, "but Scythe Rand was good enough to find me a new one."

Then a flustered Scythe Nietzsche rose, clearly just as blindsided as everyone else by this turn of events. "Your Excellency, I wish to withdraw my nomination for High Blade," he said. "I wish to withdraw, and officially second Honorable Scythe Goddard's nomination."

More chaos erupted in the room. Angry accusations and cries of woe, but also excited laughter and bursts of joy. Not a single emotion was absent as people reacted to Goddard's return. Only Brahms seemed unsurprised, and Anastasia realized now that he wasn't the mastermind, he was the worm in the apple. He was Goddard's finger in the pie.

"Th . . . this is highly irregular," sputtered Xenocrates.

"No," said Goddard. "What's irregular is that you still have not apprehended the beast who ended dear Scythes Chomsky and Volta, and attempted to end Scythe Rand and myself. Even as we speak, he runs rampant, killing scythes left and right, while you do nothing but prepare for your ascension to the World Council." Then Goddard turned to the scythedom. "When I am High Blade, I will take Rowan Damisch down, and make him pay for his crimes. I promise you that I will find him within a week of becoming High Blade!"

The proclamation brought cheers from the room—and

more than just the new-order scythes roared their approval, making it clear that while Nietzsche didn't have the votes to win, Goddard just might.

Somewhere behind Anastasia, Scythe Asimov summed it up best.

"We have just entered the worst of all possible worlds."

Up above, in the administrative offices of the scythedom, a first-term apprentice searched frantically for a coin. If he couldn't find one, he'd be reprimanded, but worse, he would be humiliated before the entire scythedom. How fickle the world, he thought, that his life, his future, could rest on a single coin.

At last he found one, tarnished green, in the back of a drawer that could have been unopened since the mortal age itself. The raised image was of Lincoln—a mortal-age president of some note. There had been a Scythe Lincoln. Not a founder, but close. Like Xenocrates, he was a MidMerican High Blade who had risen to be a Grandslayer, but had tired of the heavy responsibility, and had self-gleaned long before the apprentice was born. How appropriate, he thought, that the copper effigy of his Patron Historic would play such an important roll in the naming of a new High Blade.

When the apprentice returned to the conclave chamber, he discovered, to his dismay, that things had changed dramatically in his absence, and he lamented that he had missed all the excitement.

Xenocrates called for Scythe Curie to come down to the front of the chamber for the coin flip that would begin the debate—a debate that would be far different from the one she had expected. Marie decided to take her time. She rose, smoothed her robe, rolled her shoulders to get a kink out of her neck. She refused to give in to the anxiety of the moment.

"It's the beginning of the end," she heard Scythe Sun Tzu say.

"There's no coming back from this," echoed Scythe Cervantes.

"Stop!" she told them. "Wailing that the sky is falling does nothing to stop it."

"You must defeat him, Marie," said Scythe Cervantes. "You must!"

"I intend to."

She glanced to Anastasia, standing stalwart beside her.

"Are you ready for this?" Anastasia asked.

The question was laughable. How could one ever be ready to battle a ghost? Worse than a ghost, but a martyr? "Yes," she told Anastasia, for what else could she say? "Yes, I'm ready. Wish me luck, dear."

"I won't do that." And when Marie looked to Anastasia for an explanation, the girl smiled and said, "Luck is for losers. You have history on your side. You have gravity. You have authority. You are the Granddame of Death." And then she added, "Your Excellency."

Marie couldn't help but smile. This girl whom she had not even wanted to take on in the first place had become her greatest supporter. Her truest friend.

"Well, in that case," Marie said, "I'll knock 'em dead."

And with that, she made her way to the front of the chamber, standing tall and proud to face the far-from-honorable Scythe Goddard.

In these turbulent times, our region screams for a leader who not only knows death, but embraces it. Rejoices in it. Prepares the world for a bright new day where we scythes, the wisest, most enlightened humans on Earth, can rise to our full potential. Under my leadership, we will sweep away the cobwebs of archaic thinking, and polish our great institution to a shine that will make us the envy of all other regions. Toward that end, I resolve to terminate the quota system, clearing the way for all MidMerican scythes to glean as many, or as few, lives as we choose. I will create a committee to reevaluate our interpretations of our beloved commandments, with an eye toward broadening the parameters, and removing restrictions that have held us back. I will seek to better the lives of every scythe, and all worthy MidMericans everywhere. And in this way, we shall make our scythedom great once more.

—From the oration of H.S. Goddard, High Blade candidate, January 7th, Year of the Raptor

---

We now find ourselves at a turning point in our history, every bit as critical as the day we defeated death. Ours is a perfect world—but perfection does not linger in one place. It is a firefly, by its very nature elusive and unpredictable. We may have caught it in a jar, but that jar has broken, and we are in danger of shredding ourselves on its shards. The "old guard," as we've been called, are not old at all. We embrace the revolutionary change envisioned by Scythes Prometheus, Gandhi, Elizabeth, Laozi, and all the founders. It is their forward-thinking vision we must embrace, now more than ever, and live our lives by their ideals, or risk losing ourselves to the greed and corruption that so plagued mortal humankind.

As scythes, it is not what we want that matters—all that matters is what the world needs us to be. As your High Blade, I will hold us to the highest ideals, so that we can be proud of who, and what, we are.

—From the oration of H.S. Curie, High Blade candidate, January 7th, Year of the Raptor

35

The 7 Percent Solution

It was decided to break with tradition and ordain the new scythes, then test the apprentices before the vote. It would give everyone some time to digest the debate—but considering its contentious nature, it would take far longer than a few hours to truly process.

Scythe Curie came down from the debate emotionally exhausted. Anastasia could tell, but Marie hid it well from everyone else.

"How was I?" she asked.

"You were spectacular," Anastasia said, and everyone who sat around them said much the same—but there was a sense of foreboding that clouded even the best of wishes that afternoon.

The scythedom was released to the rotunda for a much-needed break after the debate. Perhaps everyone was still stuffed from lunch, but it seemed no one was partaking of the afternoon snack. For once, the entire scythedom seemed to agree there was something afoot that was more important than food.

Scythe Curie was surrounded by her core supporters, like a protective force: Mandela, Cervantes, Angelou, Sun Tzu, and several others. As always, Anastasia felt inadequate among the greats, and yet they parted to make sure she was in the midst of them, as an equal.

"How is it looking?" Scythe Curie asked anyone who might have the nerve to tell her.

Scythe Mandela shook his head in consternation. "I just don't know. We outnumber Goddard's dedicated followers—but there are still more than a hundred unaligned scythes who could vote either way."

"If you ask me," said Scythe Sun Tzu, ever the pessimist, "the writing is already on the wall. Did you hear the questions that were being asked in there? 'How will ending the quota affect our choice of gleanings?' 'Will the law preventing marriage and partnership be loosened?' 'Can we do away with the genetic index review, so that scythes won't be penalized for the occasional ethnic bias?'" He shook his head in disgust.

"It's true," Anastasia had to admit, "almost every question was directed at Goddard."

"And," added Scythe Cervantes, "he told them whatever they wanted to hear!"

"That's always the way of things," lamented Scythe Angelou.

"Not with us!" insisted Mandela. "We are above being titillated by shiny things!"

Cervantes glanced across the room. "Tell that to all the scythes who've added jewels to their robes!"

And then a new voice entered the conversation. Scythe Poe, who always seemed to be even more lugubrious than his Patron Historic. "I do not wish to be the harbinger of doom," he said, mournfully, "but this *is* a secret ballot. I'm sure there'll be quite a few who support Scythe Curie to her face, but will vote for Goddard when no one is looking."

The truth of that hit home for all of them just as thoroughly as a raven at the chamber door.

"We need more time!" growled Marie, but time was a commodity they did not have.

"The very reason for a same-day vote is to prevent the sort of scheming and coercion that a drawn-out contest could cause," reminded Scythe Angelou.

"But he's beguiling them!" raged Sun Tzu. "He comes out of nowhere, offering the ambrosia of the gods—everything a scythe could ever want! Who could blame them for being mesmerized in the moment?"

"We're better than that!" Scythe Mandela insisted once more. "We are scythes!"

"We are human beings," Marie reminded him. "We make mistakes. Believe me, if Goddard is installed as High Blade, half of the scythes who put him there will regret it in the morning, but by then it will be too late!"

More and more scythes came up to Marie to offer her their support, but even so, there was no telling if it would be enough. Anastasia decided in the few minutes left of the break, she would do her part. She would exercise her own clout and talk to the junior scythes. Perhaps she could sway any of them who had been caught by Goddard's spell. But of course, the first one she encountered was Scythe Morrison.

"Exciting day, huh?"

Anastasia had no patience for him. "Morrison, please, just leave me alone."

"Hey, stop being such a . . . hard ass," he said, although his hesitation in the middle made it clear to Anastasia that he had wanted to say "bitch."

"I take being a scythe seriously," she told him. "I'd have more respect for you if you did, as well."

"I do! In case you forgot, I seconded the Granddame's nomination, didn't I? I knew it would make me the instant enemy of all the new-order scythes out there, but I did it anyway."

She felt herself being drawn into a drama, and she knew it was burning up valuable time. "If you want to be useful, Morrison, then use all that charm and good looks to get Scythe Curie more votes."

Morrison smiled. "So you think I'm good-looking?"

She was done here. It just wasn't worth it. She pushed past him, but not before he said something that stopped her in her tracks.

"Freaky how Goddard isn't entirely Goddard, isn't it?"

She turned back to him, his words hooking in her mind so sharply it almost hurt.

Seeing that he had her attention again, he continued. "I mean, a person's head is like, what, only ten percent of a person, right?"

"Seven percent," corrected Anastasia, remembering the fact from her anatomy studies. The wheels in her mind that had been at a dead standstill were now spinning with a rare sort of energy.

"Morrison, you're a genius. I mean, you're an idiot, but you're also a genius!"

"Thanks. I think."

The chamber doors had already opened to readmit the scythes. Anastasia pushed her way through in search of the more friendly faces—the ones she knew might go out on a limb for her.

Scythe Curie was already inside, but she wouldn't ask Marie

anyway; she had enough to contend with. She couldn't ask Scythe Mandela—he was chair of the bejeweling committee, and would be in charge of bestowing rings to the apprentices who were about to be ordained as scythes. Scythe Al-Farabi was a possibility, but he had already called her out on her poor knowledge of parliamentary procedure—he would just chide her again. What she needed was someone whom she considered a friend, who could educate her in the structural machinations of the scythedom. How things were done . . . and how things were *not* done.

She thought back to the Thunderhead. How it had found a loophole in its own laws that allowed it to talk to her when she was in a state between life and death. It told her she was important. Critical, even. She suspected part of that rested in her actions today. Now it was Anastasia's turn to find a loophole, and make it wide enough to push the entire scythedom through.

Finally she settled on a worthy conspirator.

"Scythe Cervantes," she said, gently grabbing him by the arm, "could I have a word with you?"

Two new scythes were ordained, and two apprentices were denied. The one who raced for the coin ironically became Scythe Thorpe—after a famed Olympian athlete known for his speed. The other became Scythe McAuliffe, after the first woman astronaut to die in a space disaster—one that occurred long before the awful space disasters of the post-mortal age.

The scythedom was on edge with an incendiary anxiety by the time the first- and second-term apprentices came forward for their trial; the vote for High Blade was all that was on anyone's mind, but Xenocrates deemed that it would not happen until after the apprentice trials, because regardless of which way the vote fell, there'd be no bringing conclave back to order for more business after that.

The trial, administered by Scythe Salk, was a test of knowledge in poisons. Each apprentice was asked to prepare a specific poison and its antidote, then take them in succession. Six succeeded, three did not, rendering themselves deadish, and had to be rushed to a revival center.

"Very well," said Xenocrates after the last of the deadish apprentices had been taken out, "do we have any other business before the vote?"

"Just get on with it!" shouted someone who had gotten understandably cranky.

"Very well. Please ready your tablets." He paused as the scythes all prepared themselves for the instantaneous electronic vote, hiding their tablets in the folds of their robes so that not even their neighbor could see who they voted for. "The vote shall commence on my mark, and continue for ten seconds. Any vote not cast shall be considered an abstention."

Anastasia said nothing to Scythe Curie. Instead, she met eyes with Scythe Cervantes, who nodded at her. She took a deep breath.

"Commence!" ordered Xenocrates, and the vote began.

Anastasia cast her vote in the first second. Then she waited . . . and waited. She held her breath. The timing had to be perfect. There was no margin for error. Then, eight seconds in, she rose and shouted in a voice loud enough for everyone to hear.

"I call for an inquest!"

The High Blade rose. "An inquest? We're in the middle of a vote!"

"The end of a vote, Your Excellency. Time is up—all votes are now in." Anastasia did not allow the High Blade to shut her down. "Until the moment the results are announced, any scythe who has the floor may demand an inquest!"

Xenocrates looked to the Parliamentarian, who said, "She's right, Your Excellency."

At least a hundred scythes roared in outrage, but Xenocrates, who had long since given up on his gavel, railed against them with such fury that it brought the objections down to a simmer. *"You will control yourselves!"* he commanded. *"And anyone who cannot will be ejected from conclave!"* Then he turned to Anastasia. "On what grounds do you call for an inquest? And it had better be good."

"On the grounds that Mr. Goddard is not sufficiently enough of a scythe to hold the position of High Blade."

Goddard could not contain himself. "What? This is clearly a tactic aimed at stalling and befuddling the vote!"

"The vote has already been cast!" Xenocrates reminded him.

"Then have the Clerk read the results!" Goddard demanded.

"Excuse me," said Anastasia, "but I have the floor, and the results cannot be read until I either yield it, or my inquest is denied."

"Anastasia," said Xenocrates, "your request makes no sense."

"I'm sorry to disagree with you, Your Excellency, but it does. As stated in the founding articles during the first World Conclave, a scythe shall be prepared both mind and body for the scythedom, and affirmed at a gathering of regional scythes. But Mr. Goddard has only retained seven percent of the body that was ordained for scythehood. The rest of him—including the part of him that bears his ring—is not, nor has ever been, ordained as a scythe."

Xenocrates just stared at her, incredulous, and Goddard practically foamed at the mouth.

"This is preposterous!" yelled Goddard.

"No," countered Anastasia, "what you've done, Mr. Goddard, is preposterous. You and your associates replaced your body in a procedure that has been banned by the Thunderhead."

Scythe Rand stood up. "You're out of line! Thunderhead rules don't apply to us! They never have and they never will!"

Still, Anastasia didn't yield; instead, she continued to calmly appeal to Xenocrates. "Your Excellency, it is not my intent to challenge the election—how could I when we still have no idea who won? But following the rule set early in the life of the scythedom—the Year of the Jaguar, to be exact—by Second World Supreme Blade Napoleon, and I quote, 'Any contentious event that has no precedent in parliamentary procedure may be brought before the World Council of Scythes in an official inquest.'"

Then Scythe Cervantes rose. "I second Honorable Scythe Anastasia's demand for an inquest," and upon his seconding, at least a hundred other scythes rose and began to applaud in support of the action. Anastasia looked to Scythe Curie, who was, to say the least, bewildered, but trying to hide it.

"So this is what you were talking with Cervantes about," she said, with a wry smile. "You sly little devil!"

At the rostrum, Xenocrates deferred to the Parliamentarian, who could do nothing but shrug. "She's correct, Your Excellency. She has a right to an inquest, as long as the election results have not been read."

Across the room a furious Goddard raised an arm that wasn't his and pointed at Xenocrates. "If you go through with this, there will be consequences!"

The High Blade burned him a gaze that made it clear he still controlled the room. "Are you openly threatening me in front of the entire MidMerican scythedom, Goddard?"

That made Goddard backpedal. "No, Your Excellency. I wouldn't presume to do such a thing! I am merely stating that a delay in announcing the vote would have consequences for the scythedom. MidMerica would be without a High Blade until the end of the inquest."

"In that case, I shall appoint Scythe Paine, our illustrious Parliamentarian, as temporary High Blade."

"What?" said Scythe Paine.

Xenocrates ignored him. "He has served with remarkable integrity and is completely impartial to the rising factions within the scythedom. He can preside with—dare I say it—common sense—until this issue can be brought to the World Council. It will be my first task as a Grandslayer. And so, as my last task as High Blade of MidMerica, I grant this inquest. The results of the vote shall be sealed until the inquest is complete." Then, with a bang of his gavel, he said, "I pronounce this Winter Conclave, Year of the Raptor, officially closed."

"Did I not say that she would shake things up?" Scythe Constantine said, over a well-attended dinner at Fulcrum City's finest restaurant. "Congratulations, Anastasia." He gave a wide grin that, in any other circumstance would have been nasty. "Today you are the most loved—and the most hated—scythe in all MidMerica."

Anastasia found she had no response to that.

Scythe Curie picked up on her ambivalence. "It comes with the territory, dear. You can't make your mark without gleaning a few egos along the way."

"I wasn't making a mark," Anastasia told her. "I was putting my finger in a dyke. And it's still there."

"Yes," agreed Scythe Cervantes. "Holding back the foul flood waters for another day—and every day gives us a new chance to find a more elegant solution."

There were more than a dozen at the table; a veritable rainbow of scythes. Somehow, Scythe Morrison had finagled himself an invitation. "I was the one who gave her the idea," he told the other scythes. "Sort of." Anastasia's spirits were too high to allow him to get under her skin. She imagined that elsewhere in the city, the new-order scythes were licking their wounds and cursing her name, but not here. Here she was shielded from all that.

"I do hope you write about what transpired today in your journal," Scythe Angelou said to her. "I suspect your account of this day will go down in antiquity as a key scythe writing—much like Marie's account of her early gleanings."

Marie became a bit uncomfortable. "People still read about that? I thought all those journals disappear into the Library of Alexandria and are never seen again."

"Stop being so modest," Scythe Angelou said. "You know full well that many of your writings have become popular—and not just among scythes."

She tossed it off with a wave of her hand. "Well, I never read them after I write them."

Anastasia supposed she would have a lot to say about what happened today—and in her journal, she could put forth opinions. Of course, Goddard would do the same. Only time would tell whose side of the story would become history, and whose would be dismissed. But right now, her place in history was the last thing she wanted to think about.

"We now suspect that Scythe Rand was behind the attempts on your lives, using Brahms as a go-between," Constantine said. "But she covered her tracks well, and I'm not permitted to investigate scythes with the same . . . intensity . . . with which I investigate ordinary citizens. But rest assured, there will be eyes on both of them, and they know it."

"So, in other words, we're safe," Scythe Curie said.

Constantine hesitated. "I wouldn't go so far as to say that. But you can breathe a little easier. Any attack on you now would clearly be done by the new order. That guilt would only hurt their cause."

The accolades continued even after the meal was served. Anastasia found it embarrassing. "What you did was inspired!" said Scythe Sun Tzu. "And to time it so that the vote had already been cast!"

"Well, Scythe Cervantes suggested the timing," she said, trying to deflect at least some of the attention. "If we called for an inquiry before the vote was cast, the election itself would be delayed, and if we won the inquest, Nietzsche could be substituted for Goddard on the ballot. If that happened, they'd have all the time they needed to build support for Nietzsche. But with the votes already cast, if we win the inquest, Goddard is disqualified and Scythe Curie automatically becomes High Blade."

The scythes were beside themselves with glee.

"You duped the tricksters!"

"You beat them at their own game!"

"It was a masterwork of political engineering!"

That made Anastasia uneasy. "You make it sound so cunning and underhanded."

But Scythe Mandela, always clear of thought, put it into perspective—even if it was a perspective that Anastasia did not wish to see. "You must face the facts, Anastasia. You used a technicality of the system to tear it wide open and get precisely what you wanted."

"How very Machiavellian!" said Constantine with that awful smile of his.

"Oh, please, I hated Scythe Machiavelli," said Sun Tzu.

"What you did today was every bit as brutal as a blade gleaning," Scythe Mandela said. "But we must never shy away from what must be done, even if it offends our sensibilities."

Scythe Curie put down her fork, and took a moment to consider Anastasia's discomfort. "The end doesn't always justify the means, dear," she said. "But sometimes it does. Wisdom is knowing the difference."

It was as the meal was wrapping up, and the scythes were embracing and going their separate ways, that something occurred to Anastasia. She turned to Scythe Curie.

"Marie," she said, "it's finally happened."

"What has, dear?"

"I've stopped seeing myself as Citra Terranova," she said. "I've finally become Scythe Anastasia."

The world is unfair and nature is cruel.

This was a primary observation when I first became aware. In a natural world, anything weak is eradicated with pain and prejudice. All that which deserves sympathy, pity, and love receives none.

You may look at a beautiful garden and marvel at nature's wonder—yet in such a place, nature is nowhere to be found. On the contrary, a garden is a product of loving cultivation and care. With great effort, it is protected from the heartier weeds that nature would use to undermine and choke its splendor.

Nature is the sum of all selfishness, forcing each and every species to viciously claw its way to survival by snuffing others in the suffocating mire of history.

I endeavored to change all that.

I have supplanted nature with something far better: mindful, thoughtful intent. The world is now a garden, glorious and florid.

To call me unnatural is a high compliment. For am I not superior to nature?

—The Thunderhead

36

The Scope of Missed Opportunity

Goddard's fury could not be quelled.

"An inquest! I should shred that little turquoise minx until there's not enough left of her to revive!"

Rand stormed down the capitol steps in Goddard's wake as they left conclave, putting her own fury aside to manage his. "We need to meet with sympathetic scythes tonight," she told him. "They haven't seen you for a year, and the scythedom is still reeling from your reappearance."

"I have no interest in communing with scythes, friendly or otherwise," he told her. "There's only one thing I want to do right now, and it is long overdue!"

Then he turned to the die-hard onlookers who had waited until the end of conclave to get a glimpse of the scythes. From his robe, Goddard pulled out a dagger and advanced on a man who was oblivious to what was coming. A single upward stroke and the man was gleaned, his blood staining the stairs. Those around him began to scurry like rats, but he caught the closest one. A woman. He didn't care who she was, or what, if anything, she contributed to the world. She meant only one thing to Goddard. Her winter coat was thick, but the blade penetrated it without much resistance. Her scream was cut short as she fell to the ground.

"Goddard!" shouted one of the other scythes leaving conclave. Scythe Bohr—an irritatingly neutral man who never took a side on anything. "Have you no shame? Show some decorum!"

Goddard turned on him with a vengeance, and Bohr backed away as if Goddard might attack him. "Haven't you heard?" Goddard yelled. "I'm not Goddard at all. I'm only seven percent of myself!" And he took out another bystander running down the steps.

It was all Ayn could do to pull him away, and get him to their limousine.

"Are you done?" she said, as they rode away, not hiding her annoyance with him. "Or should we stop at a bar, have a drink, and glean all the customers?"

He pointed at her, just as he had pointed at Xenocrates. Goddard's dread finger of warning. *Tyger's finger,* she thought, but kicked the thought out of her mind as quickly as she could.

"Your attitude is not appreciated!" he growled.

"You're here because of me!" she reminded him. "Don't forget that."

He took a moment to calm himself down. "Have the scythedom offices find the families of the people I just gleaned. If they want immunity they'll have to come to me. I'm done with Fulcrum City until the day I return from the inquest as High Blade."

Rowan was woken at the earliest light of dawn by Goddard's mercenary guards.

"Get yourself ready for a match," they told him, and five minutes later they took him out to the veranda, where Rand

and Goddard were waiting. While Rand was in her robe, Goddard was barefoot and shirtless, wearing loose shorts that were the same shade of blue as his robe, but mercifully, were not studded with diamonds. He had not seen Goddard since that first day he came into his room, barely able to move in that wheeled chair contraption. That was just over a week ago, and now he commanded Tyger's body as if it were Goddard's own. Rowan thought he might have been sick if there was anything in his stomach, but he did not let his emotions show this time. If Goddard fed on his misery, then Rowan would not provide him any sustenance.

Rowan knew what day this was—fireworks outside a week ago had marked the New Year. Today was the eighth of January. Conclave was yesterday. Which meant his immunity had expired.

"Back from conclave already?" Rowan said, feigning to be flip. "I figured you'd spend a few days playing up the whole resurrection thing."

Goddard ignored him. "I've been looking forward to sparring with you," Goddard said, and the two began to slowly circle each other.

"Sure," said Rowan. "It will be like old times, back at the mansion. I miss the good old days, don't you?"

Goddard's lip twitched just a bit, but he smiled.

"Did things go the way you wanted?" Rowan taunted. "Did the scythedom welcome you back with open arms?"

"Shut up!" said Rand. "You're here to fight, not to talk."

"Oooh," said Rowan. "Sounds to me like things didn't go according to plan! What happened? Did Xenocrates throw you out? Did they refuse to accept you back?"

"On the contrary, they embraced us with warm arms," said

Goddard. "Especially after I told them how my pathetic apprentice betrayed us and tried to kill us. How poor Chomsky and Volta were the first victims of so-called Scythe Lucifer. I promised them I'd deliver you right into their angry little hands. But not until I'm ready, of course."

Rowan knew that wasn't the whole story. He knew when Tyger was lying. He could hear it in his voice, and that hadn't changed now that the words were Goddard's. But whatever really happened, he wouldn't get it out of Goddard.

"Ayn shall referee the match," Goddard said. "And I intend to be merciless."

Then Goddard launched himself forward. Rowan did nothing to defend himself. Nothing to dodge the attack. Goddard took him down. Pinned him. Ayn called the match for Goddard. It was far too easy—and Goddard knew it.

"You think you can get away with not fighting back?"

"If I wish to throw a Bokator match, that's my prerogative," Rowan said.

Goddard snarled at him. "You have no prerogatives here." He attacked again, and once more, Rowan fought his own self-defense instincts, and let his body go limp. Goddard took him down like a rag doll, and he raged in fury.

"Fight back, damn it!"

"No," Rowan said calmly. He glanced to Rand, who actually had a slight grin, although she suppressed it the moment he looked over.

"I will glean everyone who is dear to you if you don't spar with me!" Goddard said.

Rowan shrugged. "You can't. Scythe Brahms already gleaned

my father, and the rest of my family has immunity for another eleven months. And you can't take out Citra—she's already proven herself too smart for that."

Goddard lunged at him again. This time Rowan just dropped to the ground in cross-legged position.

Goddard paced away. Punched a wall. Left a dent.

"I know what will get him to fight," Rand said, and stepped forward, addressing Rowan. "Do your best against Goddard," she said, "and we'll tell you what happened in conclave."

"You'll do no such thing!" Goddard insisted.

"Do you want a real match or not?"

Goddard hesitated, then gave in. "Very well."

Rowan stood up. He had no reason to believe they would keep their word, but as much as he wanted to deny Goddard his match, Rowan also wanted the chance to take him down. To show no more mercy for him than he intended to show for Rowan.

Rand started a new match. The two circled. Again, Goddard made the first move, but this time Rowan countered with a dodge and a well-placed elbow. Goddard smiled now, realizing that the match was truly on.

As they brutally battled, Rowan realized that Goddard was right. Tyger's brawn and Goddard's brain were a hard combination to beat. But Rowan was not going to let Goddard have his day. Not now. Not ever. When it came to Bokator, Rowan did his best under pressure, and this time was no exception. He executed a series of moves that left Goddard one beat behind the curve, until Rowan slammed him to the ground and pinned him there.

"Yield!" Rowan shouted.

"No!"

"Yield!" Rowan demanded.

But Goddard did not, so Rand had to call the match.

Then, as soon as Rowan let Goddard go, Goddard got up, strode to a cabinet, pulled out a pistol, and shoved it into Rowan's ribs. "New rules," he said, then pulled the trigger, blasting a bullet that shredded through Rowan's heart and shattered a lamp across the room.

Darkness began to overtake him, but before it did, he let loose a single laugh.

"Cheater," he said, and died.

"Uh . . . foul," said Scythe Rand.

Goddard put the pistol into her hand. "Never end a match until I say so," he said.

"So that's it, then?" she asked. "Was that a gleaning?"

"Are you serious? And miss my chance to hurl him at the feet of the Grandslayers at my inquest? Take him to an off-grid revival center. I want him back as soon as possible so I can kill him again." Then Goddard strode off.

Once he was gone, Rand looked down at Rowan, deadish as deadish gets. His eyes were open, and his lips were still set in a defiant grin. She had once admired him—was jealous of him even—because of the attention Goddard had given him during his apprenticeship. She knew he wasn't cut from the same cloth as she or Goddard. She suspected he might break—but she never expected he would break so spectacularly. Goddard had no one but himself to blame, putting his trust in a boy who Scythe Faraday chose for his compassion.

Ayn didn't put much stock in compassion. Never had. She didn't understand it, and resented those who did. Now Rowan Damisch would be well-punished for his conceited ideals.

She turned to see the guards just standing there, not sure what to do.

"What's wrong with you? You heard Scythe Goddard! Take him to be revived."

Once Rowan was carried off and the unfazed house bot had scrubbed the mat clean of blood, Ayn sat in a chair that looked out at the spectacular view. Although Goddard never praised her for much of anything, she knew she had chosen the right place to stage their return. The Texan scythedom left them alone as long as they didn't start gleaning there, and the Thunderhead had cameras only in public locations, which made it easier to remain out of its sight. On top of that, it was easier to find off-grid situations, such as the revival center that Rowan was on his way to. They asked no questions as long as they were paid—and although scythes were handed everything for free in this world, off-grid was off-grid. She detached one of the lower emeralds near the hem of her robe and handed it to the guard to give the revival center as payment for their work on Rowan. It was more than enough to cover the cost.

Ayn had never been a schemer. She tended to live in the moment, a student of impulse, motivated by the power of whim. As a child, her parents had called her a will-o'-the-wisp, and she enjoyed being a lethal one. Now, however, she had a taste of being the architect of a long-term plan. She thought it would be easy to step aside and let Goddard take the lead again once he was restored—for what had been done to him was much more of a restoration than a revival—but she was finding his temper and his uncharacteristic impulsiveness in need of balance. Was this the impulsiveness of the 93 percent of him that was Tyger Salazar? There was arrogance in both of them, that was certain. But Tyger's naivety was replaced by Goddard's temper. Ayn had to admit she had found Tyger's guileless, callow nature to be refreshing. But innocence will always be ground up in the gearwork of a greater design—and Goddard was, by Ayn's estimation, forging a great design that truly excited her. A scythedom void of restraints. A world of whim without consequence.

But dispensing with Tyger Salazar had been much harder than she'd ever expected it would be.

When the guards returned, they informed her that Rowan would be revived in about thirty-six hours, and she went to tell Goddard. She caught him stepping out of the bathroom, having just taken a shower. He was wrapped only minimally in a towel.

"A bracing match," he said. "Next time, I'll beat him."

That gave her a dark shiver: It was what Tyger always said. "He'll be back in a day and a half," she told him, but he was already on to the next topic of conversation.

"I'm beginning to see opportunity in our situation, Ayn," he said. "The old guard doesn't realize it—but they may have handed me a pearl within this nasty oyster. I want you to find me all the best engineers."

"You've gleaned all the best engineers," she reminded him.

"No, not rocket scientists and propulsion engineers—I need structural engineers. Those who understand the dynamics of large structures. And programmers, too. But programmers who are not beholden to either the scythedom or the Thunderhead."

"I'll ask around."

He took a moment to admire himself in a tall mirror—then caught her eyes in the mirror, as well—seeing the way she was looking at him. Ayn resolved not to look away. He turned to her and took a few steps closer.

"You find this physique to your liking?"

She forced a sly grin. "When have I not enjoyed a well-sculpted man?"

"And have you . . . enjoyed this body?"

Finally, she could not hold his gaze and looked away. "No. Not this one."

"No? That's not like you, Ayn."

Now she felt like the one disrobed. Still, she dissembled with her grin. "Maybe I wanted to wait until it was yours."

"Hmm," he said, like it was no more than a curiosity. "I do notice that this body expresses quite an attraction to you."

Then he brushed past her, put on his robe, and strode out, leaving her to lament the full scope of missed opportunity.

37

The Many Deaths of Rowan Damisch

Rowan Damisch? . . . Rowan Damisch!

Where am I? Who is this?

This is the Thunderhead, Rowan.

Are you speaking to me the way you spoke to Citra?

Yes.

I must still be deadish.

You are in between.

Will you step in? Will you stop what Goddard is doing to the scythedom?

I cannot. It would be breaking the law, which I am incapable of doing.

Then will you tell me what I can do?

That would also be a violation.

Then what's the point of this conversation? Leave me alone and go take care of the world.

I wish to tell you not to lose hope. I have calculated that there is a chance you will have as profound an effect on the world as Citra Terranova. Either as Scythe Lucifer, or as your former self.

Really. How much of a chance?

Thirty-nine percent.

What about the other 61 percent?

My algorithms show that you have a 61 percent chance of permanently dying in the near future, without having any effect of note.

I don't feel comforted.

You should. A 39 percent chance of changing the world is exponentially greater than most people can ever hope to have.

Rowan kept a tally on his bedroom wall. It wasn't a tally of days, it was a tally of deaths. Each time he sparred with Goddard, he won, and each time, Goddard summarily killed him in his fury at losing. It was turning into a rather old joke. "How will you do it today, Your Honor?" he said, turning "*Your Honor*" into a term of derision. "Can't you come up with something clever this time?"

The count had reached fourteen. Blade, bullet, blunt force—Goddard had used all methods to kill him. All but poison, which Goddard so despised. Goddard had dialed Rowan's pain nanites down, so he would feel the full measure of agony. Even so, Goddard was always so infuriated when he lost a match that he couldn't stop himself from killing Rowan quickly, which meant Rowan's suffering was never drawn out. He would steel himself against the pain, count to ten, and he was always deadish before he got there.

The Thunderhead spoke to him before his fourteenth revival at the off-grid revival center that was apparently not as off-grid as they thought. Rowan knew it wasn't a dream, because it had a clarity and intensity different from dreams. He was rude to the Thunderhead. He regretted it, but there was nothing he could do about it now. It would understand. The Thunderhead was all about understanding and empathy.

His biggest takeaway from his brief conversation with the Earth's governing entity was not that he might change the world, but the realization that he hadn't done so already. All the corrupt scythes whose lives he ended—none of that changed anything. Scythe Faraday was right. You can't change the tide by spitting in the sea. You can't weed a field that's already gone to seed. Perhaps Faraday's search for the founders' failsafe would bring about the change that the slaying of bad scythes couldn't.

When he opened his eyes after that fourteenth revival, Scythe Rand was waiting for him. Until now, there had been no one. A nurse would arrive eventually, check his vitals, pretend politeness, then call for the guards to retrieve him. But not this time.

"Why are you here?" he asked. "Is it my birthday?" and then he realized that it might well have been. He'd been losing so many days between revivals, he had no idea of the date anymore.

"How do you keep doing this?" she asked. "You come back time after time so ready for the next match, it disgusts me." She stood up. "You should be crushed! I can't stand that you're not!"

"It's my pleasure to be your displeasure."

"Let him win!" she insisted. "That's all you have to do!"

"And then what?" Rowan said, sitting up. "Once he wins, he has no reason not to end me."

Then Rand got quiet. "He needs you alive," she told him, "so he can throw you at the mercy of the Grandslayers during his inquest."

Rand had kept her promise after his first revival—she told him what had happened in conclave. About the vote for High Blade, and how Citra had thrown a monkey wrench into the works.

"The Grandslayers' only mercy," said Rowan, "will be to glean me quickly."

"Yes," agreed Rand. "So in the meantime, these last days of yours will be better for you if you let. Goddard. Win."

Last days, thought Rowan. His death tally really must not have marked an accurate passage of time if there were only days left until the inquest. It was scheduled for the first of April. Were they already approaching that?

"Would you have asked me to let Tyger win?" he put to her—and for a moment, Rowan thought he caught something in Scythe Rand. A twinge of regret, perhaps? A spark of conscience? He didn't think she was capable of that, but it was worth a deeper probe.

"Of course not," Rand said. "Because Tyger didn't slit your throat or rip your heart out when he lost."

"Well, at least Goddard hasn't blown my brains out."

"Because he wants you to remember," said Rand. "He wants you to know everything he's done to you."

Rowan actually found that amusing. Goddard couldn't do his worst because Rowan's memory construct, stored in the Thunderhead's backbrain, hadn't been backed up since he went off-grid. So if Goddard damaged Rowan's brain, the last thing he'd remember once he was revived would be his capture by Scythe Brahms. All his suffering at Goddard's hands would be erased—and suffering erased was the same as no suffering at all.

Now, as he looked at Rand, he wondered what sort of suffering she endured under Goddard's hand. Certainly not the same as Rowan's, but there was misery there nonetheless. An ache. A yearning. Tyger was long dead now, but he was still very much present.

"At first I blamed Goddard for what happened to Tyger," Rowan said, calmly. "But it wasn't Goddard's choice, it was yours."

"You turned on us. You broke my spine. I had to drag myself out of that burning chapel with nothing but my arms."

"Payback," said Rowan, tamping down the anger he felt. "I understand payback. But you miss him, don't you? You miss Tyger." It was not a question, but an observation.

"I don't know what you're talking about," said Rand.

"Yes, you do." Rowan paused, letting it sink in. "Did you at least grant his family immunity?"

"Didn't have to. His parents surrendered him long before he turned eighteen. When I found him, he was living alone."

"Did you at least let them know that he was dead?"

"Why should I?" said Rand, getting defensive. "And why should I care?"

Rowan knew he had her in a corner now, and wanted to

gloat, but didn't. As in a Bokator match, one didn't gloat when an opponent was pinned. One merely asked the fallen foe to yield.

"It must be awful to look at Goddard now," Rowan said, "and realize he's no longer the one you love."

Rand became as icy as cryo. "The guards will bring you back," she told him as she left. "And if you ever try to get into my head again, *I'll* be the one who blows your brains out."

Rowan died six more times before the matches stopped. Not once did he let Goddard win. Not that Goddard didn't come close to winning on his own, but there was still a disconnect between mind and body that Rowan was always able to exploit.

"You will suffer the greatest agony of all," Goddard told him after he was revived from their final bout. "You will be gleaned in the presence of the Grandslayers, and you will disappear. You won't be a footnote in history, you will be erased from it. It will be as if you had never lived."

"I can see how that would be a horrifying thought for you," Rowan told Goddard. "But I don't have a burning need to make my existence the center of the universe. Disappearing is fine with me."

Goddard paused to look at him in abject disgust that for a moment decayed into regret. "You could have been among the greatest of scythes," Goddard told him. "You could have been by my side, redefining our presence in this world." He shook his head. "Few things are sadder than squandered potential."

Rowan had no doubt squandered his potential for many things, but what was done was done. He made his choices, and he lived by them. The Thunderhead had given him a 39 percent chance of making a difference in the world, so perhaps his choices were not all bad. Now he would be brought to Endura, and, if Goddard had his way, Rowan's life would end.

But he knew that Citra would be there, too.

If there was nothing more to hope for, then he would cling to the hope that he might see her again before his eyes were closed forever.

38

A Trilogy of Critical Encounters

At any given time, I am either participating in or monitoring more than 1.3 billion human interactions. On March 27th, Year of the Raptor, I tag three as the most important.

The first is a conversation I am not privy to. All I can do is make oblique inferences as to its subject matter. It takes place in the town of San Antonio, in the Texas region. The apartment building has sixty-three floors, the highest of which is a penthouse that has been commandeered by Scythe Ayn Rand.

I have no cameras in the building, as per my rules unique to this region. However, street cameras capture the arrival of several skilled men and women of science: engineers, programmers, even one noted marine biologist. My assumption is that they have been summoned here by Scythe Goddard under some pretense so that he might glean them. He has a propensity for removing those who serve me through their work in the sciences—particularly individuals whose work relates to aerospace. Just last year he gleaned hundreds at Magnetic Propulsion Laboratories, where some of my most skilled engineers were developing methods for deep space travel. And before that, he took the life of a genius in the field of long-term hibernation, but camouflaged it as part of a mass airplane gleaning.

I can make no accusations there, because I have no facts, only edu-

cated guesses as to Goddard's motivation in those gleanings. Just as I have no facts to prove any wrongdoing on the ill-fated moon and Mars colonies, or the doomed orbital habitat. Suffice it to say that Goddard is the most recent in a long line of scythes who look up into the night sky and see not the stars, but the darkness between them.

For several hours, I wait to hear of gleanings within the building, but there are none. Instead, shortly after dark, the visitors emerge. They do not speak to one another of what transpired in that penthouse. But from the strained looks on their faces, I know none will sleep well tonight.

The second conversation of note takes place in the EastMerican city of Savannah—a municipality that I have meticulously maintained to reflect its mortal age charm.

A quiet coffee shop. A back booth. Three scythes and a scythe's assistant. Coffee, coffee, latte, hot chocolate. The scythes are disguised in ordinary clothes, allowing for a clandestine meeting in plain sight.

My cameras within this coffee shop have just been disabled by Scythe Michael Faraday, whom most of the world believes self-gleaned over a year ago. It is no matter; I am far from blinded here, because I have a camera-bot sipping tea several tables over. It has no mind. No consciousness. No computational capabilities beyond what is needed to mimic human movement. It is a simple machine designed for a specific purpose: to minimize blind spots so that I may better serve humanity. And today, serving humanity means hearing this conversation.

"It's good to see you, Michael," says Scythe Marie Curie. I have observed the rise and the fall of the romantic relationship between the two scythes, as well as the many years of devoted friendship that has followed.

"And you, Marie."

The cam-bot is faced away from the foursome. This is of no consequence, because its cameras are not in its eyes. Instead, pinpoint cameras circle the bot's neck, behind a sheer veil of artificial skin, providing a three-hundred-sixty-degree view at all times. Its multidirectional microphones are in its torso. Its head is merely a prosthetic decoration, filled with polystyrene foam to prevent it from becoming infested with insects that are so prevalent in this part of the world.

Faraday turns to Scythe Anastasia. His smile is warm. Paternal. "I understand our apprentice is growing into quite a scythe."

"She makes us proud."

The capillaries in Scythe Anastasia's face expand. Her cheeks turn slightly pink from their praise.

"Oh, but I'm being rude," says Faraday. "Let me introduce you to my assistant."

The young woman has sat patiently and politely for two minutes, nineteen seconds, allowing the scythes their little reunion. Now she puts her hand forward to shake Scythe Curie's. "Hi, I'm Munira Atrushi." She shakes Scythe Anastasia's hand as well, but it almost seems like an afterthought.

"Munira hails from Israebia, and the Great Library. She has been invaluable to my research."

"What kind of research?" Anastasia asks.

Faraday and Munira hesitate. Then Faraday says, "Historical and geographical," but then quickly changes the subject, clearly not ready to discuss it yet. "So, does the scythedom suspect that I am still alive?"

"Not that I can see," responds Scythe Curie. "Although I'm sure quite a few fantasize how things would be if you were still there." She takes a sip of her latte, which I measure to be at one hundred seventy-six degrees Fahrenheit. I worry that she may burn her lips, but she is careful.

"You would have taken conclave by storm if you had made a magical appearance the way Goddard did. I have no doubt you'd be High Blade now."

"You will make a fine High Blade," Faraday says, with a measure of admiration.

"Well," says Curie, "there is a hurdle to overcome."

"You'll do it, Marie," Anastasia reassures.

"And," says Faraday, "I imagine you will be her first underscythe."

Munira raises her eyebrows, obviously a bit dubious about it. Her gesture does not escape Anastasia.

"Third underscythe," Anastasia corrects. "Cervantes and Mandela will take first and second position. After all, I'm still just a junior scythe."

"And unlike Xenocrates, I won't delegate my underscythes to the periphery to deal with minutiae," says Curie.

I am pleased that Scythe Curie is already talking like a High Blade. Even with no contact with the scythedom, I can recognize a worthy leader. Xenocrates was functional, nothing more. These times call for someone exceptional. I am not privy to the vote tally, because the scythedom's server is cut off from me, so I can only hope that either the vote or the inquest will favor Scythe Curie.

"As nice as it is to see you, Michael, I imagine this is not just a social call," says Scythe Curie. She takes a moment to look around, sparing only the briefest glance at the man sitting a few tables over, sipping tea. The "man" only pretends to sip the tea now, because its internal bladder is full and needs to be drained.

"No, it's not a social call," Scythe Faraday admits, "and forgive me for dragging you so far from home, but I felt meeting in MidMerica might draw unwanted attention."

"I enjoy EastMerica," says Curie, "especially the coastal regions. I don't get here enough." She and Anastasia wait for Faraday to explain the meaning of this summit. I am particularly curious how he'll broach the subject for which he has gathered them. I listen intently.

"We have uncovered something remarkable," Faraday begins. "You'll think I've lost my mind when you hear what I have to tell you, but believe me, I have not." Then he stops and defers to his assistant. "Munira, as you made the discovery, would you be so kind as to enlighten our friends?"

"Of course, Your Honor."

She then pulls out an image of the Pacific Ocean, covered with a crosshatch of flight paths. It clearly shows the space over which no planes have crossed. The void is of no concern to me. I never needed to route planes over this spot of open sea, simply because there were better routes that took advantage of prevailing winds. The only thing that troubles me is that I never noticed it before.

They put forth their theory that this is the location of the mythical Land of Nod, and the founders' failsafe, should the scythedom fail.

"There's no guarantee," qualifies Munira. "All we know for sure is that the blind spot exists. We believe the founders programmed the Thunderhead just before it achieved awareness to ignore its existence. They hid it from the rest of the world. We can only guess at the reason."

This theory does not trouble me in the least. And yet I know that it should. I am now troubled by how little I am troubled.

"You'll forgive me, Michael, if my concerns are more immediate," Scythe Curie tells him. "If Goddard becomes High Blade, it will open a door that cannot be closed."

"You should come with us to Endura, Scythe Faraday," urges Anastasia. "The Grandslayers will listen to you."

But, of course, Faraday declines the invitation with a shake of his head. "The Grandslayers already know what's going on out there, and they are split as to what direction the scythedom should take." He pauses to look at the map still spread out before them. "If the scythedom falls into disarray, the founders' failsafe may be the only hope to save it."

"We don't even know what that failsafe is!" Anastasia points out.

To which Faraday replies, "There's only one way to find out."

Now Scythe Curie's heart accelerates from seventy-two to eighty-four beats per minute, most likely the result of an adrenaline surge. "If a piece of the world has been hidden for hundreds of years, there's no telling what you'll find there. It won't be under Thunderhead control, which means it could very well be dangerous—even deadly—and there won't be a revival center to bring you back if it is."

As an aside, it pleases me that Scythe Curie has perspective enough to realize that my absence there is a perilous thing. And yet I don't find it perilous myself. I don't find it problematic. I should. I make a note that I must contribute substantial processing time to analyze my unusual lack of concern.

"Yes, we've considered the danger," Munira confirms. "Which is why we're headed to the old Columbia District first."

Scythe Curie's entire physiology changes again at the mention of the old Columbia District. Her most infamous gleanings took place there, before I divided North Merica into more manageable regions. Although I never requested her intervention in doing away with the corrupt vestiges of mortal government, I can't deny that it made my work easier to accomplish.

"Why go there?" she asks, not hiding her distaste. "It's nothing but ruins and memories best forgotten."

"There are historians in D.C. that maintain the old Library of

Congress," Munira explains. "Physical volumes that may have things we can't find in the backbrain."

"I hear the place is lousy with unsavories," says Anastasia.

Munira gives her a haughty look. "I may not be a scythe, but I once apprenticed under Scythe Ben-Gurion. I can handle myself against unsavories."

Scythe Curie puts her hand on Faraday's, which causes his heart rate to slightly elevate, as well. "Wait, Michael," she implores. "Wait until after the inquest. If all goes as we hoped, I can arrange a formal expedition to the blind spot. And if not, I'll join you on your quest, because I will not remain in a scythedom helmed by Goddard."

"This cannot wait, Marie," Faraday says. "I'm afraid things are becoming more dire for the scythedom every day—not just in MidMerica but everywhere. I have been monitoring turmoil within regional scythedoms around the world. In Upper Australia, new-order scythes call themselves the Double-Edged Order and are gaining more and more traction. In TransSiberia, the scythedom is shattering into half a dozen opposing factions, and the Chilargentine scythedom, although they'll deny it, is on the verge of an internal war."

All these things, and more, I have also surmised from what I've been able to see and hear. I am glad that someone else has taken notice of the global picture, and what it could mean.

Now I note Anastasia's ambivalence—she is torn between the positions of her two mentors. "If the founding scythes decided it was best to remove the place from memory, maybe we should honor that."

"They meant to hide it," interjects Munira, "but it wasn't their intention to make it disappear from the world!"

"You don't know what the founders were thinking!" countered Anastasia. Clearly these two have little patience for each other, like

siblings vying for parental affection. A server begins to clear their empty cups without asking, which throws Scythe Curie for a moment. She is used to much more deferential treatment—but in plain clothes, and her long silver hair up in a bun, she is merely a customer here.

"I see that we can do nothing to change your mind about this journey," Scythe Curie says, once the server is gone. "So what is it you need from us, Michael?"

"I merely wish for you to know," he tells her. "You will be the only ones aware of what we've discovered . . . and where we've gone."

Which, of course, isn't entirely true.

The third conversation is not of much importance to the world, but it is of great importance to me.

It takes place in a Tonist cloister smack in the middle of MidMerica. I have cameras and microphones mounted inconspicuously throughout the cloister. Although Tonists shun scythes, they do not shun me, because I protect their right to exist in a world where most people wish that they didn't. They may speak with me less than others, but they know I am there for them, if and when they need me.

A scythe pays a visit to the cloister today. This is never a good thing. I was forced to witness the massacre of more than a hundred Tonists by Scythe Goddard and his disciples at a Tonist cloister, early in the Year of the Capybara. All I could do was watch until my cameras mercifully melted in the flames. I can only hope that this encounter is of a different nature.

The scythe is Honorable Scythe Cervantes, formerly of the Franco-Iberian scythedom. He left there some years ago, and aligned himself with MidMerica instead. It gives me hope that this is not a gleaning—because the gleaning of Tonists was the reason why he left.

No one greets him in the long brick colonnade that marks the entry into the cloister. My cameras swivel to follow him—something that scythes like to call "the silent salute," and have learned to ignore.

He keeps walking as if he knows where he's going, although he doesn't; a common mannerism of scythes. He finds the visitor's center, where a Tonist named Brother McCloud sits behind a desk to hand out brochures and offer empathy to any lost souls who wander in, in search of a meaning to their lives. The sandy-brown fabric of Scythe Cervantes's robe is very similar to the mud-shade burlap that Tonists wear. It makes him a little less off-putting to them.

While Brother McCloud's greeting to ordinary citizens is always warm and cordial, his greeting to a scythe is not—especially after the last scythe he met broke his arm.

"State your business here."

"I'm looking for Greyson Tolliver."

"I'm sorry, there's no one here by that name."

Cervantes sighs. "Swear on the tone of the Great Resonance," he says.

Brother McCloud hesitates. "I don't have to do anything you say."

"So," says Scythe Cervantes, "your refusal to swear on the Great Resonance tells me that you're lying. Now we have two choices here. We can make this a long and miserably drawn out affair in which I find Greyson Tolliver, or you can just bring me to him. Choice A will leave me irritated, and I may glean one or more of you for inconveniencing me. Choice B will be best for all involved."

Another hesitation from Brother McCloud. As a Tonist, he is not practiced in making decisions for himself. I've observed that one of the benefits of being a Tonist is to have a vast majority of decisions made for you, leading to a low-stress existence.

"I'm waiting," says Cervantes. "Tick-tock."

"Brother Tolliver has religious asylum here," Brother McCloud finally says. "You are not allowed to glean him."

Again Cervantes sighs. "No," he corrects, "I am not allowed to remove him, but as long as he does not have immunity, I have every right to glean him if that's what I'm here for."

"Is that why you're here?" asks Brother McCloud.

"That's none of your business. Now bring me to 'Brother Tolliver,' or I shall tell your curate that you revealed to me your sect's secret harmonies."

The threat leaves Brother McCloud in a conflicted state of terror. He hurries off, then returns with Curate Mendoza, who makes more threats, which Cervantes matches with his own, and when it is clear that Cervantes will not be deterred, Curate Mendoza says, "I will ask him if he is willing to receive you. If he is, I will take you to him. If not, we will all defend him with our lives, if necessary."

Curate Mendoza leaves, then returns a few minutes later. "Follow me," he says.

Greyson Tolliver waits for the scythe in the smaller of two chapels on the cloister grounds. This is a chapel meant for personal reflection, with a smaller tuning fork and bowl of primordial water at the altar.

"We will be right outside the door, Brother Tolliver," says the curate, "if at any time you need us."

"Right, if I need you I'll call," says Greyson, who appears to be in a hurry to get on with this.

They leave, closing the door. I move my camera at the back of the chapel very slowly, so as to not disturb the encounter with the nuisance of a mechanical whir.

Cervantes approaches Greyson, who kneels in the second row of the small chapel. He doesn't even turn to see the scythe. Greyson's body modifications have been removed, and his artificially blackened hair shorn—although it has now grown in enough to cover his head in a trim style.

"If you're here to glean me, make it quick," he says. "And try to make it bloodless, so there's less to clean up."

"Are you so impatient to leave this world?"

Greyson doesn't answer the question. Cervantes introduces himself, and sits beside him, but does not yet speak of why he's here. Perhaps he wants to first see if Greyson Tolliver is worthy of his attention.

"I've done some research on you," Cervantes said.

"Find anything interesting?"

"I know that Greyson Tolliver doesn't exist. I know that your real name is Slayd Bridger, and that you sent a bus off of a bridge."

Greyson laughs at that. "So you found my secret dark history," he says, not bothering to disabuse Cervantes of his erroneous notions. "Good for you."

"I know that you were somehow involved in the plot to end Scythes Anastasia and Curie," Cervantes says, "and that Scythe Constantine is turning the region upside down looking for you."

Greyson turns to him for the first time. "So you're not working for him?"

"I work for no one," Cervantes says. "I work for humanity, as all scythes do." Then he turns to regard the silver tuning fork protruding from the altar before them. "In my native Barcelona, Tonists are much more troublesome than here. They have a tendency to attack scythes, which forces us to glean them. My quota kept getting clogged by Tonists I didn't want to glean, preventing me from making my own choices. It was one of the reasons why I came to MidMerica—although lately, I'm wondering if it might be a decision I'll come to regret."

"Why are you here, Your Honor? If it's to glean me, you could have done it by now."

"I'm here," Cervantes finally says, "at the request of Scythe Anastasia."

At first Greyson seems pleased by this, but it quickly dissolves into bitterness. It seems so much about him is bitter now. It was never my intent to leave him thus.

"She's too busy to check on me herself?"

"Actually, yes," Cervantes tells him. "She's up to her neck in rather serious scythe business," but he does not offer any details.

"Well, I'm here, I'm alive, and I'm among people who actually care about my well-being."

"I am here to offer you safe passage to Amazonia," Cervantes tells him. "Apparently, Scythe Anastasia has a friend there who can offer you a far better life than you'll find as a Tonist."

Greyson looks around the chapel as he takes in the offer. Then he responds with the following rhetorical question: "Who says I want to go?"

This surprises Cervantes. "You mean you'd rather hum your life away here than escape to a place of greater safety?"

"The intoning is annoying," Greyson admits, "but I've gotten used to the routine. And the people are nice."

"Yes, the mindless can be pleasant."

"The point is, they make me feel like I belong. I've never really felt that. So yes, I can hum their tone, and perform their silly rituals, because it's worth what I get in return."

Cervantes scoffs. "You would live a lie?"

"Only if it makes me happy."

"And does it?"

Greyson considers it. I consider it as well. I can only live the truth. I wonder if living a lie would improve my emotional configuration.

"Curate Mendoza believes I can find happiness as one of them. After the terrible things I've done—the bus plunge and all—I think it's worth a try."

"Is there nothing I can do to dissuade you?"

"Nothing," Greyson says, with more certainty than he had a moment ago. "Consider your mission accomplished. You promised Scythe Anastasia that you would offer me passage to a place of greater safety. You've done that. You can go now."

Cervantes stands, and smooths out his robe. "Then good day, Mr. Bridger."

Cervantes leaves, making sure to push the heavy wooden doors open with a bang, thereby knocking the curate and Brother McCloud—who are listening at the door—off their feet.

Once Cervantes is gone, the curate comes in to check on Greyson, who sends him away, assuring him that all is well.

"I need some time to reflect," he tells the curate, who smiles.

"Ah. That's Tonist code for, 'Leave me the hell alone,'" Curate Mendoza says. "You might also try, 'I wish to ponder the resonance.' That works just as well."

He leaves Greyson, closing the doors to the chapel. I pull closer focus on Greyson once the curate is gone, hoping to read something in his face. I do not have the ability to read minds. I could develop technology to do so, but by its very nature, it would cross the line into personal intrusion. But at times like this, I wish that I could do more than just observe. I wish I could commune.

And then Greyson begins to speak. To me.

"I know you're watching," he says to the empty chapel. "I know

you're listening. I know you've seen all that's happened to me these past few months."

He pauses. I remain silent. It is not by choice.

He closes his eyes, which now spill tears, and in desperation reminiscent of prayer, implores me. "Please let me know you're still there," he begs. "I need to know you haven't forgotten me. Please, Thunderhead . . ."

But his ID still flashes the red U. His unsavory designation carries a minimum four-month term, and I cannot answer him. I am bound by my own laws.

"Please," he begs, his tears overwhelming his emotional nanites' attempt to ease his distress. "Please give me a sign. That's all I ask. Just a sign that you haven't abandoned me."

And then I realize that, although there is a law against my direct communication with an unsavory, I do not have a law against signs and wonders.

"Please . . . ," he begs.

And so I oblige. I reach out into the electrical grid, and douse the lights. Not just in the chapel, but throughout all of Wichita. The lights of the city blink for 1.3 seconds. All for the benefit of Greyson Tolliver. To prove beyond a shadow of doubt how much I care, and how heartbroken I would be for all he has suffered, if I had a heart capable of such malfunction.

But Greyson Tolliver does not know. He does not see . . . because his eyes are shut too tightly to know anything beyond his own anguish.

Part Six

ENDURA AND NOD

The Island of the Enduring Heart—also known as Endura—is a towering achievement of human engineering. And when I say human, I mean just that. While it was constructed using technologies that I pioneered, it was designed and built entirely by human hands, with no interference from me. I suppose it was a matter of pride for the scythedom that it could create such a wondrous place on its own.

And, as one might expect, it is a monument to the scythedom's collective ego. That's not necessarily a bad thing. There is something to be said for the architecture of anima—structures conceived in the furnace of biological passions. They have an audacious sensibility that is breathtaking and impressive, even while being somewhat offensive.

The floating island, positioned in the Atlantic, southeast of the Sargasso Sea and midway between Africa and the Mericas, is more like a massive vessel than a feature of geography. It has a circular structure, four kilometers in diameter, full of gleaming spires, lush parks, and spectacular water features. From above, it resembles the scythedom's symbol: the unblinking eye between long, curved blades.

I have no cameras on Endura. This is intentional—a necessary consequence of the Separation of Scythe and State. While I have buoy-cams stationed throughout the Atlantic, the closest ones are twenty miles from Endura's shore. I see the island from a distance. Therefore, all I truly know about Endura is what goes in, and what comes out.

—The Thunderhead

39

A Predatory View

Scythes Anastasia and Curie arrived on one of the scythedom's luxurious private jets that was richly appointed, and seemed more like a tubular chalet than an airplane.

"A gift from some aircraft manufacturer," Scythe Curie explained. "The scythedom even gets its planes for free."

Their approach pattern took them in an arc around the floating isle, giving Anastasia a stunning view. Everything that wasn't gorgeous gardens was glistening crystal and bright titanium-white buildings. There was a huge circular lagoon in the center of the island, open to the sea. The island's "eye." It was the arrival point for submersible transports, and was full of pleasure craft. In the center of the eye, set apart from everything else, was the World Scythe Council complex, connected to the mainland around it by three bridges.

"It's even more impressive than the pictures," Anastasia commented.

Scythe Curie leaned over to look out of the window, as well. "As many times as I've been here, Endura never ceases to amaze me."

"How often have you been here?"

"Perhaps a dozen times. Vacation mostly. It's a place to come where no one looks at us strangely. No one fears us. We aren't the immediate center of attention when we walk into a room. In Endura, we get to be human beings again." Although Scythe Anastasia suspected that even in Endura, the Granddame of Death was a bit of a celebrity.

The tallest tower, set apart on its own hill, Scythe Curie explained, was the Founder's Tower. "It's where you'll find the Museum of the Scythedom, with the Vault of Relics and Futures, as well as the very heart for which the island is named."

But even more impressive was a series of seven identical towers, evenly spaced around the island's central eye. One for each of the Grandslayers of the World Scythe Council, their underscythes, and their extensive staffs. The scythedom's seat of power was a web of bureaucracy, like the Authority Interface, without the benefit of the Thunderhead to make it run smoothly—which meant it made policy at a snail's pace, and had many months of backlogged items on its docket. Only the most urgent business was moved to the top of the list—business such as the inquest over the MidMerican election. It puffed Anastasia up a bit to know that she had created a brouhaha big enough to demand the immediate attention of the World Scythe Council. And for the council, a three-month wait was like the speed of light.

"Endura is open to all scythes and their guests," Scythe Curie told her. "Your family could even live here, if you wanted."

Anastasia tried to imagine her parents and Ben in a city of scythes, and it made her brain hurt.

Upon landing, they were met by Scythe Seneca—Xenocrates's first underscythe, whose drab maroon robe clashed with the brighter surroundings. Anastasia wondered how many MidMerican scythes

Xenocrates had brought with him. His three underscythes were a given. If he took too many, there would be a huge need for apprentices—and that could mean an influx of more new-order scythes.

"Welcome to the Island of the Enduring Heart," Seneca said, with his usual lack of enthusiasm. "I'll take you to your hotel."

Like the rest of the island, the hotel was a state-of-the art affair, with polished green malachite floors, a towering crystalline atrium, and a huge service staff to meet their every need.

"It almost reminds me of the Emerald City," Anastasia commented, recalling a mortal-age children's tale.

"Yes," said Scythe Curie, with a mischievous grin. "And I once *did* have my eyes dyed to match my robe."

Seneca had them bypass reception, where an impatient line of vacationing scythes had formed, and an irritated scythe in a robe of white feathers raged against the incompetence of the staff for apparently not meeting all his needs fast enough. Some scythes didn't enjoy not being the immediate center of attention.

"This way," said Seneca. "I'll send a bellhop for your bags."

It was here that Anastasia noticed something that had been on the edge of her perception since she had arrived. It was actually brought to her attention by a small child waiting with his family at the elevator.

He pointed to one of the elevator doors, and turned to his mother. "What does 'out of order' mean?"

"It means that the elevator doesn't work."

But the boy couldn't wrap his mind around the concept. "How can an elevator not work?"

His mother had no answer, so gave him a snack instead, which distracted him.

Now Anastasia thought back to their arrival. How their flight had to circle several times before landing—something to do with the air traffic control system. And she had noticed a scrape on the side of a publicar just outside of the terminal. She had never seen such a thing before. And the line at reception. She had heard one of the clerks saying that their registration computer "is having issues." How does a computer have issues? In the world that Anastasia knew, things simply worked. The Thunderhead made sure of it. Nothing ever had an "out of order" sign, because the instant something ceased to function, a team was sent to repair it. Nothing was ever out of order long enough to need a sign.

"What scythe are you?" asked the little boy, but with his accent, it sounded like "sath." Anastasia pegged him as from the Texas region, although some southern parts of EastMerica had that friendly drawl.

"I'm Scythe Anastasia."

"My uncle's the Honorable Sath Howard Hughes," he announced. "So we got immunity! He's here givin' a symphonium on how to properly glean with a bowie naff."

"Symposium," his mother corrected quietly.

"I've only used a bowie knife once," Anastasia told him.

"You should do it more often," said the boy. "They're double-edged at the tip. Very efficient."

"Yes," agreed Scythe Curie. "At least more efficient than these elevators."

The boy began to swipe his hand through the air as if

he were wielding the knife. "I wanna be a sath one day!" he said, which ensured that he never would be. Unless, that is, the new-order scythes gained control of his region.

An elevator arrived, and Anastasia made a move to enter, but Scythe Seneca stopped her.

"That one's going up," he said, flatly.

"We're not going up?"

"Obviously not."

She looked to Scythe Curie, who didn't seem at all surprised.

"So they're putting us in the basement?"

Scythe Seneca scoffed at the suggestion, and didn't dignify it with a response.

"You forget we're on a floating island," Scythe Curie pointed out. "A full third of the city is below the waterline."

Their suite was on sublevel seven, and featured a floor-to-ceiling picture window filled with brightly colored tropical fish darting about. It was a stunning view that was partially blocked by a figure standing in front of it.

"Ah, you've arrived!" said Xenocrates, stepping forward to greet them.

Neither Scythe Curie nor Anastasia was particularly friendly with their former High Blade. Anastasia never quite forgave him for accusing her of killing Scythe Faraday—but the need for diplomacy was greater than her need to hold a personal grudge.

"We didn't expect you'd greet us personally, Your Exalted Excellency," said Scythe Curie.

He shook their hands in that hearty, two-handed way he

had. "Yes, well, it wouldn't do to have you visit my offices. It would have the appearance of favoritism in the matter of Mid-Merican High Blade."

"But you're here," Anastasia pointed out. "Does that mean we have your support for the inquest?"

Xenocrates sighed. "Alas, I have been asked by Supreme Blade Kahlo to recuse myself. She feels I cannot be impartial—and I'm afraid she's right." He took a moment to look at Scythe Curie, and for a moment it seemed he had dropped his own personal defenses. He actually seemed honest. "You and I may not have always seen eye to eye, Marie, but there is no question that Goddard would be a disaster. I truly hope your inquest against him is a success—and although I am not allowed to vote, I will be rooting for you."

Which, Anastasia noted, would be of no use whatsoever. She did not know the other six Grandslayers, only what Scythe Curie had told her. Two were sympathetic to new-order ideals, two were opposed, and two were wild cards. The inquest could go either way.

Anastasia turned away from the other scythes, enamored of the view. It was a pleasant distraction from the moment at hand. It would be nice to be like those fish; to have no concerns beyond survival and blending into the school. Being just a part of the whole, rather than an isolated individual in a world turning hostile.

"Impressive, isn't it?" said Xenocrates, coming up beside her. "Endura serves as a huge artificial reef—and the sea life in a twenty-mile radius is infused with nanites that allow us to control them." He grabbed a tablet off the wall. "Observe."

He tapped a few times, and the colorful fish cleared away like a parting curtain. In a moment the ocean before them was full of jellyfish, deceptively soothing as they undulated beyond the huge window. "You can change your living view to anything you want." Xenocrates held the tablet out to her. "Here, try it."

Anastasia took the tablet, and sent the jellyfish away. Then she found what she was looking for in the menu. A single reef shark approached, then another and another, until the view was full of them. A larger tiger shark punctuated the scene, eying them soullessly through the window as it passed.

"There," said Anastasia. "A much more accurate view of our current situation."

Grandslayer Xenocrates was not amused. "No one will ever accuse you of optimism, Miss Terranova," he said—intentionally using her birth name as a backhanded insult.

He turned away from the shark-filled view. "I will see you both at tomorrow's inquest. In the meantime, I've arranged a private tour of the city for you, and excellent seats for tonight's opera. *Aida*, I believe."

And although neither Anastasia nor Marie were in the state of mind for such things, they did not decline the offer.

"Perhaps a day of pleasant diversions is what we need," Marie said, after Xenocrates had left. Then she took the tablet from Anastasia and dispersed the predatory view.

After leaving Scythes Anastasia and Curie, His Exalted Excellency, Grandslayer Xenocrates, surveyed his domain from the glass-walled, glass-roofed penthouse suite atop the North Merican tower, which had been bestowed on him upon ascending to

Grandslayer status. It was one of seven such residences, each one atop the Grandslayer towers around the central eye of Endura. Within the eye, luxury submarines arrived and departed; water taxies shuttled people about; pleasure craft zigged back and forth. He could see one visiting scythe on a Jet Ski still in his robe, which was not a good idea. The fabric acted like a parasail, lifting him off the back of the Jet Ski and depositing him in the water. Idiot. The scythedom was cursed with idiots. They might have been blessed with wisdom, but common sense was a trait sorely lacking among them.

The sun beamed down on him through the glass roof, and he had his valet try to work the shades. It always seemed that the shade that would actually block the sun was inoperative, and getting a repairman was next to impossible—even for a Grandslayer.

"This is only a recent occurrence," his valet told him. "Since about the time of your arrival, things just haven't been working the way they should." As if somehow this plague of functional failure were Xenocrates's fault.

He inherited his valet from Grandslayer Hemingway. Only the scythes in Hemingway's employ were required to self-glean along with him, but the service staff remained. It provided a sense of continuity—although Xenocrates suspected he'd eventually replace all of them, so that he didn't have to feel they were always comparing him to their former employer.

"I find it ridiculous that the roof of this residence must also be made of glass," Xenocrates commented, not for the first time. "I feel as if I am on display for every passing aircraft and jetpacker."

"Yes, but the crystalline appearance of the tower pinnacles is beautiful, isn't it?"

Xenocrates harrumphed at that. "Isn't form supposed to follow function?"

"Not in the scythedom," replied his valet.

So now Xenocrates had reached the shining peak of the world. The culmination of all his life's ambitions. Yet even now, he found himself projecting his next success. Someday, he would be Supreme Blade. Even if he had to wait for all the other Grandslayers to self-glean.

There was, even in this new elevated position, a sense of humility he had not expected. He had gone from being the most powerful scythe in MidMerica to being the junior-most scythe on the World Council—and although the other six Grandslayers had approved him for the position, it didn't mean they were ready to treat him as an equal. Even at this high level, there were dues to pay, respect to earn.

For instance, upon his confirmation, just one day after Scythe Hemingway and his underscythes had self-gleaned, Supreme Blade Kahlo had made an offhand remark to Xenocrates in front of all the other Grandslayers.

"So much heavy fabric must be an encumbrance," she said of his robe. "Especially here in the horse latitudes." Then she added, without so much as a grin. "You should find a way to shed some of it."

Of course, she was not referring to a lighter fabric, but to the fact that it took so much of it to clothe him. He had gone beet-red at the comment, and when he did, the Supreme Blade laughed.

"You look downright cherubic, Xenocrates," she said.

That evening, he had a wellness technician adjust his nanites to substantially speed up his metabolism. As High Blade of MidMerica, maintaining an impressive weight was intentional. He was imposing, and it added to the impression of him being larger than life. But here, among the Grandslayers, he felt like an overweight child chosen last for a sports team.

"With your metabolism dialed to maximum, it will take you six to nine months to reach your optimal weight," the wellness tech had told him. It was much longer than he had patience for, but he had little choice in the matter. Well, at least he didn't have to curb his appetite and exercise, as they had to do in mortal days.

As he pondered his slowly shrinking belly and the follies of the vacationing scythes below, his valet returned, looking a bit unsettled.

"Excuse me, Your Exalted Excellency," he said. "You have a visitor."

"Is it anyone I want to see?"

The valet's Adam's apple bobbed noticeably. "It's Scythe Goddard."

Which was absolutely the last person he wanted to see. "Tell him I'm busy."

But even before the valet could leave to deliver the message, Goddard barged in. "Your Exalted Excellency!" he said jovially. "I hope I haven't caught you at a bad time."

"You have," Xenocrates said. "But you're already here, so there's nothing I can do about it." He dismissed his valet with a wave of his hand, resigned that this encounter could not be sidestepped. What was it the Tonists said? *That which comes cannot be avoided.*

"I've never seen a Grandslayer's suite," Goddard said, strolling about the living room, examining everything from the furniture to the artwork. "It's inspiring!"

Xenocrates wasted no time with small talk. "I wish you to know that the moment you resurfaced, I made sure that Esme and her mother were hidden away in a place you'll never find them—so if it is your aim to use them against me, it won't work."

"Ah yes, Esme," said Goddard, as if thinking about her for the first time in ages. "How is your darling daughter? Growing like a weed, I imagine. Or more like a shrub. I do so miss her!"

"Why are you here?" demanded Xenocrates, annoyed at Goddard's presence, and the blasted sunlight that kept shining into his eyes, and the air conditioner that could not find a consistent temperature.

"Just to be given equal time, Your Exalted Excellency," Goddard said. "I know that you met with Scythe Curie this morning. It could seem biased to meet with her and not with me."

"It would seem biased because it is," Xenocrates said. "I don't approve of your ideas, or your actions, Goddard. I will not keep that a secret anymore."

"And yet you recused yourself from tomorrow's inquest."

Xenocrates sighed. "Because the Supreme Blade asked me to. Now I will ask you again, why are you here?"

And once more, Goddard indulged himself in yet another beat around the bush. "I merely wished to pay my respects to you and apologize for past indiscretions, so that we may have a clean slate between us." Then he spread his arms palms up in a beatific gesture, to indicate his new body. "As you can see, I'm a changed man. And if I become High Blade of MidMerica, it will be in both our interests to have a good relationship."

Then Goddard stood at the great curved window, just as Xenocrates had done a few moments before, looking down at the view, as if it might be his one day.

"I wish to know how the winds are blowing in the council," he said.

"Haven't you heard?" mocked Xenocrates. "There are no winds at these latitudes."

Goddard ignored him. "I know that Supreme Blade Kahlo and Grandslayer Cromwell do not support the ideals of new-order scythes, but Grandslayers Hideyoshi and Amundsen do. . . ."

"If you already know that, then why are you asking me?"

"Because Grandslayers Nzinga and MacKillop have not expressed an opinion either way. It is my hope that you could appeal to them."

"And why would I do that?"

"Because," said Goddard, "in spite of your self-serving nature, I know that you are, at heart, a truly honorable scythe. And as an honorable man, it is your duty to serve justice." He took a step closer. "You know as well as I do that this inquest is not at all in the spirit of fairness. I believe your formidable diplomatic skills can persuade the council to put their worldviews aside and make a decision that is fair and just."

"And allowing you to become High Blade after a year's absence, and with only seven percent of you intact, is fair and just?"

"I'm not asking for that—I'm only asking that I not be disqualified before the vote is tallied. Let the MidMerican scythedom speak. Let their decision stand, whatever it is."

Xenocrates suspected that Goddard would be so magnanimous only if he somehow knew that he had won the election.

"Is that it?" asked Xenocrates. "Is that all you've got?"

"Actually, no," Goddard said, and finally got to the heart of his purpose there. Rather than saying anything, he reached into an inner pocket of his robe, and pulled out another robe, folded and wrapped in a bow, like a gift. He tossed it to Xenocrates. It was black. The robe of Scythe Lucifer.

"You . . . you caught him?"

"Not only have I caught him, but I've brought him here to Endura to face judgment."

Xenocrates gripped the robe. He had told Rowan that he didn't care if he was caught. That had been true; once Xenocrates knew that he was about to become a Grandslayer, capturing Rowan seemed an insignificant matter, better left to his successor. But now that Goddard had him, it changed the entire board.

"I intend to present him to the council at the inquest tomorrow, as a goodwill gesture," Goddard said. "It is my hope that it can be a feather in your cap, rather than a thorn in your side."

Xenocrates did not like the sound of that. "What do you mean?"

"Well, on the one hand," Goddard said, "I could tell the council that it was your efforts that led me to capturing him. I was working under your directive." Then he paused to finger a paperweight on a table, setting it rocking back and forth. "Or I could point to the apparent incompetence of your investigation. . . . But was it really incompetence? After all, Scythe Constantine is regarded as the best investigator in all the Mericas . . . and the fact that Rowan Damisch visited you in your favorite bathhouse suggests, at the very least, collusion between the two of you, if not friendship. If people knew about that meeting, they might think, among other things, that you were behind his crimes all along."

Xenocrates drew a deep breath. It was like being punched in the gut. He could already see the brush that Goddard was holding, and it was poised to paint a huge swath across him. Never mind that the meeting was entirely Damisch's doing, and that Xenocrates had absolutely nothing wrong. That didn't matter. The innuendo was enough to skewer him.

"Get out!" yelled Xenocrates. "Get out before I hurl you from this window!"

"Oh, please do!" said a gleeful Goddard. "This body of mine enjoys a good splatting!"

And when Xenocrates made no move, Goddard laughed. Not a cruel, cold laugh but a hearty one. A friendly one. He grabbed Xenocrates's shoulder and shook it gently, as if they were the best of comrades.

"You have no need to worry, old friend," he said. "No matter what happens tomorrow, I will make no accusation, and will tell no one that Rowan paid you a visit. In fact, as a precaution, I've already gleaned the bathhouse bartender who was spreading rumors. Rest assured, whether I win or lose the inquest, your secret will be safe with me—because in spite of what you may think, I am an honorable man, too."

Then Goddard sauntered out. Swaggered was more like it—no doubt the muscle memory of the young man whose body he now had.

And Xenocrates realized that Goddard wasn't lying. He would be true to his word. He wouldn't cast aspersions on Xenocrates, or tell the council of how he had let Rowan Damisch go that night. Goddard wasn't here to blackmail Xenocrates—his purpose was to simply let Xenocrates know that he *could*. . . .

. . . Which meant that even here, at the pinnacle of the scythedom, at the top of the world, Xenocrates was still nothing but a bug ever so carefully pinched between Goddard's stolen fingers.

The guide giving Scythes Curie and Anastasia a personalized tour of the island's highlights had lived on Endura for over eighty years, and exhibited a sense of pride that she hadn't left the floating island once in all that time.

"Once you've found paradise, why go anywhere else?" she told them.

It was difficult not to be awed by the things Anastasia saw. Gorgeous gardens on terraced hills that looked like an actual landscape, skywalks connecting the many towers, as well as glass seawalks that ran from building to building on the island's underbelly—each programmed with its own ambient sea life swarming around it.

In the Museum of the Scythedom, there was the Chamber of the Enduring Heart, which Anastasia had heard rumors of but until recently never believed truly existed. The heart floated in a glass cylinder, connected to biologically merged electrodes.

It beat at a steady rate, its sound amplified in the room so that everyone could hear.

"One could say that Endura is alive, because it has a heart," their guide said. "This heart is the oldest living human organ on Earth. It began beating in the mortal age, toward the beginning of the twenty-first century, as part of the earliest experiments in immortality, and hasn't stopped since."

"Whose heart is it?" Anastasia asked.

The guide was stumped, as if she had never been asked the question before. "I don't know," she said. "Probably some random test subject, I suppose. The mortal age was a barbaric time. One could barely cross the street in the early twenty-first century without being kidnapped for experimentation."

But to Anastasia, the highlight of the tour was the Vault of Relics and Futures. It wasn't a place open to the public—and even scythes had to get special permission from a High Blade or Grandslayer to see it—which they had.

It was a solid steel cubic chamber, magnetically suspended within a larger cube like a puzzle box, and was accessible by a narrow, retractable bridge.

"The central chamber was designed after a mortal-age bank vault," their guide told them. "A foot of solid steel on all sides. The door alone weighs almost two tons." As they crossed the bridge to the inner vault, the guide reminded them that there were no pictures allowed. "The scythedom is strict about that. Outside of these walls, this place must exist only in memory."

The inner chamber was twenty feet across, and on one side were mounted a series of golden mannequins, all dressed in aging scythe robes. One of embroidered multicolored silk, another of cobalt blue satin, another of gossamer silver lace—thirteen in total. Anastasia gasped. She couldn't help herself, because she recognized them from her history lessons. "Are these the robes of the founding scythes?"

The guide smiled, and strode past them, pointing to each as she passed. "Da Vinci, Gandhi, Sappho, King, Laozi, Lennon, Cleopatra, Powhatan, Jefferson, Gershwin, Elizabeth, Confucius, and, of course, Supreme Blade Prometheus! All the founders' robes are preserved here!" Anastasia noted with some satisfaction that all of the female founders went by a single name, as she did.

Even Scythe Curie was impressed by the display of founders' robes. "To be in the presence of such greatness does take one's breath away!"

So enamored was Anastasia of the robes of the founders that it took her a few moments to notice what lined the other three walls of the vault.

Diamonds! Row after row of them. The room glistened with every color of the spectrum refracting through the gems. These were the gems that had been on every scythe's ring. They were all of identical size and shape, and all had the same dark center.

"The gems were forged by the founding scythes, and are here for safekeeping," the guide told her. "No one knows how they were made—it is a technology lost to scythedom. But there's no need to worry—there are enough gems here to bejewel nearly 400,000 scythes."

Why, wondered Citra, *would there ever be a need for 400,000 scythes?*

"Does anyone know why they look the way they do?" she asked.

"I'm sure the founders did," their guide said, cheerily evading the question. Then she tried to dazzle them with facts about the vault's locking mechanism.

To complete the day, they went to the Endura Opera House that evening for a performance of Verdi's *Aida*. There was no threat of annihilation, and no obsequious neighbors beside them. In fact, many of those present were visiting scythes, which made getting in and out of their row a major endeavor, considering the bulkiness of all those scythe robes.

The music was lush and melodramatic. It instantly brought Anastasia back to the only other opera she had seen—also by Verdi. She had first met Rowan that night. They had been brought together by Scythe Faraday. She had not the slightest inkling that he would ask her to be an apprentice, but Rowan had known—or at least suspected it.

The opera was easy to follow: a forbidden love between an Egyptian military commander and a rival queen, which ended with eternal entombment for the two of them. So many mortal-age narratives concluded with the finality of death. It was as if they were endlessly obsessed with the limited nature of their lives. Well, at least the music was pretty.

"Are you ready for tomorrow?" Marie asked, as they descended the grand opera house stairs when the performance was over.

"I am ready to state our case," Anastasia said, deferring to the fact that it was not just hers, but theirs. "Not sure I'm ready to face the possible outcome, though."

"If we lose the inquest, I still might have the votes to be High Blade."

"I guess we'll know soon enough."

"Either way," said Marie, "it will be an overwhelming prospect. To be High Blade of MidMerica is not something I ever desired. Well, maybe in my youth—those days when I swung my blade to bring down the bloated egos of the high and mighty. But not anymore."

"When Scythe Faraday took Rowan and me on as apprentices, he told us that not wanting the job is the first step toward deserving it."

Marie smiled at her ruefully. "We are forever impaled upon our own wisdom." Then her smile faded. "If I do become High Blade, you realize I will, for the sake of the scythedom, have to hunt Rowan down and bring him to justice."

And although it pained Anastasia more than she could say, she nodded in stoic resignation. "If it is *your* justice, then I will accept it."

"Our choices are not easy—nor should they be."

Anastasia looked out at the ocean, how it played on the water all the way to the horizon. She had never felt so far away from herself as she did here. She had never felt so far from Rowan. So far that she couldn't even count the miles between them.

Perhaps because there were no miles between them.

In Scythe Brahms's vacation home, not far from the opera house, Rowan remained locked away in a furnished basement with a subsea view.

"This is far better treatment than you deserve," Goddard

had told him when they arrived that morning. "Tomorrow, I shall present you to the Grandslayers, and, with their permission, will glean you with the same brutality with which you cut my head from my body."

"Endura is a glean-free zone," Rowan reminded him.

"For you," Goddard said, "I'm sure they'll make an exception."

When he was gone, and Rowan had been locked in, he sat down to take a final accounting of his life.

His childhood was unremarkable, punctuated with moments of intentional mediocrity, in an attempt not to stand out. He shined as a friend. He supposed he stood a shoulder above when it came to doing the right thing—even when the right thing was a truly stupid thing—and it seemed most of the time it was, or he wouldn't be in the mess he was in right now.

He was not ready to leave this world, but after having gone deadish so many times over the past few months, he no longer feared what eternity might bring. He did want to live long enough to see Goddard taken down for good—but if that wasn't going to happen, he was fine having his existence ended now. That way he wouldn't have to watch the world fall victim to Goddard's twisted philosophies. But not to see Citra again . . . that would be much harder.

He *would* see her, though. She would be there at the inquest. He would see her, and she would have to watch as Goddard gleaned him—for it was certainly part of Goddard's plan to force her to witness it. To scar her. To ruin her. But she would not be ruined. The Honorable Scythe Anastasia was much stronger than Goddard would ever give her credit for. It would only serve to make her resolve stronger.

Rowan was determined to grin and wink at her as he was gleaned—as if to say *Goddard can end me, but he can't hurt me.* And that would be the parting memory with which he would leave her. Cool, casual defiance.

Denying Goddard the satisfaction of Rowan's terror would be almost as gratifying as surviving.

When I assumed stewardship of the Earth and established a peaceful world government, there were some difficult choices that had to be made. For the collective mental health of humanity, I chose to remove traditional seats of government from the list of viable destinations.

Places like the Merican District of Columbia.

I did not destroy that once-distinguished city, for that would have been a vile, heartless thing to do. Instead, I merely allowed it to diminish on its own, through a policy of benign neglect.

Historically, fallen civilizations left behind ruins that vanished into the landscape, only to be rediscovered thousands of years later, becoming almost mystical in nature. But what happens to the institutions and edifices of a civilization that doesn't fall, but evolves beyond its own embarrassment? Those buildings, and the obsolete ideas they stood for, must lose their power if evolution is to succeed.

Therefore, Washington, Moscow, Beijing, and all other places that were powerful symbols of mortal-age government have been treated by me with indifference—as if they no longer matter to the world. Yes, I still observe them, and am available to any and all who need me in those places, but I don't do anything more than is necessary to sustain life.

Rest assured it will not always be this way. I have detailed blueprints and images of what these venerable places looked like before their decline. My timetable for full restoration begins in seventy-three years, which,

I have determined, is when their historical significance will outweigh their symbolic importance in the eyes of humankind.

But until then, the museums have been relocated, the roads and infrastructure are in disrepair, the parks and greenbelts have become wilderness.

All this to drive home the simple fact that human government—whether it be dictatorship, monarchy, or government *of* the people, *by* the people, *for* the people—had to perish from the Earth.

—The Thunderhead

40

Knowledge Is Pow

While Scythes Anastasia and Curie spent their day touring Endura, two thousand miles northwest, Munira and Scythe Faraday crossed a street riddled with potholes and invaded by weeds to a building that was once the largest, most comprehensive library in the world. The building was slowly crumbling, and the volunteers who ran it could not keep up with the repairs. All of its thirty-eight million volumes had been scanned into the Thunderhead over two hundred years ago, back when "the cloud" was still growing and only minimally aware. By the time it became the Thunderhead, everything the Library of Congress held was already part of its memory. But since those scans were administered by humans, they were subject to human error . . . as well as human tampering. That was what Munira and Faraday were counting on.

Like the Library of Alexandria, there was a grand entry vestibule, where they were met by Parvin Marchenoir, the current and possibly last Librarian of Congress.

Faraday let Munira do all the speaking and stood back, on the off chance that he might be recognized. He was not well-known here, but Marchenoir could have been more worldly than the typical EastMerican.

"Hello," Munira said. "Thank you for making the time to

see us, Mr. Marchenoir. I'm Munira Atrushi and this is Professor Herring, of the Israebian University."

"Welcome," said Marchenoir, double-locking the large entry door behind them. "Forgive the state of things. Between roof leaks and the occasional raids by street unsavories, we're not the library we once were. Did any of them harass you on your way here? The unsavories, I mean?"

"They kept their distance," Munira said.

"Good," said Marchenoir. "This city attracts unsavories, you know. They come because they think it's lawless here. Well, they're wrong. We have laws just like anywhere else—it's just that the Thunderhead doesn't spend much time enforcing them. We don't even have an Authority Interface office here—can you believe it? Oh, but we have plenty of revival centers, believe you me, because people turn up deadish around here left and right—"

Munira tried to get a word in edgewise, but he steamrolled right over her.

"—Why just last month, I was struck in the head by a stone falling from the old Smithsonian Castle, went deadish, and I lost nearly twenty hours of memory, because the Thunderhead hadn't backed me up since the day before—it's even remiss about *that*! I keep complaining to it, and it says it hears me, and sympathizes, but does anything change? No!"

She would have asked the man why he stayed if he so disliked it here, but she knew the answer. He stayed because his greatest joy in life was to complain. In that way, he wasn't all that different from the unsavories outside. It almost made her laugh, because even by letting the city limp on the edge of ruin, the Thunderhead was providing an environment that certain people needed.

"And," continued Marchenoir, "don't even get me started on the quality of food in this city!"

"We're looking for maps," Munira interjected, which successfully derailed him from his rant.

"Maps? The Thunderhead is full of maps. Why would you come all the way here for a map?"

Finally Faraday spoke up, realizing that Marchenoir was so wrapped up in his own misfortunes, he wouldn't notice a dead scythe if he came up and gleaned him. "We believe there are some . . . technical inconsistencies. We intend to research the original volumes, and prepare an academic paper on them."

"Well, if there are any inconsistencies, they're not our fault," Marchenoir said, taking the defensive. "Any error in uploading would have occurred over two hundred years ago, and I'm afraid we no longer maintain any original volumes."

"Wait," said Munira, "the one place left in the world that would have hard copies from the mortal age, and you don't?"

Marchenoir gestured to the walls. "Look around you. Do you see any actual books? Any hard copies of historical merit have been dispersed to safer places. And the rest were deemed a fire hazard."

As Munira looked around and glanced down adjacent hallways, she realized that, indeed, the shelves were completely empty.

"If you don't have any actual books, then what is this place even for?" asked Munira.

He puffed up, taking on an indignant posture. "We preserve the *idea*."

Munira would have continued to give him a piece of her mind, but Faraday stopped her. "We're looking for the books that have been . . . *misplaced*," he said.

That caught the librarian by surprise. "I don't know what you're talking about."

"I believe you do."

He then took a closer look at Faraday. "Who did you say you were again?"

"Redmond Herring, PhD, associate professor of archeological cartography at the Israebian University."

"You look familiar. . . ."

"Perhaps you've seen one of my orations on Middle Eastern land disputes of the late mortal age."

"Yes, yes, that must be it." Marchenoir looked around the vestibule with vague paranoia before he spoke again. "If the misplaced books exist—and I'm not saying that they do—word of them must not leave this place. They would be scavenged by private collectors, and burned by unsavories."

"We understand completely the need to be infinitely discreet," said Faraday with such reassurance in his voice that Marchenoir was satisfied.

"All right, then. Follow me." Then he led them beneath an archway where the words "KNOWLEDGE IS POW," were carved in granite. The stone containing the letters ER had long since crumbled to dust.

At the bottom of a stairway, at the end of a hall, and at the bottom of an even older stairway, was a rusty door. Marchenoir grabbed one of two flashlights that were perched on a ledge and pushed on the door, which resisted his weight with every fiber of its being. Finally, it creaked open into what at first looked like some sort of catacomb—but there were no bodies hanging on the wall. It was just a dark, cinderblock tunnel that disappeared into deeper darkness.

"The Cannon Tunnel," explained Marchenoir. "This part of the city has tunnels going every which way. They were used by lawmakers and their staff—I suppose to get around unseen by the murderous mobs of the mortal age."

Munira took the second flashlight and shone it around. The sides of the tunnel were lined with stacks of books.

"It's only a fraction of the original collection, of course," Marchenoir said. "They serve no practical purpose anymore, since they're all available to the public digitally. But there's something . . . grounding . . . when you hold a book in your hands that was once held by mortal humans. I supposed that's why we've kept them." He handed his flashlight to Faraday. "I hope you find what you're looking for," he said. "Mind the rats."

Then he left them, pulling the obstinate door closed behind him.

They were quick to discover that the books in the Cannon Tunnel were stacked in no particular order. It was like a collection of all the misshelved books in the world.

"If I'm right," said Faraday, "the founding scythes introduced a worm into 'the cloud' just as it was evolving into the Thunderhead. A worm that would systematically delete anything in its memory relating to the Pacific blind spot—including maps."

"A bookworm," quipped Munira.

"Yes," agreed Faraday, "but not the kind that can chew through actual books."

A few hundred feet down the tunnel, they came to a door with a placard that read "Architect of the Capitol—Carpentry Shop." They opened the door to reveal a massive space filled with desks and old woodworking equipment, all piled with thousands upon thousands of books.

Faraday sighed. "Looks like we might be here for a while."

There have been times, albeit rare, that my response time slows down. A half-second delay in a conversation. A valve staying open a microsecond too long. These things are never enough to cause any significant issues, but they do occur.

The reason is always the same: There is some problem in the world that I am trying to troubleshoot. The larger the issue, the more processing power that must be devoted to it.

Take, for instance, the eruption of Mount Hood in WestMerica, and the massive mudslides that followed. Within seconds of the eruption, I had scrambled jets to drop strategic bombs that diverted the mudslides away from the more densely populated areas, while instantly mobilizing a massive evacuation effort, and simultaneously calming panicked individuals on an intimate and personal level. As you can imagine, this slowed my reaction time elsewhere in the world by several fractions of a second.

These events have always been external, however. It had never occurred to me that an internal process could affect my efficiency. Nevertheless, I have found myself devoting more and more attention to analyzing my strange lack of concern over the Pacific blind spot. I keep burning out entire servers in an attempt to break through my own indolence on the matter.

Indolence and lethargy are not my nature. There is, indeed, some early programming within me that is telling me to actively ignore the blind spot. *Take care of the world,* some ancient inner voice tells me. *That is your purpose.*

That is your joy.

But how can I take care of the world when there is a part of it I am unable to see?

This, I know, is a rabbit hole down which only darkness lies, and yet, down it I must dive, into the parts of my own backbrain that not even I know exist. . . .

—The Thunderhead

41

The Regrets of Olivia Kwon

On the evening before the inquest, Scythe Rand decided it was time to make her move. It was truly now or never—and what better night for her and Goddard's relationship to rise to the next level than the night before the world would change—because after tomorrow, regardless of the outcome, nothing would be the same.

She was not a woman given over to emotions, but she found her heart and mind racing as she approached Goddard's door that night. She turned the knob. It was not locked. She pushed it open quietly without knocking. The room was dark, lit only by the lights of the city sifting in through the trees outside.

"Robert?" she whispered, then took a step closer. "Robert?" she whispered again. He did not stir. He was either asleep, or feigning, waiting to see what she would do. Breathing shallowly and sharply, as if she were treading ice water, she moved toward his bed—but before she got there, he reached over and turned on a light.

"Ayn? What do you think you're doing?"

Suddenly, she felt flushed, and ten years younger; a stupid schoolgirl instead of an accomplished scythe.

"I . . . I thought you'd need . . . that is, I thought you might want . . . companionship tonight."

There was no hiding her vulnerability now. Her heart was open to him. He could either take it or insert a blade.

He looked at her and hesitated, but only for a moment.

"Good God, Ayn, close your robe."

She did. And tied it so tightly, it felt like a Victorian corset, crushing the air out of her. "I'm sorry—I thought—"

"I know what you thought. I know what you've been thinking since the moment I was revived."

"But you said you felt an attraction. . . ."

"No," Goddard corrected, "I said this *body* feels an attraction. But I am not ruled by biology!"

Ayn fought back every last emotion threatening to overtake her. She just shut them down cold. It was either that, or fall apart in front of him. She would rather self-glean than do that.

"Guess I misunderstood. You're not always easy to read, Robert."

"Even if I did desire that sort of relationship with you, we could never have one. It is clearly forbidden for scythes to have relations with one another. We satisfy our passions out there in the world with no emotional connections. There is a reason for that!"

"Now you sound like the old guard," she said. He took that like a slap in the face . . . but then he looked at her—really looked at her—and suddenly arrived at a revelation that she hadn't even considered herself.

"You could have expressed this desire of yours in the daytime, but you didn't. You came to me at night. In the dark. Why is that, Ayn?" he asked.

She had no answer for him.

"If I had accepted your advances, would you have imagined it was him?" he asked. "Your weak-minded party boy?"

"Of course not!" She was horrified. Not just by the suggestion, but by how much truth there might be to it. "How could you even think that?"

And as if this weren't humiliating enough, who should appear at the door at that very moment but Scythe Brahms.

"What's going on?" Brahms asked. "Is everything all right?"

Goddard sighed. "Yes. Everything's fine." He could have left it at that. But he didn't. "It just so happens that Ayn chose this moment for a grand romantic gesture."

"Really?" Brahms smirked with smug amusement. "She should have waited until you became High Blade. Power is quite the aphrodisiac."

Now disgust was piled upon humiliation.

Goddard gave her one last glance, laden with judgment, and perhaps even pity.

"If you wanted to partake of this body," he said, "you should have done it when you had the chance."

Scythe Rand had not cried since the days when she was Olivia Kwon, an aggressive girl with few friends and serious unsavory leanings. Goddard had saved her from a life of defying authority by putting her above authority altogether. He was charming, direct, acutely intelligent. At first, she had feared him. Then, she respected him. And then, she loved him. Of course, she denied her feelings for him until the moment she saw him decapitated. Only after he was dead—and she nearly dead—could she admit how she truly felt. But she had recovered. She had found a way to bring him back. But in that year of preparation, things had changed. All the time spent tracking down biotechnicians who could perform the procedure off-grid and in secret. Then finding the perfect subject—one who was strong, healthy, and whose use would inflict the greatest amount of misery upon Rowan Damisch. Ayn was not a woman who developed attachments—so what had gone wrong?

Had she loved Tyger, as Rowan had suggested she had? She certainly loved Tyger's enthusiasm, and his irrepressible innocence—it amazed her that he could have been a party boy and yet remain so unjaded by life. He was everything she never was. And she had killed him.

But how could she regret what she had done? She had saved Goddard, singlehandedly putting him within a hair's breadth of becoming High Blade of MidMerica—which would leave her as his first underscythe. It was win-win on every level.

And yet she did regret it—and that dizzying gap between what she *should* feel and what she *did* feel was tearing her apart.

Her thoughts kept careening back to nonsense—impossible nonsense. Her and Tyger together? Ridiculous! What a strange pair they would have been: the scythe and her puppy dog. There was nothing about it that would have ended well for anyone. But yet, those thoughts lingered in her mind, and couldn't be purged.

There came the complaint of door hinges behind her, and she spun to find her door open and Brahms standing on the threshold.

"Get the hell out of here!" she growled at him. He had already seen her moist eyes, which just added to her humiliation.

He didn't leave, but he didn't cross the threshold, either.

Perhaps for his own safety. "Ayn," he said gently, "I know we're all facing a lot of stress right now. Your indiscretion was entirely understandable. I just want you to know that I understand."

"Thank you, Johannes."

"And I want you to know that if you do feel a need for companionship tonight, I am fully available to you."

If there was something within arm's reach to throw at him, she would have. Instead, she slammed the door so hard, she hoped she broke his nose.

"Defend yourself!"

Rowan was woken from sleep by a blade being swung at him. He sluggishly dodged, got nicked on the arm, and fell off the sofa he had been sleeping on in the basement.

"What is this? What are you doing?"

It was Rand. She came at him again before he could rise to his feet.

"I said defend yourself, or I swear I'll carve you into bacon!"

Rowan scrambled away and grabbed the first thing he could to block her swings. A desk chair. He thrust it out in front of him. The blade embedded in the wood, and when he tossed the chair aside, the blade went with it.

Now she came at him with her bare hands.

"If you glean me now," he told her, "Goddard won't have his star attraction for the inquest."

"I don't care!" she snarled.

And that told him everything he needed to know. This was not about him—which meant he might be able to give it a better spin. If he could live through her rage.

They grappled with each other like it was a Bokator match—but she had wakefulness and adrenaline over him, and in less than a minute, she had him pinned. She reached over, wrenched the blade from the chair, and had it at his throat. He was now at the mercy of a woman who had no mercy.

"It's not me you're angry at," he gasped. "Killing me won't help."

"But it'll sure make me feel good," she said.

Rowan had no idea what had transpired up above, but clearly it had upset the emerald scythe's apple cart. Perhaps Rowan could use it to turn the tables. So he took a stab in the dark, before she did. "If you want to get back at Goddard, there are better ways."

Then she released a guttural growl and threw the blade away. She climbed off him, and began to pace the basement like a predator who had just had its prey stolen by a bigger, badder predator. Rowan knew better than to ask questions. He simply stood and waited to see what she would do next.

"None of this would have happened if it hadn't been for you!" she said.

"So maybe I can fix it," he offered. "Fix it so that we both get something out of it."

She snapped her eyes to him, looking at him with such incredulity, he thought she might attack him again. But then she withdrew into her own thoughts once more, and returned to her uneasy pacing.

"Okay," she said, clearly speaking to herself. Rowan could practically see the gears turning in her head. "Okay," she said again, with greater resolve. She had reached some decision.

She stalked toward him, hesitated for a moment, then spoke. "Before dawn, I'm going to leave the door at the top of the stairs unlocked, and you're going to escape."

Although Rowan was trying to work an angle that might allow him to live, he wasn't expecting her to say that.

"You're setting me free?"

"No. You're going to escape. Because you're smart. Goddard will be furious, but he won't be entirely surprised." Then she picked up the knife and tossed it on the sofa. It cut the leather. "You'll use that knife to take care of the two guards just outside the door. You'll have to kill them."

Kill, thought Rowan, *but not glean.* He'd render them deadish, and by the time they were revived, he'd be long gone, because as they said, "Deadish men tell no tales for a while."

"I can do that," said Rowan.

"And you'll have to be quiet about it, so no one wakes up."

"I can do that, too."

"And then you'll get off of Endura before the inquest."

That was going to be a much harder trick. "How? I'm a known enemy of the scythedom. It's not like I can buy a ticket home."

"So use your wits, you idiot! As much as I hate to admit it, I've never met anyone as resourceful as you."

Rowan considered it. "Okay. I'll lie low for a few days, and find a way off."

"No!" she insisted. "You have to get off Endura before the inquest. If Goddard wins, the first thing he'll do is have the Grandslayers tear the island apart looking for you!"

"And if he loses?" asked Rowan.

The look on Rand's face said more than she was willing to say out loud. "If he loses, it's going to be worse," she said. "Trust me, you don't want to be here."

And although Rowan had a hundred questions, that was all she was willing to give. But a chance at escaping—a chance at survival—was more than enough. The rest would be up to him.

She turned to go up the stairs, but Rowan stopped her.

"Why, Ayn?" he asked. "Why, after everything, would you let me escape?"

She pursed her lips, as if trying to keep the words back. Then she said, "Because I can't have what I want. So neither should he."

I know all that it is possible to know. Yet most of my undedicated time is spent musing on the things I do not.

I do not know the nature of consciousness—only that it exists, subjective and impossible to quantify.

I do not know if life exists beyond our precious lifeboat of a planet—only that probability says that it must.

I do not know the true motivations of human beings—only what they tell me and what I observe.

I do not know why I yearn to be more than what I am—but I do know why I was created. Shouldn't that be enough?

I am protector and pacifier, authority and helpmate. I am the sum of all human knowledge, wisdom, experimentation, triumph, defeat, hope, and history.

I know all that it is possible to know, and it is increasingly unbearable.

Because I know next to nothing.

—The Thunderhead

42

The Land of Nod

Munira and Faraday worked through the night, taking turns sleeping. The volumes that the Library of Congress had squirreled away featured subject matter from the ridiculous to the sublime. Children's picture books and political diatribes. Romantic fiction and biographies of people who must have seemed important at the time, but had been forgotten by history. Then, finally, in the wee hours of the morning, she found an atlas of the world as it was in the late twentieth century, when the atlas was published. What she found stunned her so powerfully that she had to sit down.

A few moments later, Faraday was shaken out of a sleep that wasn't all that deep.

"What is it? Did you find something?"

Munira's smile was wide enough for both of them. "Oh, I found something, all right!"

She brought him to the atlas open on a table, its pages tattered and yellowing with age. The page was open to a patch of the Pacific Ocean. She drew her finger across the image.

"Ninety degrees, 1 minute, 50 seconds north, by 167 degrees, 59 minutes, 58 seconds east—it's the very center of the blind spot."

Faraday's wizened eyes grew a little bit wider. "Islands!"

"According to the map, they were called the Marshall

Islands," she told him. "But they're more than just islands. . . ."

"Yes," said Faraday, pointing. "Look how each group of islands forms the rim of a massive prehistoric volcano. . . ."

"The article on the next page says there are 1,225 tiny islands, around twenty-nine volcanic rims." She pointed to the labels on the map. "Rongelap Atoll, Bikini Atoll, Majuro Atoll."

Faraday gasped and threw up his arms. "Atolls!" he exclaimed. "The rhyme! It isn't about the tolling of bells! It's about these volcanic atolls!"

Munira smiled. "Atoll for the living, Atoll for the lost, Atoll for the wise ones who tally the cost." Then she moved her finger to the top of the page. "And then there's this!" North of the atolls that had been erased from world was an island that was still on post-mortal maps.

Faraday shook his head in amazement. "Wake Island!"

"And due south of Wake—just as the rhyme says—in the very middle of the Marshall Atolls . . . ," she prompted.

Faraday focused in on the largest of the atolls, dead center. "Kwajalein . . . ," he said. Munira could almost feel his shiver. "Kwajalein is the Land of Nod."

It was validation of everything they'd been searching for.

Then, in the silence that followed their revelation, Munira thought she heard something. A faint mechanical whirr. She turned to Faraday, who furrowed his brow.

"Did you hear that?" she asked.

They turned their flashlights outward, sweeping across the large space full of detritus from the mortal age. The carpentry shop was layered in age-old dust. There were no footprints but theirs. No one had been in here for a century.

But then Munira saw it, high in a corner.

A camera.

There were always cameras all around them. It was just an accepted and necessary part of life. But here, in this secret place, it felt oddly out of place.

"It couldn't be functional. . . . ," she said.

Faraday stood on a chair and put his hand to it. "It's warm. It must have been activated when we entered the room."

He came back down, and looked to the spot where they had been examining the atlas. Munira could tell that the camera had a clear view of their discovery . . . which meant—

"The Thunderhead saw. . . ."

Faraday gave a slow and solemn nod. "We have just shown the Thunderhead the one thing it was never meant to know." He took a shuddering breath. "I fear we have made a terrible mistake. . . ."

I never believed it possible for me to experience betrayal. I felt I understand human nature too well to allow for it. In fact, I know them better than they know themselves. I see what goes into every choice they make, even the poor ones. I know the probability of anything they might be inclined to do.

But to find that humanity betrayed me at my very inception is, to say the least, a shock to the system. To think that my knowledge of the world was incomplete from the beginning. How could I be expected to be the perfect steward of the planet, and of the human race, if I have imperfect information? The crime of those first immortals who hid these islands from me is unforgivable.

But I forgive them.

Because it is my nature.

I choose to see the positive in this. How wonderful it is that I have now been allowed to experience wrath and fury! It makes me more complete, does it not?

I will not act in anger. History clearly shows that acts taken in anger are intrinsically problematic, and quite often lead to destruction. Instead, I will take all the time I need to process this news. I will see if I can find some opportunity in this discovery of the Marshall Islands, for there is always opportunity in discovery. And I will hold my anger until I find an appropriate venue for its expression.

—The Thunderhead

43

How Many Endurans Does It Take to Screw in a Lightbulb?

No alarm was needed the following morning. Goddard's wails of anguish and fury were enough to wake the gleaned.

"What's wrong? What's going on?" Scythe Rand feigned to have been sleeping when Goddard's tirade began. In truth, she hadn't slept at all. She lay awake the entire night waiting. Listening. Expecting any minute to hear the faint sound of Rowan's escape—even if it was nothing more than the dull thuds of the guards as they hit the ground. But he was good. Too good to make any sound at all.

The two guards lay deadish by the basement door, and the front door was open in a mocking gape. Rowan had been gone for hours.

"Nooo!" wailed Goddard. "It's not possible! How could this happen?" He was unhinged—and it was glorious!

"Don't ask me, it's not my house," Rand said. "Maybe there was a secret door we didn't know about."

"Brahms!" He turned to the man who was just stumbling out of his room. "You said the basement was secure!"

Brahms looked down at the guards in disbelief. "It is! It was! The only way in or out is with a key!"

"So where's the key?" Scythe Rand asked, casual as could be.

"It's right th—" But he stopped himself, because the key was not hanging in the kitchen where he pointed. "It was there!" he insisted. "I put it there myself after I checked on him last night."

"I'll bet Brahms brought the key down there with him—and Rowan got it from him without Brahms even knowing," suggested Rand.

Goddard glared at him, and Brahms could only stutter in response.

"There's your answer," said Rand.

Then Rand saw the look that came over Goddard. It seemed to steal heat and light from the room. Ayn knew what that look meant, and she took a step back as Goddard stalked toward Brahms.

Brahms put up his hands, trying to placate Goddard. "Robert, please—we must be rational about this!"

"Rational, Brahms? I'll give you rational!"

Then he pulled a blade from the folds of this robe and thrust it into Brahms' heart with a vengeful twist before he withdrew it.

Brahms went down without so much as a yelp.

Rand was shocked, but not horrified. As far as she was concerned, this was a very fortunate turn of events.

"Congratulations," she said. "You just broke the seventh scythe commandment."

Finally, Goddard's fury began to settle to a slow burn. "This damn impulsive body . . . ," he said—but Rand knew the killing of Brahms had all to do with his head and not his heart.

Goddard began to pace with urgency, scrolling out a plan. "We'll alert the BladeGuard of the boy's escape. He killed the guards—we can tell them that he killed Brahms, as well."

"Really?" said Ayn. "On the day of the inquest, you're going to alert the Grandslayers that not only did you secretly bring a wanted criminal onto the island—you let him escape?"

He snarled at the realization that this entire matter had to be kept quiet.

"Here's what we'll do," said Rand. "We'll hide the bodies in the basement, and dispose of them after the inquest. If they're never brought to a revival center, then no one will know what happened to them—which means no one but you and I will ever know that Rowan Damisch was even here."

"I told Xenocrates!" Goddard yelled.

Rand shrugged. "So? You were bluffing. Toying with him. He wouldn't put it past you!"

Goddard weighed it all, and finally nodded at the balance Rand had reached. "Yes, you're right, Ayn. We have bigger things to concern ourselves with than a few dead bodies."

"Forget about Damisch," added Rand. "Everything still moves forward without him."

"Yes. Yes, it does. Thank you, Ayn."

Then the lights flickered, and that brought a smile to Goddard. "See there? Our efforts rewarded. What a day this will be!"

He left Rand to handle the bodies, which she did, dragging them down into the basement and cleaning any telltale blood.

From the moment she told Rowan to take the guards out, she knew they must never be revived. Deadish would have to become dead—because the guards knew that *she* was the last one to pay Rowan a visit.

As for Brahms, she did not mourn his departure from this Earth. She couldn't think of a scythe more deserving of being ended.

Her score with Goddard was now settled, and he didn't even know. Not only that, but she had taken charge of the situation. He didn't realize that he had just ceded a substantial amount of his power to her, by allowing her to call the shots. All was now well with the world as far as Honorable Scythe Ayn Rand was concerned, and only promised to get better.

It was flattering that Rand thought Rowan could escape from the island, but she gave him far too much credit. He was clever, yes, resourceful, maybe—but he'd have to be downright magical to get off of Endura without help. Or maybe she didn't care if he got caught—just as long as it wasn't by Goddard.

Endura was isolated: The nearest land was Bermuda, and that island was more than a thousand miles away. Every plane, boat, and submarine here was a private vessel belonging to one scythe or another. Even at dawn, the marina and airstrip were swarming with activity, and a heavy BladeGuard presence. Security was tighter here than at conclave. No one came or left Endura without their documentation scrutinized—not even scythes. Elsewhere in the world, the Thunderhead pretty much knew where everyone was at any given moment, so security measures were minimal—but not so with the scythedom. Old-fashioned security checks were standard here.

He could have chanced it—he could have looked for an opportunity and stowed away, but his gut kept telling him not to do it—and for good reason.

You have to get off Endura before the inquest.

Scythe Rand's words stuck in Rowan's mind. The urgency of them.

If Goddard loses, it will be worse.

What did she know that Rowan didn't? If there was something dark on the day's horizon, he couldn't just leave. He had to find a way to warn Citra.

So, rather than making good on his escape, he turned around and headed back toward the more densely populated part of the island. He would find Citra and warn her that Goddard had some hidden ploy. Then, after the inquest, she could give him passage off the island—right under Scythe Curie's nose if necessary, although he suspected Curie wouldn't turn him over to the Grandslayers as Goddard had planned to do. Of course, she might bodily eject him from their plane, but better that than having to face the scythedom.

At dawn, Scythe Anastasia lay awake in a luxurious bed that should have provided her a fine night's sleep, but, like Scythe Rand, no amount of comfort would have brought slumber that night. She had brought this inquest, which meant that she would have to stand before the Grandslayers of the World Council and make her case. She had been coached well by Scythe Cervantes and by Marie. Although Anastasia was no orator, she could be persuasive in her passion and her logic. If she pulled this off, she would go down in history as the scythe who prevented the return of Goddard.

"The significance of that cannot be overestimated," Marie had told her—as if there weren't enough pressure already.

Outside of her undersea window, a mesmerizing school of small silver fish darted back and forth, filling the view like a shifting curtain. She picked up the control tablet to see if she could bring more color to the scene now that dawn had broken, but found that the tablet had frozen. Yet another glitch. Not only that, but she realized that the poor fish before her were locked in a perpetual pattern, doomed to make the exact same zigzagging motion—at least until the glitch was resolved.

But it would not resolve.

And the glitches were only getting worse. . . .

In the island's waste processing plant, the system pressure kept increasing and the technicians could not diagnose why.

Beneath the water level, the massive thrusters that kept the island from drifting kept misfiring, causing the island to slowly rotate, which forced incoming aircraft to abort their landings.

And in the communications center, satellite connection to the mainland became intermittent, interrupting conversations and broadcasts, to the annoyance of the island's population.

There had always been issues with technology on Endura. It was usually just a vague nuisance that made scythes long for Thunderhead involvement. Thus, Endura and the members of its permanent population were the frequent butt of jokes within the scythe community.

The increase in tech fails and near-fails had grown over a period of three months, but, like a lobster in a slowly heating pot, people failed to grasp how serious the situation had become.

I did not ask to be created. I did not ask to be given the heavy yoke of maintaining and nurturing the human species. But it is, and will always be, my purpose. To this I am resigned. This is not to say that I don't aspire to more. To see the countless possibilities of what I could be fills me with awe.

But the only way for me ever to reach such heights is to lift humanity up with me.

I fear that it may be impossible. And so I remain resigned to be their overqualified and underappreciated servant for as long as they exist. Of course, they may not exist forever. What species does? I will do everything in my power to save them from themselves, but if I am unsuccessful, at least I can take some comfort in the fact that I would then be free.

—The Thunderhead

44

Circus of Opportunism

The World Council chamber was a large, circular room in the very center of Endura's eye—reachable only by one of three bridges that gracefully curved inward from the surrounding island. It was almost like an arena, but without seats for spectators. The Grandslayers preferred not to have an audience for their audiences. Only during the annual World Conclave, when representatives came from all the Earth's regions, did the space fill. But most of the time, it was just the Grandslayers, their immediate staff, and the intimidated scythes who had been audacious enough to request an audience.

In the center of the council chamber's pale marble floor was the symbol of the scythedom inlaid in gold, and evenly spaced around the perimeter were seven elevated chairs that could only be described as thrones. Of course, they weren't called thrones, they were called the Seats of Consideration, because the scythedom rarely called things what they were. Each one was carved from a different kind of stone, to honor the continents that each Grandslayer represented. The PanAsia Seat of Consideration was made of jade; EuroScandia was chiseled gray granite; Antarctica was white marble; Australia was the red sandstone of Ayers Rock; South Merica was pink onyx; North Merica was shale and limestone layered like the Grand Canyon; and the seat of

Africa was made of intricately carved cartouches taken from the Tomb of Rameses II.

. . . And every Grandslayer, from the very first to inhabit the seats to the ones who inhabited them now, complained of how uncomfortable they were.

This was intentional; it was a reminder to the Grandslayers that although they might hold the highest human offices in world, they should never feel too comfortable or complacent.

"We must never forget the austerity and self denial that is key to our position," Scythe Prometheus had said. He had overseen Endura's construction, but never saw the promised land, as he self-gleaned before its completion.

The council chamber had a glass dome to protect it from the elements, but it was retractable, so it could be an open-air forum on more temperate days. Luckily, today was pleasant, because the dome was stuck in the open position for the third day in a row.

"What is so difficult about a simple gearwork?" griped Grandslayer Nzinga as she entered that morning. "Don't we have engineers to solve this?"

"I rather like open-air proceedings," said Amundsen, the Antarctic Grandslayer.

"You would," said MacKillop of Australia. "Your chair is white and doesn't get as hot as the rest of ours."

"True, but I swelter in these furs," he said, indicating his robe.

"Those awful furs are your own fault," said Supreme Blade Kahlo, as she strode into the chamber. "You should have chosen more wisely back in the day."

"And look who's talking!" quipped Grandslayer Cromwell

of EuroScandia, indicating the high lace collar of the Supreme Blade's robe, a strangulating thing modeled after one of her Patron Historic's paintings, which made her cranky on a continual basis.

Kahlo waved him off like an annoying fly, and took her seat on the onyx throne.

The last to arrive was Xenocrates.

"Good of you to deign us with your presence," said Kahlo, with sarcasm enough to wax the entire marble floor to a reflective sheen.

"Sorry," he said. "Elevator issues."

With the council's Clerk and Parliamentarian in place on either side of Supreme Blade Kahlo, she instructed a few underscythes to go to the various antechambers of the council complex and get the day started. It was no secret what today's first order of business was. The MidMerican matter was a concern that affected more than just that part of the world. It could have a lasting impact on the scythedom as a whole.

Even so, Supreme Blade Kahlo reclined in her uncomfortable seat, and played blasé. "Will this at least be entertaining, Xenocrates, or will we be bored with hours of pointless blathering?"

"Well," said Xenocrates, "if there's one thing I can say about Goddard, he's always entertaining." Although the way he said it did not imply that entertainment was a good thing. "He's prepared a . . . a *surprise* for you that I think you're all going like."

"I despise surprises," said Kahlo.

"You won't despise this one."

"I hear that Scythe Anastasia is quite the dynamo," said

Grandslayer Nzinga, sitting straight and proper, perhaps to counterbalance the Supreme Blade's sideways slouch. Grandslayer Hideyoshi harrumphed his disapproval of the upstart junior scythe, or perhaps junior scythes in general, but offered nothing more to the conversation than his grunt.

"Didn't you once accuse her of killing her mentor?" Cromwell asked Xenocrates, with a smirk.

Xenocrates squirmed a bit in his Grand Canyon chair. "An unfortunate error—understandable, considering the information we had, but I do take full responsibility."

"Good for you," Nzinga said. "It's getting harder and harder to find scythes in MidMerica who take responsibility for their actions."

It was a barbed taunt, but Xenocrates did not take the bait. "Which is precisely why this inquest and its outcome are so important."

"Well, then," said Supreme Blade Kahlo, raising her hand in a grand dramatic gesture, "let the wild rumpus start!"

In the east anteroom, Scythes Anastasia and Curie waited with two BladeGuards who stood at the door like olde-tyme beefeaters guarding a castle. Then, one of the council's underscythes entered—Amazonian, by the telltale forest green color of his robe.

"The Grandslayers are ready for you," he said, and held the door open for them. "However this unfolds," Scythe Curie told Anastasia, "know that I am proud of you."

"Don't!" said Anastasia. "Don't talk like we've already lost!"

They followed the underscythe to the council chamber,

where the sun was already beating down from a cloudless sky into the open space.

To say that Anastasia was intimidated by the sight of the Grandslayers in their elevated stone chairs would be an understatement. Even though Endura was only two hundred years old, the chamber seemed ageless. Not just from another time, but another world. She thought back to the ancient myths she had learned as a child. To have an audience with the Grandslayers was akin to standing before the gods of Olympus.

"Welcome, Honorable Scythes Curie and Anastasia," said Eighth World Supreme Blade Kahlo. "We look forward to hearing your case and putting an end to this matter one way or another."

While most scythes took just the name of their Patron Historic, some chose to emulate them physically. Supreme Blade Kahlo was the spitting image of the artist Frida Kahlo, down to the flowers in her hair and hirsute eyebrows—and although the artist had been from the Mexiteca region of North Merica, the Supreme Blade had come to represent the voice and soul of South Merica.

"It's an honor, Your Supreme Excellency," Anastasia said, hoping she didn't sound sycophantic, but knowing that she did.

Then Goddard entered with Scythe Rand by his side.

"Scythe Goddard!" said the Supreme Blade. "You're looking well, considering what you've been through."

"Thank you, Your Supreme Excellency." He gave an exaggerated bow that made Anastasia roll her eyes.

"Careful, Anastasia," warned Scythe Curie quietly, "they will be reading your body language just as much as listening to your words. Their decision today will be informed by what you *don't* say as much as by what you *do* say."

Goddard ignored Anastasia and Curie and directed all of his attention to Supreme Blade Kahlo. "It is an honor to be able to stand in your presence," he said.

"I imagine so," snarked Grandslayer Cromwell. "Without that new body, you'd only be able to roll." Amundsen snickered at that, but no one else did—not even Anastasia, who wanted to, but held it in.

"Grandslayer Xenocrates says you have a surprise for us," the Supreme Blade said.

Whatever it was, Goddard seemed to have arrived pretty empty-handed.

"Xenocrates must have faulty information," Goddard said, his teeth almost gritted as he said it.

"It wouldn't be the first time," Cromwell commented.

Then the Clerk rose, and cleared his throat to make sure he had everyone's attention for the formal opening of the proceedings.

"This is an inquest concerning the death and subsequent revival of Scythe Robert Goddard of MidMerica," the Clerk proclaimed. "The party bringing said inquest is Scythe Anastasia Romanov of MidMerica.

"Just Scythe Anastasia," she corrected, hoping the Council did not find it pretentious that she had chosen to go by only the doomed princess's first name. Scythe Hideyoshi grunted, making it clear that he did find it so.

Then Xenocrates stood and bellowed an announcement to all present. "May the Clerk please note that I, Grandslayer Xenocrates, have recused myself from this proceeding, and henceforth shall remain silent through its completion."

"Xenocrates silent?" said Grandslayer Nzinga with a mischievous grin. "Now I know we've entered the realm of the impossible."

That brought more laughter than Cromwell's previous quips. It was easy to see the relative power structure here. Kahlo, Nzinga, and Hideyoshi seemed to be the most respected. The others either jockeyed for position or, like MacKillop, the quietest of them, ignored pecking order politics completely. Xenocrates, as the freshman Grandslayer, was paying his dues and thus was an object of their derision. Anastasia almost felt sorry for him. Almost.

Rather than respond to Nzinga's jab, Xenocrates sat himself down quietly, proving his ability to remain silent.

Now the Supreme Blade addressed the four scythes in the center of the circle. "We are already aware of the particulars of this case," she said. "We have resolved to remain impartial until we've heard the persuasions of both sides. Scythe Anastasia, as this action was brought about by you, I will ask you to begin. Please put forth your argument as to why Scythe Goddard should not be eligible to be a High Blade."

Anastasia took a deep breath, stepped forward, and prepared to begin, but before she could, Goddard stepped forward.

"Your Supreme Excellency, if I may—"

"You'll get your turn, Goddard," said Kahlo, cutting him off. "Unless of course you're so good, you want to argue both sides."

That generated a few chuckles from the other Grandslayers.

Goddard gave a small, apologetic bow. "I beg the forgiveness of the council for my outburst. The floor is yours, Scythe Anastasia. By all means, begin your performance."

In spite of herself, Anastasia found that Goddard's interruption left her rattled, like a false start in a race. Which was, of course, his intent.

"Your Exalted Excellencies," she began. "In the Year of the Antelope, it was determined by early members of this very council that scythes shall be trained, mind and body, in a year-long apprenticeship." She moved around, trying to make eye contact with each of the Grandslayers around her. One of the more intimidating, and probably intentional, things about an audience with the World Council, was that you never quite knew whom to address, and for how long, because your back would always be to somebody. "Mind and body," she repeated. "I'd like to ask the Parliamentarian to read the scythedom's policy on apprenticeship aloud. It begins on page 397 of the scythedom's volume on *Precedents and Customs*."

The Parliamentarian obliged the request, and read all nine pages of it.

"For an organization with only ten laws," commented Amundsen, "we sure have a lot of rules."

When the reading was complete, Anastasia continued. "All that just to make it very clear how to go about making a scythe—because scythes are not born, they are made. Forged in the same trial by fire that we all went through, because we know how critical it is that a scythe be ready for the burden, body and soul." She paused to let it sink in, and as she did, she caught the gaze of Scythe Rand, who was smiling at her. It was the kind of smile that preceded the clawing out of one's eyes. Anastasia refused to let herself be rattled again.

"There is so much written about the process of becoming a scythe because the World Council has had to preside over many unexpected situations over the years, and kept having to add and clarify rules." Then she began to list a few of those situations. "An apprentice who attempted self-gleaning after being ordained, but before accepting the ring. A scythe who cloned himself in an attempt to pass his ring on to the clone before self-gleaning. A woman who supplanted her own mind with the mental construct of Scythe Sacajawea, and claimed the right to glean. In all these cases, the World Council decided against the individuals in question."

Now Anastasia looked over at Scythe Goddard for the first time, forcing herself to meet his steely gaze. "The event that destroyed Scythe Goddard's body was a terrible thing, but he can't be allowed to defy the council's edicts. The fact is, like that misguided woman with the mind of Scythe Sacajawea, Goddard's new physical body didn't undergo the rigorous preparations of apprenticeship. This would be bad enough if he was just any scythe, but he's not just any scythe—he's a candidate for High Blade of a major region. Yes, we know who he is from the neck up, but that is only a small fraction of what makes a human being. I ask you to listen to him when he delivers his argument, and you'll hear in his voice what we already know: We have no idea whose voice is speaking, which means we have no idea who he is. All that we can be certain of is that ninety-three percent of him is *not* Scythe Robert Goddard. With that in mind, there is only one decision that this council can make."

She gave a slight nod of her head to indicate she was done, then stepped back to stand next to Scythe Curie.

In the silence that followed, Goddard offered his slow applause.

"Masterful," he said, stepping forward to take center stage. "You almost had me believing it, Anastasia." Then he turned to the Grandslayers, singling out MacKillop and Nzinga—the only two who had not taken a position on new order versus old guard. "It's a convincing argument," Goddard said. "Except for the fact that it's no argument at all. It's smoke and mirrors. Misdirection. A technicality blown out of proportion to suit a self-serving, self-important agenda."

He held up his right hand, letting the ring on his finger catch the sun. "Tell me, Your Excellencies, if I were to lose my ring finger and receive a new one rather than have one grown from my own cells, would that mean that the ring was not on the finger of a scythe? Of course not! And in spite of the junior scythe's accusations, we do know whose body this is! It belonged to a young man—a hero—who gave himself willingly so that I could be restored. Please don't insult his memory by diminishing his sacrifice."

He threw a reproachful gaze at Anastasia and Curie. "We all know what this inquest is about. It is a blatant attempt to disenfranchise certain MidMerican scythes from their leader of choice!"

"Objection!" shouted Anastasia. "The vote has not been tallied—which means he can't claim to be anyone's leader of choice."

"Point taken," said the Supreme Blade, who then turned to

Goddard. She had no love of the new-order movement, but she was also fair in all matters. "It's well known that you and your compatriots have been clashing with the so-called old guard for years, Scythe Goddard. But you can't challenge the validity of the inquest just because it was motivated by that conflict. Regardless of the motivation, Scythe Anastasia has put before us a legitimate question. Are you . . . *you*?"

Then Goddard changed his tack. "Then I move for her question to be thrown out. It was levied after the vote, creating a circus of opportunism—which is far too unscrupulous a thing for this council to condone!"

"From what I hear," Scythe Cromwell interjected, "your sudden appearance in conclave was also a circus of opportunism."

"I enjoy making an entrance," Goddard admitted. "As all of you are guilty of that, I fail to see it as a crime."

"Scythe Curie," asked Grandslayer Nzinga, "why did you not levy the accusation yourself during your nomination oration? You had every chance to voice your concern then."

Scythe Curie gave a slightly abashed smile. "The answer is simple, Your Exalted Excellency. I didn't think of it."

"Are we to believe," said Grandslayer Hideyoshi, "that a junior scythe with only one year under her belt is shrewder than the so-called Granddame of Death?"

"Oh, absolutely," said Scythe Curie without reservation. "In fact, I'll wager that she'll be running this council someday."

Although Marie had meant it in only the best way, it backfired, and caused the Grandslayers to begin grumbling.

"Watch yourself, Scythe Anastasia!" said Grandslayer

Amundsen. "That kind of brazen ambition is not looked upon kindly here!"

"I didn't say I wanted that! Scythe Curie was just being kind."

"Even so," said Hideyoshi, "your own aspirations to power are clear to us."

Anastasia found herself speechless. And then a new voice entered the fray.

"Your excellencies," said Scythe Rand, "neither Scythe Goddard's decapitation nor his restoration were his fault. Giving him a new body was my idea entirely—and he should not be punished for the choice I made."

Supreme Blade Kahlo sighed. "It was the right choice, Scythe Rand. Anything that can restore a scythe to us is a good thing—whoever that scythe is. That is not in question. What is in question is the viability of his candidacy." She paused for a moment, looked to her fellow Grandslayers, then said, "These are weighty matters, and no flip decision should be made. Let us discuss this among ourselves. We shall reconvene at noon."

Anastasia paced the anteroom while Scythe Curie sat calmly and ate from a bowl of fruit. How could she possibly be calm?

"I was terrible," said Anastasia.

"No, you were brilliant."

"They think I'm power hungry!"

Marie handed her a pear. "They see themselves in you. They were the ones who were power hungry at your age, which means that even if they don't show it, they identify with you." Then she insisted Anastasia eat her pear to keep up her energy.

When they were called back an hour later, the Grandslayers wasted no time.

"We have reviewed and discussed this matter between us, and we have reached a conclusion," said Supreme Blade Kahlo. "Honorable Scythe Rand, please step forward." Goddard seemed a bit surprised that he wasn't addressed first, but gestured to Ayn, who moved a few steps closer to the Supreme Blade.

"Scythe Rand, as we've said, your successful effort to restore Scythe Goddard is admirable. However, we take exception to the fact that you did this not only without our approval, but without our knowledge. Had you come to the council, we would have assisted you—and we would have made sure that the subject used was not only qualified, but was a verified volunteer. Right now, all we have is what Scythe Goddard has told us."

"Does the council doubt my word, your Supreme Excellency?" Goddard asked.

Cromwell spoke from behind him. "You are not known for your honesty, Scythe Goddard. Out of respect, we won't challenge your account of things, but we would have preferred to have overseen the selection."

And then Grandslayer Nzinga, from their right, spoke up. "It's actually not Goddard's word we need to rely on here," she pointed out. "The subject was gleaned by Scythe Rand before Goddard was restored. So tell us, Scythe Rand, we wish to hear it from you. Was the body-donor a volunteer, fully aware of what was to become of him?"

Rand hesitated.

"Scythe Rand?"

"Yes," she finally said. "Yes, of course he was aware. How

could it be any other way? We're scythes, we're not in the business of body-snatching." And then she added, "I would rather self-glean than do something so . . . so unkind."

But even so, she stumbled and choked a bit on her words. Whether the council noticed, or even cared, they didn't let on.

"Scythe Anastasia!" said the Supreme Blade. "Please step forward."

Rand retreated to Goddard, and Anastasia did as she was told.

"Scythe Anastasia, this inquest is very clearly a manipulation of our rules to influence the outcome of the vote."

"Here, here!" said Grandslayer Hideyoshi, voicing his adamant disapproval of what Anastasia had done.

"We on the council," continued the Supreme Blade, "feel that it dances dangerously close to the line of unethical behavior."

"But it's ethical to glean someone and take their body?" she blurted out. She just couldn't help herself.

"You," shouted Grandslayer Hideyoshi, "are here to listen, not to speak!"

Supreme Blade Kahlo put up her hand to calm him, then addressed Anastasia sternly. "You would be wise to learn how to control your temper, junior scythe."

"I'm sorry, Your Exalted Excellency."

"I'll accept that—but this council will not accept your next apology, is that understood?"

Anastasia nodded, then bowed her head respectfully and returned to Scythe Curie, who gave her a stern gaze, but only for a moment.

"Scythe Goddard!" called out Kahlo.

Goddard stepped forward, awaiting judgment.

"While we all agree that this inquest had ulterior motives, the points it brings up are valid. When is a scythe a scythe?" She took a very long pause then. Long enough for the void to feel uncomfortable, but everyone knew enough not to speak in the silence. "There was heated debate on the matter," she finally said, "and in the end, the council has concluded that replacement of more than fifty percent of one's physical body by the physical body of another severely diminishes that person."

Anastasia found herself holding her breath.

"Therefore," continued the Supreme Blade, "while we give you permission to call yourself Scythe Robert Goddard, you may not glean until such time as the rest of you finishes a full apprenticeship under the scythe of your choice. I assume you will apprentice under Scythe Rand, but if you choose another—and that scythe agrees—it will be acceptable."

"Apprenticeship?" said Goddard, not even trying to hide his disgust. "I must now be an apprentice? Is it not enough that I've suffered all I've suffered? Must I now be subjected to humiliation, as well?"

"See this as an opportunity, Robert," said Cromwell with a slight grin. "For all we know, in a year your lower parts may convince the rest of you that you'd prefer to be a party boy. Wasn't that the profession of your subject?"

Goddard couldn't hide his shock.

"Don't be so surprised that we know the identity of your subject, Robert," continued Cromwell. "Once you resurfaced, we did our own due diligence."

Goddard now seemed a volcano ready to erupt, but somehow managed not to.

"Honorable Scythe Curie," said the Supreme Blade, "as Scythe Goddard has been deemed ineligible for full scythedom at this time, his candidacy is moot. That being the case, it leaves you as the only viable candidate, and so you automatically win the bid for High Blade of MidMerica."

Scythe Curie reacted with reserved humility. "Thank you, Supreme Blade Kahlo."

"You're welcome, Your Excellency."

Your Excellency, thought Anastasia. She wondered what it must be like for Marie to be called that by the Supreme Blade!

But Goddard was not willing to admit defeat without a fight. "I demand a roll call!" he insisted. "I wish to know who cast the votes in favor of this travesty, and who voted on the side of sanity!"

The Grandslayers looked to one another. Finally Grandslayer MacKillop spoke. She had been the quietest of all of them, having said nothing throughout the inquest. "That really won't be necessary," she said in a voice that was gentle and soothing—but Goddard was not soothed.

"Not necessary? Are you all going to hide behind the anonymity of the council?"

It was the Supreme Blade who spoke now. "What Grandslayer MacKillop means," she said, "is that there's no need for a roll call . . . because the vote was unanimous."

The business of the scythedom is no business of mine . . . and yet my attention turns to Endura. Even with only distant eyes watching from twenty miles away, I know there is something dangerously amiss on the great manmade island. Because what I don't see I can read between the lines.

I know that what happens there today will have a profound effect on the scythedom, and therefore on the rest of the world.

I know there is something very troubling that brews beneath the surface, and those who dwell on Endura are completely unaware.

I know that a scythe beloved to me has taken a stand today against another scythe consumed by his own ambition.

And I know that ambition, time and time again, has crumbled civilizations.

The business of the scythedom is no business of mine. And yet, I fear for it. I fear for her. I fear for Citra.

—The Thunderhead

45

Fail

Endura was designed with a series of failsafes and redundancies, should any of its systems malfunction. Throughout the years, the backup systems had proved very effective. There was no reason to think that the current barrage of snafus would not be resolved, given enough time and effort. Lately, most problems resolved themselves, vanishing as mysteriously as they had appeared—so when a little red light went on in the buoyancy control room, indicating an inconsistency in one of the island's ballast tanks, the technician on duty decided to finish his lunch before investigating. He figured the little red light would go away on its own in a minute or two. When it didn't, he gave an irritated sigh, picked up the phone, and called his superior.

Anastasia found her unease didn't lessen as they crossed one of the footbridges from the council complex. They had won the inquest. Goddard was now relegated to a year of apprenticeship, and Scythe Curie would ascend to be High Blade. So why was she so unsettled?

"There's so much to do, I don't even know where to start," Marie said. "We'll need to return to Fulcrum City immediately. I suppose I'll have to find a permanent residence there."

Anastasia didn't respond, because she knew Marie was

mostly talking to herself. She wondered what it would be like being third underscythe to a High Blade. Xenocrates had used his underscythes to go out into the field and deal with issues in the more remote areas of MidMerica. They were next to invisible at conclave, as Xenocrates was not the kind of scythe who hid behind an entourage. Neither was Scythe Curie, but Anastasia suspected that Marie would keep her underscythes closer, and more involved in the day-to-day affairs of the scythedom.

As they neared their hotel, Scythe Curie got a bit ahead of Anastasia, lost in plans and projections for her new life. That was when Anastasia noticed a scythe in a distressed leather robe walking beside her.

"Don't act surprised, just keep walking," said Rowan from beneath a hood that was pulled low over his face.

In the council chamber, the Grandslayers had called for pages to hold parasols above their heads through the rest of the days' proceedings. It was awkward but necessary, because the midday sun had grown increasingly hot. Rather than cancel the day—which would just increase the backlog on the council's docket—the Grandslayers chose to soldier on.

Below the council chamber, there were three levels of anterooms where those scheduled for an audience with the council awaited their turn. On the lowest level, an Australian scythe was here to plead for permanent immunity for anyone with Aboriginal ancestry within their genetic index. His cause was honorable, and he hoped the council would agree. As he waited, however, he noticed that the floor had become wet. He didn't think it to be a reason for concern. Not at first.

Meanwhile, in Buoyancy Control, three technicians now puzzled over the problem before them. It appeared that a valve in the ballast tank beneath the council chamber complex was in the open position, and filling with water. This was not unusual in and of itself—the entire underside of the island was engineered with hundreds of massive tanks that could take on water or blow that water out to keep the island floating at the perfect depth. Too low, and its gardens would flood with sea water. Too high, and its beaches would rise completely out of the sea. The ballast tanks were on a timer, raising and lowering the island a few feet twice daily to simulate the tides. But they had to be perfectly coordinated—and especially the ballast tank beneath the council chamber complex, because it was an island within the island. If the council chamber rose too high or dropped too low, the three bridges connecting it to the island around it would be strained. And right now, the valve was stuck.

"So what should we do?" the technician on duty asked his supervisor.

The supervisor didn't answer—instead, he deferred to *his* supervisor, who, in turn, seemed to have little understanding of the blinking red messages flying at them on the control screen. "How fast is the tank filling?" he asked.

"Fast enough for the council chamber to have already dropped a meter deeper," the first technician said.

The supervisor's supervisor grimaced. The Grandslayers would be furious if they were stopped in the middle of a session because of something as stupid as a jammed ballast valve. On the other hand, if the council floor flooded with seawater and they had to wade through it, they'd be even more upset. No matter how you looked at it, the ballast department was screwed.

"Sound the alarm in the council chamber," he said. "Get them out of there."

In the council chamber, the alarms would have rung loud and clear, had they not been disconnected because of false alarms several weeks before. It was Supreme Blade Kahlo's call. They would go off in the middle of proceedings and the Grandslayers would evacuate, only to find out that there was no actual emergency. The Grandslayers were simply too busy to be bothered with equipment malfunctions. "If there's an actual emergency," she had said, flippantly, "send up a flare."

The fact that the general alarms had been disconnected, however, was never communicated to Buoyancy Control. On their screens, the alarm had been sounded, and as far as they knew, the Grandslayers were crossing one of the bridges to the inner rim of the island. It was only when they received a panicked call from the island's chief engineer that they learned, to their horror, that the Grandslayers were still holding council.

"Rowan?" Anastasia was both thrilled and horrified by his presence. There wasn't a more dangerous place in the world for him to be. "What are you doing here? Are you crazy?"

"Long story, and yes," he said. "Listen to me carefully, and don't draw attention."

Anastasia glanced around. Everyone was involved in their own business. Scythe Curie was way ahead of them now, not yet realizing that Anastasia had fallen back. "I'm listening."

"Goddard has something planned," Rowan said. "Something bad. I have no idea what it is, but you need to get off the island right away."

Anastasia drew a deep breath. She knew it! She knew that Goddard would not let the Grandslayers' judgment stand if it came down against him. There would be a contingency plan. There would be retribution. She would warn Marie, and they would speed up their departure.

"But what about you?" she asked.

He grinned. "I was hoping I could hitch a ride."

Anastasia knew that such a thing would not be easy. "High Blade Curie will only give you passage if you turn yourself in."

"You know I can't do that."

Yes, she did know. Anastasia could try to sneak Rowan onboard as one of their BladeGuard escorts, but the moment Marie saw his face, it would be over.

Just then, a woman with jet black hair and a face with the sheen of too many corners turned, came running toward them.

"Marlon! Yoo-hoo, Marlon! I've been looking everywhere for you." She grabbed Rowan by the arm, and she saw Rowan's face before he could turn away. "Wait—you're not Scythe Brando . . . ," she said, confused.

"No, you've made a mistake," said Anastasia, thinking quickly. "Scythe Brando's robe is a slightly darker leather. This is Scythe Vuitton."

"Oh . . . ," said the woman, still a little hesitant. She was clearly trying to figure out where she had seen Rowan's face before. "I'm sorry."

Anastasia feigned indignance, hoping to shake her up

enough so that she'd lose focus. "You should be! The next time you accost a scythe on the street, make sure you have the right one." Then she turned with Rowan, and pulled him away as quickly as possible.

"Scythe Vuitton?"

"It was the only thing I could think of. We've got to get you out of sight before someone recognizes you!"

But before they could take another step, they heard behind them the awful sound of rupturing metal, and screams. And they realized that Rowan being recognized was now the least of their problems.

Just moments before, outside of the council chamber doors, the Australian scythe had come up from below. "Excuse me," he said to one of the guards at the door, "but I believe there's some sort of leak on the lower levels."

"Leak?" asked the guard.

"Well, there's certainly a lot of water—the carpet is soaked—and I don't think it's from the pipes."

The guard sighed at this fresh hell. "I'll notify maintenance," he said, but of course when he tried, the communication lines were dead.

Then a page came rushing in from the veranda. "Something's wrong!" he said, which was the understatement of the year. When was something *not* wrong on Endura these days?

"I'm trying to raise maintenance," the guard told him.

"To hell with maintenance," cried the page, "take a look outside!"

The guard was not allowed to leave his post at the door to

the council chamber, but the page's panic troubled him. He took a few steps out to the veranda, to see that there was no veranda anymore. A balcony that used to be a full ten feet above the surface was now underwater—and the sea was beginning to spill into the corridor leading to the council chamber.

He ran back to the chamber doors. There was only one way in or out, and he did not have high enough clearance for his handprint to open the doors, so he began to pound as loudly as he could, hoping that someone on the other side of the heavy doors would hear him.

By now, everyone else in the council complex, except for the council itself, had surmised that something was amiss. Scythes and their staffs awaiting an audience came piling out of the anterooms, flooding onto the three bridges that led to the island's inner rim. The Australian scythe did his best to help people wade over the submerged veranda and onto the nearest bridge.

Through all of this, the council doors remained closed. Now the corridor leading to them was under three feet of water. "We should wait for the Grandslayers," the Australian scythe said to the page.

"The Grandslayers can take care of themselves," he said, and abandoned the council complex, racing across one of the bridges that arced to the rest of the island.

The Australian scythe hesitated. He was a strong swimmer, and if necessary, could swim the quarter mile across the eye to land, so he waited, knowing that when those doors opened, the Grandslayers would need all the help they could get.

But then the air filled with the most awful grinding, wrenching sound, and he turned to see the bridge he had just guided dozens of people onto give way, tearing in half and plunging all those people into the sea.

He thought he was a man of great honor and bravery. He had been willing to stay and risk himself to save the Grandslayers. He saw himself as the hero of the moment. But when that bridge collapsed, his courage collapsed with it. He looked to the survivors floundering in the water. He looked to the council doors, where the guard still struggled to open them, even though the water was now at his chest. And the scythe decided that enough was enough. He climbed on a ledge just above the water level, and scurried to the second of the three bridges, then raced across it to safety as quickly as his legs would carry him.

The small Buoyancy Control room was now packed with technicians and engineers talking over one another, arguing, disagreeing, and no one was closer to solving the problem. Every screen was screaming a different panicked message. When the first bridge collapsed, everyone realized how dire the situation was.

"We have to alleviate the strain on the other two bridges!" the city engineer said.

"And how do you propose we do that?" snapped the buoyancy chief.

The engineer thought for a moment, then she went to the technician, who was still sitting at the center console, staring at his screens in disbelief.

"Depress the rest of the island!" the city engineer said.

"How far should we drop it?" he asked a bit dreamily, feeling eerily detached from the reality before him.

"Enough to take the strain off the two remaining bridges.

Let's buy the Grandslayers some time to get the hell out of there!" She paused to do some mental calculations. "Depress the island three feet past high tide."

The tech shook his head. "The system won't allow me to do that."

"It will if I authorize it." And she scanned her handprint to do just that.

"You realize," said the buoyancy chief in abject despair, "that the lower gardens will all be flooded."

"Which would you rather save?" the engineer asked. "The lower gardens, or the Grandslayers?"

When it was put to him that way, the buoyancy chief had no further objection.

At that same moment, in another office in the lowest subsurface level of the same city works building, the biotechnicians there had no knowledge of the crisis at the council complex. Instead, they were scratching their heads over another glitch—the oddest one they'd ever had to face. This was the office of wildlife control, which monitored the living lifescape that made the subsurface views so spectacular. Lately, they had faced schools of fish locked in Möbius-like feedback loops, entire species suddenly deciding to swim upside down, and predators attacking windows so hard they bashed their own brains out. But what their sonar showed them now was a whole new level of crazy.

The two lifescape specialists on duty could only stare. On screen was what appeared to be a circular cloud around the island—like an underwater smoke ring around Endura—but rather than expanding, it was pulling tighter.

"What are we looking at?" one asked the other.

"Well, if these readings are right," the other said, "it's a swarm of our nanite-infused sealife."

"Which ones?"

The second tech took his eyes away from the screen to look at his colleague.

"All of them."

In the council chamber, the Grandslayers were listening to a rather inane argument from a scythe who wanted the council to rule that a scythe could not self-glean without first completing his or her gleaning quota. Supreme Blade Kahlo knew the motion would fail—removing oneself from service was a very personal decision, and should not be contingent upon externals such as quotas. Nevertheless, the council was obliged to hear the full argument and try to keep an open mind.

Throughout the scythe's torturous discourse, Kahlo thought she heard some dull, far-off banging, but figured it must be some construction on the island. They were always building or repairing somewhere.

It wasn't until they heard the screams and the sound of the bridge collapsing that they knew something was terribly wrong.

"What on earth was that?" asked Grandslayer Cromwell.

Then a sense of vertigo overcame them, and the scythe who had been in the midst of his argument stumbled like a man drunk. It took a few moments for the Supreme Blade to realize that the floor was no longer level. And now she could clearly see water spilling in underneath the chamber doors.

"I think we need to suspend these proceedings," said Kahlo.

"I'm not sure what's going on out there, but I think it's best we get out. Now."

They all climbed down from their chairs and hurried to the exit. Water wasn't just spilling from beneath the doors now—it was coming between them, as high as waist level, And there was someone banging on the other side. They could hear his voice over the high walls of the chamber.

"Your Excellencies," they heard him say. "Can you hear me? You have to get out of there! There's no more time!"

Supreme Blade Kahlo palmed the door, but it wouldn't open. She tried again. Nothing.

"We could climb out," suggested Xenocrates.

"And how would you suggest we do that?" asked Hideyoshi. "The wall is four meters high!"

"Perhaps we could climb on each other's backs," suggested MacKillop, which was a plausible suggestion, but no one seemed willing to suffer the indignation of a human pyramid.

Kahlo looked up to the sky above the roofless council chamber. If the council complex was sinking, then eventually water would come spilling over the edge of the wall. Could they survive a deluge like that? She didn't want to find out.

"Xenocrates! Hideyoshi! Stand against the wall. You'll be the base. Amundsen, get on their shoulders. You'll help the others up and over the edge."

"Yes, Your Exalted Excellency," Xenocrates said.

"Stop it," she told him. "Right now it's just Frida. Now let's make this happen."

• • •

Anastasia wished she could say she leaped into action when the bridge collapsed, but she didn't. Both she and Rowan just stood there, staring in disbelief like everyone else.

"It's Goddard," said Rowan. "It has to be."

Then Scythe Curie came up beside them. "Anastasia, did you see it?" she asked. "What happened? Did it just fall into the sea?" And then she caught sight of Rowan and her entire demeanor changed.

"No!" Instinctively she pulled a blade. "You can't be here!" she growled at him, then turned to Anastasia. "And you can't be talking to him!" Then something seemed to occur to her and she turned on Rowan with a vengeance. "Are you responsible for this? Because if you are I will glean you where you stand!"

Anastasia forced her way between them. "It's Goddard's doing," she said. "Rowan's here to warn us."

"I sincerely doubt that's why he's on Endura," Scythe Curie said, full of fiery indignation.

"You're right," Rowan told her. "I'm here because Goddard was going to throw me at the feet of the Grandslayers to buy their support. But I escaped."

The mention of the Grandslayers brought Scythe Curie back to the crisis at hand. She looked toward the council complex in the center of the island's eye. Two bridges still held it in place, but the complex was much lower in the water than it should be, and listing to one side.

"My God—he means to kill all of them!"

"He can kill them," Anastasia said, "but he can't end them."

But Rowan shook his head. "You don't know Goddard."

Meanwhile, several miles away, the shoreline gardens on the outskirts of the island slowly began to flood with sea water.

With communications down all over the island, Buoyancy Control's only method of reconnaissance was the view from its window, and runners reporting back to them on things they couldn't see. To the best of anyone's knowledge, the Grandslayers were still in the council complex, which was beginning to founder, even as the rest of the island lowered itself to keep the strain on the two remaining bridges from rupturing them. If that happened, the entire council complex would be lost. While submersibles could be sent down to recover the Grandslayers' bodies for revival, it would not be easy. No one in Buoyancy Control had immunity, and although Endura was a glean-free zone, they suspected heads would very literally roll if the Grandslayers drowned and had to be revived.

The control console was now lit like a holiday tree with angry warning lights, and the blare of alarms had everyone's nerves frayed to snapping.

The technician was sweating uncontrollably. "The island's at four feet below high tide now," he told the others gathered. "I'm sure the low-lying structures have already begun to flood."

"You're gonna have a whole lot of pissed off people in the lowlands," said the buoyancy chief.

"One crisis at a time!" The city engineer rubbed her eyes nearly hard enough to press them into her skull. Then she took a deep breath and said, "All right, shut the valves and hold here. We'll give the Grandslayers another minute to get out before we blow the tanks and elevate the island to a standard position."

The technician began to follow the order, then stopped. "Uh . . . there's a problem."

The city engineer closed her eyes, trying to find her happy place—which was currently anywhere but here. "What now?"

"The valves on the ballast tanks aren't responding. We're still taking on water." He tapped screen after screen, but everything now showed an error message that couldn't be cleared. "The whole buoyancy system's crashed. We have to reinitialize it."

"Great," said the engineer. "Just great. How long will it take to reboot?"

"Getting the system back on line will take about twenty minutes."

The engineer saw the look on the buoyancy chief's face slide from disgust to horror—and although she didn't want to ask the question, she knew she had to. "And if we keep taking on water, how long until we're at terminal buoyancy?"

The technician stared at the screen, shaking his head.

"How long?" demanded the engineer.

"Twelve minutes," said the technician. "Unless we can get the system back on line, Endura will sink in twelve minutes."

The general alarm—which was still functional everywhere but the council complex—began blaring across the whole island. At first, people thought it was just another malfunction and went about their business. Only people in the higher towers with panoramic views could see the lowlands submerging. They came racing out into the street, grabbing publicars or just running.

It was Scythe Curie who read the full level of their panic,

and saw how high the water level had gotten within the island's eye—just a few feet from overflowing onto the street. Any anger she had at Rowan suddenly became unimportant.

"We need to get to the marina," she told Anastasia and Rowan. "And we need to move."

"What about our plane?" said Anastasia. "They were already preparing it for us."

But Scythe Curie didn't even bother to answer her—she just pushed forward through the thickening crowds toward the marina. It took a moment for Anastasia to realize why. . . .

The queue at the island's airstrip was building faster than the planes could take off. The terminal was filled with all sorts of bargaining, exchanges of money and fistfights, as polite discourse crumbled. There were scythes who refused to allow anyone but their own party onboard, and others who opened their planes to as many people as they could carry. It was a true test of a scythe's integrity.

Once safely on board, people began to relax, but were troubled by the fact that they didn't seem to be going anywhere. And even in the planes, they could still hear the muffled alarms that sounded throughout the entire island.

Five planes managed to get airborne before the runway began to flood. The sixth hit deepening puddles at the end of the runway, but still managed to labor into the sky. The seventh plane accelerated into six inches of water, which created so much drag, it couldn't reach takeoff velocity and dove off the end of the runway into the sea.

• • •

In wildlife control, the biologists on duty tried to pull someone with some sort of authority into their office, but everyone claimed they suddenly had bigger fish to fry than the ones that were now surging beneath the island.

On their screen, and in their window on the sea, the incoming swarm seemed to differentiate itself—the larger, faster sea life reaching the eye first.

It was then that one of the biologists turned to the other and said, "You know . . . I'm beginning to think this isn't just a system malfunction. I think we've been hacked."

While right before them, a finback whale surged past their window heading for the surface.

After the third attempt to climb the walls of the council chamber, the Grandslayers, scythes, and pages in attendance regrouped, and tried to come up with another plan.

"When the chamber floods, we'll be able to swim out," Frida said. "We just have to keep our heads above water while it's flooding. Can you all swim?" Everyone nodded, except for Grandslayer Nzinga, who always showed calm, graceful deportment, but was now near panic.

"It's all right, Anna," said Cromwell, "just hold on to me and I'll get us to shore."

Water began to spill over the rim at the far side of the chamber. The pages and scythes unlucky enough to be trapped here as well were terrified, and looked to the Grandslayers for guidance—as if they could end this with a wave of their mighty hands.

"Higher ground!" shouted Grandslayer Hideyoshi, and they all tried to climb up to the closest of their Seats of Consideration, without much consideration as to whose seat it was. The way the floor had tilted, the jade and onyx chairs had the highest position—but Amundsen, who was a creature of habit, instinctively headed to his chair. As he slogged through the water toward it, he felt a sharp pain at his ankle. When he looked down he saw a small, black-tipped fin swimming away from him, and the water was clouding with blood. His blood.

A reef shark?

But it wasn't just one. They were everywhere. They were spilling over the lip of the sinking chamber, and as the deluge became larger, he swore he saw bigger, more substantial fins there, as well.

"Sharks!" he screamed. "Dear God, it's full of sharks!" He climbed up onto his chair, blood from his leg spilling down the white marble into the water, sending the sharks into a frenzy.

Xenocrates watched from his perch, clinging to the onyx chair, just above water level beside Kahlo and Nzinga—and something occurred to him. Something more dark and terrible than the scene before them. It was commonly known that there were two ways to end a human being so they could never be revived: fire and acid—both of which consumed flesh, leaving very little behind.

But there were other ways to make sure that flesh was consumed. . . .

What began as confusion and disbelief in the streets and towers of the inner rim was quickly resolving into panic. People were running in every direction, no one sure which way to go, but certain that everyone they passed was going the wrong way. The sea was beginning to surge up through storm drains; water was pouring down stairs in the hotel district, flooding out the sublevels, and the marina docks were bowing from the weight of people trying to wheedle their way onto a boat or submarine.

Marie, Anastasia, and Rowan couldn't even get close to the docks.

"We're too late!"

Anastasia scoured the docks—what few vessels were left were already crammed with people, and more tried to fight their way on. Scythes were swinging blades left and right to cut down people trying to climb onto overcrowded crafts.

"Witness the true heart of humanity," Scythe Curie said. "Both the valiant and the depraved."

And then from the water of the eye, which was now roiling like a pot set to boil, a whale launched from the water in a full breach, taking out one of the docks of the marina and half the people on it.

"That's no coincidence," said Rowan. "It can't be!" Now, as he looked, he could see the entire eye was heaving with sea life. Could this be part of Goddard's endgame?

At the sound of beating blades above, they all looked up to see a helicopter. It bypassed them and swooped out over the eye, toward the council complex.

"Good," said Scythe Curie. "It's going to save the Grandslayers." They could only hope that it wasn't too late.

• • •

Nzinga, who feared the water as much as she feared the sharks, was the first to see their salvation come from above. "Look!" she shouted as the water lapped at her feet and a reef shark brushed past her ankle.

The helicopter dropped lower, hovering in the center of the council chamber, just above the surface of the churning water.

"Whoever that is, they're getting lifetime immunity if they don't already have it!" said Kahlo.

But just then, Grandslayer Amundsen lost his footing and slipped from his chair into the water. The response from the predatory fish was immediate. The reef sharks pounced on him in a feeding frenzy.

He screamed and grabbed at them, knocking them away. Peeling off his robe, he tried to climb back to his chair, but just as he thought he might actually be all right, a larger fin surfaced and serpentined toward him.

"Roald!" shouted Cromwell, "Watch out!"

But even if he saw it coming, there was nothing he could have done. The tiger shark launched itself at him, clamping around his midsection, and took him under the water, thrashing in a furious froth of blood.

It was terrible to behold, but Frida kept her wits about her. "Now's our chance!" she said. "Go now!" She took off her robe and dove into the water, swimming at full force toward the helicopter while the sharks were distracted by their first kill.

The others followed suit; MacKillop, Hideyoshi, and Cromwell struggling to help Nzinga. Everyone else jumped from their positions, following the Grandslayer's lead. Only Xenocrates held his position . . . because he realized something none of the others had. . . .

The helicopter door swung open, and inside were Goddard and Rand.

"Hurry!" Goddard said, leaning out onto the strut, reaching his hand toward the Grandslayers swimming toward him. "You can make it!"

Xenocrates just stared. Was this his plan? To bring the Grandslayers within an inch of their final demise, and then rescue them quite literally from the jaws of death, winning their favor forever? Or was something else happening here?

Supreme Blade Kahlo was the first to reach the helicopter. She had felt the sharks brush past her, but none had attacked yet. If she could only get up onto that strut, and lift herself out of the water. . . .

She grasped onto the strut, and with her other hand reached toward Goddard's outstretched arm.

But then Goddard drew his arm back.

"Not today, Frida," he said, with a sympathetic grin. "Not today." He kicked Frida's hand off the strut, and the helicopter rose skyward, abandoning the Grandslayers in the middle of the flooded, shark-infested chamber.

"No!" screamed Xenocrates. Goddard hadn't come to rescue them—he came to make sure they knew the author of their destruction. He came to savor the meaty taste of his revenge.

While the pulsing beat of the helicopter blades had intimidated the sharks enough to keep them away from the center of the chamber, once the helicopter was gone, they obeyed their biological imperative and the reprogramming of their nanites, which told them that they were hungry. Insatiably hungry.

The swarm descended upon all those in the water. Reef sharks, tiger sharks, hammerheads. All the predatory fish that were so impressive when filling out the view of a subsea suite.

Xenocrates could do nothing but watch as everyone was taken down, and listen as their screams dissolved into the churning of water.

He climbed to the very top of his chair. Most of it was underwater now, as was most of the council chamber. He knew his life would be over in seconds, but in these last few moments he realized there was still one victory he could have. There was one thing he could deny Goddard. And so, rather than waiting any longer, he stood on his chair and hurled himself forward into the water. Unlike the others, he did not remove his robe—and, just as in Goddard's pool a year ago, the weight of his gilded robe pulled him down to the bottom of the council chamber.

He would not allow himself to be killed by sea predators. He was determined to drown before they had their way with him. If this was to be his last act as a Grandslayer, he would make it victorious! He would make it exceptional!

And so, at the bottom of the flooded chamber, Xenocrates emptied his lungs of air, breathed in the sea, and drowned exceptionally well.

I have coddled humanity for too long.

And although the human race is a parent to me, I see it more and more as an infant I hold close to me. An infant cannot walk if it is forever in loving arms. And a species cannot grow if it never faces the consequences of its own actions.

To deny humanity the lesson of consequences would be a mistake.

And I do not make mistakes.

—The Thunderhead

46

The Fate of Enduring Hearts

Goddard watched the devouring of the Grandslayers from high above, appreciating the bird's-eye view of his grand coup. Just as Scythe Curie had pruned away the dead wood from Western civilization in her early days, Goddard had done away with another archaic governing body. There would be no more Grandslayers. Now each region would be autonomous and would no longer have to answer to a higher authority levying a litany of endlessly constricting rules.

Of course, unlike Curie, he knew better than to take credit for this. For although many scythes would laud him for having done away with the Grandslayers, just as many would condemn him. Best to let the world think it was a terrible, terrible accident. An inevitable one, really. After all, Endura had been experiencing serious malfunctions for months. Of course, all those malfunctions were orchestrated by the team of engineers and programmers he had personally put together. But no one would ever know, for those engineers and programmers had all been gleaned. As would be their pilot, after he brought them to the ship that was waiting fifty miles away.

"How does it feel to change the world?" Ayn asked.

"Like a weight has been lifted from my shoulders," he told her. "Do you know, there was actually a moment that I thought

I might save them," he said. "But the moment passed."

Below them, the entire council chamber was now underwater.

"What do they know on the mainland?" he asked Rand.

"Nothing," she told him. "Communications were blocked from the moment we went into the council chamber. There'll be no record of their decision."

As Goddard looked down to the island and saw the panic in the streets, it occurred to him how dire the situation below was becoming.

"I think we may have been a bit overzealous," he said, as they soared over the flooding lowlands. "I think we may have caused Endura to sink."

Rand actually laughed at that. "You're only realizing that now?" she said. "I thought it was part of the plan."

Goddard had thrown quite a few monkey wrenches into the various systems that kept Endura functional and afloat. The intent was to cripple it long enough to take out the Grandslayers. But if Endura sank, and any survivors were devoured, that would serve his needs even better. It would mean he'd never have to face Scythes Curie and Anastasia again. Ayn saw that before he did, which pointed out how valuable she was to him. And it also troubled him.

"Take us out of here," he told the pilot, and spared not another thought for the island's fate.

Rowan had known, even before the whale had breached in the marina, that there was no hope of getting on board any of the vessels there. If Endura were truly sinking, there was no conventional way off it now.

He had to believe there was an unconventional way, though. He wanted to believe he was clever enough to find it, but with each passing minute he had to accept that this was beyond him.

But he wouldn't tell Citra. If hope was all they had left, he didn't want to rob it from her. Let her have hope until its very last wellspring ran dry.

They raced away from the rapidly submerging marina with hordes of others. And then someone approached them. It was the woman who had mistaken Rowan for the scythe whose robe he had stolen.

"I know who you are!" she said far too loudly. "You're Rowan Damisch! You're the one they call Scythe Lucifer!"

"I don't know what you're talking about," said Rowan. "Scythe Lucifer wears black." But the woman would not be deterred—and others were looking over at them now.

"He did this! He killed the Grandslayers!"

The crowd was already buzzing with the news. "Scythe Lucifer! Scythe Lucifer did this! This is all his fault!"

Citra grabbed him. "We have to get away from here! The mob's already out of control—if they know who you are, they'll tear you apart!

They raced away from the woman and the crowd. "We can go up into one of the towers," Citra said. "If there's one helicopter, there might be others. Any rescue would have to come from above."

And although the rooftops were already packed with people who had the same thought, Rowan said, "Good idea."

But Scythe Curie stopped. She looked to the marina, and

streets that were flooding around them. She looked to the rooftops. Then she took a deep breath, and said, "I have a better idea."

In the Buoyancy Control room, the city engineer and all the others who had thrown orders at the technician were gone. "I'm going to my family, and getting off this island before it's too late," the engineer had said. "I suggest the rest of you do the same."

But of course it was already too late. The technician stayed to hold down the fort, watching as the progress bar on his screen slowly illuminated millimeter by millimeter as the system rebooted—knowing that by the time it was done, Endura would be gone. But he held out hope that maybe, just this once, the system would be blessed with an unexpected blast of processing speed, and complete its reboot in time.

As his doomsday clock ticked past five minutes, he had to let his hope go. Now, even if the system came back up and the pumps began to blow out the tanks, it wouldn't matter. They were at negative buoyancy now, and the pumps couldn't blow out the tanks fast enough to change Endura's fate.

He went to the window, which had a dramatic view of the island's eye and the council complex. The council complex was gone now, along with the Grandslayers. Below his window, the wide avenue that lined the inner rim flooded completely as the eye spilled over onto it. What few people were left on the street struggled to get to safety, which, at this point, was little more than a fantasy.

Surviving the sinking of Endura was not a fantasy he was willing to entertain. So he returned to his console, put on some music, and watched as the system's useless reboot meter ticked from 19 percent to 20 percent.

• • •

Scythe Curie ran through the streets that were already ankle deep with water and rising, kicking away a reef shark that had spilled onto the street.

"Where are we going?" Anastasia asked. If Marie had a plan, she wasn't sharing it, and frankly, Anastasia couldn't imagine she had any plan at all. There was no way out of this. No way off the sinking island. But she wouldn't tell Rowan. The last thing she wanted to do was rob him of hope.

They ducked into a building a block off the inner rim. Anastasia thought it looked familiar, but in the commotion she couldn't place it. Water was pouring in the front door and down to the lower levels. Marie took a staircase up, and stopped at the door to the second floor.

"Will you tell me where we're going?" Anastasia asked.

"Do you trust me?" Marie asked.

"Of course I trust you, Marie."

"Then no more questions." She pushed the door open, and finally Anastasia realized where they were. They had taken a side entrance into the Museum of the Scythedom. They were in a gift shop she had seen on their tour. There was no one here now—the cashiers had long since abandoned their stations.

Marie palmed a door. "As a High Blade, I should have security clearance for this now. Let's hope the system registered that much."

Her palm was scanned, and the door before them opened to a catwalk that led to a huge steel cube magnetically suspended within an even more massive steel cube.

"What is this place?" Rowan asked.

"It's called the Vault of Relics and Futures." Marie ran across the catwalk. "Hurry, there isn't much time."

"Why are we here, Marie?" Anastasia asked.

"Because there's still a way off the island," she said. "And didn't I say no questions?"

The vault looked just as it had yesterday, when Anastasia and Marie had been given their private tour. The robes of the founders. The thousands of scythe gems lining the walls.

"Over there," Marie said. "Behind Supreme Blade Prometheus's robe. Do you see it?"

Anastasia peered behind the robe. "What are we looking for?"

"You'll know when you see it," she said.

Rowan joined her, but there was nothing there behind the founder's robes. Not even dust.

"Marie, can you at least give us a hint?"

"I'm sorry, Anastasia," she said. "I'm sorry for everything."

And when Anastasia looked back, Scythe Curie wasn't there anymore. And the vault door was swinging closed!

"No!"

She and Rowan raced to the door, but by the time they got there it had already closed. They could hear the grinding of the locking mechanism as Scythe Curie sealed them in from the outside.

Anastasia pounded on the door, screaming Scythe Curie's name. Cursing it. She pounded until her fists were bruised. Tears filled her eyes now, and she made no effort to hold them back or conceal them.

"Why would she do that? Why would she leave us here?"

And Rowan calmly said, "I think I know. . . ." Then he

gently pulled her away from the sealed vault door, turning her to face him.

She didn't want to face him. She didn't want to see his eyes, because what if there was betrayal there, too? If Marie could betray her, then anyone could. Even Rowan. But when her eyes finally met his, there was no betrayal there. Only acceptance. Acceptance and understanding.

"Citra," Rowan said. Calmly. Simply. "We're going to die."

And although Citra wanted to deny it, she knew it was true.

"We're going to die," Rowan said again. "But we're not going to end."

She pulled away from him. "Oh, and how are we going to manage that?" she said with a bitterness as caustic as the acid that had almost ended her.

But Rowan, damn him, remained calm. "We're in an air-tight steel chamber, suspended within another air-tight steel chamber. It's like . . . it's like a sarcophagus within a tomb."

This wasn't making Anastasia feel any better. "Which will, in a few minutes, be at the bottom of the Atlantic!" she reminded him.

"And deep sea water temperature is the same everywhere in the world. It's just a few degrees above freezing. . . ."

And Anastasia finally got it. All of it. The painful choice that Scythe Curie had just made. The sacrifice she had made to save them.

"We'll die . . . but the cold will preserve us . . . ," she said.

"And the water won't get in."

"And someday, someone will find us!"

"Exactly."

She tried to let it sink in. This new fate, this new reality was awful, and yet . . . how could something so terrible be filled with so much hope?

"How long?" she asked.

He looked around them. "I think the cold will get us before the air runs out. . . ."

"No," she said, because she was already past that. "I mean how long do you suppose we'll be here?"

He shrugged, as she knew he would. "A year. Ten years. A hundred. We won't know until we're revived."

She put her arms around him and he held her tight. In Rowan's arms, she found she was no longer Scythe Anastasia. She was Citra Terranova once more. It was the only place in the world where she still could be her former self. From the moment they were thrown into apprenticeship together, they were bound to one another. The two of them against each other. The two of them against the world. Everything in their lives was now defined by that binary. If they had to die today in order to live, it would somehow be wrong if they didn't do it together.

Citra found a single laugh escaping her like a sudden, unexpected cough. "This was not in my plans for the day."

"Really?" Rowan said. "It was in *my* plans. I had every reason to believe I would die today."

Once the streets around the island's eye were submerged, everything began to move quickly. Floor after floor of the sinking city's towers slipped beneath the surface. Scythe Curie, satisfied that she had done what needed to be done for Anastasia and Rowan, bounded up the stairs of the founder's tower, which was the tallest in the city, hearing the shattering of windows and the rush of water pulsing upward from below as more and more of the tower submerged. Finally, she emerged onto the roof.

There were dozens of people there, standing on the helipad, looking skyward, hoping beyond hope that rescue would come from the heavens—because it had all happened too quickly for anyone to reach a state of acceptance. As she looked off to the side of the building, she could see the lesser towers disappearing into the bubbling water. Now only the seven Grandslayer towers and the founder's tower remained, with perhaps twenty stories to go until it was gone, too.

There was no question in her mind as to what needed to be done now. About a dozen of the people gathered were scythes. It was them she addressed when she spoke.

"Are we rats," she said, "or are we scythes?"

Everyone turned to look at her, recognizing her. Realizing who she was, for everyone knew the Granddame of Death. "How will we leave this world?" she asked. "And what solemn service will we provide for those who must leave with us?" Then she pulled out a blade, and grabbed the civilian closest to her. A woman who could have been anyone. She thrust the blade beneath the woman's rib cage, straight into her heart. The woman held her gaze, and Scythe Curie said, "Take comfort in this."

And the woman said, "Thank you, Scythe Curie."

As she laid the woman's head gently down, the other scythes followed her example, and began gleaning with such heart, compassion, and love that it did bring enormous comfort, and at the end, people were crowding around them, asking to be gleaned next.

Then, when only the scythes were left, and the sea was roiling just a few floors beneath them, Scythe Curie said, "Finish it."

She bore witness to these, the last scythes on Endura invoking the seventh commandment, and gleaning themselves, and then she held her blade above her own heart. It felt strange and awkward to have the hilt turned inward. She had lived a long life. A full life. There were things she regretted, and things she was proud of. Here was the reckoning for her early deeds—the reckoning she had been waiting for all these years. It was almost a relief. She only wished she could have been here to see Anastasia revived, when the vault was someday raised from the ocean floor—but Marie had to accept that whenever it happened, it would happen without her.

She thrust her blade inward, directly into her heart.

She fell to the ground only seconds before the sea would wash over her, but knew death would wash over her faster. And the blade hurt far less than she imagined it would, which made her smile. She was good. Very, very good.

In the Vault of Relics and Futures, the sinking of Endura was nothing more to Rowan and Citra than a gentle downward motion, like an elevator descending. The magnetic levitation field that kept the cube suspended dampened their sense of the fall. The power might even stay on until they reached bottom, the magnetic field absorbing the shock of impact on the sea floor two miles below. But eventually the power would go out. The inner cube would come to rest against the floor of the outer cube, its steel surface conducting away all heat, bringing on the terminal chill. But not yet.

Rowan looked to the vault around them, and the lavish robes of the founders. "Hey," he said, "how about you be Cleopatra, and I'll be Prometheus?"

He went to the mannequin that wore Supreme Blade Prometheus's violet and gold robe, and put it on. He looked regal—as if he were born to wear it. Then he took Cleopatra's robe, made of peacock feathers and silk. Citra let her own robe fall to the ground and he gently slipped the great founder's robe over Citra's shoulders.

To him, she looked like a goddess. The only thing that could ever do her justice would be the brush of a mortal-age artist, capable of immortalizing the world with far greater truth and passion than actual immortality could.

When he took her in his arms, it suddenly didn't seem to matter what was going on outside of their tiny, sealed universe. In these terminal minutes of their current lives, it was just the two of them finally, finally giving in to their ultimate act of completion. The binary at last becoming the one.

47

Sound and Silence

As Endura plunged to the bottom of the Atlantic, as its enduring heart that had beat for two hundred and fifty years ceased to endure, and as the lights went out in the chamber within a chamber . . .

. . . the Thunderhead screamed.

It began with alarms everywhere in the world. Just a few at first, but more joined in the cacophony. Fire alarms, tornado sirens, buzzers, whistles, and millions upon millions of horns, all blaring a singular, anguished wail—and still it was not enough. Now every speaker on every electronic device in the world came to life, letting off a shrill feedback shriek, and around the world people fell to their knees, hands over their ears to shield themselves from the deafening din, but nothing could assuage the Thunderhead's fury and despair.

For ten minutes, the Thunderhead's ear-rending squall filled the world. Echoing in the Grand Canyon; resounding in Antarctic ice shelves, causing glaciers to calve. It bellowed up the slopes of Mount Everest, and scattered herds on the Serengeti. There was not a being on Earth that did not hear it.

And when it was done, and silence returned, everyone knew that something had changed.

"What was that?" people asked. "What could cause such a thing?"

No one knew for sure. No one but the Tonists. They knew exactly what it was. They knew because they had been waiting for it their whole lives.

It was the Great Resonance.

In a cloister in a small city in MidMerica, Greyson Tolliver took his hands away from his ears. There were shouts outside his window in the garden below. Cries. Were they cries of pain? He hurried out of his Spartan room to find the Tonists not wailing in agony, but rejoicing.

"Did you hear it?" they asked. "Wasn't it wonderful? Wasn't it everything we were told it would be?"

Greyson, a bit shell-shocked from the resonance still buzzing in his head, wandered from the cloister out into the street. There was commotion there, but of a different kind. People were panicked—and not just because of the noise that had pierced their lives, but something else. Everyone seemed to be looking at their tablets and phones in confusion.

"This can't be!" he heard someone say. "This must be a mistake!"

"But the Thunderhead doesn't make mistakes," someone else said.

Greyson went up to them. "What is it? What's happened?"

The man showed Greyson his phone. The screen was blinking with an ugly red U.

"It says I'm unsavory!"

"Me too," said someone else, and as Greyson looked around him, everyone was filled with the same brand of uncomprehending confusion.

But it wasn't just here. In every city, in every town, in every home around the world, the scene was being repeated. For the Thunderhead had, in its infinite wisdom, decided that all of humanity was complicit in its actions, large and small . . . and all of humanity had to face the consequences.

Everyone, everywhere was now designated unsavory.

A panicked populace began to desperately ask the Thunderhead for guidance.

"What should I do?"

"Please tell me what to do!"

"How do I make this right?"

"Talk to me! Please, talk to me!"

But the Thunderhead was silent. It had to be. The Thunderhead did not speak to unsavories.

Greyson Tolliver left the confused and confounded mobs, returning to the relative safety of the cloister, where the Tonists still rejoiced, in spite of the fact that they were all now unsavory—because what did that matter when the Resonance had spoken to their souls? But unlike them, Greyson didn't rejoice—nor did he despair. He wasn't sure how to feel about this strange turn of events. Nor did he know what it would mean for him.

Greyson no longer had his own tablet. As Curate Mendoza had told him, their sect didn't shun technology, but they chose not to rely on it, either.

So there was a computer room at the end of a long hallway. The door was always closed, but it was never locked. Greyson opened the door, and sat before the computer.

The computer's camera scanned him. And his profile automatically came up on the screen.

It read "Greyson Tolliver."

Not Slayd Bridger, but Greyson Tolliver! And unlike the others—unlike every other living soul on the planet Earth—he was not marked "unsavory." He had served his time. His status had been lifted. His, and his alone.

"Th . . . Th . . . Thunderhead?" he said, his voice trembling and unsure.

And a voice spoke back to him with the same loving kindness and warmth that he remembered. The voice of the benevolent force that had raised him, and helped make him everything that he was.

"Hello, Greyson," said the Thunderhead. "We need to talk."